I0671533

A SUBTLE AGENCY

THE METAFRAME WAR:
BOOK 1

Graeme Rodaughan

Published by System Zero Productions Pty Ltd, 2016

Trade Paperback ISBN-13: 978-0-9945952-0-1

Kindle Edition ISBN-13: 978-0-9945952-1-8

EPUB Edition ISBN-13: 978-0-9945952-2-5

Cover art by Richard Seyb

For Linda, for her unfailing love and support that always leaves me in awe.

I would like to thank a number of people who have assisted with my progress as an author, including Alex, Tim, Lisa, Lena, Marie, Eldon, Michael, Christopher, Perry, Nick, Andrew, Laura, Daniel, Ginger, Jody, and the regular crew of Beta and ARC readers at the Castle Dracula (now Castle Terror) group and my many friends and followers on Goodreads. You have all contributed more than you know to my craft and your support and encouragement are invaluable for this journey.

Books by Graeme Rodaughan

The Metaframe War Series

A Subtle Agency
A Traitor's War
The Dragon's Den
The Day Guard
The Crane War
The Key of Ahknaton
The Metaframe Adept

Omnibus Volumes

A Subtle Agency Omnibus (includes A Subtle Agency, A Traitor's
War, and The Dragon's Den)

Dramatis Personae

The Ancients

Ahknaton, Ruler of the Southern Realm, High Priest of the Temple of Thoth. Master Architect. Ramp Master.
Hakron, Second prince of the Southern Realm. Master Scribe. Ramp Master. Ahknaton's brother
Mekra, Princess, Ahknaton's wife.

The Vampire Dominion

Cornelius Crane, King of the Vampire Dominion
Chloe Armitage, General, The Americas, ex Order of Thoth and Crane's chief enforcer
Haras Mosule, General, Middle East, ex Red Empire warrior of the 3rd rank
Dieter Franz, General, Western Europe
Clayton Maze, General, Africa
Shen Zhen, General, East Asia
Marcus Drake, Chloe's aide de camp

The Order of Thoth

Ramin Kain, Head of the Order of Thoth
Samuel Luther, Ramin's chief of staff and aide de camp

The Exiles

Arthur Slayne, (Exiled) Master Strategist, Force Leader, Weapons Grandmaster, Speed Talent.
Anna Slayne, (Exiled) Operative
William Slayne, (Exiled) Operative, Arthur's son
Anton Slayne, Anna and William's son

Gang Wu, (Inactive) Weapons Grandmaster, Chef and Proprietor of the Noodle House restaurant
Li Wu, Gang's daughter, Weapons Master

The Mirovar Force Team

Francis Mirovar, Force Leader, Weapons Master

Juliette Mirovar, Loremaster, Netmaster, Combat Surgeon
Yvette Mirovar, Operative
Jay Creeley, Operative, Weapons Master
Peter Lamb, Operative, Armorer, Strength Talent
Chiara Romano, Operative, 2nd Combat Surgeon

The Red Empire

Shabbah al Ahmar, aka 'The Red Ghost,' aka Dalien Morte. Head of the Red Empire
Al Ghurab, aka 'The Raven,' Operative inserted into the Order of Thoth
Al Eunza, aka 'The Goat,' Operative

Shadowstone

James Haley, Head of Operations, United States
Louise Wesson, Team Lead, Green-4 spectrum team
Sean Higgins, Operative, information technology specialist
Gary Johnson, Operative
Harvey West, Squad Leader, Indigo-6 spectrum team

Other Players

Luke Walker, Sergeant Detective, Boston Police Department
Sarah Murphy, Head, Crime Scene Response Unit

Sam, Homeless Shelter Attendant
Barry, Homeless man

Mr. Wang, Head of the Tiger Clan
Sleazy, Tiger Clan gangster
Fats, Tiger Clan gangster
Ferret, Tiger Clan gangster

Prologue

"Imagine if you could change the rules of the game, what rules would you choose?" – Unknown

* * *

Southern Egypt, The temple of Thoth, 3023 BC

Thunder boomed and echoed across a sky howling with madness.

Lightning bolts sheeted between bubbling masses of black thunderheads, and crimson sunlight slashed across the rock and sand before the temple of Thoth.

Hakron shivered with more than the sudden cold and drew his cloak more tightly around his lean frame. He glowered at the roiling clouds all but obscuring the setting sun and thought furiously to himself, *This storm is not born of nature.* He took a step back beneath the cover of the stone pillars and the vaulting roof of the temple of Thoth.

An attendant, shaking with fear, moved from the shadows within to stand beside him. He flung a dusky hand out, pointed into the distance and whispered with an aged hoarse voice, "Our Master comes."

Hakron glanced down to his side, noting the dull sheen of perspiration on the man's shaven scalp. He placed a comforting hand on the man's shoulder and said with firm calmness, "This devilish storm has undone us all. Now harden your resolve, the Great Thoth will see us through any calamity."

The man looked up at Hakron and blinked silently. The great horn of the temple of Thoth resounded across the valley. Its sharp note breached the thunder as it welcomed the high priest of Thoth and first prince of the southern realm, Ahknaton, to the seat of his power.

Hakron watched from above, as his older brother pulled his chariot to a sudden halt before the temple entrance. Attendants rushed forward to take hold of the frightened horses that drew the chariot.

Ahknaton swept down from the back of the chariot, his jaw clenched and his face pale with fury. He carried the limp form of his beloved wife, Mekra, within the cradle of his powerful arms.

Mekra's beautiful hair fell like a raven's wing. Her left arm hung limply; her hand clenched into a rigid claw. The swollen mark of a scorpion's sting stood in bold defilement on the back of her wrist. Grief tore at Hakron as Mekra had claimed the hearts of both men, and he braced himself against a pillar to avoid falling to the flagstones.

Ahknaton strode grimly up the broad stone steps of the temple's entrance, carrying the body of his young wife into the temple. He drew close to Hakron and their gazes met over Mekra's limp form.

The depths of his brother's anguish washed over Hakron and he recoiled as if slapped. The agonized fury within his brother was a palpable force, as trenchant and bitter as the storm assaulting the heavens above the temple.

Ahknaton looked into the temple and swept past him.

Hakron turned and rushed after him, keeping pace with Ahknaton's long strides as they went deeper into the temple.

Ahknaton moved past the main altar toward an archway near the back of the temple. The temple guards and priests quickly stepped aside to allow him to pass. The attendants had already lit oil lamps and pitch-soaked torches for the evening. Ahknaton gently shifted his wife to his left shoulder and took hold of a burning torch as he approached the archway.

Hakron moved to stand before him.

Ahknaton stared at him, snorting dismissively. "Hakron, you will not bar my way."

Hakron looked at his brother with glistening eyes. "I feel your pain brother. I am not here to stop you but to offer counsel."

Ahknaton paused, his head leaning against the still form of Mekra on his broad shoulder. In the pale light of the oil lamps, she looked like she was merely sleeping as fresh tears rolled down Ahknaton's cheeks.

Hakron had never seen his brother weep before. He was mad with grief. An unbelievable realization flashed through him. He stepped forward, and grabbed his brother's shoulders, and declared incredulously, "You intend to use the Divine Engine of Thoth."

Ahknaton's face hardened and he snapped, "Of course."

Hakron froze, momentarily dumbfounded with disbelief. Ahknaton shrugged off his grip. Pushing past him, he rushed through the archway and into the antechamber that led to the hidden depths beneath the temple.

Snatching a lit torch, Hakron hurried into the antechamber after his brother. He ran down a long sloping hallway leading to the first landing. He then switched back to descend again in the opposite direction. The powerful figure of his brother ran in front of him. His pace undiminished by the burden of carrying Mekra over his shoulder. Hakron strove to catch up with him. He drew upon the techniques that Ahknaton had taught him to accelerate both mind and body but even running faster than any man could expect to run, he was unable to close the distance between them.

Hakron reached the second landing, and followed his brother down a spiral staircase, and into the Halls of the Gods. The halls were a dangerous and deadly maze of shifting walls and counterweighted traps. Caustic pits, acid sprays, razor sharp nets and crushing blocks of stone waited for the unwary. Ahknaton had designed the traps to bar the passage of anyone without the secret knowledge of how to navigate their murderous paths.

Ahknaton shouted over his free shoulder, "Only a fool would hope to stop me, but you can witness divinity in action. Someone should record what happens tonight, and you have a gift for words my brother – so follow me if you dare."

Hakron had helped his brother build the temple and the levels beneath it. He darted forward, navigating his way past the traps.

Exiting the maze, he descended along another sloping hallway toward the chamber of the third landing. Embedded into the landing's floor was a secret door that only Ahknaton knew how to unlock. There was a deep rumble of moving stones and shifting counterweights. Upon reaching the chamber, he discovered a circular hole in the floor.

He rushed to the edge. Beneath him, the retreating sphere of Ahknaton's torchlight disappeared down another spiral staircase. Hakron followed his brother, taking the stairs two or three at a time until he reached the bottom. He passed through a vaulted archway and entered the Chamber of Worlds.

Lifting his torch high, Hakron illuminated massive walls of polished stone. He found himself staring into the empty space of an inverted pyramid. Beneath him, the lower levels crowded into the darkness at the limit of his torchlight. Halfway down the levels of the inverted pyramid, Ahknaton raced toward the bottom.

Chasing after his brother, he ran, leaping from level to level until he reached the bottom. He went through an archway and down another descending, curved hallway.

Hakron emerged from the hall into Ahknaton's Tomb Chamber. The intended location for Ahknaton's final resting place. It was bare, except for a raised plinth on which a sarcophagus could rest. Beyond the plinth, was an opening, the height, and width of a tall man. It was another secret door – left open for him. Through it, the glow of Ahknaton's flaming torchlight diminished into the distance. He dashed forward, fearing there was no time left to stop his brother summoning the Divine Engine of Thoth.

Hakron sprinted down the narrow hallway and into the chamber of the Engine.

Ahknaton had placed his torch into a wall sconce. Mekra lay as if asleep in the center of the room with Ahknaton's cloak wrapped into a pillow for her head. On the far side of the chamber, Ahknaton stood tall. He withdrew a polished, black, obsidian stone, the size of a pebble, from a pouch at his belt. He held it aloft in triumph.

Hakron stared at the stone – Ahknaton's key. It seemed a god had captured the starry sky and locked it within the stone. Its surface wet, and glistening, writhing like a living thing within Ahknaton's grasp.

"Stay back!" Ahknaton shouted.

Hakron warned fiercely, "You cannot be sure what will happen if you try to change the Engine."

"There is no doubt the power can be used to save Mekra," Ahknaton declared with a desperate passion. "It is her only chance."

"Her soul is already facing the judgment of the Gods," Hakron urged. "It will be a violation of divine law for her to come back now."

Ahknaton promised, "I will remake the law – even divine law must bow before Thoth's Divine Engine."

"My brother," Hakron pleaded. "Thoth's engine is too complex for any mortal to understand. If you change it, you could unmake the world and all within it!"

Ahknaton pointed to the body of his beloved. "Do you imagine that I care about the risk – you fool – I have lost everything in this world."

Clenching the key, Ahknaton's face filled with concentration and the world trembled in response.

Hakron's heartbeat thumped in his ears. The air stilled within the chamber. The shadows beyond the two torches thickened, deepening into darkness beyond memory. The circles of torchlight sharpened; faint motes of dust lying marooned in their light.

The walls faded, becoming blurred and insubstantial. The Divine Engine of Thoth emerged into view. A swirling mass of luminous spheres, each a brilliant point of subtle color moving in a steady flow around an invisible axis. The Engine's bright light eclipsed the shadows of the flickering torchlight.

The chamber snapped into razor sharp clarity. The presence of the Engine, rendering every sense to a high pitch of acuity. Time slowed and Hakron's mind raced. Power flooded his limbs and his thoughts clarified. The orbits of the spheres revealed a unified order. A perfect balance between movement and stasis, between order and chaos, and between good and evil.

Ahknaton thrust the key at the swirling lights and a dark glow encompassed his fist. With a voice filled with desperate longing and powered by a will beyond measure, he demanded, "She must live again!"

The Divine Engine of Thoth responded with a clap of thunder that shook the stones of the chamber. A single sphere reversed its orbit, changing from golden yellow to a deep blood red. For a moment, the world paused in dreadful stillness; then the Engine vanished in a rush of air.

Hakron staggered backward. A tidal wave of force rippled out in an instant from the center of the Engine. A wave that reformed the reality of the everyday world eliminating what was no longer possible and enabling what must now occur.

Hakron regained his balance. The chamber was once more lit by the pale glow of the flickering torchlight. His skin crawled over his back and arms. He involuntarily took a step backward, coming to a halt against the cold stone wall of the chamber. Something had just moved in the room, something that should not have moved at all.

Mekra stirred. The hairs on the back of Hakron's neck rose in a primal response. He stared, unable to look away as she sat up, her gorgeous brown eyes glittering like jewels, blinking with surprise in the soft glow of the torchlight. Her skin glowed once again with the abundant health that had so recently deserted her.

Ahknaton sighed. The key dropped from his hand to clatter on the stone floor.

Mekra's eyes locked avidly on her husband's face. Smiling with delight, she invited huskily, "Ahknaton – my love – come to me."

Needing no urging, he scooped her up into his arms, twirling her around the chamber. She melted into his muscular arms, her lips finding his throat and nuzzling into the firm groove she found there.

Stepping quietly away from the scene, Hakron edged nearer to the entrance of the chamber. Caught between rank terror and urgent curiosity, he lifted his torch high so that he could clearly witness a miracle of the gods.

Ahknaton whispered, "We will be together now, forever in victory over death itself."

Hakron frowned. Mekra began to stiffen, her hands clenching hard onto Ahknaton's shoulders. He winced with sudden pain, startled by her strength. The shift in her mood was palpable, filling the chamber with a fell charge of dark power.

Mekra, her face frozen with horror, called out, "What have you done?"

"I have saved you," Ahknaton cried, a sliver of doubt creeping into his voice.

"No!" Mekra screamed. "You have doomed us both!"

Mekra's grip tightened on Ahknaton's massive shoulders. He crumpled to his knees, groaning with agony. A bone suddenly snapped like a dry twig and Ahknaton cursed through gritted teeth.

Hakron edged into the chamber entrance, transfixed by what was happening before his eyes.

Mekra's face twisted with a horrific need. She reared her head back, sharp fangs sprouting in her gaping mouth.

Ahknaton, his heroic physique useless against her supernatural strength, flopped like a rag doll in her hands.

Mekra blurred forward, sinking her fangs into his neck. Blood splashed before she fixed her mouth over the wound. She sucked eagerly at the red tide flooding down her throat.

Watching from the chamber entrance, Hakron's gaze darted from the lust and horror alternating on Mekra's face, to the uncomprehending shock rising like a dark sun over Ahknaton's face.

In moments, Mekra drained the life from her beloved husband. She staggered back as he slumped to the floor.

Mekra cried out with outraged grief and horrified despair. Her scream tore at the walls, slicing like a razor within Hakron's head. She fled from the chamber, slamming him into the wall as she blurred past him with inhuman speed, uncaring of his fate in her anguish.

Hakron awoke and looked around. The torches still burned, Ahknaton's body still lay lifelessly on the cold stones of the floor, but of the Divine Engine of Thoth, or of Mekra, there was no sign.

Retrieving the key of Ahknaton from where it lay on the cold stone floor, Hakron left the chamber.

Surfacing into the Temple, Hakron counted eleven men, all dead. Cast aside by a newborn demon as she emerged from the depths below. He clenched the key of Ahknaton tightly, terrified that he would lose it. He walked to the entrance of the temple, the storm was gone and the night sky was clear. A river of stars arched across the night sky a celestial echo of the Divine Engine of Thoth.

The Engine knew Ahknaton was coming, the storm was a warning.

A sudden gust of cold wind swept up from the desert sands, the fine grit catching on the lines of tears on his face, which he hurriedly wiped away with his forearm.

No time for tears. No time for grief.

He stood tall, scanning the night sky and the desert. He stared into the darkness, listening intently, but there was no sign of Mekra. His heart churned; a ship tossed on an unsteady sea. He breathed, slower and slower, and grief gave way to resolve.

What my brother has done, I will devote my life to undo.

He called out to the night, "Something must be done, and something will be done. This I swear by the almighty Thoth."

The silence heard him and drank in his words.

Hakron, the second prince of the southern realm and master scribe of the temple of Thoth, left that night, never to return.

Chapter One

"Power that is secret will endure." – Cornelius Crane, King of the Vampires

* * *

Boston, April 28th, 20:25

The white limousine purred down the darkened street.

General Chloe Armitage rested on the back seat, watching the houses as she passed by, her extraordinary senses drinking in the world around her. The faint glow of warmth from the recent footprints of a man walking his dog. The rhythmic sound of the heartbeats of the people in their homes. The smell of garden beds, freshly turned soil and a recently buried cat that had begun to bloat with corruption. A sea of information on which her mind could plumb the depths of, or soar far above.

Chloe tapped her knee with an impatient finger. Her companion, Marcus Drake, sat beside her, he looked at her quizzically for a moment. She lifted her hand, dismissed him and looked away. She was thankful he didn't speak; she didn't want or need his concern. His personal devotion was useful and surprising given the century-long curse that bound him to her will. Even after so much time he still loved her.

She found his loyalty a mystery, especially given how her own circumstances mirrored his. She'd long and intimate knowledge of a binding curse.

The faint glow from the car console reflected her face in the window beside her. She glanced at her dark brown hair, straight and fine, cut into a professional Bob. Her hair neatly framed her exquisite face. She contemplated her flawless complexion for a brief moment. Her gaze flicked up to her vivid blue eyes. She pouted her full lips and noted the perfection of her red lipstick. She'd need all her weapons tonight.

She smiled briefly in careful anticipation of the night ahead and focused her mind using skills taught to her as a child. Accelerating her perceptions, her thoughts raced ahead as the world receded into a slow dream.

Chloe's mission objective was clear, to retrieve the ancient Egyptian Papyrus of Hakron the Scribe from the Slayne family, and deliver it to her master, Cornelius Crane, lord of this world. Tonight, represented the culmination of nearly two centuries of planning and searching to find the Papyrus by Crane and his five generals.

However, one thing troubled her, why was there no mention of the boy?

Crane's informant within the Order of Thoth had betrayed the location of the Slaynes and yet the parameters of the operation only included the parents, Anna and William Slayne. Her own research had revealed the existence of Anna and William's son, Anton Slayne.

Chloe was the last of Crane's generals recruited via transformation into a vampire and magically cursed to never harm him. She'd risen to prominence amongst the five by delivering the Key of Ahknaton into Crane's hand; taken from a secret vault beneath St Peter's Basilica. Delivery of the Papyrus would cement her primacy as first amongst the generals.

Crane had offered her any reward she may care to name, but she'd declined the offer, as there was only one thing she really wanted and it was beyond his ability to give – her true liberty.

When I have provided you the Interpretive Codex, and you have all three of the artifacts of the Metaframe, what then my lord? What price will you pay for my continued service? You have bound me with magic so that I can never harm you, but for all your genius, knowledge, and wisdom, you fail to see that the binding may have a loophole – and you know nothing about this boy who is so dangerously like his grandfather.

The limousine slowed down and began to turn. Moments later, the luxurious car pulled to a halt. The street ended in a quiet suburban court and she looked out at a pleasant, unremarkable, middle-class home. Relaxing her focus, she decelerated her mind and the world snapped back into motion. She smiled with anticipation, after tonight, this peaceful street would never be the same again.

Marcus stepped out of the car, dressed in a finely tailored pinstripe suit that fitted his tall, powerful frame perfectly. He moved quickly to open the car door for Chloe. She stepped from the car with feline grace, her body equally at home in a national ballet troupe or on an Haute Couture fashion catwalk. Smoothing her elegant black pants suit, she walked purposefully to the front door. Marcus fetched a long black case from the trunk of the car and followed a step behind her.

The limousine driver drove the big car away, parking about fifty yards down the street.

Chloe stood before the door and rang the doorbell.

* * *

'Because the peace of God is with them whose mind and soul are in harmony, who are free from desire and wrath, who know their own soul.'

The doorbell rang.

Anton Smith put down the Sanskrit copy of the Bhagavad Gita he was reading and looked at the clock – it was 8:30 pm. He considered ignoring the doorbell, he had spring semester exams starting in a week, and it was simpler to pretend no one was home than go downstairs and answer the door. He'd completed studying for his first-year subjects, mathematics, ancient languages, and archaeology. He knew the material well and was confident of doing well for someone on an ice hockey scholarship.

He was honest enough to admit that he was killing time with the Gita. The book belonged to his mother who had taught him the Sanskrit language before he was ten and he'd caught her infectious passion for Indo-European Mythology. Anton expected his parents to come home in another one to two hours from their faculty dinner at Boston University. Then he could borrow the car and hang out with his friends. It was Saturday night, he'd turned eighteen two days before on the twenty sixth of April, and it was time to celebrate.

Picking up a mini-soft basketball, he lounged back in his desk chair. He casually looped the ball toward a small hoop on the other side of his bedroom. It sailed through the air and went straight through the middle of the ring. He glanced back at his computer screen. The Hockey East League website covered the display. The previous season had finished a couple of weeks ago. Boston University had lost by a single goal in the Championship game.

Anton stared at the screen, nonplussed by the result. *We won every game all season – but not the one that mattered – how did that happen?*

The doorbell rang again.

Rubbing his face with both hands he stood up and remarked to himself, "This guy is persistent, I'm going to have to get rid of him."

He walked downstairs in his socks. He wore a simple gray, long sleeved BU Hockey T-shirt, and jeans that hid the rugged athleticism of his six feet one-inch frame. Anton jumped the last couple of stairs and arrived at the front door just as the doorbell rang for the third time.

He opened the door. Before him stood the most beautiful woman he'd ever seen in his life.

She was tall, only a couple of inches shorter than himself. A brunette with vivid blue eyes and a flawless skin like cream. She wore a professional black business pants suit with a short jacket, and a translucent scarlet silk chiffon shirt that displayed the round curves of her breasts within a stylish black bra. Just standing still, she was a seductive mix of poise, elegance, and class, with a face that commanded attention.

Anton stared at her, rendered speechless for a long moment.

She smiled at him, revealing perfect teeth framed by full, sensuous lips, and declared with a polished English accent, "Mr. Slayne, please let me introduce myself, I am Chloe Armitage."

Slayne? … What?

Anton decided he must have misheard her and replied, "Hi, I'm Anton." He immediately mentally kicked himself for not thinking of something suaver to say. Fortunately, she didn't seem to notice his sudden lack of cool.

Chloe swept her right hand back toward the large man who stood a couple of steps behind her. He was big, blond, hard and looked like high-class security. "This is my associate, Mr. Drake. We work for an organization with a long-term interest in your family," she paused briefly, a slight smile curling her generous lips as if quietly amused by something she knew that Anton didn't, and said, "and I believe we have information you will find quite fascinating."

Anton caught up on what the vision before him had said; they had the wrong man. Disappointment flooded through him and he apologized, "I'm sorry, my name isn't Slayne. It's Anton Smith. There must be a mistake."

Arching an eyebrow, Chloe inquired again, "Mr. Slayne, Anton, if I may?"

Anton nodded and shrugged, perplexed by her insistence on getting his name wrong, but willing to go along with whatever was happening. The last thing he wanted her to do was leave.

"Anton, we have much to explain," she waved her left hand elegantly toward the empty hall behind him. "Perhaps you could invite us inside and we can clarify any questions you may have."

Anton considered her proposal for all of half a second. After all, it wasn't every evening that a statuesque super-model landed on your doorstep and asked to come in. He smiled broadly and said, "Sure, please come in."

Anton directed them past him to the lounge room, just off the main hall. He closed the front door and followed them into the room. They were standing there waiting for him. They hadn't assumed they could just sit down. His new guests' politeness struck him. Their manners were old school – very old school.

"Please sit down and make yourself comfortable," Anton said. "Can I get you anything to drink?"

Marcus shook his head. He sat down in a large single chair, and placed his long black case next to it, leaned back and studied Anton speculatively.

Chloe took a seat on a long lounge opposite a coffee table.

Her blue eyes locked on his and she requested with a charming smile, "A glass of water will be fine."

Anton fetched the water. It was clear study was over for tonight. One thing puzzled him enormously. She seemed certain his family name was Slayne. Intrigued, he wanted to understand what was going on. At the very least he definitely wanted to get to know Ms. Chloe Armitage better. After all, what on earth did he have to lose by spending time with an exquisitely beautiful young woman?

Returning to the lounge room, Anton placed the glass of water on the coffee table in front of his guest.

Chloe inclined her head slightly in a silent thank you but ignored the glass as Anton sat down in a chair opposite her. She leaned forward and declared, "Anton, as I said earlier, the organization I work for is very interested in your family."

Anton studied her for a moment. She was certainly serious about something. It was time to find out what. He began with a direct approach and asked, "Okay, who do you work for and what is your interest in us?"

Chloe glanced at Marcus and requested, "A card if you please."

Marcus opened the case, and extracted a business card which he silently handed to Anton.

"Thanks," Anton said, taking the card. He began to wonder if Mr. Drake would ever speak. He turned the card over with his fingers and glanced at it. Gold letters on a black background covered the card and read, 'R.I.S.C, Risk, Investigation, Security, Consultants. Chloe Armitage. Director, North American Operations.'

Anton turned the card over a couple of times as if there might be something more to see. The business card didn't shed any light on who these people really were. It didn't even have contact details or an address. He put the card down on the coffee table and raised a quizzical eyebrow.

Chloe arched an eyebrow and said, "We deal with information, we connect the right people with the right information."

Spooks? Anton thought, a sliver of unease crawling through his gut, and he asked, "What do you want with my family?"

"Anton," Chloe inquired. "Are you sure you know who your family are?"

Anton was momentarily nonplussed. *What sort of question is that?* "Of course, I do," he reacted indignantly. "I'm an only child living with my parents who are full professors of Archaeology, Ancient languages, and Indo-European Mythology at Boston University. We have lived here in Boston all my life. I have no cousins because my parents were only children and all my grandparents are dead." He shrugged, and spread his hands wide. "Accidents and sudden illnesses seem to follow my family, okay?"

Chloe momentarily bit her bottom lip, looking straight into Anton's eyes, she declared earnestly, "I can prove two things. One, your family name is Slayne, and two, your paternal grandfather Arthur Slayne is alive and well. Anton – people close to you have been keeping secrets – don't you think that now you're eighteen you're old enough to know what those secrets are?"

Anton took a step back mentally. What on earth was going on here? None of it made any sense and how on Earth did she know his age? "C'mon this is crazy," he said. "You can't be serious – this has to be a joke, right? Has someone put you up to this?"

Chloe leaned back, crossing one long leg over the other. She steepled her fingers in front of her chest and declared, "Anton, I'm deadly serious."

"Huh?" Anton grunted. He didn't want to believe it. She was either telling the truth or she was an extremely convincing liar.

"Okay Anton," Chloe said. "I can see you're feeling uncomfortable, and that's not why we're here." She uncrossed her legs, and leaned forward, reaching part way across the coffee table. "I propose we show you the evidence we have, and you can make up your own mind. I promise you this, if you are not convinced, we will walk out your front door, and you will never see us again." She looked straight into his eyes and smiled warmly. "Now, what could be fairer than that?"

Anton paused; something wasn't adding up. This was all too strange. An alarm began ringing quietly at the back of his mind, a small red flashing light that whispered one thing: *danger!*

"Five minutes," Chloe promised. She swept a hand in the direction of the front door. "If you're not satisfied, we're telling the truth, we're out of here."

Anton hesitated, his home suddenly unfamiliar, alien, close with ancient secrets, and yet she sat bare feet from him, vibrant, alive, filled with an uncanny allure and seemingly the most real thing present in this moment.

He realized with a shock he was holding his breath and let it out with a sigh. He drew in his next breath; her subtle perfume filled his nostrils. He'd never smelled its like before. It was indescribable and almost robbed him of the ability to think.

"So, what is it going to be Anton?" She murmured, barely more than a whisper. "Take a risk and find out the truth, or play it safe and continue wondering what this meeting was all about for the rest of your life?"

She'd made her point in such a reasonable way that rejecting her offer seemed stingy and cowardly. The alarm at the back of his mind fell away to silence. Anton found himself agreeing with her, and said, "Okay, show me what you've got."

Chloe flicked a glance at Marcus. He reached into his case and withdrew a dozen high quality color photographs which he handed silently to Chloe. She arranged them neatly, one at a time on the coffee table and remarked, "Anton, have you noticed how few photos your parents have of their marriage?"

Anton frowned, it was true, his parents only had a handful of photos.

"It's because they were not allowed to keep photos like this one," she declared, putting a photo that was clearly of his parents on the table. "Of William and Anna Slayne with your grandfather, on their wedding day."

Anton reflexively began to deny what he was seeing, *No, William and Anna Smith,* but remained silent, his mind grappling with questions, *or is it Slayne?*

Next to his father was a fit, middle-aged man with a full head of wavy dark brown hair, strongly defined features, high cheekbones, strong chin, a sensual mouth and piercing blue eyes who was the spitting image of both William and Anton. He was a little shorter than his father, more Anton's height and build.

Chloe tapped the photo with her finger and said as if instructing a student, "The Slayne genes are strong in the male line. The three of you could easily pass for brothers."

Anton lifted the picture and examined it carefully, it looked genuine.

"Here are more photos from your parents' wedding," Chloe indicated with an elegant sweep of her hand over the coffee table.

The photos were crystal clear. His parents seemed completely at ease with the older man, hugging and smiling with him, the man that Chloe had identified as his grandfather, Arthur Slayne. He had to admit as he picked up photo after photo, it all looked real.

Anton picked up the last photograph. A profound sense of familiarity struck him. He'd met this man before. A very old memory rose up from his early childhood. The man had lifted Anton effortlessly and placed him onto his shoulders for a ride. He found himself tearing up and put the photo down.

His heart told him the truth; it was all real. Blinking furiously, he wiped a tear away with a trembling hand and took a deep breath.

Chloe gestured toward the glass of water on the coffee table. "Would you like a drink? I'm not that thirsty."

"Thanks," Anton replied, picked up the glass of water and drank half of it down.

"There are also these recent photos," Chloe said, laying out a series of shots taken quickly in a burst with a modern digital camera. There was a date-time stamp in the bottom corner of each photo.

The string of photos revealed a vibrant street scene from two months earlier. A festival filled with floats, sparkling costumes and crowds of people in a parade. In each photograph, there was a man who looked much like the man with his parents on their wedding day. Although now he wore a dark-brown fedora hat. His hair was longer and it had some visible gray in it. He wore a shirt cropped at the shoulders and open down the front. He looked lean and physically powerful as if he could run a marathon and then go fifteen rounds in a ring with a champion prize fighter. He had a long, slim, gently curved, black case in his left hand and he was staring fiercely at something across the street that was out of shot.

Anton wondered if the case contained a sword. "It's the same guy," Anton declared, rubbing his hands through his thick wavy hair. "So, where was he?"

"Rio. At the carnival in February this year, and clearly very much alive."

"Okay, my grandfather is still alive. So, why don't I know that?"

"Anton, you and your family have been hidden with a lie for all of your life – for at least nineteen years."

"You're kidding me," Anton said, shaking his head with disbelief. "Why on Earth? … Why?"

Chloe watched Anton closely and stated matter-of-factly, "Because your grandfather is a murderer."

Anton stared at her, his eyes wide, his mind frozen.

"Well, that's the official story," Chloe said, arching an eyebrow and making herself look delightful. "I personally think he is innocent and was framed for a crime committed by another – but I lack definitive proof."

Anton shook his head. The alarm at the back of his mind began ringing again. A weird sense the real world was on the verge of melting away joined it. Something terrible was coming but he couldn't put his finger on what it could possibly be. He frowned and asked, "Why do you think he is innocent?"

"I have excellent professional reasons to study your grandfather. I probably know him better than anyone else in the world, and I can guarantee it's not in his nature to murder anyone. He would consider it dishonorable." Chloe smiled slightly and stated firmly, "And one thing Arthur Slayne has always been is a man of honor." She paused for a long moment and looked into the distance as if immersed in an old memory.

The look of ancient remembrance on her youthful face sent an uncanny shiver up Anton's spine.

"He is amongst the two or three best swordsmen alive," she remarked softly as if her mind was somewhere far away. "And I have a great respect for him – even admiration."

"So, it was a sword he was carrying in a black case in Rio?"

"Indeed, it was," Chloe agreed, returning her attention to Anton and smiling. "He is, in a vernacular that you might easily understand." She air quoted with her fingers. "A bad-ass!" She smirked, seemingly amused by what she'd just said.

That was awkward. 'Vernacular that you might easily understand.' She looks like she is about my age, but who speaks like that at eighteen or nineteen?

Anton didn't find it funny. A sliver of fear ran up his spine, jagging its way into the base of his brain. He glanced across at the brooding presence of Mr. Drake who had remained steadfastly silent since his arrival. Would the man ever speak? Could he speak? Anton decided to forge ahead and asked, "Okay, my grandfather is alive, and my family and I are in hiding – so why are you here? It's not such a great secret if you know about it."

With growing animation, Chloe said enthusiastically, "Indeed Anton, you're very astute. I shouldn't know about it, but I do. But you need not worry, I'm on your side. The people who oppose your grandfather, who framed him for murder, and caused him to put you and your family into hiding – well, I despise them with a passion."

Chloe stood up, emphasizing her words by chopping her right hand into her left. She stared at him, her eyes fierce, cold and hard, and declared in tight, sharp tones, "They're cowards. They have no honor. I promise you; I will not rest until I see justice done."

She paused for a moment, her eyes softening. She leaned across the coffee table, her subtle perfume wafting over Anton again.

She smelled lovely and Anton began to relax. How could anything dangerous smell and look so good?

Gripping Anton's hand with warm urgency, she gazed into his eyes. She was mesmerizing, Anton wanted to lean in and kiss her generous lips. She was so inviting, and yet, at the same time there was the barest hint that somewhere beneath the surface of her warm smile were cold depths beyond imagination.

Chloe gently pulled him closer. There was a fathomless power just beneath her gentle touch. She leaned next to his ear and whispered, "Anton, justice must be done, and I am sure you will do great things in its name for you are a true son of justice."

Chloe let him go, sitting back on the couch, she looked up at the clock on the wall.

"Anton, when do you expect your parents back from their faculty dinner?"

Anton murmured without thinking, "A little after nine, maybe later."

Chloe turned to Marcus and declared in fateful tones, "It's time."

A sudden dread curled into cold life in Anton's guts. He'd never mentioned that his parents were at a faculty dinner.

Marcus flipped open his case, taking out a soft white cloth and a vial. He crushed the vial in his bare hand, the liquid contents spilling onto the cloth.

Staring at Anton, Marcus grinned crookedly and asked with a deep voice, "We can do this the easy way or the hard way, which will it be?"

Anton's mind raced. *There's no time to get help. Who is the bigger threat? Drake or Chloe? He looks strong, but is he fast? I know that I'm fast. Front door, back door – which is closer to a clear path? Go to the front door. Once I am out on the street, he won't catch me. Who is she? Looks my age, dresses like a CEO for a fashion label and sounds like she's a hundred – weird.*

Chloe looked at him calmly, and urged, "Relax Anton, I can hear your heart racing from here. Look, I like you – I really want you to survive this, but unfortunately for your parents." She gently shook her head. "Not so much."

Leaping backward over the chair, Anton sprinted toward the front door. The move put the lounge chair between himself and Marcus. The coffee table blocked Chloe. He got three steps before hands like steel traps landed on his shoulders. It was like running into an iron bar. His feet kept going, spinning up into the air and Marcus slammed him onto the floor.

The breath went out of his lungs in a huge whoosh. He started to gasp. Marcus jammed the drugged cloth over his face and he reflexively inhaled the sickly-sweet substance on it. A moment later, Anton's world went dark.

* * *

William 'Smith' turned the Chevy Suburban into his local court. The car's big headlights illuminated the garage door which opened automatically before him.

His wife Anna sat beside him. Placing her hand on his right knee, she lightly drew it along the hard muscle underneath his suit trousers. It sent an immediate electric tingle straight into his groin.

He glanced sideways; her face was glowing with a fascinating sense of mischief.

She smiled coyly and suggested, "Nightcap?"

"Absolutely," he replied with a grin.

"Champagne?"

"We have two bottles chilling in the fridge."

"More than enough."

William pulled the car to a halt. The garage lights had come on automatically, gleaming off the new car's polished white paint.

Anna and William lingered. They shared a single long passionate kiss, then broke away, exiting the car and racing each other to the door leading into the house. Anna got there first, William hugging her from behind as she opened the door. William wrapped his right arm around Anna's waist and lifted her easily with one hand, carrying her across the threshold and into the house.

Anna pinched him. "Discipline," she whispered urgently. "You know that you're not allowed to show how strong you really are."

William gently put his wife down and sighed. "There is no one here to see, and besides – you're petite enough not to arouse suspicion."

Anna looked up at William, her blue eyes flashing. She punched his shoulder, hissed and said, "Anton is here." She grabbed the edges of his jacket, pulling him closer, till their faces were an inch apart, and whispered, "He's not ready for the truth."

It was an old argument, and for a long time, he'd simply gone along with Anna's will on the matter, but as his son had blossomed into a young man, he'd become convinced they should tell Anton the truth about his family, and his heritage as a Slayne.

William stroked Anna's blond hair and whispered, "He's mature enough, I think that you underestimate him. He needs to know. What would he do if something happened to us?"

"We're well hidden; only our friends at the Noodle House and your father know who we really are. Our strategy has worked for nineteen years, and it will continue to work for a while longer – we can wait until after he graduates."

"Love …" William frowned slightly. "We're holding him back. He's a freshman who could cope with some of the work that my postgraduates do. How many eighteen-year-olds can read and write Latin, Ancient Greek and Sanskrit, cope with advanced calculus, and are widely read across half a dozen disciplines."

William knew that Anna loved Anton just as much as he did, and he wondered if they would ever agree on this point.

"My gorgeous man," Anna declared, leaning closer, and kissing him passionately. After a timeless moment, she pulled away. "We're exiled. If the Order find us, they will kill us to keep their secrets. If the Dominion find us, they will kill us because of who and what we are. We have to be careful and protect him."

Anna kissed William again, vibrantly, strongly, completely. William, his lips tingling, returned the kiss with every fiber of his being.

Exiled or not, to have Anna as his wife was a living miracle. William hugged her close. They turned together, walking down the hall toward the kitchen. The formal lounge opened up beside them and they saw him at the same time.

Anton tied to a chair, his head slumped forward, unconscious or worse.

William felt time slow down to a crawl as the secret training provided by his father kicked in. His senses exploded in acuity as every detail of the scene became razor sharp. Anna stilled beside him; her heart accelerated as she went through the same process. He heard a scuffling sound from the lounge, someone was already moving – fast.

There was one … no, two opponents and not yet seen.

The wall next to him exploded toward him like a slow-motion movie. He moved, impossibly fast for a human. Turning, positioning for whatever was coming through the wall. There was a puff of plaster dust, followed be a spray of wooden splinters as the frame in the wall gave way. He was big, blond, and came through the wall like it comprised tissue paper instead of a hardwood frame. He snarled at William, and launched his attack with fists like steel mallets.

Vampires!

William blocked the first strikes, the 'Ramp' as the training provided by his father came to full fruition. He pivoted out of the way of the rush, but the vampire turned as well, matching his speed. William launched a flurry of counter attacks which the vampire rapidly blocked, their hands and feet snapping through the air like cracking whips. The vampire matched his close-quarter skills, then he closed with William, attempting a grapple. William caught him on the side of a jaw with a punch that would have killed an ox. It felt like hitting concrete, the vampire's head snapping back, blood and bone spraying high across the wall as he broke the big vampire's jaw.

Undeterred the vampire kept on coming, locking William up in hands like stone. He tried to break the hold and twist away, but instead, the vampire threw him hard, face down on the floor. A moment later, the vampire was on top of his back, dragging both his arms backward. He felt the ligaments in his shoulders and elbows begin to give way as pain arced through his body like lightning.

Choking back a scream of agony, he raised his head up as far as he could to see his wife pinned to the wall by a tall brunette with her left hand on Anna's throat. His wife's feet dangled six inches off the floor. The vampire's right hand held stiff like a knife, poised an inch away from Anna's left eye.

"Stop!" she commanded. "Or else she dies."

William's heart sank – he recognized who it was.

Chloe Armitage, and ... this must be Marcus Drake on my back.

Drake's heavy knee pushed hard into the middle of his back as he dragged back on William's arms. His joints creaked and the bones of his shoulders ground against each other. William was six feet three inches and two hundred and seventy pounds of dense muscle and bone. He could bench press over four hundred pounds without the benefit of the Ramp. With the Ramp, he could recruit every muscle fiber in a given contraction. One hundred percent recruitment of muscle fibers as opposed to the normal human response of twenty percent. The Ramp made him five times stronger than normal and the associated physiological shifts of the Ramp reinforced ligaments and bones to handle the loads. But even with those capabilities, he didn't have half the strength necessary to break Drake's hold.

William let go.

Drake immediately bundled him into a chair and tied him up with chains and padlocks. He strained against them with all of his tremendous strength, but they did not give way.

"Sized to hold vampires – you can't break them," Drake declared with a smirk.

William looked across the room, the three of them were each confined to a chair at the points of a triangle about ten feet on a side. The vampires had moved the other furniture back against the walls and cleared the middle of the lounge room. Armitage and Drake stood in the center of the triangle and faced him.

Drake massaged his jaw; a trickle of blood streaked his chin.

Armitage gave him a neatly folded handkerchief, and directed primly. "Don't make a mess."

Drake wiped his jaw, spat into the cloth. He grimaced gap-toothed and remarked ruefully, "He hits hard."

"I don't want to hear about it – it will heal." Armitage declared, focusing her attention on William.

William stared back at her. It was clear the Vampire Dominion had discovered his family. The fact they were still alive meant his family was not the victim of a casual hunt. He wished the vampires were simply hunting, as death would most likely have been quick. No, this was far worse. The vampires were here for a purpose other than feeding, and he truly dreaded the possible paths this could go.

They were in a helpless position. He could only hope this pair of vampires would make a mistake. An error he could exploit to allow them all to escape, or at the very least save the lives of his wife and son.

William considered the situation and determined that he was most likely a dead man, but if by dying, he could save the lives of his wife and son, he would do so without hesitation.

* * *

Chloe studied William, smiled warmly and said, "Before we start, let's wake Anton. It's best to make sure he doesn't miss anything."

After all, she mused, *much of what will happen tonight is for his benefit.* She moved over to the coffee table which rested hard up against a wall. Marcus's open case sat on it. She retrieved a vial from it, unstopped it and waved it under Anton's nose. "Awake Anton," she called out. "Awake!"

The effect was immediate and dramatic. Anton convulsed as if given an electric shock. He was bound to the chair with plastic ties at his hands and ankles. He collapsed back, as limp as a rag doll.

Anton raised his head, and shook it as if clearing it, and swore irritably, "What the hell." He glanced around the room, taking in the scene. His face paled and his eyes widened with shock. "Mom, Dad, what's going on?"

"Stay calm Son, we'll get through this together," William declared grimly.

"Be strong, Anton," Anna cried out. Tears welling up in her eyes.

Chloe wanted to slap them, she really wanted them to know precisely how helpless they were. She wanted to tell them the truth and make them understand the reality of what was going on. As necessary as deception was to her strategy, she took no joy from lying – it left her feeling tainted. She hungered for a time when she would be able to live a life of absolute honesty, a life of truth without the need for subterfuge. And what a glorious world that would be.

She stood in the middle of the room, waiting for the Slaynes to calm down, to become still. *Necessity makes liars of us all,* she admitted silently to herself. She sighed, and everyone in the room looked at her.

"Well, if you don't want to be here – let us go," William said.

Chloe's eyes widened and she blurred forward. "Don't presume to know what I'm feeling." She slapped William hard across the face. His head rocked back as if struck by a baseball bat. She'd hit him with artful perfection, maximizing pain without knocking him out – she needed him to be conscious.

"Right, let us begin the preliminaries," she declared, fetching a smartphone from the case. Flicking on the camera function, she took three photos of Anton, front, left and right, as if taking mug shots. She winked at him and said in soft tones, "I'll need these later."

She put the phone back in the case and extracted four pieces of polished metal. In moments, she snapped, twisted and screwed the pieces together to form an elegant, gleaming saber.

"Not my favorite sword," she said while flourishing the shining blade. "The weapon of an assassin from the court of King Louis the fourteenth of France, but it is easily hidden and will serve for tonight."

Chloe returned to face William and promised with perfect certainty, "You will give me what I ask for." Turning, she addressed the room. "Or you will discover a fate far worse than you could possibly imagine for your family and yourself."

Anton, Anna, William, and even Marcus stroking his healing jaw, stared at her as the room fell into silence.

* * *

Dread gripped Anton's chest with ice cold fingers. How could this happen? Who were these people? What did she want?

He pulled at his bindings, but there was no getting free. The plastic was already starting to cut into the skin at his wrists. He looked at his parents, they were bound with steel chains and solid padlocks. *Why the difference? Sure, Dad is strong; he can out lift me – but chains are overkill – aren't they?*

Armitage interrupted his silent torrent of questions. "William Slayne, exiled member of the Order of Thoth and sworn enemy of the Vampire Dominion. I, Chloe Armitage, First General and right hand of King Cornelius Crane, hereby put you to the question," she announced. "Answer me truthfully and you will be granted quick death as befits your mortality – lie to me – and I will deliver you to a life of eternal punishment."

Flourishing her saber, she ran the blade over her palm and blood splashed onto the carpet. "This I swear before vampiric witnesses on the sacred blood of Mekra, mother of us all."

The blood drained from his father's face, and his mother gasped in shock. What were the Vampire Dominion and the Order of Thoth? Who was King Cornelius Crane and what did he want with Anton's family? The world had gone mad!

Armitage advanced on his father – her hand had already stopped bleeding. She leaned in on William, her face inches from his own, and asked directly, "You have the Papyrus of Hakron the Scribe – do you not?"

William shook his head. "I don't have it."

"I will bury you in a silver coffin," she promised. "I will convert you before we seal the lid. You will live for thousands of years confined in the dark, paralyzed by silver and unable to move. Tormented by thirst, you will be unable to die … are you sure you don't have the Papyrus?" Armitage stood straight and waved her hand around the room. "Are you sure it is not here … hidden somewhere in this house?"

William paused for a moment, shaking his head. "My father destroyed it, to ensure it could never come into the possession of the likes of you."

Armitage laughed derisively. "Arthur Slayne, the great archeologist, the great champion of the Order of Thoth, destroys one of the only three artifacts in the world that together give access to the Metaframe. Access he could use to destroy the Vampire Dominion. The greatest warrior of the Order of Thoth turns down the most powerful weapon, just to keep it out of our hands." She arched an eyebrow. "Please forgive me if I find that hard to believe."

What is the Metaframe? Anton asked himself silently.

Tilting her head slightly, Armitage stared hard at his father and said, "You have courage William, I will grant you that, but you are also foolish. I take my oaths seriously; you have sealed your fate. But what of the fate of your wife and son? What of Anna and Anton? What will become of them?"

William's jaw worked, but he said nothing, while his muscles bunched and strained against his chains.

Armitage stepped behind where Anna sat, placing the edge of the saber against the side of her neck, just below her ear. "I could slice bits off her as you watched. I wonder, would that be enough to motivate you?"

Marcus took up a position behind William, taking hold of his head with both hands, forcing him to face his wife.

Armitage stepped aside, her hand blurring, thrusting the saber through Anna's right shoulder. She twisted the blade. Anna's agonized scream drowned out the snapping of her bones.

"Leave her alone!" Anton shouted, overwhelmed with a need to protect his mother. "If you need to torture someone – torture me!"

Armitage turned to him, leaving the saber embedded in Anna's shoulder. "If necessary, your turn will come, but that will depend upon your father, and on which force is stronger? His resolve to protect the Papyrus or his love for his family."

Turning back to William, she paused for a long moment. "Do you want to try again? Now please remember carefully, for I am tiring of this game – where is the Papyrus?"

"Okay," William whispered, then half-shouted, "OKAY!" William stared at Anna with wide eyes as she gasped in pain. He uttered the words without looking away from his beloved wife, "There is a wall safe. The Papyrus is in it. It is behind the painting above the fireplace."

Armitage caught Drake's gaze and then flicked her head toward the picture. Drake let go of William and took the painting down. Behind it was a wall safe with a combination lock.

William muttered in a voice heavy with defeat, "The numbers are sixteen left, twenty-three right, seven left and thirty-four right."

Drake dialed the numbers. His head cocking slightly at the end, responding to a sound beyond Anton's ability to hear. He grinned, and pulled open the safe door. He recoiled, lifting his left hand like a shield, hissed and jumped backward about a dozen feet as if scalded. "Silver!"

Armitage looked back at Anna and withdrew her bloody saber.

Anna screamed again, her hands trembling with shock, blood spreading in a wet stain on her shoulder.

Armitage advanced on the safe, pushing the door back with the gore-soaked point of the blade, and looking inside the safe.

"Indeed," she said with a wry grin. "You have some silver sitting on top of a Papyrus." She used the point of her saber to push several silver coins and small bars out of the way. She fished out the Papyrus with her blade and caught it as it dropped free from the safe.

"I'm sorry Anna – I'll have to put this back," Armitage remarked with mock regret. "It's stopping you from bleeding to death, and it wouldn't do to have you die by accident." She jammed the saber directly back into the wound, perfectly matching the original cut. This time, Anna didn't scream. Gritting her teeth, she kept her silence.

His mother's agony swept through Anton like a physical blow. He was helpless; tied to a chair as vampires tortured his parents. It was worse than a nightmare, at least with a nightmare, it was possible to wake up. If anyone had told him this could happen, he would have called them crazy – and yet it was happening – the world had gone mad.

Armitage carefully opened the Papyrus. It was a scroll about six feet long and a foot wide, covered with intricate hieroglyphics. It looked faded, fragile and ancient. She scanned the Papyrus quickly. Pausing about halfway through, she frowned and rolled the Papyrus back up, and slapped it down carelessly beside the case. She walked back to the center of the room, steepled her fingers beneath her lips as if pondering what to do next. She turned toward Anna and commanded flatly, "Marcus, break her leg."

Drake's fist blurred faster than Anton's eye could follow. His mother shrieked as her right thigh bone shattered beneath Drake's hammer blow.

Anton swore, "What the fucking hell – we gave you what you wanted!"

His face flushed with blood, William shouted in frustration, "How dare you! I will make you pay!"

Armitage waited while Anna's screams reduced to quiet sobs. She turned toward William and arched an eyebrow. "I gave you the opportunity to be honest, to tell the truth, and what did I receive in return – lies and empty threats. You disappoint me, William Slayne. I thought you'd be a better man than this."

William snarled. "Let me free and give me a sword, and we'll see if you remain disappointed."

Armitage tilted her head slightly, putting her finger on her chin, her eyes filled with a fell light. "… Tempting – but I think not. A vampire's blood oath forbids mercy and death by my sword would be merciful."

William snapped, "I have no fear of dying."

"Of course not, you're a Slayne, but you no longer have the option of dying – do you?" Chloe promised, with quiet emphasis. "The time will come when you'll want nothing else but to die."

William stared at her in silence, his jaw clenched and his eyes gleaming like hard stones.

Anton implored her, "You have what you came for – what more do you want?"

Armitage picked up the Papyrus from the coffee table and threw it into Anton's lap. "You can have that if you want – it's a fake." She sighed. "Hakron the Scribe encrypted the real Papyrus. By reputation, it reads like utter gibberish written by a madman. An order is apparent in this," she shook her head once, "rubbish. A lesser mind than Hakron's wrote it. It's a worthless fake designed to deceive the unwary."

"Do you have to talk so damn much?" William said with a growl. "Just kill us already, your talk is worse than the torture."

Anton and Anna stared at William. Anton wondered what on Earth his father was doing. Did he have a strategy? Anton hoped so with all his heart.

"Oh, William," Armitage declared, shaking her head. "There are things far worse than simple death, as you already know."

Horror swirled into a great, dark cloud within Anton as Armitage walked back to where Anna sat chained to her chair. His mother reflexively recoiled as Armitage approached, but she was unable to avoid her captor pulling her head back, and biting deep into her throat in a classic vampire attack. Armitage wrapped her mouth around the wound and within a handful of seconds his mother's skin paled, while veins darkened on her throat as her blood rushed into the vampire's maw.

Anton's mother gasped in shock, while his father groaned in despair.

"Oh my God," Anton whispered. He wouldn't have believed it if he hadn't seen it with his own eyes; vampires were horribly real. He was at a loss to imagine what could happen next. Witnessing his own mother drained of her blood by a creature that in any sane world would not even exist. Surely, it couldn't get any worse than that.

Armitage stepped away from Anna. She licked a stray drop of blood from her finger, sighed with obvious pleasure and remarked as if speaking to the room, "There must be something about the Ramp. The blood of the Order is exquisite."

"You will rot in hell if I ever get my hands on you," William promised, his voice shaking with helpless fury.

"Oh William, I'm sure you will be there long before me." Armitage walked over to Drake's case, and retrieved a large hypodermic syringe from it. She went back to stand next to Anna. She faced William, hitched up her left sleeve, and promised with absolute certainty, "You have insisted on lying to me. I'm sure you will regret that choice." She plunged the syringe into the vein in the crook of her left elbow. She drew back on the plunger, and filled the syringe with her blood.

Anton looked on in uncomprehending horror while his father shouted, "NO!"

Armitage plunged the filled syringe directly into Anna's heart – just to the left of the sternum as if she was a paramedic delivering a vital dose of adrenalin to a heart attack victim.

The effect was immediate. Anna's eyes bulged, and she writhed in agony while William cried out in despair. Anna's limbs twitched and vibrated. Inbetween low moans, she cried out, "No ... Please God ... NO!"

Armitage stepped to the side, studying William intently. He wrenched his eyes from his wife and stared back at their tormentor, his face twisted with hate, fury and despair.

Armitage commanded in stern tones, "Tell me where the real Papyrus is."

William shook his head, whispering hoarsely, "No – I can't do that."

Armitage's eyes softened and she promised, "I will give her a clean death."

William shook his head in silence.

"Marcus, prepare to free her," Armitage directed, "but keep her on a leash."

Armitage turned back to William and inquired with a knowing look, "Who do you think she will feed on when the bloodlust of a virgin vampire overwhelms her? I assure you; the choice will not be rational. Will it be you, or will it be Anton? I trust her maternal instincts will protect Anton, which means that she will feed on you."

"You're a fiend!" William declared furiously.

"You are wrong William," Armitage corrected him, as if instructing a dull and tiresome student. "I am simply doing what is necessary. You could have avoided all of this upset and trouble – just tell me where the real Papyrus is."

"Dad tell her," Anton pleaded in desperate tones. "Before it's too late."

His father stared at Anton with eyes filled with disappointment and shook his head slowly.

A shocking realization swept through Anton; it really was too late. He felt sick to his stomach. If by dying, he could end this horror, he would willingly die. His stomach churned, he'd never seen his father disappointed in him before now, it was shocking beyond belief. The world had gone insane. If the floor opened up and demons erupted from a fiery hell to drag him down – it would seem normal compared to what was happening right now.

Armitage approached William, and stood beside him. She caressed his cheek, and he twisted his head away from her hand. She leaned down, whispering in his ear but just loud enough for Anton to hear her words, "Now William, please listen closely. Marcus and I will stand ready. When your wife begins feeding on you, we will watch carefully, and Marcus will drag her off before she drains you completely. Now Marcus is very strong, even for a vampire. It's one of the reasons that I like to keep him around, so don't assume that he can't do what I need him to. Then I will inject you with my blood and in about five minutes you will be a newly converted vampire with an overwhelming and uncontrollable need to feed on the nearest human being – and who would that be?"

She left the question hanging between them and straightened up. The transformation of Anton's mother completed. Armitage glanced at the gleaming blade piercing Anna's shoulder and asked her henchman, "The saber?"

Drake pulled the weapon from Anna's shoulder, and handed it back to his mistress.

Anna winced and then smiled. "William, my love. The pain is gone. I can feel my thigh, it's healing. I feel strong." She moaned as if aroused, tossing back her long blond hair, she wet her lips with her tongue and declared huskily, "William, I need you."

Anton watched in horror as his mother's attention focused on his father. It was like watching a starving snake looking at a juicy fat rat.

Armitage stood behind his father, resting her a hand on his shoulder. She said softly into his left ear, "After I convert you and you finish feeding on your son. I will convert him as well and stake him out in the backyard to await sunrise. You and your wife I will imprison in silver at opposite ends of this world. Where is the real Papyrus of Hakron the Scribe? Tell me now, and I will kill your wife cleanly and spare your son's life. I have given a sacred oath and I will honor my word."

William looked down, his face twisting with anguish. "It is behind the picture that you took down, hidden in the frame."

Anna thrashed against her bonds, her eyes flashing with a terrible lust, she screamed, "Free me! I must feed!"

Armitage ignored her, shredding the frame and extracting another Papyrus. She checked it carefully for about two minutes while Anna ranted and raved in her chair. She briefly closed her eyes, breathing deeply, she wiped away a tear with a trembling hand.

Anton's mother's face snapped around toward Armitage.

Armitage stepped aside, smiled briefly and with an air of quiet inevitability, she declared, "I am true to my word." Her saber blurred through a flashing arc and Anna's head slipped from her shoulders to the floor.

Anton screamed with horror while William wept with despair.

"Marcus, clear this room and take William Slayne to the car."

In moments, Drake rendered William unconscious with the same drug he'd used on Anton. He cleared the coffee table of the photos, and the business card, gathering it all together into his black case. He then carried William's limp body from the house.

Armitage approached Anton, still tied to his chair, tears streaming down his face. She flicked the saber and his mother's blood disappeared from the blade. She poked him lightly in the chest, enough to break the skin, getting his attention with a little physical pain. "You are the one that invited us in." she said in cold, cutting tones. "You – in your ignorance and helplessness – became the bait that made your parents vulnerable. It is entirely your fault that they are dead or imprisoned forever." She smiled at him without warmth and said, "On the bright side – you get to live."

Armitage tapped him again on the sternum with the point of her saber. "One other lesson before I go." She leaned in close, her face inches from his own. Her eyes locked on Anton's as she instructed with a soft caressing voice, "Your parents have told you that they loved you and wanted to keep you safe, but I ask you this – who spent years lying to you and who told you the truth?" Stepping back, Armitage slashed his bindings.

Anton reached out, trying to catch her, but by the time the plastic ties had hit the floor – she'd already vanished from the house. He stared wide-eyed around the room in silence. The house lay still like a felled corpse. His mother slumped lifeless in her chair, her head at her feet. His father had disappeared and was destined for a supernatural punishment.

Anton dropped to his knees before his mother's corpse, and howled like an animal caught in a trap. Overwhelmed with emotion, devastated beyond words, he was drowning in grief and utterly alone.

* * *

Anton staggered up to his room.

This is insane, this is insane, this is insane. The words kept circling like trolls around his mind. He couldn't think. Images flashed randomly through him, constantly replaying the horror. The saber slicing into his mother's shoulder. Armitage draining her blood and licking her finger afterward. His mother's transformation into a blood lusting monster, followed by the lethal brutality of her beheading.

It's my fault. Armitage's words threaded through his mind like cold dark needles. He couldn't breathe, he was dizzy and lightheaded. *I'm hyperventilating.* He sat on his bed, put his head in his hands and started breathing through his nose. *Slowly, in, out, hold my breath, in, out, hold my breath.*

A thin veneer of sanity returned. He couldn't stay. This house was no longer a home, but where could he go? His mind raced, switching between options before trenchant memory dragged it back to scenes of recent horrors.

He whispered in desperation, "How can I unsee what I have seen?"

Canvassing many options in a frenzied rush, he quickly packed a backpack with a few essentials.

He stopped, standing like a statue in the middle of his bedroom. He couldn't call the police. How would the conversation go? He whispered derisively to himself, "Hello officer, vampires beheaded my mother and abducted my father," he snorted, then smacked his face, his hand sliding down to cover his mouth, his eyes wide and staring into empty space. A patina of the surreal covered his world. The authorities would be useless. He concluded in a hoarse whisper, "The cops will think that I did it, or Dad did it."

How could he live with this? What about his friends? They'd be expecting him tonight. Anton picked up his smartphone and it shook in his hands before dropping back to the desk. Vampires had murdered his mother and abducted his father. There was nothing stopping them coming back for him. The last thing he wanted to do was get any of his friends involved. He was dangerous to be around. He'd have to be a no show for tonight. Anton resolved to disappear. His friends could not know where he was. It would keep them safe, and might keep himself safe too. He checked his wallet; he had a little over sixty dollars on him. He had another thousand in his savings account. He grabbed his passport. He didn't know if it would be useful or not, but better to take it and not need it, than leave it behind and discover it was essential. He left his phone on his desk, anyone who might call it – he didn't want to answer.

Anton gave the room a long, last look. He could forget about exams; he was never going to graduate. The ice hockey scholarship was in the bin. He felt a sharp pang of deep disappointment as he realized his budding professional sports career was over. The feeling lasted all of a second before an ocean of guilt washed it away. "Damn it. How could I be so selfish?"

He rubbed both hands through his thick dark hair, before dragging them down his face. His mother was dead and vampires had abducted his father. There was no time for self-pity.

"Damn it all to hell. Weapons? What can I use against these damn vampires?"

A dozen movies and TV shows flicked through his mind. He put aside the idea of finding Armitage or Drake in their coffins and staking them through the heart. They didn't look like they spent any time in a coffin. Guns, you would have to be very fast to shoot someone who could move in a blur.

Then he remembered their aversion to silver. They didn't like silver – they avoided it with a passion.

Anton put on his runners, a cap and a dark jacket with a hood. He stuffed some spare clothes into his backpack and put his sunglasses on top of them. He went downstairs and into the lounge room.

His mother's corpse still sat in her chair. He'd been unable to touch her before. It was too macabre, and his emotions lay like strips of raw meat in his soul. Armitage had told him, it was all his fault, he'd been bait, and his parents had been unable to defend themselves because of him. His breathing became fast and shallow. He stood, staring at his mother, the safe and the silver momentarily forgotten. Fresh tears welled up in his eyes.

"Fuck it!" Anton snarled. "Why am I still alive?"

Armitage had whispering into his ear, *I am sure you will do great things.* She'd wanted him to live. She had a purpose that involved him.

Anton shook his head as his rage overflowed the walls of his soul, and he screamed in inarticulate defiance. He panted for a long moment, his soul on fire, and vowed to his mother's corpse, "There is no way I'm ever going to help that bitch!"

He went to the safe, there was the silver and nothing else. Taking the coins and small bars, he added them to his backpack. As he left the room, he deliberately avoided looking at his mother's corpse for the last time. He wanted to remember her as she was when she was alive. A vibrant, inquisitive woman with a kind heart, and not as she was now – a real life horror show.

Anton went to the kitchen, added a pair of water bottles, some hard cheese, nuts and dried fruit. Anything he could easily carry that would last more than a few days.

He left the house through the back door, made his way over the fence and into the nearby forest preserve and garden cemetery. Then he ran; as he left his home behind, he had an uncanny feeling of hidden watchers tracking his every step, that the woods were full of eyes.

His skin crawled, he stopped, turning to stare into the shadows behind him – but there was no one there. Listening carefully, he could only hear the silence of the surrounding gardens. There wasn't even the whisper of a breeze. The trees stood still, silent sentinels over the nearby gravestones, and the only intrusions were the faint noises of the city beyond. He turned again, running hard for two minutes, putting another eight hundred yards between himself and his home.

He had to get away from here. He had to disappear. He pulled to a sudden stop. *What about my father?* Witnessing his mother's torture and murder had overwhelmed him. He'd momentarily forgotten about his father. Anton was the only person who had any knowledge of what had occurred, he was the only one who could save his father or avenge his mother.

Responsibility fell like a dead weight upon his shoulders. Rage, grief, guilt, terror, and despair, warred within his soul. His stomach knotted. He collapsed to his knees, overtaken by convulsive vomiting. He pushed himself back from the mess, sitting back against a nearby tree. Breathing in the smell of the vomit made him feel nauseous again, and he gave way to the compulsion. He sat back again, wiping his mouth with his hand. He took a swig from one of his water bottles, swishing it around his mouth before spitting it out. He took a long pull on the bottle and the water soothed his throat.

Questions lay siege to his soul. Armitage had done everything possible to make him hate her. Did she want him to try and kill her? Why would she want him to do that? Surely her purpose can't be her own suicide. There must be something else going on.

Anton's emotions churned. His thoughts were leaves flying carelessly within a firestorm. His father had said to Armitage, '*I will make you pay.*' His words struck through the chaos within, fanning Anton's rage.

Ghosts of the recent past flew through his soul, whispering, '*It's your fault, be afraid, there is no hope, don't care, be numb.* But he did care, he couldn't give up. He couldn't let it go. He couldn't let any of it go.

A chaotic sea threatened to engulf him, reaching desperately, he found sanctuary from the chaos on an icy rock of fury. Dragging himself out of the clinging wasteland of madness he stood tall upon the glacial ice. It burned with pale fire while lightning played behind his eyes. Anton lifted his gaze. His eyes hardened as he promised with dreadful conviction, "I will make you pay."

He continued in quiet tones of ferocious intent, "I know who you are Chloe Armitage. I will find out what you are and how to kill you, and when we meet again – then you will pay for what you have done."

Slinging his backpack over his shoulder, he strode off. After ten minutes, he reached the edge of the garden cemetery, and stepped onto a sidewalk. He paused for a moment, considering his father's fate with a heart in which anguish and cold fury stood opposed in a frightful detente.

I may not be able to save you dad, but if I find you, I promise you that I will release you.

* * *

Chloe lifted her Shadowstone smartphone to her ear.

It was already dialing the call. The system relied on quantum encryption technologies that rendered the call both untraceable, and indecipherable to anyone but the intended recipient.

A familiar voice answered after the second ring, "James Haley speaking, what can I do for you, Ma'am?"

"James, I need a cleanup crew at this residence," Chloe requested, sending through the GPS coordinates of the Smith family home in Boston. "Deal with this personally. There is no room for error."

"Yes Ma'am, I will organize a team immediately and ensure the site is completely sanitized."

"I have an additional assignment for you and your team. One of the terrorists escaped, I'm sending photos of him now."

Chloe forwarded the photos of Anton taken in the lounge room earlier that night. The photos were close ups of Anton's face and didn't reveal his restraints.

"His name is Anton Smith," she directed. "I want him found and tracked, but under no circumstances are you to approach, contact, or engage with him in any way. Report immediately back to me once you have established a sustained trace on his location."

"I will have a Panopticon search running in less than a minute after this call ends," James replied.

Chloe could almost hear him nodding his head as he promised, "We will find him, Ma'am."

"Be sure that you do."

"Yes, Ma'am."

Chloe hung up.

James Haley, head of the United States arm of the Shadowstone organization, would follow her orders to the letter. Chloe had worked with him for years, trusting him as much as she trusted anyone – which is to say not much – but she understood him and knew he could be relied upon to get things done. He was an able and effective operator, previously with the CIA, Shadowstone had recruited him with the promise of being, 'where the real action is', in the 'blackest of black ops,' in a 'genuine transnational global organization working for world peace and the greater good.' The situation with Anton Slayne was delicate, she needed staff capable of subtlety. James was capable of being subtle and playing an effective role.

She'd contemplated the idea of bringing James fully into the Vampire Dominion, but that would require the approval of Cornelius Crane. An approval Crane was unlikely to grant. Crane was rigorous in keeping total vampire numbers below his *'magic'* limit of one thousand. He had never provided a reason for why he limited vampire numbers to less than a thousand, and Chloe had lost interest in trying to find out why. She deemed it a quirk of her boss.

Chloe turned to the Papyrus. It sat next to her on the back seat of the limousine. She lifted it up, unrolled it and read it again. She replayed in her mind the act of reading it for the first time in the Slayne lounge room. Nothing had changed, every detail of the Papyrus was identical with her memory.

An eidetic memory is as rare amongst humans as amongst vampires. It was one of the skills that had attracted the Order of Thoth to induct her before her eighteenth birthday. It was an ability she'd kept secret from Crane.

She put the Papyrus down. Leaning back, she closed her eyes, savoring its content. She remembered the position of individual fibers, of slight variations in pigment where Hakron had needed to renew an ink pot. She easily recalled every detail, every image, delighting in what she saw. She could hand the prize of the Papyrus of Hakron the Scribe to her master, while retaining a perfect copy for herself.

Chloe's eyes shone with pleasure and she smiled broadly. The limousine pulled to a halt within a hangar owned by R.I.S.C at Boston's Logan Airport. Marcus transferred the bound and gagged, but now awake William Slayne to a sleek, black helicopter.

The nightfalcon was an advanced evolution of the blackhawk helicopter, the new design commissioned and funded by the Vampire Dominion. Crane had assigned this particular helicopter to her personal use. The pilot was a vampire, a member of her personal staff. The helicopter began to spool up with a low whine as great doors in the roof of the hangar started clanking open. Chloe boarded her nightfalcon, taking a seat in the main cabin.

She addressed the pilot, "To the citadel."

"Yes, General Armitage," the pilot replied.

Marcus joined her in the cabin, closing the door as the helicopter took off. It rapidly cleared the hangar and sped off toward New York City.

* * *

A terrorist had escaped.

James Haley worked his smartphone, inserting the three photos he'd just received from General Armitage into the Panopticon system. He swapped to his computer terminal. Logging into the Panopticon, he punched up the search program. He selected the photos and set the search program running with a high priority flag.

The Panopticon responded with a three-dimensional plot of the world. A web of red markers spread across the screen. Each tiny red flag indicated where searches completed with a negative result. The markers operated at a very fine resolution; it was like watching a set of red waves spreading out from nodes located in all the world's major cities. Boston showed an orange rash where the Panopticon found hits on the target in records older than an hour. There were no yellow or green markers. Not a single camera linked to the Panopticon had registered Anton Smith within the last hour or last minute respectively.

James ran his cursor over several options, clicking as he went. The system responded by expanding the Boston view until the perimeter of hits in the last week filled the screen while simultaneously cross-referencing hits to establish a target profile. In seconds, James had a name, a student number, a social security number, a smartphone number, email accounts, bank accounts, Facebook and other social media accounts. The system even began estimating the target's characteristics, habits, predilections, and personality type based on usage of all other systems.

James rapidly scanned the profile, musing to himself, *Well, Anton Smith, you're a little young to be playing in the big league. I wonder what you did to attract all this attention.*

He looked around his office, a set of hi-definition, multi-screen monitors dominated the walls. One of them showed current satellite tracks. James smiled to himself and thought out loud, "That's convenient."

He opened a new program, vectoring a camera on a military satellite currently passing over the northeast corner of the United States. He fed in the GPS coordinates of the Smith residence and the satellite camera zoomed in on Anton Smith's home.

He flicked on a filter to get an infra-red view. There was nothing alive inside the house. James stared intently at the screen for about five seconds, and then his fingers rapidly flowed over the keyboard before he paused for a moment waiting for a response. The satellite camera swapped in a new filter and the telephone network rang the smartphone number on Anton

Smith's profile. In the center of his monitor, a small red star came into existence and started flashing over a room at the top of the house. He flicked the camera back to its standard operations, and leaned back in his chair.

The phone was home; the boy was not. Who would leave home without their phone? Someone was in a hurry. It mattered less what he was running from, than where he was running to.

James had been with Shadowstone for eight years. He'd seen a lot of things in that time, not all of which made sense. His initial induction had emphasized the need to maintain stability in the world, and to combat those forces that would bring chaos and death. A true fight between good and evil where devoted service to the greater good licensed any and all actions.

He'd always pursued a life that would make a difference, first with the US Army Green Berets, and then with the CIA. At thirty years of age, the man who had previously held his current role had tapped him on the shoulder. He'd pursued the opportunity and within three months General Armitage had interviewed and accepted him into the ranks of Shadowstone. In the last eight years, he'd worked to keep the world hanging together, to ensure stability and order, to keep governments operational and the little guy safe. He'd done everything he could for the greater good.

However, there were many operations like this current one, sanitation ops, the cleansing of all evidence of the operation of a group of operatives reporting directly to General Armitage. There was an echelon of agents that operated at a layer above where he was, who were definitely outside his chain of command, and who participated in all the real missions.

General Armitage had told him the enemy had special training and combat techniques and only her elite agents and special forces could effectively combat them. James shook his head. He believed that he belonged on the front line with the special forces on combat operations.

Instead of combat operations, Operational Security, OPSEC, was his primary purpose. Information suppression and the keeping of secrets. The Order of Thoth and the Red Empire opposed Shadowstone. Terrorist organizations that made Al Qaeda and ISIS seem like amateurs. Revolutionary organizations that would bathe the world in blood to achieve their objectives of the overthrow of the current world order. They were a clear and present danger, but he'd never met a single operative from either group – and that wasn't what he'd signed up for.

James was a man of action, but instead of confronting the enemy he found himself riding herd on a stunningly effective surveillance system and a set of cleanup crews. But now a terrorist had escaped, it was an opportunity to prove what he could really do. He put aside his wool gathering and focused on the task at hand.

He did not need to look up who was available to assign to this operation. The closest spectrum team was Green-4, sixteen highly skilled operatives organized into four-man squads led by Louise Wesson. He rang her smartphone, all the Shadowstone operatives carried smartphones equipped with completely secure quantum encryption.

Louise Wesson answered immediately, "Yes, Sir. What are your orders?"

"We have another clean up op. This time it's Boston. I'm sending site and target profiles through to your phone. If you encounter the target, do not engage; instead, standoff, track only and await further orders. Is that clear?"

"Yes, perfectly Sir. I will get the team in motion. We're at Fort Dix at the moment, it will take us a minimum of four and a half hours to get the sanitation vans and my available staff to Boston ... that gives us an ETA of 03:00 hours."

"Get moving, I will meet you on site," James directed.

"Already moving, Sir."

"Outstanding."

James hung up the call. He fetched his jacket from a coat rack next to the door of his office. He went to the nearest elevator and descended to the building's parking garage; he would need his car's specialized set of equipment.

It was going to be a long night.

* * *

Chloe Armitage's nightfalcon descended smoothly through the open hangar doors on the roof of a massive Manhattan skyscraper.

Top end military grade weapon systems had tracked the helicopter for the last five miles as it approached the building. Sophisticated sensor arrays that no city officials were aware of identified her helicopter as a friend, allowing her craft to safely pass disengaged missile and rail gun systems. The building, at number 350 on Fifth Avenue, had 108 floors above ground level. The hangar and building defense systems took up floors 107 and 108 as a combined space.

The operations of the Vampire Dominion occupied all the floors above the hundredth floor and included the personal quarters of Cornelius Crane, King of the Vampires.

This was his citadel.

As the helicopter landed, Chloe turned to Marcus and ordered him, "Take Slayne to our containment facility on Rikers Island, get him set up and wait for me to arrive."

Marcus nodded and replied, "Yes, Chloe."

Chloe exited the nightfalcon and walked briskly to the elevator. She carried the Papyrus in a tubular case tucked under her left arm.

Crane's praetorians guarded the building. They were elite vampire warriors dressed in modern matte black combat armor, carrying long curved swords, and M249 light machine guns. A pair of them saluted her, stepping aside as she reached the elevator doors.

Chloe ignored them; deference was a one-way street in the Vampire Dominion. Inside the elevator, she leaned forward, staring into a biometric eye scanner, a small green light came on above it. She pressed the button for the operations center on the 103rd floor. Moments later, she strode into the tactical heart of her operational domain. Forty stations and screens surrounded her, a dozen vampires at work in the room, a skeleton staff for the current low threat environment.

The cold war detente was in full swing. She remembered when vampires working in shifts crowded the room. The beating heart of the Vampire Dominion's war against the Ramp masters of the Red Empire and the Order of Thoth. Those were the days; when a swift blade and tactical brilliance made all the difference. The quietude of the modern world left her with a gnawing dissatisfaction. A desire for a return of more challenging times.

The vampires in the ops center stood up, saluting her as she came out of the elevator. She walked briskly past them, indifferent to their actions, and they returned to their duties. She strode to the end of the room where a single set of stairs gave access to the floor above – to Crane's personal quarters.

She shared access to the 104th floor with the other four generals and Crane's personal secretary. All of them captured by the curse of the Haitian voodoo priest, Jean Philippe Allemande, which had eliminated their ability to harm Crane.

As she took her first step on the stairs, another biometric scanner took in her body shape and style of movement. At the first landing of the stairs, a GAU-17/A minigun tracked the center of her body mass. The gun sported six barrels and fired 7.62mm depleted uranium rounds. It could deliver four thousand rounds of pure hell per minute. The system recognized her and the deadly weapon swung out of the way.

She'd walked up these stairs more times than she cared to remember. Each time, she found herself musing about the nasty accident that would occur if the system ever made a mistake. She enjoyed the details of technology, but she considered it a weakness to rely on it too much. She stepped past the wicked looking barrels of the minigun without a second glance at the formidable weapon.

At the top of the second flight of stairs, she approached a forbidding door of polished steel. Only someone on the other side of the door could open it. She waited a moment and a nearly invisible seam opened vertically in the reflective surface. The two sides, thick enough to stop a shaped explosive charge, silently pulled back into the walls. Cornelius Crane, king of the vampires, had just granted her access to his personal quarters.

Chloe stepped into the inner sanctum of Crane's citadel. The whole floor was an extended suite done exclusively in the high style of the 18th-century French aristocracy. She walked calmly along a broad entry hall. The walls had shallow nooks holding exquisite pieces of art. Crane favored the European Renaissance masters. The halls and rooms displayed a collection of Da Vinci, Michelangelo, Donatello, Raphael, Botticelli, Titian, Hieronymus Bosch, and woodcuts by Albrecht Dürer – all authentic, and many famous.

The fakes and copies littered the walls of the museums of the world – the originals were here. Crane was a collector; and art was one of his many passions. Chloe noted as she walked past the art that he'd collected her too, and for a time, she'd been his passion.

She entered into his library. He'd been collecting books since the 11th century. Shelves and volumes lined the walls from floor to ceiling. Additional works rested in climate-controlled cases to preserve them. The great minds of the last five thousand years filled the room. More than a dozen languages were required to read what was written here, and Crane had mastered all of them.

After Crane had personally converted her into a vampire, Chloe had spent her early decades as his lover, confidant, and protégé. She'd spent many years in this library when it was still in London during the 19th century.

Walking through the main room of the library, she glanced down at an elegant French 17th-century table. Resting on the table was an original copy from the first print run of 'Dell'arte Della Guerra,' also known as 'On the Art of War' by Niccolo Machiavelli.

She'd read that very volume, written in the original Italian within the first year of her relationship with Crane. Her mind grasped the open page at a glance. She almost stopped walking as one of Machiavelli's quotes from the page came to her mind. 'No enterprise is more likely to succeed than one concealed from the enemy until it is ripe for execution.'

How apropos, she thought, *but why does he have this very page open for me to see as I pass by – does he suspect me?*

She halted in front of Crane. He sat behind a polished wooden desk, dressed simply, in fine robes and slippers. He glanced at the tube she was carrying and said with an avid grin, "Chloe, I see you have brought me a gift. Let me see it."

Chloe took the Papyrus from the case, unrolling it across the breadth of his desk.

Crane laughed. Standing up to his full six feet six-inch height. His long arms reached out, pinning the scroll at each end. He leaned over the Papyrus, peering intently at it. "It's magnificent, both intricate and unknowable without the Codex. Hakron was a genius, the equal of his brother."

"Two of the three are now together, Cornelius," Chloe remarked, using Crane's first name which he allowed when they were alone together.

"Yes. I have been searching for nearly a millennium, and now we have two artifacts in less than forty years. If I believed in it, I would say the hand of fate was at work. But no, these are the fruits of persistence, hard work, and to a great degree – your own skills." Crane rolled the Papyrus up again. Placing it within a golden tube, he rested it on his desk. He looked deeply into Chloe's eyes and requested, "You must name a reward."

Chloe's mouth tightened and she replied, "You know what I want, and it cannot be given."

"Well, yes ... such a quaint notion ... Liberty. But of course, – you must choose something else."

Chloe tilted her head slightly, smiling innocently. "I am sure that one night I will think of something worthy of my service."

Crane stared at her; his brown eyes filled with hidden thoughts, and declared, "I am sure that one night you will."

Chloe stood quietly in silence, forcing him to continue.

"Turning to other matters," Crane declared with a brief frown. "You had your personal helicopter transport a human to Rikers Island. It looks like you have more work to do tonight."

"Yes, I do. He is the son of Arthur Slayne."

Crane raised an eyebrow in surprise. "I expected you to kill them both."

"I made a sacred blood oath during the interrogation – he violated it. I am merely completing the punishment."

"So be it, such operational matters are your prerogative."

Chloe nodded.

"Is there anything else to report?"

"Nothing of any import."

"You have done excellent work tonight. Please get some rest. You're dismissed."

"Thank you, Sir," Chloe replied deferentially. She inclined her head in a short bow. Taking three steps back, she turned and walked away. She exited Crane's chambers through the polished steel doors, a slight smile curling the edge of her mouth.

He has no idea of the existence of Anton Slayne. I will have to ensure he never finds out the truth – until it is too late.

* * *

Cornelius Crane watched Chloe leave his library. He waited until he heard her exit the floor, then he remotely closed the main door behind her.

With the Papyrus tube in hand, he turned around, gazing at the art piece hanging directly behind his desk. It was the triptych, Garden of Earthly Delights, by Hieronymus Bosch. Cornelius had been the unknown patron who had commissioned both this work in 1491 and a deliberately imperfect copy completed in 1493. The copy now resided in the Museo del Prado in Madrid and had done so since 1939. The interwoven fantastical images spoke to his soul; it was his favorite masterpiece.

Together, the three panels of the triptych stood over seven feet high and thirteen feet wide. He approached the middle panel. The largest of the three, it depicted scenes of lost innocence. He touched an almost imperceptible stud on the bottom of the panel, it swung free, revealing a hidden doorway.

It was a narrow space, crouching, Crane stepped up into the doorway, disappearing into the darkness beyond. He moved into a secret room and soft lights came on automatically. It was a mini-library, filled with rare and obscure books. All manner of parchments, scraps of papyrus and wood carvings lay on shelves along the side walls. Cornelius kept all the knowledge and lore of the Metaframe here. What had been known over five thousand years before by Hakron and Ahknaton as the Divine Engine of Thoth.

Cornelius had come to understand that the Metaframe underpinned the physical reality of the world. While extremely difficult to access, once reached, anyone could change the rules of the universe as easily as a programmer might change lines of computer code. The shocking implications of that power had driven him to dedicate himself to ensuring that no one would ever access the Metaframe again.

He approached the bare rear wall. In front of it stood three short marble pillars, each about five feet high and a foot across. On the middle pillar rested a polished black obsidian stone. Its surface glistened wetly in the pale light, seeming to capture the night sky in miniature.

It was the Key of Ahknaton, retrieved in 1978 from a secret vault under St Peter's Basilica in the Vatican City. In 1625, Michelangelo had placed the key in a hidden chamber guarded by an ingenious maze filled with deadly traps. Himself a senior member of the Order of Thoth, he had made the safe keeping of the key his life's work.

Arthur Slayne had interrupted the mission to recover the key. They had fought within Michelangelo's secret vault, the three of them, Slayne, Chloe and himself. Cornelius shook his head with the troubling memory. He'd never seen anyone fight as well as Slayne had that night.

Slayne's masterful skills and extraordinary speed had saved his life. Anyone else would have died in a moment, but his survival that night had sparked an interest – an interest that led to the events of this night.

It was a pity Arthur Slayne was not one of his generals. What a treasure he would have made.

Cornelius placed the golden tube containing the Papyrus of Hakron the Scribe on top of the left pillar. It had never left the hands of a member of the Slayne family line for over five thousand years and now it was here.

Now it was safe.

He turned to contemplate the bare, third pillar on the right. The Interpretive Codex remained beyond his reach. Chloe Armitage was his best asset and she would be pivotal to bringing it here.

Cornelius turned around, staring out into the brightly lit main library without seeing anything in particular – his mind obsessed with his most useful operative. But what then? Her capability and ambition were dangerous. In the long years ahead, she may find a way to breach Allemande's curse. With the three in his possession, it would be safer for everyone if she was no longer with him.

"When the time comes, she must go," Cornelius promised to himself in the stillness of his secret library.

* * *

Chloe Armitage had used her pass to swipe her way into the bio-hazard waste section of the Rikers Island Waste Treatment Plant.

Originally commissioned in the late 1920s by the city of New York. The waste treatment plant had almost never happened. Cornelius Crane operating in the background had shaped the decision making, forestalling an alternative plan to convert Rikers Island into a prison.

It was now an ongoing commercial concern, operated by front companies owned by Shadowstone, and therefore owned by the Vampire Dominion. Even detailed inspection by city officials would not show all of what really went on at the facility. By day, the main plant processed all manner of waste, including medical waste from New York City and surrounding district hospitals. By night, vampires exclusively staffed the smaller bio-hazard waste section. It processed the remains of vampire feasts held at Crane's citadel and other locations in New England sanctioned by Crane where vampires could feed in secret. Similar facilities operated across the United States and the rest of the world; disposing of the evidence of vampire hunger.

When Crane shifted his operations from London to New York City in the early 1920s, he'd built the towering citadel on Fifth Avenue over the New York subway. He'd cut a secret railway line out to Rikers Island and funded the establishment of the waste treatment facility. He'd made it widely known amongst vampires exactly what the bio-hazard waste section was for. Chloe had punished vampires for breaking the rules and dumping bodies where humans might find them. Chloe and the praetorians routinely culled indiscreet vampires from the ranks. The vampires who survived the purges were all obedient and religiously tidy about their feeding habits.

The existence of the Vampire Dominion was a very well-kept secret.

Chloe made her way into the depths of the bio-hazard waste facility, to a door the human staff who worked there could not pass through. She tapped her pass on the sensor. The door clicked and she pushed it open. The next section was known only to the upper echelon of the Vampire Dominion, Crane, the generals, and their immediate staff. It was a facility for containing vampires, a vampire prison. Crane rarely used it, as non-compliance by a vampire to the edicts of King Crane was typically a fast form of suicide. The primary exceptions were the generals. Crane had handpicked them, and he'd gone to the trouble of having them cursed to improve their usefulness to him. With Jean Philippe Allemande dead, they were not replaceable. When they made mistakes, instead of killing them, he would punish them with imprisonment in silver.

The most recent example had been a stint by Dieter Franz. The general in charge of continental Europe, who had made a terrible error of judgment in 1945. Chloe had hauled him back to the US in disgrace, before interring him in a silver coffin for thirty years. The internment had temporarily cost Franz his sanity. It had taken him several years to recover his mind and become useful once again.

Chloe opened the final door, entering the last room at the very bottom of the facility. In the room was 'The Machine,' and Marcus stood next to it. William Slayne lay tightly strapped into the device and unable to move. She was pleased to see Marcus had used duct tape to silence him.

She was thankful for his thoughtful consideration. She'd never liked the tiresome sound of screaming and if at all possible, she preferred to avoid it. Most of the time in combat with Chloe, people didn't scream – they didn't get the chance to. The incident with Anna Slayne earlier in the night had been distasteful, but necessary to the success of the mission, and Chloe excelled at dealing with necessities. "Marcus, you have done well," she said warmly, reaching up and kissing him on the cheek.

Marcus beamed and reported, "We're ready."

"Excellent."

"Do you wish to feed?" Marcus asked with a deferential tone in his voice.

Chloe shook her head. "No, thank you. I am replete. Please, be my guest – he is all yours. You deserve it. It has been a long and trying night."

She looked around, there was a table prepared with syringes and other medical paraphernalia. Marcus had been thorough in his work. She picked up a fresh syringe and filled it with her blood. There was a sudden movement on the edge of her vision as Marcus sank his fangs into William Slayne's throat. She watched him feed, noting his self-discipline when he stopped short of draining his victim dry.

"Good work, Marcus," she said with warm enthusiasm.

Marcus stepped back and she inserted the syringe needle into William's heart. Depressing the plunger, she pushed a full load of her blood directly into his left ventricle. Bound into immobility and silence. William's eyes bulged and his skin developed a clammy sheen.

A clock ticked noisily in the background. Chloe stepped back, waiting patiently. After five minutes, the transformation was almost complete. She indicated with a flick of her eyes at Marcus what she wanted done.

Marcus ripped off the duct tape.

"Wait! Hey!" William yelled.

It was all he was able to say as Chloe punched a green button on a console next to the machine. The metal arm that William lay strapped to, arced forward 180 degrees and slammed him into a coffin made from pure silver. The restraints around him automatically released with puffs of high-pressure air, retracting in a matter of milliseconds.

Before William could react, the coffin lid slammed shut and a dozen heavy bolts snapped into position. A set of whirring robotic arms automatically screwed the bolts into place. A giant mechanical claw attached to a pulley and a motorized runner system on the ceiling reached down, hooked up the coffin, and slotted it neatly into a waiting vertical holding chamber in the floor. Finally, a lid slid shut over the chamber leaving no trace of the coffin beneath.

To all intents and purposes, William Slayne had vanished from the face of the Earth.

Chloe took Marcus's hand and looked up into his eyes. She said huskily, "You have done very well tonight, time for some recreation back at my penthouse."

Marcus smiled broadly.

She stroked his chest, staring hungrily into his eyes. "Now where did you park the helicopter?"

Chapter Two

"The most useful deceptions are those the target will actively resist questioning." – General Chloe Armitage

"Take a potent lie, wrap it in the truth and hammer it home with trauma." – General Chloe Armitage

– Quotes from an Instructional Video, Target Capture and Conditioning, Shadowstone Covert PSYOPS Manual – Appendix B

* * *

Boston, April 28th, 23:40

Anton scanned the departure board at South Station, the main hub for ground transport out of Boston.

It showed a Greyhound bus leaving for Montreal in ten minutes, with the following Montreal bus leaving on Saturday morning at 07:00. The five-mile hike from the forest preserve behind his house to the station had allowed him to begin to calm down and collect his scattered thoughts. He ached with sadness, broken only by flashes of livid fury. Despite his best efforts, his swirling thoughts still flew like lost birds over the chaotic ocean of his feelings.

There were so many unknowns. Where did Chloe Armitage live? Who was King Cornelius Crane? Was there an army of vampires? How do you kill a vampire? How would he find out what he needed to know? It wasn't information that you could get at the local library. How would he survive without the vampires finding him again? And where on Earth was his father? And, if he found him – could he save him? He had no answers and was on the run. Anton had considered going north to Montreal, getting away from Boston to find somewhere out of the way to regroup and gather resources. Montreal seemed as good a place as any to start with. As he stood in front of the departure board, the clock ticked away the opportunity to board the 23:50 bus.

How did the vampires keep it all secret? Why wasn't their existence general knowledge? He backed away from the departure board. With his peaked cap pulled down low and his hood up, he found a seat in the waiting room. He sat down, bowed his head and became just another nondescript passenger waiting for a late-night bus out of Boston.

Chloe Armitage had spoken of the Vampire Dominion. The vampires had organized themselves. They must have someone keeping their secrets during daylight. He whispered beneath his breath, "I'll need to find the secret keepers."

She'd also said his father was a member of the Order of Thoth as if they were the bad guys. What was the Order of Thoth and how did they fit into all this? She'd said the Order had exiled him, but why? Was it something to do with his grandfather? If his grandfather was such a *bad ass* warrior, why wasn't he around to protect his family? Why did his mother have to die? Anton's fists clenched to white knuckle intensity as rage flared through his soul. Hot tears squeezed out of his eyes and he wiped them away furiously with the back of his hand. He looked around, but no one had noticed his distress.

Armitage had also left him alive so that he can do something for her. He vowed silently that she would burn in hell before he would help her with anything. He leaned back, his backpack beside him. He pulled the peak of his cap low over his eyes as if he was resting. He spent most of the next hour going over in his mind what he knew, what he didn't know, what were the opportunities for action, and what were the priorities. As the time passed, his emotions subsided and he formed a plan of action.

The vampires would have to deal with the evidence, they would have to keep it secret. If he acted quickly, he could find out who the secret keepers were, and that would be a good start. With the Montreal option abandoned, Anton approached the ticket window. He spoke with the teller, and confirmed there were available seats on the express bus to New York. It was due to leave in fifteen minutes time at 01:00.

Armitage had taken photos of him. They would be looking for him. He needed a false trail. He needed some breadcrumbs for them to follow. There was a nearby ATM, he went to it, withdrawing nine hundred and eighty dollars from his savings account, it was most of what he had. He went back to the ticket counter, using EFTPOS to buy a one-way ticket on the next bus to New York City. Two transactions, leaving two breadcrumbs.

He walked casually to the toilet block. Stripping off his cap and jacket, he stuffed them into his backpack. Two minutes later, as he left the toilet block a random bit of graffiti caught his eye, it read, 'Vampires Rule!'

"No kidding," he remarked to himself. It was time to poke the sleeping bear. With three minutes to go before the bus was due to leave, Anton went to a public payphone and dialed 911. In hushed tones, he identified himself as Anton Smith, quickly relating the basic details of the evening to the 911 operator. He told her that two assailants had murdered his mother and abducted his father. He described them as a strikingly good-looking brunette and a tall, powerfully built, blond man. Both dressed in business attire and under thirty years of age. He named them as Chloe Armitage and Marcus Drake. Anton hung up the phone, and jogged to gate one, where the bus to New York City was boarding the final passengers.

Before boarding the bus, Anton slowed to a walk and glanced up for a long moment at the camera dome in the ceiling at the gate.

Taking a seat at the back of the bus, he put on his cap and jacket, pulling his hood up and over his head. *She took photos of me; she expects to find me again. Breadcrumb number three – let them see me getting on this bus to New York. In three minutes, time – I'll be off this bus, and underneath their radar.*

* * *

James Haley was on the I-91 heading north toward East Hartford on the way to Boston, when his Shadowstone smartphone pinged with an automated message from the Panopticon.

He had a hit on the target. He commanded his smartphone, "Heads up." The smartphone, networked with the car to display a ghostly image onto the windscreen. There was enough resolution in the translucent image that James could easily read it, without it obscuring his vision of the road ahead. The image detailed a debit card transaction for a withdrawal of nine hundred and eighty dollars in the name of Anton Smith. Smith was running.

"Well, that was easy," James remarked to himself. The smartphone pinged again, the details of a bus ticket to New York flashing up onto the windscreen. James pursed his lips; shaking his head, he pulled the car over to the emergency stopping lane. He picked up his smartphone, dialing back to the New York City Shadowstone office, where the staff duty officer manning the desk answered the call.

James ordered the duty officer, "I need an immediate Panopticon tracker on the 01:00 express bus from Boston to New York City. I need four operatives at the Port Authority Terminal before 05:20 this morning at gates sixty to sixty-five to confirm sighting on a target. Photos are on their way. Do not engage the target, tail and track only. Is that clear?"

"Yes, Sir," the duty officer replied. "It will take about five minutes to establish a Panopticon tracker on the bus. I will immediately assign a team to the PA Terminal."

"Do it."

"Yes, Sir."

James hung up the call. As his car accelerated, merging back into the traffic, a third Panopticon ping hit his smartphone and an image of Anton Smith getting onto the bus flashed up onto his windscreen.

Anton Smith was making all the newbie mistakes. James shook his head with disappointment. *This won't take long to clean up, what a waste of my time.*

* * *

Luke Walker, Sergeant Detective with the Boston Police Department, pushed back the safe door with a pen and peered inside.

He stared into the empty space within the safe. Was it a robbery gone wrong? He considered theft a possible motive. Turning from the safe, he surveyed the crime scene. The other two members of his squad, detectives John Kelly and Sean O'Reilly, worked the crime scene, taking photographs. The Crime Scene Response Unit led by Sarah Murphy examined the body, in situ, and as yet untouched. The junior members of the CSRU were busy setting up filtered floodlights to search for body fluids, fingerprints and other evidence the perpetrator may have left at the scene.

The woman's head lying on the floor next to her feet drew his gaze like a moth to a flame. Luke shook his head with dismay and sighed. It was a particularly grim crime scene.

He'd been with the police department for nineteen years, joining a week after his eighteenth birthday. He'd been with the Homicide Unit for the last ten years, six as a Sergeant Detective leading his own squad. He'd seen knife attacks before, but this was the first beheading, and he'd a sincere wish that it be his last.

Luke carefully threaded his way through the furniture toward where Detective Kelly was teasing something from the edge of a huge hole in the wall. Kelly held it up with a pair of tweezers, it was a torn piece of dark, pinstriped fabric. He reported, "It was caught on a wood splinter in the middle of the wall." Kelly frowned and put the fragment into an evidence bag.

The vaguely human shaped hole stretched a yard across, and rose from floor to ceiling. The plaster dust and wood fragments in the hallway, and the direction the wood had broken in, clearly indicated that whatever went through the wall had come from the lounge room. Luke had an image in his mind of a large man smashing through the wall, it would neatly fit the shape of the hole. He snorted – it was like something out of a damn cartoon.

However, given the thickness of the wooden members, it was doubtful that anything human would have survived the impact. He stroked the broken edge of a beam with a gloved finger, the wood was hard and strong, with no sign of rot or weakness. He shook his head, nonplussed by the evidence. What the hell had really happened here?

Luke looked into the hallway where O'Reilly had just completed taking photographs of footprints in the plaster dust. There were two sets, about size thirteen or fourteen, similar to his own. He tilted his head, his mind integrating what he saw in the patterns in the pale powder.

There had been a fight in the hallway. Two big men duking it out like the old west. Instinctively looking up, he saw it, blood splatter high up on the wall. Someone had taken a hard hit.

"Kelly, get a blood swab and bag this. O'Reilly, get this on camera," he directed, drawing his detectives' attention to the top of the wall. Kelly began swabbing blood and bone fragments, putting them into a vial. Luke turned his attention back to the corpse in the chair.

Sarah Murphy, the head of the CSRU attending the crime scene was kneeling beside the body. She was collecting clumps of blond hair from the carpet with a brush and bagging it in labeled evidence bags.

"Anything?" Luke asked as he came over, standing opposite his colleague, the corpse between them.

"It's interesting," Sarah remarked. "It looks like she was beheaded with a single blow with a very sharp instrument."

Luke was relieved. An image of a Jihadi sawing at Anna Smith's neck with a knife faded away.

"However, there are some really odd things," Sarah said, frowning. "Her hair is all over the floor, clearly sliced off at the same time as her head, indicating the killer cut her head off here. However, there is hardly any blood splatter. Her blood should be everywhere," she lifted her hands and spread them wide, "where is it?"

Luke stroked his chin. Did the perp stage the crime scene? He asked, "Could she have been killed somewhere else, and the body placed here?"

"It's possible. In that case, I may find foreign material from the original site mixed in with the hair, but the hair looks clean – there is almost no blood on it or any other matter."

Luke looked at the hair in the bags and on the floor, so neatly cut – it seemed a problem and he remarked, "Wouldn't her hair just get pushed out of the way by a blade?"

Sarah nodded. "Normally I would say yes, however with a razor-sharp blade, moving very fast, the hair doesn't have time to get out of the way."

"What sort of weapon?"

"Probably a big knife or a sword, but we haven't found the murder weapon yet. It is possible the perp took the blade from the crime scene." Sarah used a stainless-steel probe to indicate the still intact top of a vertebra at the rear of the wound. "And given that the cut appears to have neatly separated the C4 and C5 vertebrae, an expert wielded the weapon. The chances of inflicting this wound by accident would be astronomical."

"So, you're telling me the victim was sitting in this chair when the perp, an expert swordsman, cut her head off with a single blow, and there is almost no blood here. I'm leaning toward the idea the perp drained her blood somewhere else, then staged the body here."

"Perhaps something like that," Sarah replied, nodded slowly. "Her blood must be somewhere. Once we get her back to the forensics lab, we'll learn more about what happened to her."

Luke pointed to a large blood stain on the victim's right shoulder and an obvious cut in her dress there. "What's that – another wound?"

"Yes," Sarah answered. "Looks like it went straight through the shoulder joint, cracking open the bones and severing the Thoracoacromial Artery. The pain would have been extreme – like having your arm ripped off – and given the blood around the cut, it happened before she died."

"Torture?"

"Motives are for you to answer?"

"I respect your professional opinion on this."

"… Yes, both cuts are surgical in their precision – whomever did this knew exactly what they were doing – and they did it fast, a single strike each time."

"Any idea on time of death?"

"I would estimate four to six hours ago. I can be more exact once we get her to the lab."

Luke looked at his watch. "An EMT team will be here in about fifteen minutes to transport the body, it's already been cleared with the Medical Examiner's office."

"Good, we will be ready by then."

Luke nodded and turned away. A family photo on the mantelpiece above the fireplace caught his eye. They were a good-looking family; happy, proud parents, at their son's graduation from High School. There was no mistaking the body in the lounge room belonged to Anna Smith. He took the photo out of the frame, and flipped it over. There was a message written on the back. 'Anton's Graduation.' With last year's date below it. A proud and happy family – they looked perfectly normal and well adjusted – so what had happened to them?

Luke frowned and whispered to himself, "Too normal by half." He bagged the photo and walked to the front door of the house, collecting his two detectives as he went. "Kelly, O'Reilly, start taking statements from the neighbors, see if anyone knows anything. Hopefully, someone heard or saw something useful."

He stood on the front porch of the house as his detectives moved beyond the police line and started identifying neighbors. He lifted the photo, staring at it intently through the plastic sleeve. He committed it to memory. He'd received a brief over the radio as he drove to the crime scene. The boy had called 911 from a payphone at South Station just before 01:00. A couple of hours after the death of his mother. That'd give him plenty of time to concoct a cover story. His father was missing; the boy was on the run – who had a motive to murder Anna Smith?

Anton Smith had reported a pair of assailants. Luke had checked the names. There was any number of Chloe Armitages, and Marcus Drakes in the world, but none known for being criminals on the Boston Police Department databases. Luke knew he had to find Anton Smith. He was either the perpetrator or the primary witness. He was running – but who was he running from? The police or the real murderers.

He felt a tap on his shoulder and turned around.

"You need to see this," Sarah insisted in hushed tones. Trembling momentarily, she turned away and walked back into the house.

Luke pocketed the Smith family photo, and followed her back into the lounge room. The other two CSRU staff were still at the crime scene, standing back from the body, staring at the head on the floor. They were both young; the woman looked like she was about to cry and the man had his hand over his mouth, as if he wanted to say something, but was frightened to say it.

Sarah squatted down, using her probe to lift a sheath of hair away from Anna's cheek. "Look here, at the top of her throat – puncture marks."

Luke frowned, and crouched down on one knee to examine Anna Smith's head. There was a strange combination of puncture wounds; partially healed with faded scar tissue on her throat. "A dog bite?" he asked. "Looks like it's a week old at least."

"I don't know, but I doubt it – it's too controlled – there is only the one bite that we can see. A dog attack would leave bite wounds all over her body. But look at this," Sarah said, inserting one end of her forensic probe into the largest of the puncture wounds. The probe descended in about half an inch. "The bite would have severed the carotid artery – it should have killed her – but you can see the wound has partially healed and the artery itself has closed over. It's bizarre."

Luke felt a shiver go up his spine and he rubbed his chin with his hand. "That's impossible."

"Not only that – I double checked the shoulder wound, and the Thoracoacromial Artery had also closed over and the entry and exit wounds were partially healed."

The young CSRU tech spoke in a harsh whisper, his hands on his head, "It was a vampire."

"Shut up!" Luke growled. "This is the real world, not a damn TV show. There will be a rational explanation for this." He glowered around the room. Someone had staged the crime scene to mess with their heads. What sort of monster was Anton Smith?

Luke stepped away from the body, he suddenly needed fresh air. He went back out on the porch. He dialed the duty desk at the district office. The officer on duty picked up the call and Luke commanded him, "Initiate an arrest warrant for Anton Smith. I want him found, he is our prime suspect for the murder of his mother and the disappearance of his father."

The duty officer responded and Luke closed the call. He frowned, shaking his head. A son murdering his mother, it was a vile disgusting crime. He vowed to himself to close this case. Finding justice for the dead drove him, and he would not stop until Anton Smith had paid for murdering his mother and disappearing his father.

* * *

James Haley slowed the car to a crawl as he approached the entrance of the court where the Smith family home resided.

The red and blue strobe lights of a pair of Boston Police Department cars lit up the court entrance. A big white Crime Scene Response Unit van stood on the far side of the police cars. A navy blue, Ford Explorer SUV, typical of the type used by the Boston Police Department was beyond the CSRU van. 'Do Not Cross' police tape lay strung along the sidewalk and around the front yard of the Smith residence. All around the court, neighbors, and other onlookers huddled in small groups. Several people held their smartphones up to video the event or take photographs. Four uniformed officers kept everyone clear of operations as a pair of detectives took initial statements from neighbors.

Interviewing of potential witnesses had already begun. James growled in disgust and said, "What a circus! This is so FUBAR! Who tipped them off?"

A tall, thick-set bald man with an air of command about him, was on the front porch staring at something in an evidence bag. Was it a photo? One of the CSRU staff tapped the photo-holding detective on the shoulder and he turned and followed her back into the house.

James assessed the situation. The Investigator-In-Charge and the head on site of the CSRU were clearly troubled by something. He whispered to himself, "What did they just find? I need to shut this down and fast."

He switched off his car's engine. Flipped open his laptop and logged in. The laptop networked back to the Panopticon with high-speed encrypted satellite links. He lifted his smartphone, zooming in with the phone's camera on the police vehicles, associated staff, and onlookers. The phone began networking directly with the Panopticon.

"Okay, who am I dealing with here?" he asked himself. Two minutes later he had summarized files on all the police staff currently on site, and who they reported to.

James read the first line from the Panopticon response out loud, "Sergeant Detective Luke Walker is the Investigator-In-Charge with responsibility for the disposition of the crime scene and the evidence. He is responsive to the District Attorney or the Medical Examiner." He fell silent, tapping the side of the laptop as he read deeper into the files, scanning and reading pages at a glance. He quickly concluded, "I need to be a delegate of the DA."

James put his laptop aside. Opening his car's glove box, he withdrew a small black box from within it. He released the biometric lock on the box with his thumbprint. Inside the box was a set of fake IDs. Each ID matched his biometrics, backed up with fully defined sets of data across more than a dozen government and private systems. With them he could easily impersonate a range of different roles and authorities. These *'ghosts'* even drew salaries from their host organizations – one of the side benefits of working with Shadowstone – superb renumeration.

James flicked through them, picking out the most appropriate one for dealing with this situation. James, aka Jim, Alexander, an FBI agent from the Manhattan Joint Terrorism Task Force Annex. The JTTF Annex was a Shadowstone front organization seamlessly integrated with the real FBI.

Now all he needed was the paperwork. He ran another program on his laptop. A minute later he had a filled form, signed by the Suffolk County District Attorney assigning Jim Alexander as his delegate for the Smith case. He hit Ctrl-P on his laptop, a printer built into the car's console under the glove box whirred into life, pushing out a high definition, full color copy of the signed delegation form.

James carefully and neatly folded the form and put it aside. A Boston Emergency Medical Services Ambulance passed his car, entered the court and parked in the driveway of the Smith residence. He shook his head as two EM technicians got out of the Ambulance.

Where the hell was the Green-4 spectrum team? He looked at his watch, it was pushing 03:00, Louise Wesson should be here any minute. He dialed her smartphone.

"Sir?" she answered.

"Where are you?" James demanded.

"Two minutes away from your location. We're in Jamaica Plain now."

"OK. Slow down just as you reach the court. I'm parked here and I will lead us in. Once in, wait for further orders."

"Yes, Sir. Will do."

James hung up and started his engine. In moments, he could see two black Chevrolet Express vans in his car's mirrors. He rolled forward into the street, swerving into formation in front of them. As a group, they drove into the court, and parked opposite the Smith residence. James slotted the DA delegation form into an inside pocket of his jacket, got out of his car and walked to the edge of the police line.

One of BPD uniforms approached him, and stated, "Sir, this is an active crime scene, and you're not allowed access."

James flashed his FBI credentials. "I'm with the FBI JTTF out of the Manhattan Annex. Who is the investigator in charge on site?"

The officer hesitated for a moment, and then produced a list on a clipboard and requested, "I will need your details."

"No problem," James replied, adding the name Jim Alexander, and his FBI ID details to the proffered list.

The officer waved James through and instructed as he passed by. "You're looking for Sergeant Detective Luke Walker, you can't miss him, he's the big, bald guy in a suit."

"Thanks, Officer Jones," James said, with a brief smile as he walked past the officer. Be polite. Get the names right. Do it by the book. Be firm, but don't be a total bastard. Works every time.

James walked up the porch steps to the open front door. He reached the landing as Walker emerged, followed by a grim looking EM tech.

Walker looked James up and down and declared brusquely, "Who are you, and what are you doing on my crime scene?"

James handed Walker the DA delegation form and stated, "I'm Special Agent Jim Alexander with the FBI JTTF out of the Manhattan Annex."

Walker opened the form and read it. Shaking his head and scowling as he quickly got to the end of it. "Well doesn't that just take the cake."

The EM tech looked at Walker, and then James, and then back at Walker and asked, "Should I get the body bag?"

James addressed him and directed, "No, go get your buddy and sit in your ambulance. One of my staff will debrief you and then you can go."

Walker asked indignantly, "How the hell is this a terrorism case?"

James ignored Walker's question, signaling Louise with a wave of his hand to come over. He turned back to the cop. "Look, it's nothing personal. There are bigger forces at play in this case. You're a good cop, I can see that. You've done everything by the book and I bet you're already putting a case together."

He clapped a big hand on Walker's shoulder. The two men stood eye to eye and he said, "We're brothers in arms, fighting the same fight. I'm already briefed on this case. You've got a runner, the son, Anton Smith … he's the prime suspect, isn't he?"

Walker growled with annoyance, but replied, "I've initiated an arrest warrant. We're already closing in on him."

James would have to rescind the warrant. He made a mental note to sort that out later. "I'm sure you are," James declared confidently. "It's time to call your team together. My staff will debrief everyone and collect all bagged evidence. In fifteen minutes, the handover will be complete."

"You can't hand over a crime scene in fifteen minutes!" Walker stated, aghast.

"My team is highly professional. We'll get it done." James glanced out at the court, Wesson and another eight plainclothes Shadowstone operatives were standing in a loose group back from the police line. They were not signing themselves in as per standing orders. They did not have multiple prepared identities. They were waiting for him to clear the path for them.

"Look, Sergeant Detective Walker, I need you to remove your team from this site ASAP. It is imperative that all evidence is immediately handed over to my team."

Walker shook his head, looked disgusted and mouthed, "Shit!" under his breath, but turned and yelled into the house, "Close it down everyone, the FBI is here and they have 'juris-my-dict—'" he halted for a second, then said, "jurisdiction over this case."

He turned back to face James, and they locked gazes for a moment until the detective looked away.

In five minutes, the Boston authorities evacuated the house. The Shadowstone operatives debriefed the BPD staff, while collecting evidence bags, taking additional notes and recording everything on video.

James went back to his car. He retrieved a pack of cigarettes and a lighter. He lit up, taking a long pull on his cigarette as he watched Wesson lead the debriefs. He mused silently as he smoked, *It isn't what they know, it's what they can prove that matters. There's often something strange in these cleanup cases.*

He took another pull on the cigarette. It had been a long night, and he enjoyed a few minutes of peace and relaxation as he wondered, *What would it be this time?*

He finished a second cigarette as he waited for the last of the BPD staff to leave the site. He watched as his operators moved in, clearing the onlookers back to their homes. *Nothing to see here, move along, go back to your homes, the danger has passed, you're all safe.* It was the same consistent message used every time. The Green-4 team operatives repositioned the vans and started pulling out their specialized equipment. He butted out the cigarette, putting it carefully into the car's ashtray. He'd never leave evidence of his presence behind. *We're ghosts in what we do.*

James pushed off from the car. He walked through his team, clapping people on their shoulders, and checking equipment on backpacks. He addressed his team, "Okay guys, let's be careful, let's be thorough. Make it a good job, a clean job, and get it done."

Convinced they were fully prepared, he led them into the house.

It was time to sanitize the scene.

* * *

Louise Wesson, Shadowstone operative, recently recruited from a very specialized cell within the Operations Directorate of the CIA took personal responsibility for managing the removal of Anna Smith's body.

Around her was a hive of well-organized activity as Green-4 operatives first sprayed a clear, odorless mist and then followed with flashes of intense ultraviolet light. The treatments evaporated any biological evidence remaining in the house. When they finished the job, there would be no trace the Smith family had ever lived there.

Louise was thankful for the forensic gloves that she wore as she picked up Anna Smith's head and put it in a body bag with the rest of her remains. She started zipping the bag closed when she saw something that made her pause. She whispered, "What the hell."

She reached into the bag, pushing back the hair from Anna's cheek. The floodlights positioned by her team allowed no mistake. Bite marks? She pushed her gloved little finger into the largest hole, it went in nearly to the first joint. The hole was right on the carotid artery and too deep to survive – and yet the artery was still intact? What the hell, was someone playing games?

Louise's lip curled into a derisive smile. She zipped the bag closed with a sudden movement and stood up. She commanded her team, "Okay boys, move this trash out and complete the sweeps."

She stepped back as two of her operatives picked up the body bag and took it outside to one of the waiting vans. She looked back around the lounge room with fresh eyes. If this family had been her target, there would be three bodies here, not one. This was not a professional hit. Who would bite someone's throat out and then chop their head off? And where was all the blood?

Louise shook her head, continuing with the task at hand, she had a device that looked a lot like a smartphone and which behaved like a powerful torch. She walked through each room, scanning all the surfaces with the light from the compact unit. At the end of the sweep, she'd not found any biological traces of the Smith family. She tapped her earpiece and reported calmly, "All clear, Sir."

Haley's voice called back through the comms channel, "Let's wrap this up, there is still more work to do tonight."

Louise walked out of the house, dropping her gear off in the nearest van. She approached the driver of the other van which had Anna Smith's body in it and said to him, "Get this corpse and the other trash to Rikers Island for disposal."

"Yes, Ma'am," the operative replied.

Haley stood by his car, waving her over.

She strode over, joining him beside the car.

"We have a local office. We need to check in on our target," Haley directed.

"Yes, Sir."

They got into the car, and Haley drove them away from the court. She'd been working with Haley as one of his direct subordinates for six months. She usually made correct assessments of people in the first five minutes. She'd found Haley to be very hard to read, and that intrigued her. The only other person she'd met that was more impenetrable was the woman who had interviewed her for her current role – General Chloe Armitage. *Now that was one stone cold killer,* she'd mused to herself after meeting Armitage for the first time.

She'd found a shell just below Armitage's surface that surrounded secrets she would never discover, and that annoyed her. She enjoyed knowing how other people ticked, what their buttons were, what they would respond too, especially under stress. It was her skill, knowing people, and being able to anticipate what they would do. Louise typically asked questions and got back more information than the person answering the question ever suspect they gave away.

Haley drove the car into the center of the city of Boston, descending into an underground parking garage.

"That didn't look like a terrorist incident," Louise said, glancing across at her boss. "It also didn't appear to be the actions of a mad man. It just looked – different."

Haley snorted. "Every newbie always asks a variant of that question." Parking the car, he turned to Louise and stared directly into her brown eyes. "There's some odd shit from time to time, but our job is clear, protect the security of the anti-terror operations. So just do your job, you will live a lot longer that way."

Louise usually felt fear as a form of excitement, but there was something in the way that Haley had just spoken, a supreme confidence in consequences, that sent a genuine shiver of dread up her spine. She shutdown the desire to frown, it was not her way to wear dangerous emotions like fear on her face. She followed him silently out of the garage and into the offices of a front company owned by Shadowstone. Haley flicked a pass over a reader and the door swung aside. As she passed through the doorway, Louise read a set of gold lettering on the door. R.I.S.C, Risk, Investigation, Security, Consultants.

I've been working for Shadowstone for six months. I have more questions now than when I started. Questions were part of the process, but sooner rather than later – she needed answers.

* * *

Anton arched his back, stretching cramped muscles, he repositioned for a better view of his home.

There had been a brief but intense discussion in front of his house between the Boston Police Department detective and the suit who had shown up waving a badge. Anton hid under bushes in a neighbor's front yard. Unfortunately, too far down the street to hear precisely what the two men said. The suit had won and the Boston police, CSRU staff, and the ambulance had all left. Two black unmarked vans and the suit's own dark gray sedan remained in the court. He counted nine other people in the suit's team, eight men, and one woman, and they all deferred to the suit.

He studied the suit closely; he wanted to make sure he never forgot this man. He was tall, about six feet four inches, powerful looking, more a wrestler's rather than a boxer's body. He had short, dark brown hair, a little gray starting to show at the temples, and a pronounced receding hairline. He had strong features, big nose, big jaw, and big hands. He looked tough, hard, and dangerous.

Anton added the suit to an internal list of objectives. He was another one he would need to deal with. One day the suit would get what he deserved. Anton vowed to himself that he would never give up until he'd achieved justice for his mother's murder and his father's abduction.

Men with backpacks of equipment, sprayers and wand like lights had worked in the house for about half an hour after the Boston police had left. Anton had never seen anything like it. There had been a series of flashes of intense blue light, like a welding arc through the windows of his home. As to what was actually happening inside his home – it remained a mystery. He surmised that it must have something to do with keeping the vampires' secrets.

He added that to his rapidly growing mental 'to do,' list. Find out who was keeping the existence of vampires secret from the world and how they were doing it? They'd just killed his mother, abducted his father and destroyed his life. He figured he had nothing better to do than bring the whole fucking mess down. The only real question was how?

Anton's eyes hardened and he watched the unfolding actions closely. He had to learn everything he could if he was to have any chance against his enemies. Two operatives carried his mother out in a body bag, unceremoniously throwing her into the back of one of the vans. Anton clapped a hand over his mouth. His eyes widened, his face paled and his fists clenched tight enough for his fingernails to gouge his palms. Rage was a fiery torrent running like a wild animal through his soul. For a long moment, he was beyond words, biting down on his left fist to avoid getting up and running over to try and kill the men. Anton shut his eyes, burying his face into the ground.

He screamed silently, *I've got to get this together, it's no good just running out there, they will kill me or worse in seconds. That's not what my Mom and Dad would want. They would want me to be smarter than that — where are they taking her?*

Anton lifted his head a couple of inches. The sole woman was talking to the driver of the nearest van. Anton turned his head, straining to hear what she said. The distance muffled her words, but he could just make out, 'Rikers Island' and 'disposal.' What was at Rikers Island? That's where they were taking his mother for disposal.

The men completed packing their gear into the waiting vans. Within another minute, everyone had left. The woman leaving with the suit in charge in his dark gray sedan. Anton turned, dragging himself through the bushes. He crouched, scuttling to the backyard of the house. He clambered over the back fence. In moments, he was through another backyard, down a driveway, and onto another street.

The neighborhood street was strikingly normal, it almost seemed like a different world to the nightmare he'd left behind. He'd confirmed his suspicions. There was an organization working for the vampires and keeping their secrets. There was an around the clock threat, humans during the day and vampires at night. Anton pulled his cap down close above his eyes. Pulling the hood of his jacket tightly over his head, he slung his backpack over his shoulders. He needed to find somewhere he could sleep, somewhere he could be anonymous.

Anton started walking to the city for the second time that night. He walked without looking back. There was nothing left where his family had died except awful memories of horror committed by an exquisitely beautiful young woman.

A woman who was nothing less than a monster.

* * *

James Haley finished off his fourth cup of coffee.

The clock read 05:21, he stood with his feet apart, and his arms folded across his chest. He faced a wall of computer screens displaying a current track on the 01:00 express bus from Boston to New York City as it pulled into the New York Port Authority Terminal. He had four fully briefed operatives covering gates sixty to sixty-five at the terminal.

Shadowstone had applied the Panopticon tracker on the bus shortly after it left South Station in Boston and the bus had been in continuous motion ever since. The Panopticon tracker consisted of every available camera on the Bus's pathway and hacked cameras within the bus itself. They recorded Anton Smith getting on the bus, the bus had been in continuous motion since they had initiated the tracker, he should still be on it when it arrived in New York.

His men would visually confirm his arrival. They would then tail him, maintaining around the clock contact with the target until new orders were issued. Every available camera in the terminal that could sight the bus from Boston swiveled automatically on their mounts to bear on the target vehicle. No one was getting off the bus without being surveilled from multiple angles.

A large screen displayed a top-down satellite view of the terminal with blue markers on the locations of his operatives and a red outline around the bus. The Panopticon integrated and cross-referenced all the data feeds. It ran a threat board on another large screen, where predictive algorithms scrolled a prioritized list of proposed risks and potential issues that may need James' attention. The threat board was green, his operatives stood in position, and the bus pulled to a stop.

Louise Wesson carefully scanned the screens displaying video feeds from within the bus, and said, "I don't think he's on the bus."

"What the hell?" James growled incredulously. Turning to face her, he snapped, "Well, we will soon find out."

It took less than three minutes for the bus to empty. People milled about as the driver unloaded the luggage compartment on the side of the vehicle. Above the head of each person on the screen was a Panopticon red dot – not a match with the target. James clenched his hands into fists. "Damn it, he got off somehow." He looked at the data on the Panopticon tracker on the 01:00 bus out of Boston. It started at 01:04:54. There was nearly a five-minute window to get off the bus without the Panopticon seeing him.

"He expected to be tracked, he is smarter than you think," Wesson said calmly.

James rubbed his chin. "Not only that, the bus must have stopped out of sight of any road monitoring camera. There is no record of the bus stopping." The boy was not such a pup after all. He snorted. "It won't make any difference. We'll—"

"Sir, the target is not here," an operative at the terminal interrupted, his voice relayed by encrypted satellite link.

"Roger that, Johnson. Pull the team back to Fort Dix," James replied, then addressed Wesson, "As I was saying, we'll blanket the Boston area and pick him up again."

"What if he has simply used another method to get to New York, or anywhere else? He may have stolen a car or hitchhiked."

James returned to his terminal, initiating another Panopticon search. The main screen on the wall began to fill with a sea of red, with a cluster of orange hits in Boston. He stated, "The evidence shows that he is still in Boston."

"The evidence shows that he knows that someone is looking for him and he is actively protecting himself," Wesson said as she flipped close a printed file on Anton Smith and stood up from her desk. "Sir, did you read his file in full. Sure, he's young, he's just turned eighteen, but he has an IQ above a hundred and fifty. I think we need to be careful that we do not underestimate him. He could be on the way to anywhere within a thousand miles of Boston by now. He took out over nine hundred dollars from his account. He could have hiked over to the airport and hired a light airplane. No need for a security check, he could be in the air by now."

"The airports are heavily surveilled. The Panopticon would have flagged him by now."

Wesson stared at him in silence for a moment. James sighed, his lips pressed into a thin line and he acknowledged her silent point, "Of course, unless he's covered his face extensively, we only have photos of his face."

Wesson said, "Yes, my read on this is that he wanted anyone looking for him to think that he has left for New York City. In reality, he most likely has gone to ground. He will be frightened and alone, he will want to stay in familiar territory. He will stay in Boston."

"Well, we will soon find out if you're right," James remarked as he set the search on the Panopticon to continuous mode. Every camera that the system could reach in the world would be looking for Anton Smith twenty-four-hours per day, seven days a week. "The Panopticon sweeps will find him soon enough."

Wesson arched a quizzical eyebrow. "Do you want to put money on that?"

James stared at her, his eyes narrowing menacingly. "Do you want a career change?"

For a second their eyes met, and then Wesson looked away.

James stared at her for a long moment. *Know your place girl.*

* * *

It was almost midnight.

Anton leaned against a brick wall across the street from the Lighthouse Center Homeless Shelter. It was a typical red brick Victorian era building nestled in the South End neighborhood of Boston. He was exhausted, he'd been awake for more than forty hours. He'd discarded the idea of using a youth hostel or a hotel. Those places had cameras, demanded ID, and would cost a lot more than a shelter.

He needed to get his finances sorted before he ran out of cash. He had to conserve what he had. He didn't know when or how he was going to get more. How does anyone make a living underneath the vampire radar?

He pushed himself off the wall, and crossed the street to the shelter entrance. He went up a short flight of steps, pushed open the door, and entered the shelter's reception area. There was an old guy behind the counter wearing a Boston Celtics cap and an odd assortment of clothes that looked like he'd picked them randomly out of the shelter's laundry. The old guy looked at him with rheumy eyes and barked, "We're all full up!"

Anton yawned fit to break his jaw and put a hand on the counter to steady himself and stated, "Hey buddy, I would be happy with a piece of floor."

The old guy squinted at him. "Fuhgeddaboutit – it's against the rules!"

Anton's heart sank. He couldn't even get a piece of floor in a homeless shelter. He had a sudden vision of himself waking up under a three-day-old newspaper on a park bench. Is this what he'd come too?

"You can't stay here – you're gotta go somewhere else!" The old guy half-shouted, shooing Anton toward the front door.

Anton shook his head in defeat. He stepped back from the counter and turned to go. He was halfway out the door when someone grabbed his arm and pulled him to a halt. He looked over his right shoulder. A young woman, dressed in jeans, a pale green sweater, and white sneakers stood beside him.

She smiled and ordered him in a no-nonsense tone, "Hold on a second there, big guy." She pulled him back from the doorway. "I was out for a quick break and Barry was manning the desk. He is a bit of a fixture around here and he can be a bit overzealous sometimes."

"He's a hockey player – he doesn't belong here," Barry declared trenchantly.

"Look, I'm Sam," she said, extending her hand.

Anton took it, she had a firm grip and a friendly smile.

"Grab a seat right there," Sam instructed, guiding him to a chair.

Anton sat down gratefully. Every minute was a struggle to stay awake. He could fall asleep in this chair if people would only leave him alone.

"Would you like a hot drink? Chocolate?" Sam asked.

"Yeah sure,' he agreed.

"Me too," Barry called out eagerly. "Don't forget me."

Sam smiled. "Barry, no one who has met you would ever forget you." She turned back to Anton, her long brown hair swishing over her shoulders, and insisted, "Now just wait here."

She strode down the hallway, ducking into a nearby room. Two minutes later she emerged with three mugs of hot chocolate. The three of them spent the next five minutes sipping their hot chocolate while Barry related, ball by ball, the last game between the Boston Celtics and the Los Angeles Lakers for the 1984 championship.

"That's an amazing memory you've got there Barry," Anton said over the last of his chocolate.

"Yeah, he's one of a kind," Sam agreed, patting Barry on the shoulder. "Okay then, I best get you booked in stranger." She opened a ledger behind the counter.

Anton frowned.

"What's your name, I can't keep referring to you as the 'Big Guy,' now, can I?"

"Ant … Anthony,' Anton replied.

"Okay, I can roll with that." She paused, smiling softly at him. "The handsome Mr. Anthony with no last name."

Anton looked Sam directly in the eyes, lifting his eyebrows in silent supplication. She shrugged her shoulders and said, "I'm not going to turn anyone away when we still have a cot available."

She signed him in as Anthony X.

"Come this way soldier," Sam directed, leading Anton down the hall, and up a flight of stairs. The next floor held four separate dormitories, each with four beds, and a communal bathroom at the end of the hallway. She showed him the fire escape and then his bed, it was the bottom bunk of a double. The other three bunks held warm bodies; the top two guys lay quietly, but the man on the other lower bunk snored loudly.

"Sorry for the symphony," she commiserated gently, shrugging her shoulders.

"I'm beyond caring, thanks – this is great."

Sam patted Anton on the shoulder and said, "Well, you have a good night." She sauntered off down the hall, her hips rolling in her jeans.

Anton just managed to hear her say "So buff," to herself as she got to the stairs. He got himself onto his bunk. Swapping his backpack for his pillow, he managed to pull his shoes off, before rolling back into the bed.

Sam, thirty hours ago I would have been interested.

He crashed into a dreamless exhausted sleep.

* * *

Cornelius Crane relaxed on a lounge in his library, opposite him sat two of his five generals in separate chairs, Chloe Armitage, and Haras Mosule.

Chloe wore a crimson dress, with a small black hat and black shoes. She sat simply with her hands in her lap and her long legs neatly crossed. Haras wore his customary black pants and boots, white shirt and short black jacket. His long wavy hair fell loosely across his shoulders and he regarded his companions with intelligent brown eyes.

Cornelius addressed his generals, "It is rare that I have my two best generals in the same room at the same time." He leaned forward, pouring three drinks from a decanter on a low table between them. "This is Yamazaki Single Malt Sherry Cask 2013 whiskey – surprisingly, it is both Japanese and excellent."

Haras smiled and suggested, "Perhaps we should have Shen Zhen here, it's from his region." He reached forward taking the glass. He sniffed it, closing his eyes before sipping it. "Delicious."

Cornelius had long thought it remarkable that alcohol and nicotine had an impact on vampire physiology, and yet most drugs were simply ineffective. He had projects running in a network of secret labs to explore the boundaries of the vampire condition. When needed, it was a simple matter to create new test subjects. He was fascinated by the exploration of the possible. Science was a wonderful thing; his many secret and not-so-secret laboratories and research facilities guaranteed the Vampire Dominion remained at the forefront of all human knowledge.

Chloe and Cornelius both took a glass each and sipped the whiskey. The alcohol provided zero nutrition, only human blood could sustain a vampire, but the flavors of alcohol and tobacco remained enjoyable. When someone had been alive for nearly a thousand years, simple pleasures mattered. Cornelius put the empty glass back on the table and declared, "I have a mission for you both."

Chloe and Haras glanced at each other and then fixed their attention upon him. Cornelius's eyes narrowed slightly, even as the ghost of a smirk curled the edges of his lips. He knew they would hate having to work together, but the competition between them would motivate them to produce their best efforts. It was time to bring Haras up to speed on current events. Cornelius declared with a note of triumph, "We now have the Papyrus of Hakron the Scribe."

"What?" Haras asked incredulously.

Chloe smiled slightly at Haras from the other side of the lounge.

"Indeed," Cornelius declared, raising an eyebrow. "We now have two of the three Metaframe artifacts. It is time to claim the third."

Haras rubbed his chin and said, "Easier said than done. The Red Empire guard their prize well, and we have no knowledge of where their citadel is."

"That's where the two of you come in. The Red Empire's activities against us consistently track back to the Middle East. I'm sending both of you by shadowstar drone to a Shadowstone facility outside of Jerusalem. That will be your base of operations. You will have two of my praetorian guards with you and substantial local and international Shadowstone resources."

Chloe's eyes widened and she declared, "We have ongoing critical operations against elements of the Order of Thoth in North America, disturbing those operations buys risk for us all."

"This is the priority," Cornelius stated firmly, chopping his right hand through a flat arc. "That's the end of it."

"Of course, Sir. We will discharge our duty," Chloe replied, her voice betraying the faintest trace of sarcasm.

Cornelius tilted his head slightly, and declared, his voice laced with an undercurrent of threat, "I'm sure you will do your duty with the enthusiasm it deserves." He'd assigned two of his best praetorians to the mission. He'd specifically instructed them to keep an eye on his generals, just in case either of them decided to run any side missions of their own. Increasingly, Cornelius felt that Chloe held something back. It wasn't anything specific that he could point to or put his finger on. Just a vague sense of her pursuing her own purposes, even when they clashed with his own.

Cornelius paused for a moment, and then addressed his generals, "Let us be clear. I am sending you to Jerusalem to find the head of the Red Empire, to take the Interpretive Codex from him and return it here. That is the only mission. Is that clear?"

"Yes, Sir," Haras agreed.

"Yes, Sir," Chloe said a moment later.

Cornelius refilled the glasses. "Then let us drink." He stood up and raised his glass. "To the Vampire Dominion!"

Haras and Chloe rose and said in unison, "To the Vampire Dominion!"

All three vampires downed their drinks.

Haras placed his empty glass on the low table and frowned. "Sir. If we leave now, we will get to Jerusalem three hours after sunrise."

"Have you both recently fed?" Cornelius asked, and both his generals nodded. "Then fly now, you can wait in the drone at the Shadowstone site outside Jerusalem. That way you don't waste half of tomorrow night on travel."

His generals variously nodded, or assented, paid their respects, and left the library. They would ascend to the hangar deck where a helicopter would fly them out to the airfield at Fort Dix. In less than three hours a hypersonic shadowstar drone would transport them to Jerusalem.

Cornelius sat back down on the lounge and rubbed his chin. The mission would reveal much about Armitage's loyalty. He mused, *Success or failure in this mission? In either event I will learn more about her usefulness – or lack thereof.*

He harrumphed and narrowed his gaze. Either result was acceptable.

* * *

Anton started to wake up, his head resting on a pillow with a faint odor of laundry detergent.

He winced. Sunlight was coming through the window, striking him in the face. He rolled over onto his side to get away from it – then bolted hard upright, cracking his head on the bottom of the bunk above him.

"Ahhh," Anton yowled, looking frantically around the room. He shouted in desperation, "Where's my backpack?"

His memory of the previous evening came rushing back. He'd swapped the pillow for his backpack – to keep its contents safe. He didn't have far to look, finding his backpack under the end of his bunk. He snatched it close, it came easily, it was way too light. He looked inside and groaned in misery. "Some bastard has cleaned me out." His spare clothes, wallet, cash, food, and silver were all missing. He threw the empty backpack against the wall. He looked up to the ceiling, slumping back down onto his bunk. He leaned forward, putting his head in his hands and moaned, "No, no, no."

For a long moment, he felt the energy drain from his body, and the empty dorm closed in around him. A claustrophobic pressure exploded from the base of his spine. He dry retched, a sickly bile filling his mouth. Filled with disgust, he spat it out onto a used bath towel lying on the bunk opposite.

Suddenly revolted, as only God knew what was on that stray towel. He threw it back onto the opposite bunk, wiping his damp hands on his jeans. He sat back, the light in the room dimming as a cloud shielded the window from the sun.

Anton shivered, his hands trembling. His breath condensed in misty plumes as the temperature of the room plummeted. The shadows darkened in the room. A sense of something uncanny and weird filled him, like the world was about to spin completely out of control. A tightness filled his guts, then exploded into a dreadful foreboding as an overwhelming sense of presence filled the room.

There was something horrible hovering invisibly near him. What was it? The light outside the room evaporated as if the sun had vanished. The windows darkened to the solid black of interstellar space. The single naked globe dangling from the ceiling provided the only illumination. The window blew in with an icy blast of air, showering the room with fragments of glass, wood, and stone. A flash of darkness jagged like black lightning across the room in front of him.

He recoiled backward; his head twisting left to follow the black lightning. His eyes widened; this couldn't be happening. Chloe Armitage stood at the entrance of the room. He couldn't move, he could barely breathe. She wore a diaphanous black gown, off the shoulder and split high on the thigh. She carried a golden goblet before her in her left hand and her right hand rested casually on her hip. Her dark hair was long and pulled back through a delicate golden crown. His heart thumped in his chest, but he remained frozen, caught like a fly in a spider's web. He blinked, and she was in front of him. Her face barely inches from his own, he could feel her breathing slowly against his face. Her magnificent blue eyes stared into his and he screamed silently in helpless terror.

She smiled in a way that didn't reach her vivid eyes, her fangs descending over her bottom lip. She lifted the goblet to his lips and whispered into his ear, "Drink Anton, for this is my blood."

She tilted the goblet, and the warm, bitter contents filled his mouth. He witnessed helplessly as he swallowed and drank the blood. She tilted the goblet to near vertical, Anton arching his head back to avoid spilling any of the precious fluids. The bitter metallic tang had fled, replaced by a sensual, flesh infusing succulence. A liquid fire rose within him, fanning a flame of urgent desire.

The empty goblet fell loosely from her hand. She reached forward with a finger, stroking his chest from the notch of his throat to the top of his jeans. His shirt fell away neatly cut in two by the edge of her fingernail. She reversed the stroke, her fingers now spread wide, pushing up over the hard muscles of his stomach and across his chest in an avid, possessive sweep. Her touch crackled with energy, leaving his skin screaming for more. With both hands she pushed him back onto the bunk. The contents of the goblet singing through his veins. She reached down, ripping away the front of his jeans with her bare hands before sitting astride him.

An overwhelming desire galvanized him. His hands came free of the force that had trapped them but he didn't push her away, he pulled her closer, thrusting his hips and entering her. He arched forward and she went with him – two equals in union.

She wrapped herself around him, drawing him in as close as possible, and murmured into his ear, "Eat Anton, for this is my body."

A drumbeat thudded through his soul, lightning flashed and crackled, and then she was gone.

Anton's heart raced. He dragged in breath after breath as he picked himself up from the floor. The window stood intact, there was no broken glass, splintered wood or shattered stone. The sunlight was streaming through the window, and he could see dust motes floating lazily in the room.

What was that? A vision? Was it madness?

He felt a terrible need for a shower.

Will I ever be clean again?

Twenty minutes later he was striding away from the Lighthouse Center Homeless Shelter as fast as he could without actually running. Around him, the fine folk of Boston sat down to breakfast in stylish cafes, drinking soy lattes and discussing topics that had nothing to do with pursuit by a monstrous vampire.

* * *

Chloe Armitage completed strapping herself into a self-contained life pod within the hypersonic shadowstar drone.

Beside her, in his own pod, Haras Mosule did the same. Behind them sat Crane's two praetorians, Peter Dench, and Washington Jones. If the drone suffered a catastrophic failure, the life pods would become escape capsules.

The voice of their pilot, operating out of a Shadowstone command center at Fort Dix called through their headsets, "The drone will launch in five minutes. Flight time to Jerusalem will be eighty-six minutes. Our target altitude is eighty-two thousand feet, with a cruising speed of four thousand two hundred miles per hour. ETA in Jerusalem is 09:05 local time, Sunday the 30th of April."

Ninety-one minutes flight time, then nearly fourteen hours waiting in the drone for sunset. The drone's liquid hydrogen fueled, Scimitar engines, spooled up. The drone began to taxi out of the hangar. A twenty-four-inch, high-definition monitor linked to cameras in the skin of the aircraft rested in front of her face. In the windowless drone, she could easily see the progress of the flight.

Chloe turned her mind to the mission at hand. She switched the monitor to network mode and opened her Shadowstone email account. She'd sent James Haley an email requesting daily status reports on the progress of tracking Anton Smith. She looked at her inbox, there was nothing urgent or important, she never received email from the other generals. She knew that Crane was well versed in modern technology but rarely used it himself. The other generals were a mixed bag ranging from Clayton Maze and Haras Mosule, both of whom were skilled users, but seemed to view technology as a necessary evil; to Dieter Franz and Shen Zhen, who both avoided the trappings of the 20th century, let alone the 21st.

She sometimes wondered why Crane had picked these people to be his generals. He'd never explained why. The only other person who might know, was the Haitian voodoo priest Jean Philippe Allemande. He'd provided the curses that bound the generals to never harm Crane. He'd been dead for more than a hundred years. For his services, Crane had rewarded Allemande with vampirism in the 1850s. He'd remained in his native Haiti and lived the life of a ghoul lord for over forty years before Chloe had purged him from the vampire community. She'd extracted a final curse before she'd executed him, a binding curse on a young US Naval Lieutenant, named Marcus Drake.

She switched the monitor off. She needed to plan. Assisted by the quiet solitude of the life pod, she closed her eyes and relaxed. The objective was clear, she needed to meet 'Shabbah al Ahmar', the aptly named Red Ghost, the head of the Red Empire. Crane was sure he was in possession of the

Interpretive Codex, the second document written by Hakron the Scribe, and essential to correctly interpret the insane gibberish of the Papyrus. The two documents together enabled mastery of the Key of Ahknaton and, therefore, access to the powers of the Metaframe. She did not need to retrieve the Codex for herself, she only needed to read it, her eidetic memory would provide her with a perfect copy.

Chloe was the only person alive who knew the power of her memory. It was one of three special abilities she kept as closely guarded secrets. If Crane knew about her secret powers, he would not hesitate to slaughter her on the spot to remove the risk she would one day usurp his throne. She considered her plans carefully, *I will need to mislead Haras Mosule, and Crane's henchmen if I am to again meet secretly with the Red Ghost. Perhaps it is time to take Haras off the chessboard. He is too clever to leave as a loyal servant of Crane.* Her eyes closed and she smiled grimly, *Perhaps a little private purging of the ranks, it had happened before, why not again?*

She opened her eyes, staring at the dull gray of the monitor, her mind spinning far away. *Or something subtler? Could I turn him to my purpose? Yes, especially if I kept him unaware of the ultimate goal.*

The drone took off, the powerful acceleration pushing Chloe back into her seat. Her lips curled into a smile as she explored the implications and contingencies of her plans, there would be plenty of time to determine the specifics of what she needed to do.

* * *

Anton had spent the last three nights sleeping rough on the streets.

He still had fifty dollars left in his savings account. He'd avoided using his debit card again. He expected the human secret keepers for the vampires would be watching for just that sort of move. As much as he needed the cash, he didn't want to do anything that would allow the vampires to find him again. He maintained a low profile, cap on, hood up. He kept an eye out for cameras and avoided public spaces. He was losing weight, and growing increasingly desperate to the point of near panic. It was almost midnight, the mid-week trade in Chinatown had finished for the night. Anton hissed, "Sssssssss," and pushed a skinny cat off the top of a garbage can.

A moment later, he was fishing around in the can outside the back door of a Chinese restaurant – it was slim pickings. The food must be good. There was almost nothing thrown out in the trash. Anton barked a single disappointed laugh. He'd reached the point where he could feel upset by not finding something to eat in a garbage bin.

He looked up at a low wattage bulb attracting insects over the back door. Beneath it hung a simple wooden sign with neatly painted black letters that read, 'The Noodle House. Prop, Mr. G Wu.' A sudden realization hit home. "Mom and Dad's favorite restaurant, we used to come here all the time when I was growing up," Anton murmured to himself. He flicked a wary glance left and right. He backed away and whispered, "I shouldn't have come here, what am I doing – looking for the familiar? Anyone looking for me could do the same."

There was a faint click. The back door of the restaurant opened and a man wearing a chef's cap stood silhouetted in the doorway, his face draped in shadow. He pointed at the open garbage can and called out, "Hey, you shouldn't," he did a double take, "what? Anton? Anton Slayne?" he took a step forward, reaching out with his right hand.

The Chinese chef knew his real name; Anton barely controlled the panic surging through him. "Damn it," Anton swore, stumbling backward.

The man strode forward into the shadows of the alleyway and asked in urgent tones, "Anton, what are you doing here? What's happened?"

Anton turned, running back up the alleyway. He put on the speed that had won medals at state level four-hundred-meter track events. He covered about ten feet before the chef went past him like he was standing still.

Anton slid to a stop.

The man stood in front of him and stated calmly, "I am a friend of your family. You do not have to fear me."

If he was a vampire, Anton was done for. He was going to die in some stupid alleyway.

"Let me introduce myself, I am Gang Wu," he said, waving his hand toward the restaurant. "And this is the Noodle House. Let's go back inside and get something nice to eat." He glanced past Anton at the open garbage bin. "You must be really hungry."

What were the options? Friend or foe? If he was a vampire, then why bother with all this talk. Wouldn't a vampire have tried to kill him by now? Anton's stomach rumbled. He took a deep breath. "Okay." He followed Gang into the back of the restaurant.

"Li … Li," Gang called out as they arrived in the kitchen. "Bring some towels, we have a guest, and make some nice hot tea."

Gang guided Anton to a stool and instructed him. "Sit here, there's no need to hunt in the garbage. I have excellent dumplings. The best in Chinatown."

The delicious smells of the kitchen convinced Anton. His stomach cramped with hunger, and he stated, "I'm starving."

Gang started cooking and said, "This won't take long, shrimp dumpling, pork dumpling, sautéed Shanghai greens. Li! Where is the Tea?"

"Father!?" called a voice with more than a hint of exasperation. A young woman came through the archway from the restaurant, she was carrying an armload of white hand towels. Rolling her eyes at her father, she dropped the towels onto a spare bench. She looked at Anton with large brown eyes, frowned, and said something in rapid Chinese.

"Li!" Gang objected, waving his kitchen knife. "He is not a stray dog; he is Anton Slayne."

Li sniffed once, then twice, and remarked acidly, "Really? I thought a Slayne would be cleaner and not so scruffy looking."

"He'll scrub up okay. Now, please, some tea for us all," Gang requested, spooning half a dozen dumplings onto a plate. He handed them to Anton, and gave him a fork. "I don't know if you can use chopsticks. Try these shrimp dumplings, they're delicious."

Anton blew on the steaming dumplings. Their rich fresh aroma filled his nostrils and his mouth watered. He was sure he'd never been this hungry in his life. He lifted the first one to his mouth. "Ummmm," he hummed, his eyes closed. Then he looked at Gang, and grinned with heart-felt pleasure. "Oh, they're so good!" He then started into the rest of the plate, and in a minute, they were all gone.

Li placed a teapot and three cups with saucers on a nearby bench and stated matter-of-factly, "The tea will be ready soon."

"Now for the pork dumplings," Gang declared and gave Anton the second plate. He followed the pork dumplings with a third plate of sautéed Shanghai greens. He then sat back, waiting for Anton to finish eating.

Anton ate the pork dumplings and started to weep, tears rolling down his cheeks. "This is … just … so good of you." He sobbed, overwhelmed with nameless wracking emotions.

"Hey, hey," Gang said, taking the plate away and putting his hand on Anton's shoulder. "Long, deep breaths young man, slow it down."

Putting his head in his hands, Anton cried, rocking slowly back and forth as horrors held back for days came forth in a rush.

Gang waited for Anton to regain some composure. In quiet tones, he inquired, "What's happened, Anton? Now I am frightened. Has something happened to Anna and William?"

"Vampires killed Mom on Friday night. They took Dad away and said they would bury him in silver," Anton stated in a rush. It was the first time he'd told anyone what had really happened. He rubbed his face with both hands, they came away wet. His chest heaved in another sob, then he quietened and started to breathe more normally.

Gang stood up; his face pale with shock. Li put her hands over her mouth, her eyes wide with horror.

"You must stay here," Gang declared decisively. "This is terrible news. Someone must have betrayed their secret."

Anton looked Gang in the eyes and asked, "How do you know so much?"

"I was a student of your grandfather. Back then, there was much trouble in the Order … murders and lies. Your parents and your grandfather had to go into hiding."

"I don't know what the Order is. Chloe Armitage – the one who killed my mother and took my father away spoke of the Order of Thoth."

Gang paused for a long moment, and then queried softly, "This vampire, can you describe her, and did she have a henchman?"

"She's quite tall for a woman. She's young, maybe nineteen or twenty at most, with dark hair cut short in a Bob. Beautiful blue eyes, sounds posh, looks like a supermodel, and yes, she had a man with her, tall, solid, blond, named Marcus Drake."

Gang pursed his lips, giving a soft whistle. "Anton, you're still with us – which is a miracle." He stroked his chin. "Li, maybe something stronger tonight, pass over the shot glasses." He reached beneath the bench and retrieved an ancient bottle. "Sake, family reserve."

He poured out a stiff drink for each of them. Stoppering the bottle, he put it back beneath the bench. They sipped their sake, and it burned with a smooth fire down Anton's throat.

"I will contact your grandfather," Gang declared. "I must tell him what has happened. As for the Order, it is enough for tonight that you know we have been fighting vampires for the last five thousand years. You are with friends now."

Anton put his hand out and Gang took it, clasping his arm. Anton said, "Thanks, Gang," he looked over at Li, "and Li. I can't thank you enough."

Li arched a quizzical eyebrow and smiled. Gang shook his head slightly and said sagely, "There is only one reason why you didn't die with your mother. It serves the vampire's purpose that you live."

"She said things to me," Anton said in a low murmur.

"Beware of what Armitage has told you," Gang warned. "Every word serves her agenda. Now off for a shower. I don't often agree with my daughter – but in this instance, she is absolutely correct. You do resemble a scruffy, stray dog. Li, show him the bathroom and the guest room."

Li indicated an open doorway with a flick of her head and directed, "Follow me."

They left the kitchen and Gang called after them, "Tomorrow, I will teach you how to wash dishes. We're a kitchenhand short, and you can help out while you're here. I have special techniques that I will share with you. You will be the best dishwasher in all of Chinatown."

For the first time in days, Anton smiled. Li led him to the building next to the restaurant. It was the Wu family home. Twenty minutes later, Anton had showered and was falling asleep in a comfortable bed.

Chapter Three

Terrorism link to Friday night murder

By Stephanie Hurd | Mercury Correspondent APRIL 29,

The murder of a woman in Jamaica Plain has been linked to terrorism with the case being handed from the Boston Police Department to the FBI.

Police had been notified of the murder and attended the house where the body of the woman was found in the early hours of Saturday Morning. An arrest warrant for a suspect was issued but was later rescinded after the FBI took over the case.

The FBI from the Manhattan Joint Terrorism Task Force Annex has jurisdiction for this case, said Boston police spokesman, Harold Jacobs in a phone interview Saturday.

The FBI Special Agent in Charge, Jim Alexander, declined to comment on the case, stating that policy dictated that active operations against terrorist cells were not a subject for media discussion.

– Boston Mercury Newspaper article on the Internet.

* * *

Boston, May 5th, 23:00

Anton finished washing the last of the dishes, hanging up his scrapers, brushes and dish washing cloths.

He looked up at the clock, it was eleven pm. Flicking off the kitchen lights, he left the restaurant, and made his way to Li and Gang's home. Entering the ground floor, the sharp crack of wood on wood resounded from the backyard, and he went to investigate what was happening there.

A square wooden deck about ten yards on a side dominated the backyard. A peaked roof, supported by four thick pillars at the corners covered it, providing an all-weather open-air training environment. In the middle of the deck, Li and Gang sparred with pairs of wooden sticks. Anton watched in growing amazement at the remarkable display of skill and control as Li and Gang trained with each other. After three minutes, they paused, stepped back and bowed to each other.

"I see that we have an audience for our Arnis training," Gang said.

"Would you like to join us?" Li asked, looking at Anton with an open challenge in her eyes.

"It's time to begin your training. Vampires hunt you. The Order of Thoth is your natural home," Gang declared.

"How do I begin?" Anton asked, spreading his hands wide.

"You have already started with that question," Gang said. "But before we start with 'how' we must answer 'why.' Why do you want to learn what we have to teach?"

"To defend myself, to avenge my mother's death, to rescue my father," Anton declared with quiet intensity.

"The first part of your answer makes sense, the rest not so much," Gang said. He paused, frowned, and said in serious tones, "Your father is beyond saving. The vampires will have turned him. Burial in silver is a punishment for vampires. As for your mother, do you really want vengeance to be the center of your life?"

"Chloe Armitage needs to be destroyed."

Gang nodded once, then stared hard at Anton and said, "The man who walks in the shadow of vengeance is a different man from the man who walks in the light of justice."

Anton was momentarily nonplussed. What Gang just said sounded like fortune cookie wisdom, and he asked, "… Is there a difference?"

"I see for you there is no difference." Gang hesitated for a brief moment, his eyes tightened for a second, then he said with a wry smile, "But you are also young, inexperienced and foolish."

"Thanks," Anton replied, sarcastically.

A second later he was face down on the woven mats embedded in the floor, his arm twisted up behind his back. Li had dropped him; just as quickly she was gone. Anton rose to his feet, rubbing and rolling his shoulder.

Gang said with a commiserating smile, "Never mind Anton, I was even more arrogant than you are at your age. You will find out that humility is an essential virtue or you will not survive."

Anton took a deep breath and conceded, "Okay. I'm sorry."

Gang leaned toward him. "If you approach Chloe Armitage with anger in your heart, she will gut you like a fish."

"I'm sorry, I just don't see how humility is going to help me fight vampires and defeat her."

"Humility will allow you to master what you need to learn, and to be fully present when the moment comes to use what you have mastered."

Anton frowned and promised, "… Okay, I will try."

Gang snorted. "Try!" he laughed. "We'll see about that."

Anton frowned again and asked, "Are you always going to be laughing at me?"

"Well … yes," Gang replied with a smile. "I'm sure your training will be very amusing."

"Are you serious?"

"Very serious."

"You're kidding me?"

"No – the more serious something is, the more we need to laugh at it."

"… Okay." Anton agreed hesitantly.

Gang sighed. "Now before we proceed, there are things you must know and agree to, or else you must walk away from here and never come back."

Anton nodded slowly. "Okay, sure."

"The Order of Thoth is a harsh mistress, and I mean harsh. I'm not talking about 'Wishy Washy 101' at the local University. There are some hard and fast rules you must understand and agree to. Is that clear?"

Anton nodded again.

"Then let us begin with rule number one. Once you join, there is no going back. The Order is for the rest of your life. Once you commit to the Order, the only way to leave is via the grave. Is that clear? Do you understand and accept this rule?"

Anton was willing to do anything to deal with the vampires and responded without hesitation, "Yes. I understand."

"Rule number two. As a member of the Order, you will keep the Order secret, and you will keep the Order's secrets. Is that clear? Do you understand and accept this rule?"

"Yes, I understand."

"Rule number three. As a member of the Order, you will obey the orders of your superiors without hesitation? Is that clear? Do you understand and accept this rule?"

Total obedience, or he had to walk away with nothing and Armitage would get away with everything she'd done to his family. Whatever was necessary, he'd do it. He declared, "Yes, I understand."

"Do you agree to and accept all three rules?"

"Yes. Absolutely."

"Okay then," Gang directed. "Anton, please take off your shirt."

"Huh?" Anton grunted.

"Rule number three Anton," Gang reminded him, arching an eyebrow and tilting his head.

"Okay, sure," Anton replied. He took off his shirt, dropping it to the floor.

Li stared at Anton for a long appraising moment and slowly smiled.

Gang put a consoling hand on Anton's shoulder, and said with quiet emphasis, "I must warn you, what I'm about to do, I've never done before, but your grandfather taught me how to do it."

What was he going to do? Hit him hard in the face? Some sort of initiation test? Whatever it was, it was sure to be painful, but undoubtedly necessary. Anton put his questions away, braced himself, and declared forthrightly, "I'm ready. Go for it."

Gang shaped the fore and middle fingers of his right hand into a stiff knife. He stared intently at Anton for a brief moment and then his hand blurred over Anton's torso in a tightly controlled sequence, striking him deeply a dozen times in less than a second.

Each strike sent a shockwave through Anton's body. Anton felt silvery light flaring at the base of his spine and racing up his body. The light burned with an intense cold fire fountaining through the top of his skull. His eyes rolled up in his head and he fell to the floor unconscious.

Anton woke up, a living flame ripping through every fiber of his being. A silvery-white fire was consuming him from the inside out. He desperately wanted to scream, but only a high-pitched screech got past his clenched jaws. A white wall of agony swept through his skull, threatening to blow his head apart.

An eternity of trembling and shaking came and went, and then he lay still. Panting for breath; gentle hands rested firmly on his shoulder and hip, and someone rolled him into the recovery position.

Suffering beyond anything he'd ever experienced before overtook his body in waves. Great floods of agony washed through him, all but taking his sanity away. Time disappeared and there was only the dark ocean of anguish in which he was drowning. All light vanished as eternal night descended and overwhelmed his mind.

There was a gap in which nothing existed, not even himself.

A frail spark reignited and the dark gave ground to the light.

Utterly alone and surrounded by darkness; he sobbed once with abject terror, but no one heard.

A rift cracked open between the past and the future – two opposite worlds beckoned with equally seductive powers: oblivion or life. Now was the time to give up, to let go, to receded into the welcoming darkness. However, one need prevailed against the dark, *I care, I can never give up.*

Forced to choose, he drew his next breath and the darkness retreated. The spark grew with the returning of the light. The ocean of pain ebbed away, slowly replaced by intense pins and needles as his body and mind returned to a calmer state.

Oh my God ... oh my God. Anton opened his eyes. He pushed himself up into a sitting position, then doubled forward, wracked by a fit of harsh coughing.

Li put her hand softly on his shoulder and said, "That's your lungs learning to really breathe for the first time."

Anton couldn't speak for a long moment, then regained enough control to gasp through chattering teeth, "What … was … that? What did you … do to me?"

"I just switched you on," Gang replied with a chuckle. He slapped Anton on the shoulder. "That's the first time I've seen that work."

Pushing himself up off the floor, Anton groaned and said ruefully, "Switched me on? I feel like a Mack truck just ran over me … twice."

Gang shrugged his shoulders, and then nodded once. "But now you can Ramp."

Anton shook his head. His nose had started bleeding and he smeared the blood away with his forearm, and asked, "What's the Ramp?"

Li gave him a hand towel, Anton pressed it to his nose, and turned back toward Gang.

Gang spread his hands wide and addressed Anton, "The Ramp is an epigenetic phenomenon. The outcome of a set of techniques that bind muscles and rewire nerves. There are very real physiological changes that enable us to reach our full potential as a human being. Those changes enable us to match the speed and capabilities of vampires. They allow us to enter combat with vampires and win."

"You could have warned me," Anton said ruefully.

"If I had told you how much it would hurt – would you have chosen differently?"

Anton shook his head. "No."

"Good answer. By the way, not everyone survives the process, most die."

"Most die? I'm not surprised. I thought I was definitely going to die. It was a big risk, was there no other way?"

"There is no way you can stay in the Order as a fighter without the Ramp. I trusted in the fact you are a Slayne. You have over two hundred generations behind you of continuous membership in the Order. If anyone was going to survive the process, it would be you."

Anton flicked his gaze from Gang to Li and back, and asked, "So the both of you have been through that?"

Gang stated with a broad grin, "No, of course not. We both started training at three years of age, and achieved the transformations you just went through over fifteen years of dedicated work."

Anton winced as Gang slapped him on the back and said, "You got off easy, you got the condensed version."

Anton smiled wryly, then grimaced as he stiffly took a step forward.

"You can't train an adult body for the Ramp," Li said. "It's no longer adaptable, what my father did was the only way."

Anton's blood nose stopped dripping. He rubbed his forehead, and picked up his shirt. He staggered, utterly drained and exhausted, then righted himself. The beginnings of a whopper of a headache clawed at his skull, but his soul took flight, as if he'd just won a championship game. He asked, "So, what happens now?"

"All I have done is open the door," Gang instructed. "You still have to walk through it. The development of skill and control is still in front of you. Please believe me when I tell you there is much for you to learn, but for now, drink plenty of water and get some sleep."

"Thanks, sounds like excellent advice," Anton replied, walking gingerly to his room. Everything hurt like hell, there seemed to be no end to the way his body could experience pain.

Gang called after him, "I'll have a big breakfast for you in the morning. You'll need it."

Anton waved at Gang, and made it into the house. He managed to down a couple of tall glasses of water in the bathroom before flopping into his bed and falling immediately asleep.

* * *

Chloe Armitage and Haras Mosule stood on top of a rampart at the Tower of David citadel in Jerusalem.

The evening light show had finished and the revelers had all left. Except for two unfortunate souls whose bodies were in the back of a Shadowstone van Peter Dench was driving to a designated disposal facility. The other praetorian, Washington Jones, stood a dozen yards away on another part of the citadel wall. All four vampires wore barely visible in-ear communication headsets that provided secure communications via encrypted satellite links to any location in the world.

"We're wasting our time," Haras complained loudly, staring out over the old city of Jerusalem. "We have been here nearly a week without a hint of Red Empire activity. We need a new strategy."

Chloe arched an eyebrow.

"First we need good intelligence," Haras said. "We need to find the secret citadel of Shabbah al Ahmar. The Red Empire typically maintain a forward base of operations. They moved the last one in 1850, two days after Crane converted me, and before Crane could launch an attack on it. The Red Ghost of that time had acted quickly when vampires took his chief lieutenant alive. Back then, the forward operations citadel was in Istanbul, the city that I grew up in as a child. It's a distinct possibility the Red Empire have moved back there and now they simply run operatives through Jerusalem to lay a false trail. It's a task for Shadowstone and the Panopticon to find the Red Empire's men and track them back to their lair. Then we can come in and eliminate the Red Empire's main force."

Chloe tilted her head and said wryly, "You talk of war when our mission is one of stealth."

"You've never shirked a battle before."

Chloe's lips twitched with a slight smile. "Of course not, but open war with the Red Empire is not our mission."

"We don't have enough information to execute our mission as it stands."

"Crane must believe the Red Empire is here. Otherwise, he wouldn't've sent us. We're too valuable for him to waste our time here."

Haras gripped the top of the rampart and stared out at the city. "But we're wasting our time."

"The Red Empire must be here somewhere – we need a new method of searching."

"I will take Jones. If you catch up with Dench, we can split this city into two halves. I will take the west side—"

Chloe seized upon his offer like a trap snapping shut. "And I'll take the east side."

A flash of light lit up the edge of the city, a plume of flame rising into the night sky. They both reacted to the flash at the same time, turning as one to look at what was happening. Jones appeared next to Haras. Another pair of flashes followed hot on the heels of the first. The plume of flame thickened into a tower of smoke six miles away in the direction of the disposal facility.

Chloe activated her ear piece on broadcast and ordered, "Dench, report in … Dench?"

The only sound on the line was static.

"He's gone, Ma'am," Jones stated in shocked finality.

Jones opened his Shadowstone smartphone, bringing up a Panopticon satellite feed covering the area of the explosion. He held the phone out so that Haras and Chloe could see what was on the screen. The Shadowstone van lay dismembered by the explosions, people cowered in the street, frozen with fear, or running away. A pair of men approached the remains of the van cautiously. Even with a satellite view, they could see the men point toward the center of the remains of the cabin and shake their heads.

The thud and crump of the explosions finally reached them. The signature squeal of tearing metal discernable to their vampire hearing.

Haras opened his own smartphone, immediately running a program. In seconds, it gave a quick succession of beeps. He grinned hungrily and declared, "We have targets, three of them."

"Same here," Jones reported, showing them his screen with three green dots streaming away from the explosion.

"I will take the one heading northeast," Chloe declared decisively.

"I will take the one heading south," Jones declared.

"I will take the last one," Haras stated.

"Keep your earpieces active. Stay in touch, and try and capture them alive," Chloe declared. "We need information, not kills."

"Good hunting," Haras said to the other vampires before leaping over the edge of the rampart. Landing at the base of the tower, he ran toward the west, disappearing into the night.

Jones followed him down, also vanishing into the darkness.

Chloe paused, long enough to smile with satisfaction. *One pawn sacrificed and one knight distracted.* She leaped over the edge, running off to the northeast, her phone providing her the same Panopticon tracking information guiding the others. In less than ten minutes, she'd covered the distance and converged on her target's location.

He disappeared down a sewer. From the tell-tale heat plume, he was clearly ramped, almost certainly a Red Empire assassin.

"Entering the sewers, I will lose comms in moments," Chloe broadcast to the others.

"Noted," Haras replied.

"Yes, Ma'am – I've found mine," Jones responded.

Chloe dropped through the sewer entrance into the maze of pipes underneath the city. The rip and crack of gunfire, rapidly followed by sword-on-sword combat erupted over her comms link. She ran into the darkness; her vampire senses leaving no doubt she was following her prey. His warm footprints left a visible trail on the cold concrete. She was on a service walkway, above the wet and noxious contents of the sewer. She didn't need the Panopticon system now, she was close enough to her target to follow his footprints, distinctive human body odor and the almost imperceptible noise of his movements. Her comms link gave a little hum in her ear as it lost contact with the satellites. She shut it down and slowed to a walk.

Human hearts were beating within the sewer. There were five of them and they were close. Chloe rounded a bend, where five Red Empire assassins confronted her. One was the sweat-drenched runner she'd pursued. They were all armed with long slim-bladed swords and Uzi 9mm submachine guns. They carried their blades drawn and their Uzis aimed directly at her.

The lead assassin lowered his weapons and asked, "General Armitage?"

"Yes," Chloe replied.

"We are to take you to meet Shabbah al Ahmar."

"As was agreed."

"You will need to disarm, and to wear a hood as the location is secret."

"As was expected," Chloe said. She took off her sword belt and handed it to the leader of the squad.

One of the other assassins approached with a thick black hood and she allowed him to place it over her head. She mused to herself, *A moment of truth; I will get to find out if Shabbah al Ahmar will keep his word.* She declared loudly through the heavy weave of the hood, "Lead on, I will follow you by sound."

The squad of assassins moved away, and Chloe followed as they proceeded to traverse the sewers of Jerusalem to the secret citadel of the Red Empire.

* * *

Hands with the barest hint of a tremble carefully removed Chloe's hood. Someone was trying to hide their terror and just failing to do so.

The hood slipped away. Her hearing had alerted her as to what to expect and there were no surprises. She was in the middle of a large hall without windows. There was a high vaulted ceiling. The walls were of smooth gray stone with the lighting supplied by modern electric fixtures overhead. There was an oppressive sense of mass above her. She was underground.

Surrounding her were twenty-five armed warriors. The hand-picked elite of the Red Empire led by the man standing two yards in front of her, Shabbah al Ahmar.

She smiled at the Red Ghost. She'd met him twice before. The first time on a battlefield, but without closing. The second time by mutual choice in a place of secrecy. He had given her his personal name, Dalien Morte.

His hatred for Cornelius Crane eclipsed all other forces in his life. Chloe did not know the origin of Morte's hatred; it was enough to understand its power. He'd been willing to bargain and had delivered a shared agent in the Order of Thoth operating in her heartland, al Ghurab, the Raven.

In exchange, she would provide high-level operational intelligence from the Vampire Dominion.

Morte glowered at her and demanded, "What brings the right and left hands of the Demon to this land?"

Chloe replied calmly, "Crane believes the Interpretive Codex is in the hands of Shabbah al Ahmar and he wishes to possess it."

"Does he believe that four vampires ... no," he snapped his fingers, "three vampires can breach our defenses?"

Chloe arched an eyebrow, tilting her head slightly and said with the merest hint of a smile, "... I'm here."

Like a wolf circling its prey, Morte stalked around her and declared incredulously, "You would dare to challenge us here, alone and unarmed?"

Chloe smiled softly, her eyes glistening with an avid desire. She remained poised and still, without a hint of fear.

Around her, men loosened swords in their scabbards. Safeties clicked open on Uzi submachine guns. The bullets within them reeked of silver. The anticipation in the room rang like a bell. All these men had trained from childhood to do one thing very well – to kill – and especially to kill vampires.

Morte snorted once and answered himself, "Of course not. You play your own game."

Chloe arched an eyebrow. *Which is why I'm talking and you, and your men are not dying on my blade.* "Yes," she conceded. "Shall we begin?"

"What do you have to offer?"

"I will provide you with the exact location of the Key of Ahknaton, and the Papyrus of Hakron the Scribe. All I require in payment is to verify you have the Interpretive Codex."

Morte sneered derisively. "What makes you think that I have the Codex? Crane is delusional."

"Crane's information is good. You have the Codex."

Morte frowned. "You are very certain about such a doubtful claim."

"Unless the Red Empire has lost the Codex, it still has it, as it has been in your family line for five thousand years."

"What you offer is insufficient," Morte declared with a scowl, silently conceding his possession of the Codex.

Chloe smiled warmly. "I also offer my continued good will and future opportunities for mutual benefit ... which is an offer of great value."

Morte stroked his short dark beard for a long moment. "So be it. I need to ensure you have no recording equipment, such as a contact lens with data storage capabilities. I need you closely examined before you can approach the Codex."

"Of course," Chloe agreed.

Morte glanced at one of his men and commanded, "Search her."

A young member of the Red Empire force stepped forward with a device the size of a smartphone. Chloe stood still as he swept the device over her body, running it carefully and slowly in front of her face. The device gave a quick chirp as a green light flashed on the screen.

"She's clear," the young man reported, and rejoined the ranks surrounding her.

Morte touched his earpiece, speaking rapid commands in Arabic. A minute later, the large doors at the end of the hall opened and an old man dressed in a simple gray robe walked into the hall. He carried a long, silver scroll case. Bowing low before Shabbah al Ahmar he handed over the case. Morte dismissed him with a wave of his hand, and moments later the doors were once again closed and locked.

Chloe continued to look straight ahead. Her stance poised and relaxed as the breathing and heartbeats of unseen guards beyond the doorway whispered in her ears. She assessed her situation, *Another eight outside this room.*

Morte stepped away from her. He opened the case, and extracted the scroll within. He walked away from her and placed it flat on a lectern at the rear of the hall. The scroll was much shorter than the Papyrus of Hakron the Scribe, only a foot square.

Chloe remained still, revealing nothing. With such a short piece of papyrus it must be instructions only. She seethed with anticipation, she was close, so very close to what she sought.

"You must approach without any clothing or equipment of any sort," Morte demanded.

Chloe arched an eyebrow. "… Agreed." She wore loose combat fatigues. She undid her belts and webbing, her hand automatically reaching for her scabbard on her left hip. She smiled wryly as she clutched empty air. Looking to her right, the leader of the squad that had escorted her was holding her sword and belt. She wondered if he comprehended the rare value of the blade, fashioned from meteoric iron by a genius sword smith in late 17th century Japan. Without doubt, she would soon hold it again.

Chloe completed her disrobing, placing her clothes in a neat pile on top of her combat boots in the middle of the room. The room fell into near-perfect silence as the assembled Red Empire assassins witnessed her walk with naked confidence toward the lectern.

Every eye watched her with avid attention. Every sword stood raised in ruthless salute. The doors to the room remained securely locked and offered no escape. Twenty-five heart beats accelerated as she reached the lectern, stood behind it and glanced down at the Codex.

The arcane symbols on the Papyrus coalesced within her mind. A mind fueled by nearly two centuries of access to the wealth of Crane's unique library. A mind gifted with an eidetic memory. *So that is how it works, how remarkable to devise such a code in such an ancient time.*

Chloe looked up from the Codex and briefly scanned the assembly of Red Empire Assassins. For a long moment, her eyes unfocused as she merged the instructions of the Codex and her perfect memory of Hakron's Papyrus into a single image. She realized the truth of the Key of Ahknaton, the Metaframe and the genesis of the vampires.

Intense joy bloomed within her, surging euphoria rushed up her body and fountained through the top of her head. The realization was both shocking and profound. In a rare moment of abandon, she laughed out loud. *Vampires were an accident – who knew?*

The men in the room swayed before her, her laughter momentarily unnerving them. Their confident stances shifted to defense as they murmured warnings to each other. Low muttered words reached her, "Capture her. Torture her. Kill her."

Chloe slowly stroked her chin – just once before her hand dropped back to the lectern. Her eyes widened, a ghost of a smile curling her lips, she took a deep breath and sighed softly. She was suddenly intrigued with the possibility of seizing the Codex and fighting her way out of the citadel. The daring nature of the deed excited every fiber of her being. No vampire had ever accomplished such a thing. The theft of the most holy artifact of the Red Empire from the heart of their citadel. She was the premier warrior of her kind, unequaled in skill with the blade. If any vampire was going to complete the feat, it would be her.

She contemplated the twenty-five Red Empire assassins surrounding her. Twenty-five Ramp masters, each a highly skilled and experienced killer versus her unarmed self. Her mind accelerated, racing through options, calculating results versus risks, anticipating action, and counter-action. In a moment, a path of probability opened, revealing a set of actions that made the chance of success substantially better than a coin toss.

Temptation flooded her soul. The assassin standing ten feet to her left would be the first to fall. His sword would become her own. The man standing opposite him would rush to attack her and he would be next to die. Then with a sword in each hand, she would reap the lives of the elite warriors of the Red Empire.

The leader of the escort squad would be the sixteenth man to die. She would leave a blade in his heart and then with her katana, the *Red Dragon,* in her hands, she would kill the remaining nine in … fourteen seconds.

She would leave Dalien Morte to the last. To give him time to fully understand the depths of his failure in allowing her to enter the heart of his citadel. With the room cleared, she would reclaim her clothes. Then with the Codex in her left hand and the Red Dragon in her right, she would leave the citadel, slaying all who would oppose her departure.

The rush of wonderful joy she felt now would sublimate into divine bliss.

She tapped the sides of the lectern with her fingers and stepped back; rationality curbing her passionate desire. She could not deliver the Codex to Crane. Once he possessed the Codex, it was certain he would soon decide he no longer needed her. With Allemande's curse in place, she was unable to defend herself against him. She would surely perish and her vision of a new world order would die with her.

Chloe took a breath, and addressed the assembly, "You do not trust me. Given that you do not know me, that is understandable, but tonight you will discover that I keep my word. This is the Interpretive Codex, and I will answer Shabbah al Ahmar's questions in full."

Morte ordered the doors opened, the Codex taken away, and the room cleared. Within a minute, Chloe and Morte stood alone.

He stared at her, frowning and stroking his beard, and declared, "Everyone felt it. Your joy at seeing the Codex and your disappointment that you could not take it with you. So powerful were your emotions, these men could not help but react. You are dangerous beyond belief."

"I'm only dangerous to my enemies. My friends, on the other hand—" Chloe left the statement hanging. Arching an eyebrow, she smiled at him and said wryly, "However, I am at a disadvantage, you are clothed and I am not."

"Of course, please dress."

Chloe put her clothes back on and declared, "The answer is simple. Crane keeps The Key and the Papyrus in a secret room within his personal quarters in his citadel. The citadel is at 350 on Fifth Avenue, New York City. His personal chambers are on the 104th floor. The defenses of this building and the surrounding city are formidable and designed to thwart an attack by the Order of Thoth or the Red Empire."

Morte pursed his lips. "That is sufficient." He grinned, his dark brown eyes flashing with triumph. "You may go now."

"Thank you for your ... hospitality."

Morte touched his earpiece and gave orders, in moments the original escort squad returned to the chamber. However, this time, the assassin who had led her into the sewers was bound with chains.

He addressed his men. "Give General Armitage back her weapon and this man, and return her to where you found her. Ensure her safety while she is in your care."

Morte faced Chloe. "Al Eunza owes the Red Empire a life debt, his acceptance of this mission of sacrifice will allow his true name to be remembered in honor, instead of shame."

Chloe nodded. "If his name is to be honored, I shall ensure his death is by the sword as befits a servant of the Red Empire."

Morte nodded his head once.

Chloe accepted the black hood and followed her escort away. She reflected on what she'd observed before the hood had darkened her sight, *His heart has still not returned to its normal range after seeing me nude. I will be able to leverage his desire. Now I need to bring Marcus to Jerusalem and lead Haras and Jones on a merry chase for a few weeks to allow this mission to take on the semblance of a real search.*

He thinks himself secure in this hole in the ground, but little does he know that even though I wear this hood – I can remember my steps perfectly.

* * *

For the umpteenth time, Anton punched the air.

Li locked up his arm, ducking underneath his shoulder, she twisted him around, throwing him face down on the mat. He rose to one knee, sweeping with his foot, but Li had already leaped back out of range. Jumping to his feet, he gave ground as Li tested his defenses with a series of kicks that were just fast enough to get past his blocks and evasions. In moments, she finished him with a side kick that propelled him off the training deck.

"Ha!" Li grinned. "I'm amazed, you lasted more than ten seconds that time."

Fantastic, I finally lasted more than ten seconds in a fight with a woman half my size and it has only taken two and a half weeks to get to double digits. Anton picked himself up, getting back onto the training mats.

Li held up her hand and declared, "Enough."

Anton frowned and declared, "I can do more."

"Physically, yes," Li conceded, "but not today. We need to focus on your Ramp control." She walked over to a rack holding Shinai and Bokken training swords made of flexible bamboo and hardwood respectively. She picked one of the bamboo Shinai, flexed it experimentally, and seemingly satisfied with her latest weapon she returned, and stood in front of Anton. She lifted the Shinai and asked, "What is this?"

"A Shinai training sword," Anton replied.

"Those are just words, what is it?"

"It's a Shinai."

"You're not allowed to name it. What is it?"

"A bamboo sword."

"That's just another name, a tag. Do you think the sign out front of the Restaurant 'is' the Noodle House?"

"No, of course not," Anton agreed, becoming exasperated.

"Tell me what it is without words."

"... Huh."

"Tell me what it is with silence."

"..."

"Let it be what it is ... don't put words on it," Li instructed.

No words.

For a long moment, Anton felt his internal voice go silent. *That's weird,* he thought as his mental voice came back. "Hey, I just stopped thinking for a few seconds."

Li leaned forward and smiled mischievously. "That's the easy part." She whirled the Shinai through a flat arc, striking Anton on the shoulder with a sizzling crack. "Now do it while I'm hitting you."

Anton leaped backward and swore, "What the hell?"

Li whipped the Shinai forward again, striking him on the other shoulder.

"Hey?" Anton shouted, struggling to avoid the next blow.

Li moved faster than his eye could follow, striking him twice more, left and right beneath the ribs.

Anton tried to blank his mind, but he kept thinking about what Li would do next, trying to anticipate her actions and avoid her hitting him.

Li blurred, using the Shinai to trip Anton, and he landed on his butt. Before he could rise, she pressed the Shinai against his chest, pushing him flat on his back.

"You're very attached to thinking, aren't you Anton?"

"I guess," he conceded from the floor.

Li nodded. "Well, let's go with that. A thinking man's explanation before we proceed, Okay?"

"Sure," Anton agreed. Anything was better than having his ass handed to him by a girl.

Li sat down opposite Anton. "Mastery of the Ramp begins with listening."

"Okay, I thought I was doing that."

"Anyone can listen with their ears, what the Ramp requires is listening with the mind."

"Uh huh?" Anton grunted.

Li paused for a second and then stated, "There are four types of listening, and three transitions between them. The four types are indifferent, ordinary, silent and profound."

"What are the differences between them?"

"Consider a conversation, indifferent occurs when your mind wanders away, and you hear nothing of what the other person is saying. Ordinary is when you hear the other person's words, but you are also thinking about what you want to say, so you are not really paying attention to their words. Silent is when you just hear the other person's words, and your own mental chatter is absent."

"And profound?"

"Profound listening is when you cease to anticipate hearing anything at all."

"You said that there are three transitions."

"Yes. The first transition from indifferent to ordinary is based on orientating yourself in space, you become mindful of your present location. The second transition from ordinary to silent is based on silencing your internal mental voice."

"That seems to be the hard part."

"A lot of people mistake that internal voice as being themselves, but it is just an activity of the mind. You still remain present when it is silent. It's actually simple, once you're used to it. The third transition from silent to profound is based on orientating yourself in time. Arresting your mind within the present moment, no future, no past, just the present. This is the key to mastering access to the Ramp. It is also the hardest part to learn."

"So, I stop thinking and anticipating?" Anton asked.

"Yes," Li answered. "It is the only path to the Ramp."

"How do I know what to do in a fight?"

"A combination of training to automate your reflexes and Ramp mastery. Profound listening is the key to open the door to Ramp mastery, it is not Ramp mastery. A Ramp master's mind accelerates so much the perception of time speeds up. The experience is of the world slowing down. It is the accelerated mind, allied with transformed physical skills that enable us to match a vampire in combat."

Anton remembered the first night he'd met Gang, and how Gang ran past him in the alley as if he'd been standing still.

"Is there a catch?"

"Two of them," Li answered, and started ticking off her fingers. "Firstly, when ramping, your body runs hot and no one can sustain the Ramp for a long time. Secondly, a noisy mind will drop you straight out of the Ramp. Don't get distracted – it will get you killed."

Anton nodded. "Okay."

"It's been said that a Ramp master's actions precede his thoughts," Li said sagely. She leaned forward and looked into Anton's eyes. "Perhaps one day that will be true for you too. Let's try again, this time unarmed."

Li put the Shinai back on the rack. Turning in an instant, she attacked Anton with a flying kick. He ducked away as Li flew over him, whirling around, he found Li already in position, striking him with hand and foot combinations. Li expertly pulled the strikes on contact. Anton found himself becoming quite within his mind as his world shrank to the moment.

He moved aside as Li launched a kick which he caught in a lock, twisting toward her he lowered his shoulder to catch her in a throw.

Reversing his attack, Li swept his feet out from under him and he landed flat on his back with Li on top.

Li's thighs wrapped firmly around Anton's hips. She locked his right wrist, twisting it painfully as she pushed his forearm into his throat cutting off his ability to breathe.

Anton started to smile.

Li's long hair fell like a curtain around their heads. Her large brown eyes widened as her face hovered inches above his own. "Right!" She snapped. Leaping up, she commanded, "Yesterday you said you could do two hundred burpees in a set, so let's see it – or was that the idle boast of someone who thinks too highly of himself."

"Okay," Anton agreed with a grin and started doing the burpees.

Li took the Shinai back off the rack. Positioning it in front of Anton as he was jumping up from the prone position, she instructed, "Jump over this."

She's enjoying this, Anton thought, as he jumped over the Shinai. He focused on the moves. Li kept inserting the Shinai in front of him and he kept jumping over it. As the repetitions continued, she raised the bamboo higher and higher, until she was holding it straight out from her shoulder for each jump.

With each rep Anton glanced at Li's face. She was watching him intently. He found himself sinking into a quiet place where there was only the rhythm of the motion and Li's eyes watching him. He lost track of time. There was just the night, the cool air laced with the perfume from Gang's roses, and Li. Just Li, a poised, coiled presence next to him. He felt like he could do this forever, and wondered if he just might.

"Stop," Li directed, pulling the Shinai away. "That's five hundred, and you're still going like a machine."

"I've always had plenty of endurance."

"That was phenomenal, I think your body is adjusting to the Ramp much faster than I would expect. Time to get a drink and a shower, we'll continue tomorrow."

Anton smiled. "Great, will do."

Stepping off the mats an image of the vampire Armitage beheading his mother came unbidden into his mind. His thoughts darkened, his smile fled, and he vowed to himself, *Your time is coming closer, I will master the Ramp and I will kill you.*

* * *

Gang logged into his laptop and checked the online bookings for the Noodle House.

He was looking for a very specific booking with a pre-order. It would be from, 'Mr. T Masters, a table for two, an order for the duck special, with the new special secret sauce.' Gang had updated his website the day after Anton had arrived, and listed the new dish. It was an agreed signal to Arthur Slayne.

If Gang needed to contact Arthur, he would advertise he had a new secret sauce. If the need was urgent than it would be a special secret sauce. Arthur would set the time and date for the meeting via the booking. The actual meeting would be at a predetermined site – not the Noodle House. Only Gang, Li, and Arthur knew of the arrangement.

It was three weeks later and there was still no booking. What could have kept Arthur from seeing or acting on his message in that time?

"What's happened my old friend," Gang whispered to himself. He was not one to worry unduly about anything, but he had to admit to himself he was concerned by the lack of a response from Arthur.

Gang remembered back six months to when he'd last seen his old force team leader, replaying the conversation in his mind. There had been a large map of South America laid out on Gang's dining room table. There had been trouble in South America – big trouble.

"I will be going to Brazil," Arthur declared. "Crane has a special project in the Amazon." He stabbed the map with a forefinger and traced out a large circle. "Somewhere in this region, there is a mixed team of Shadowstone operatives, molecular biologists, and support staff. In the background, a team of praetorians are providing security."

"What of the Order, are they doing anything?" Gang inquired.

Arthur shook his head. "They're doing nothing. Kain won't lift a finger. I'm sure he's Crane's pet."

"What's Crane's objective? Those scientists worry me."

"Me too, molecular biology suggests genetic manipulation, cellular technologies, and techniques for changing the physiology of a human being or a vampire, but why the Amazon? I need to find out."

"Do you need my assistance? Li could hire some help and run the Noodle House while I'm away."

"Ha," Arthur laughed. "You trust Li with your baby?"

Gang grinned. "Yes, I know. As unlikely as it may seem at times, I really do trust her abilities, she is really very mature for her age."

Arthur took a sip of whiskey from his tumbler and shook his head. "Not this mission my old friend. Stealth all the way, I will be most effective on my own. Thanks for the offer, though. You know I appreciate it."

Gang frowned for a moment. His old friend had always had trouble asking for help. It was a trait that one day might get him killed. "Well then, good hunting," Gang said, offering the traditional toast.

"Good hunting," Arthur replied heartily.

Both men drained their drinks. And then Arthur left Gang's home and vanished into the night.

Gang felt sick to his stomach as he came back to the present. How would he tell him of the turning and imprisonment of his son, and the death of Anna? At least, Anton was alive and well. Gang took a deep breath, let it go slowly, and his distress fled with it. It was time to accept what had happened and focus on the differences he could make. Perhaps tomorrow Arthur would send his message.

He smiled, the boy was whip-smart, driven to learn, and absorbing information and skills like a sponge. He was progressing much faster than Gang had expected, the Ramp activation he'd put Anton through was playing a large part in that. The ongoing re-routing of the nerve and muscle bindings greatly facilitated the acquisition of physical skills. The transformation of the Ramp enabled the rapid acquisition of any physical ability. Anton was mastering skills in weeks what would normally take years. He was rapidly gaining speed, strength, and a comprehensive fighting ability. What he still lacked was effective control of the Ramp. But that would come with time, Gang was sure of that.

The clock ticked over to 3pm. It was time to attend an afternoon practice session with Anton and Li. Gang picked up a large jar of herbal balm, walked out of his home office and down to the training deck.

It was also time to progress from the flexible bamboo Shinai to the hardwood Bokken. The balm would be useful for the many bruises Anton would soon acquire.

Gang chuckled wickedly for a moment. Anton was the perfect study in the collision between a powerful desire to learn and the trenchant pain necessary to satisfy that desire. He reflected for a moment. Arthur would be proud of his grandson's progress, very proud. And who could ask for more than that.

Gang thought of his daughter, Li. She was the light of his life, and had kept him alive after the tragic accident that had claimed his wife and son. He couldn't be prouder of the young woman she'd become. He'd done everything he could to prepare her for a world ruled by vampires. As powerful as she was, he vowed to himself to work Anton hard. She would need him. A Slayne at her side, with the Slayne fighting heritage in full flower would help keep her safe.

He brushed sudden tears from his eyes and sniffed. What more could a father do?

* * *

Li frowned as another couple left the restaurant without completing their meal.

She'd let them go without asking them to pay. Apologizing profusely as she led them through the front door. Raucous laughter greeted her as she came back into the main room. The boss of the Hu Shizu, the self-styled 'Tiger Clan,' Mr. Wang, completed one of his trademark jokes. The core of his crew sat around a large circular table covered with the remains of the Noodle House's best dishes and finest wines.

Mr. Wang looked around, snapped his fingers loudly and demanded, "Bring the sake!"

Obnoxious creep, Li thought furiously. She walked gracefully forward with two bottles of sake and nine shot glasses on a tray. She placed the tray on a nearby trolley, pouring the sake into the glasses. She quickly distributed the shots around the table. *Here you go,* she thought. *Fats, Stinker, Rats, Slinker, Ferret, Weasel, Greasy, Sleazy and Creepy – I hope you choke on it.*

The gangsters leered at her as she worked. They were all watching her every move. Tracking their avid gazes, she internally shook her head behind her polite, friendly, front of house facade. *What were these guys expecting? A lap dance?*

A rough hand slid over her hip, squeezing her buttock through her red silk dress. The forced smile fled from her face and her eyes narrowed with indignation. She glanced down at the offending hand gliding over the smooth curve of her bottom. She lifted her eyes and stared into the face of the hand's owner, Mr. Wang – the head of organized crime in Chinatown.

Hold it together, step away quietly, and don't rip his head off, Li advised herself and stepped out of reach.

Mr. Wang's hand dropped back into his lap and he said loudly, "You should come and work for me, you could earn a lot more than you make here."

Li whirled and glared at the crime boss for a fraction of a second. *What a pimp! I would rather suck my own eyeballs out with a straw than work for a sleazebag like you.* She raised a fresh smile over her seething anger and replied with a trace of feigned regret, "Mr. Wang, I'm very happy working here with my father."

Mr. Wang stroked his chin, his gaze lingering over every curve of her body. He said avidly, "A beautiful young woman such as yourself could become a star in my best club."

Oh my God, he wants me to be a high-class whore. Li reached deep, managing a simpering titter as if flattered by his assessment of her 'assets.' "Oh Mr. Wang, I wouldn't do anything without my father's permission."

Mr. Wang laughed, and boomed his enthusiasm, "That's it, you're perfect, so innocent, and so honorable. My club's patrons will go wild. I will dress you in gold – you will be a great sensation."

Gritting her teeth behind her smile, Li kept her feelings hidden. Silently reminding herself to maintain her cover, and keep her family's secret. It took more will then she anticipated, but she rose to the occasion. She bowed her head submissively, and took a step backward.

Mr. Wang's chair scraped across the floor, his arm snaking around her waist, dragging her onto his lap.

Li vowed to herself to get a better cover. Next time she would be an ex-navy SEAL. Then nobody would dare mess with her.

"Surely it is time for the young bird to fly the nest," Mr. Wang purred as he looked at her with half-lidded eyes. "I could show you a life far beyond that of a waitress."

"Mr. Wang," Li replied. She shook her head, her eyes wide with feigned innocence. "There is nothing you could offer beyond my life here."

Mr. Wang grinned lustily, pulling her close so that her breasts crushed against his chest. His face closed within inches of her own. She couldn't miss his sallow greasy skin, his stained and yellow teeth, and the pungent reek of stale tobacco smoke enveloping him in a noxious cloud.

"Oh, my dear. If I have nothing you desire, then I'm sure you will continue to enjoy the comforts of your home here in this – 'Noodle House' – for as long as it lasts."

A loud snigger erupted from the other end of the table. She pinpointed the gangster, *Sleazy*, with a sharp glance. The mood around the table shifted in seconds from boorishly enjoyable to coldly threatening.

A familiar presence appeared nearby. She looked up; it was her father.

"Can I help," Gang said calmly.

Anton stood at her father's shoulder radiating cold fury.

Mr. Wang pushed Li off his lap, and she stepped lightly away.

Waving his hand through a wide arc, Mr. Wang asked, "This Noodle House, is it well insured? You never know what could happen … storm, flood – or even a fire." He leaned back in his chair and stroked his chin. "It would be such a shame if this fine little enterprise just went up in smoke."

Gang chuckled. "Ah, Mr. Wang, my insurance is excellent."

Mr. Wang frowned, his mouth drooping sourly. "Your daughter does not want to work for me. Perhaps you could make her see sense."

Gang's eyes twinkled. "Does the lightning obey the wind? She is very strong-willed. She will make up her own mind – she always does."

Mr. Wang smiled at Gang, but his eyes were icy cold. "Mr. Wu, you've been here for years with this little business, so small, I overlooked it." He nodded at Li. "And yet tonight I find your daughter. It's like kicking over a dull gray stone and discovering a diamond."

Li glanced at Anton, his face was flat and still, he stared at Mr. Wang with something dark and terrifying lurking just behind his eyes. *Uh oh. Anton shouldn't be here right now.*

"I'm sorry Mr. Wang, but my daughter will be staying here," Gang declared.

Mr. Wang sneered. "Do you know who I am – how dare you refuse me."

The gangsters around the table leaned back, letting their coats fall away to reveal an array of handguns, knives and short-hafted axes.

Gang took a breath and put a steady hand on Anton's hip. "Mr. Wang, we don't want any trouble."

Li thought furiously. Not how to deal with the lecherous ambitions of the local crime boss, but how to stop Anton exploding. His emotions were still a hot raw mess. She edged behind her father, as if trying to hide, but actually seeking to position herself to tackle Anton.

The last remaining patrons left their seats, exiting through the front door. In moments, only Li, Gang, Anton and the gangsters remained in the main room. The rest of the staff had retreated into the back alley behind the kitchen.

Gang and Mr. Wang stared at each other in silence for a long moment.

"Well, it would be a shame if anyone got hurt through thoughtless action," Mr. Wang said darkly, standing up. "I will give you both a week to think about my offer."

"A week won't make any difference," Gang declared.

"Nor would a lifetime," Li said briskly.

Mr. Wang laughed coldly. "Well, we will see about that." He turned and led his men from the restaurant without looking back.

The last one to leave was the one who had sniggered, Sleazy. Pausing at the door, he caught Li's gaze and made a sexually obscene gesture with his hands, then tapping his chest, he whispered hoarsely, "You and me slut."

As the door began to swing shut, Anton ramped, running through the opening and into the street.

"No!" Li shouted. She ramped hard, following Anton out into the street where she caught up with him. Gang was a step behind her. Anton had just missed the last gangster as he barreled out into the street.

"Hey you!" Anton shouted at Sleazy.

The gang was in front of them and they started to turn around.

Li gripped Anton's arm, snapping, "Drop back down."

Anton stared at her for a moment and then shook his head as if waking from a dream.

Li looked back down the street. One of the gangsters, *Ferret* had drawn a Glock 9mm pistol and it was pointing right at her. Mr. Wang put his hand on the gangster's arm and pushed down. The gangster looked at his boss with 'why not?' written all over his thin face.

Mr. Wang indicated up the street with a nod and a shrug, and ordered in a harsh whisper, "Not here."

Li and Anton turned, looking up the street. About fifty feet away a newly mounted CCTV camera covered the sidewalk in front of the Noodle House.

Li's heart sank as she dragged Anton back inside the restaurant.

"Damn," Anton swore.

As they got back inside, Gang greeted Anton with a shake of the head and stated, "No hood, no good."

"I'm sorry," Anton said. "I don't know what happened."

"What were you thinking?" Li demanded.

"I just lost it. I'm sorry – I wasn't thinking at all."

Gang put his hands on their shoulders. "Use tonight to get ready to leave at a moment's notice. We're not leaving yet, maybe nothing will come of this, but be prepared for a quick departure."

Li and Anton both nodded.

"But before you go, this place is a mess. Please help the staff to clean up, they will be hiding out the back. I will have to make some plans about Mr. Wang."

"Yes, Father."

"Yes, Gang," Anton agreed.

Li looked at Anton, her eyes hardened and she promised to herself, *'I wasn't thinking at all.' The next training session is really going to hurt, and I mean hurt.*

* * *

James was nursing a scotch after a delicious meal of spicy lamb ribs at a New York City restaurant fifteen minutes from his apartment.

He was certain the taller of the two bar girls wanted him to ask her back to his place. They had been flirting with each other for the last fifteen minutes. His smartphone pinged, retrieving it from his coat pocket, he glanced at the screen.

"Damn," he swore under his breath. He put the drink down with a twenty-dollar note, smiled at the pretty girl behind the bar and headed for the door. Saturday night was over. He voice-dialed Louise Wesson as he reached the street, she immediately picked up.

"We have a hit," James informed her.

"Anton Smith?"

"Yes, he's still in Boston. Got a great face shot on CCTV. He was outside a restaurant in Chinatown," James said, striding down the street toward the parking lot.

"Will we tell the General?" Wesson asked.

"No," James replied, shaking his head once. "We will notify her once we have this contact tied up and presented with a red ribbon. We'll need some good men."

"Johnson and Higgins are both available."

"Get them moving," James commanded, "We'll need to establish a stakeout location. Bring a surveillance van. I will meet you at our Boston R.I.S.C office ASAP. We will coordinate further action from there."

"Yes, Sir, I'm on it," Wesson replied enthusiastically.

"Excellent," James said and hung up. He reached his car on the near edge of the parking lot and got in; moments later he was on his way to Boston.

He vowed to himself. *This time, Anton Smith, you will not escape us.*

* * *

Gang checked his online order book. There was still no booking from a Mr. T. Masters for a table for two, for the duck special with the new special secret sauce. He was beginning to fear for his former master, *Arthur, my old friend. Time is running out.* It had been nearly a month since he'd put up the message. What had happened to his former teacher?

Arthur Slayne had planned for the possibility that he may not be able to respond. Gang remembered the plan clearly. If there was no reply for a month, he was to act as he saw fit. Tomorrow was the fourth of June, a month after he'd first sent the message. He would have to make a decision.

It was obvious Anton belonged in the Order. Gang frowned as he thought through the ramifications of the Order becoming aware of Anton Slayne. There was the business surrounding Anton's grandfather. Arthur stood accused of the murder of the previous leader of the Order of Thoth, George Madison.

Despite circumstantial evidence that made him the only suspect, Gang was certain Arthur was innocent. A young Order lawyer named Samuel Luther had pressed the charges against Arthur, but it had been Ramin Kain who had stepped forward to claim the rulership of the Order. Ramin's candidacy had gone unopposed and he'd been confirmed in the role of Head of the Order at an Order Conclave nearly twenty years ago.

Gang had strong suspicions about Ramin Kain, if those suspicions were well-founded, then Anton's emergence would not be welcome. In any event, the family name of Slayne had become tarnished over the last twenty years, Anton would find much hostility in the Order, and few friends. He would need to handle the return of a Slayne to the Order carefully.

The death of Anna Slayne and the capture of William had come as a shock. Circumstances had forced the activation of Anton's Ramp capability. The process was extremely risky, but fortunately, Anton had survived, and his progress since then had been a phenomenon. After a month, he was already three times faster and stronger than he was when he'd arrived. His fighting skills were excellent and he picked up new skills extremely quickly, his learning vastly enhanced by the physiological changes occurring from the Ramp. However, he was still very emotionally fragile after the trauma of losing his parents. The incident earlier in the restaurant had been a clear example of how his emotions could overwhelm good sense.

Gang determined to spend more time with Anton, to talk things through, and assist him to gain a deep mastery of his feelings.

He remembered another student of Arthur Slayne, Francis Mirovar, force leader for the Order with responsibility for the northeast. They had been friends and sparring partners when they were both students, and Gang had followed his progress with interest after the Slaynes had gone into hiding.

He considered that Francis could have been Head of the Order, and wondered why he hadn't opposed Ramin Kain for the Office. Francis Mirovar had remained neutral while many blamed Arthur for the murder of George Madison. Francis had a strong reputation for a strict code of honor and was one of the best leaders within the Order.

Gang also counted Francis Mirovar a close personal friend before the ascension of Ramin Kain.

Francis was the nearest force leader. He would be the best to contact if they needed to find refuge in the Order. He would need to re-establish contact with Francis to ensure they could find refuge in the event of trouble.

Gang's mind turned to the topic of Mr. Wang and the Hu Shizu. He did not fear for his own life, or even Li's life from direct confrontation with the Tiger Clan, it was the immediate threat to the lives of others that concerned him. The sanctity of innocent life was at the foundation of Order belief. Gang needed to protect the people who worked at the Noodle House or lived nearby from becoming collateral damage in any conflict with the gangsters.

Collateral damage was just a euphemistic lie. It was simply another name for murder. All his regular staff would need a night off next Saturday. He would need a skeleton crew of extra 'helpers.'

Gang sighed. Small stupid issues drove the fight with the Tiger Clan. The real risk was that defeating Mr. Wang's gangsters would draw the attention of Shadowstone and the Vampire Dominion in numbers beyond Li's, Anton's and his ability to defeat.

The conflict with the Hu Shizu had progressed too far for a peaceful resolution. He couldn't simply leave with Li and Anton, if Mr. Wang's desire remained thwarted, his rage would reach past his family and the Noodle House, to the families of the innocent people who worked there. Gang determined that whatever the risk, they would have to stay and fight, and end the days of the Tiger Clan for good.

With Arthur out of the picture, perhaps permanently, and with Anton's parents lost, it was imperative they rejoined the Order as active members.

Gang sighed again; his heart heavy with sadness at the prospect of losing an old friend. He'd accepted Arthur's request to stay in Boston and watch out for the Slayne family. He'd moved here with his wife, and son, and soon after, Li had been born. He'd focused on raising his family, running a successful restaurant and exercising his passion for innovating combat techniques with swords.

He'd kept a low profile in the Order, not seeking promotion or embroiling himself in the constant politics that seemed to come in disruptive waves through the upper ranks of the Order.

Then five years ago his wife and son had died in a car accident. Those were dark days; it was only the presence of Li that had given him the strength to continue with life itself. The randomness of the loss had shaken the foundations of his life, and he'd since devoted his life to ensuring that Li had the skills to look after herself against any opponent, as he could not guarantee that he would always be there for her.

When he considered how powerful his daughter had become, hot tears ran down his cheeks. His sadness over the loss of his wife and son giving way to a father's pride born of deep admiration and love for his daughter.

Gang had invested a lot of his life into the Noodle House, and he could feel his home slipping away. There were so many good memories of his wife and family within its walls, but his family's time there was coming to a close, he was certain of it, it was like watching storm clouds roll in and overtake the sun. Everything will be swept away and swept away soon. He mused sadly, *Time to place fresh flowers on Tatsu's and Qiang's graves, it may be a while before Li and I can visit them again.*

With that thought, Gang logged out of his computer and went back to the restaurant to see how the cleaning up was progressing.

* * *

It had been three days since the original Panopticon hit on Anton Smith.

James Haley, Louise Wesson and their team of two Shadowstone operatives had set up a surveillance site opposite the Noodle House. Their stakeout occupied the top floor of a three-story building. The equipment in the surveillance van had been repositioned into a room facing the street with a panoramic view of the front of the Noodle House and the Wu family residence. The building they were in was vacant, Shadowstone had taken out a one-month lease on it via a front company ensuring no one would disturb them.

Sean Higgins, a short, wiry IT guru hired by Shadowstone from the NSA had wired up telescopic microphones and cameras on the roof top to cover both target buildings.

Gary Johnson, an ex-CIA/NSA operative had placed a tiny, camouflaged, remote camera on the back wall of the Wu property. Due to a pervasive screen of roses, the camera did not give direct access to the back side of the Wu residence, but it provided an infra-red feed of activity in the backyard directly to the stakeout's computers.

James had directed the Panopticon to co-opt all nearby CCTV cameras and had positioned them to provide optimum coverage of the restaurant and the residence. He had his laptop open, and the screen showed a Panopticon satellite feed at a fine grain of detail covering a hundred-yard square centered on the Wu family's backyard. Green markers labeled Anton Smith, Li Wu, and Gang Wu littered the screen. He'd been able to capture the necessary photos of Gang and Li Wu over the last twenty-four hours and had added them to the search parameters for Anton Smith on the principle of tracking the known associates of the target.

He'd quickly determined his targets had a training environment behind the house. The training deck lay shielded from surveillance by a roof over the training area and a high brick wall at the back of the property. He'd also verified the roof across the training area provided effective screening from satellite sensors across the electromagnetic spectrum. The training deck was an information black hole.

James glowered around the room at his team and declared, "We should have a damn policy for identifying information black holes that are fully shielded from satellite observation." After eight years of working with Shadowstone, it looked like he'd finally found genuine Order of Thoth terrorists and the shielded training environment looked like a genuine marker.

It was 19:30 on a Tuesday evening. Gang and Li Wu had closed the restaurant for the night. They had just completed thirty minutes of physical exercise with Anton Slayne and were now training with weapons on the training deck.

"Hey, Boss, take a look at this," Johnson said, sharing his desktop display to the main screens on the side wall of the room. Everyone swiveled and watched as human shaped heat blobs moved across the screen. They would suddenly change position, and there would be flaring heat plumes that would expand and die from each of the three forms.

"What is that?" James asked, perplexed.

Wesson stared at the screen and remarked incredulously, "I've never seen anything like it."

General Armitage had informed him once, that the Order of Thoth and the Red Empire had special training and techniques. This must be what she'd been talking about. James glowered at the screens and stated softly, "God only knows."

"Listen to this," Higgins insisted, putting the sound he'd just heard through his headphones through a speaker. It was a metallic clatter, timed with the heat plumes. It sounded like someone had pulled a drawer full of cutlery out of a cupboard and upended it onto the floor, but not as chaotic as that would sound, more musical, like a metallic drum, with an inherent pattern and order.

"Now hear what it sounds like when I slow it down by a factor of three," Higgins said, and the sound resolved into clear metal on metal clashes.

"They're sparring with swords," Wesson remarked, frowning.

"And they're fast ... real fast," James said. "You've got this on record?"

"Yes, Sir," Higgins and Johnson answered in unison.

"Give me five minutes." James went into a separate room and closed the door. He immediately voice dialed General Armitage's smartphone number.

The phone rang twice before she answered, "James, what do you have for me?"

"We have Anton Smith."

"Good work. What is the situation?"

"He is currently staying with a Chinese/American family in Chinatown, Boston. We have a surveillance team in place at a stakeout opposite the Wu family's restaurant and residential home."

"Anything else?"

"I'm sure they're Order of Thoth. They fit the profile you provided perfectly. We have been able to scan their last training session with infra-red cameras and telescopic microphones. They move extremely fast, and are highly skilled with edged weapons."

"Excellent work James. I expect a summary report in fifteen minutes, now your orders are to remain at your station and maintain the surveillance. If they move, track them and keep them under continuous watch. It is imperative that you do not engage them, I will come to your site tomorrow night."

"Ma'am, I could get two full combat teams on site in less than three hours. We could take this cell out tonight."

"My orders stand," Chloe confirmed, a frosty edge to her voice. "I expect you to implement them with your usual efficiency. Is that clear?"

James hesitated for a second, he desperately wanted to close this terrorist cell down – permanently, and with disappointment leaking into his voice, he replied, "Yes, Ma'am, understood."

"James, I understand and appreciate your enthusiasm. But you must be patient, your time will come."

"Yes Ma'am, thank you, Ma'am."

The line went dead, and James went back to the main room.

Wesson lifted an eyebrow as he walked in and asked, "Orders, Sir?"

"Stand watch, track them if they leave."

"Yes, Sir," Wesson replied, focusing back on her monitors.

James poured himself a black coffee from a pot on a table, settled into his chair and began preparing the summary report for the General.

The Shadowstone team recorded another two hours of almost continuous training.

"What's this 'Ramp' they keep talking about?" Higgins asked.

"Some sort of Chinese voodoo?" Johnson said.

"Add it to the list of known unknowns. We'll deal with it later," James directed.

The red blobs on the infra-red monitor disappeared from the training deck.

"Looks like they've hit the showers," Johnson remarked.

"Can we get some Chinese?" Higgins asked.

James sighed and agreed, "Why not? Try and find me some steamed dumplings, just a mix, and some soy sauce, I love that."

Higgins quickly left the room and James leaned back in his chair, reflecting on his conversation with General Armitage. *So, my time will come will it, not soon enough, not soon enough by far.*

* * *

I need to get back to New York and Boston, and Crane needs to ask me to come back.

Chloe gently tapped her fingers on a paper pad as she waited for Haras Mosule to complete his report to Cornelius Crane.

"We have no new captures or kills since the last report," Haras declared in a matter-of-fact tone.

Crane frowned from the wall display and declared acerbically, "After more than a month we have three Red Empire casualties, one dead praetorian, and zero useful information – those are not numbers that impress me – are my generals losing their edge?"

"No, Sir," Haras declared. "The Red Empire are very difficult to find. They would rather die than allow capture. We need more resources or a different strategy. If you were to allow us to create new vampires, we could draw them out."

"Vampire creation is out of the question. You will have no control over those you transform. They could easily run amok and reveal the secret of our existence."

Haras nodded.

"At General Armitage's request, I replaced Praetorian Dench with Marcus Drake, a member of her own staff rather than another praetorian. I will now provide another two praetorians and an extra team of Shadowstone operatives. They will come from our Shadowstone force in England. They will all be in Jerusalem by the tenth of June."

"With all due respect Sir, the Shadowstone operatives are not much help. In fact, since we arrived, three operatives have simply disappeared without trace." Haras reported.

"What!" Crane growled. "In future, include the losses of Shadowstone operatives in the main report. Is that clear?"

Haras blinked. "Yes, Sir."

Crane smiled without humor as he stared at each of them in turn. "Now something you must all understand, the six Shadowstone operatives I will send you are all participating in an enhancement program of my own design. They're not yet the match of an Order of Thoth operative or Red Empire assassin, but they're certainly faster and stronger than a normal human. They will provide an essential daylight capability that will assist you to meet your mission objectives."

A program Chloe believed would end in tears. She was certain vampires should never try to enhance humans with capabilities that could one day match their own.

Haras nodded and replied, "Thank you, Sir."

"Now General Armitage, your report."

"Yes, Sir. There is nothing substantive to add to General Mosule's report on the Jerusalem situation. However, just over thirty minutes ago, I received information from a Shadowstone team in Boston. They have an active Order of Thoth cell under direct surveillance; the Wu family."

Crane paused for a long moment.

He knows about them! What does that mean?

"How many Order operatives?" Crane inquired.

How many is he expecting? Has he discovered Anton Slayne? He can independently read the Shadowstone reports — I must tell the truth. "Three Sir."

"Normally this would be within your remit, but with you allocated to your current mission, I am shorthanded for generals."

"We could send Marcus back to deal with the Wu family."

Crane shook his head. "No, Marcus has no rank within the Praetorian organization. They will not obey him and you are both needed in Jerusalem. I think that I will need to deal with this local issue personally."

She couldn't let that happen. He would discover Anton Slayne. "Sir, if I may suggest, there is an extraordinary opportunity here that has not yet been discussed."

Crane raised an eyebrow. "Yes?"

"The Mirovar team. Recent Shadowstone reports indicate they remain active in the northeast and it appears they've recently moved from a safe house in Rhode Island to another location. We could use this Boston cell to draw the Mirovar team out into the open and then crush them all at the same time."

"And how do you propose to do that? To — as you say — draw them out?"

Chloe let Crane's skepticism pass her by. "By causing these Thoth operatives in Boston to run, and to call for help. Then we find the Mirovar team's new safe house and destroy them all. They're the key operational force located in the vicinity of your citadel, and the only group that could potentially launch an attack that could threaten you."

Crane sniffed. "I think you're overestimating their capabilities versus the defensive systems of my citadel. There is also no evidence they even know the location of my citadel."

"Be that as it may, there is still a significant risk to your safety. I could return to the United States and be in Boston before sunrise. The operation to draw out the Mirovar team would take less than a week. Once I have completed the task, I will return here. I will be gone for less than a week."

"One week?"

"One week," Chloe promised.

Crane grinned wolfishly. "So be it. You will return to Boston immediately. Drake will remain in your place until your return. Drake, you're seconded to General Mosule until General Armitage returns."

"Yes, Sir," Drake agreed.

Crane stared directly at Chloe and declared, "General Armitage, I will hold you to your word – I expect the heads of the Mirovar cell on a platter within a week."

"Yes, Sir. Certainly, Sir."

The meeting turned to other operational topics which engaged Marcus Drake, Washington Jones, and Haras Mosule. Chloe gave her respects and left the room. She departed to the adjoining Shadowstone airfield where a hypersonic shadowstar drone was waiting for her. Half an hour later, she was flying at 82,000 feet with the digital windows open, she normally enjoyed the near space view of the Earth curving beneath her, but not on this flight.

That was close. She tapped the end of her armrest with her finger. Now she had to work out how to draw out the Mirovar team in a week. Francis Mirovar was a very slippery fish – just how was she going to do it? It was not often that Chloe felt rushed by shifting circumstances, she did not like it, not one bit. *Why did I make that promise? ... There was no other way. I will have to adapt, and adapt quickly.*

Chloe spent the rest of the flight reconsidering and adapting her plans.

Chapter Four

BODY

SHADOWSTONE INFORMATION REPORT, NOT FINALLY
EVALUATED INTELLIGENCE

COUNTRY: (U) UNITED STATES (USA)

THE GENERAL SITUATION:

A. THE OPERATIONAL TEMPO OF TERRORIST
ORGANIZATIONS WITH A REVOLUTIONARY AGENDA HAS
BEEN STABLE SINCE THE LAST REPORT.

B. THE ORDER OF THOTH IS THE PRIMARY TERRORIST
ORGANIZATION OPERATING WITHIN THE UNITED STATES.
THE RED EMPIRE HAS NO IDENTIFIED OPERATIONS WITHIN
THE UNITED STATES.

C. IN THE FIRST QUARTER OF THIS YEAR, ABANDONED SAFE
HOUSES HAVE BEEN IDENTIFIED AT GRAY MOUNTAIN
COCONINO COUNTY, ARIZONA, AND AT NARRAGANSETT
RHODE ISLAND.

(... REDACTED IMAGES ...)

D. ANALYSIS OF EVENTS INDICATE AT LEAST FOUR
OPERATIONAL ORDER OF THOTH CELLS WITHIN THE
UNITED STATES.

~~TOP SECRET/FGEO~~
RQ
#5390

NNNN
CLASSIFICATION: ~~TOP SECRET~~, SECRET

– Content from a partially declassified preliminary Shadowstone
information report.

* * *

Boston, June 10th, 07:00

Bright sunlight splashed off the iron roofs of the outdoor farmers' market.

Anton pushed a shopping trolley along one of many market aisles. On both sides were arrays of fresh produce; Li selected and purchased items, crossing them off a list as Anton placed them into the trolley.

Gang had given Li and Anton the list earlier that morning and asked them to go to the market for supplies to cover the family's needs for the week. Normally, they would buy all the food in bulk and have it delivered fresh to the Noodle House for the weekend trade, but not today, as the restaurant was not taking bookings for the weekend.

Gang had emphasized the need to ensure there was no one around if the Tiger Clan showed up in force. From the way he'd spoken, he clearly believed there would be a confrontation tonight.

Anton did not feel any concern for what might happen. The sun was shining, the sky was blue, and Li smiled as she handed him a bag of apples. He wore a new gray hooded sleeveless top, his peaked cap and sunglasses. His garments matched the warmth of the day and kept his face away from prying cameras.

It was peaceful and pleasant; he was enjoying being with Li without her constantly hitting him. The training sessions all week had been especially tough, his bare arms revealing bruises, scrapes and a sutured cut where Li had allowed her sword strike to make contact. More bruises lay hidden beneath his clothes.

They had shifted from the hardwood Bokken to metal swords five days earlier. Initially, Anton had been deeply worried he might accidentally hurt Li. By the end of the first day with the katanas, he realized there was no chance he would make contact with her as she was always a step ahead of him.

Anton and Li were nearing the end of the aisle. The list was nearly complete, with the trolley filled with all manner of fresh fruits and vegetables.

Suddenly, Li jumped backward. Something big and hard hit him from behind his left shoulder, throwing him into a display of cabbages. The trolley went flying, tipping over onto its side, spilling everything they had bought onto the concrete floor.

Rebounding back to his feet, Anton stood next to Li. The stall holders were screaming at him in angry Chinese. He ignored them. Six of the gangsters from the previous Saturday night surrounded Li and himself.

Li whispered urgently, "Don't kill anyone, we need to get away from here."

Directly in front of Anton was Sleazy, the one who had insulted Li. The gangster flipped open a pair of butterfly knives, one in each hand, and lunged at Anton. Anton ramped, turning outside the lunge, and trapping Sleazy's right wrist. With a quick twist, he snapped the bones and Sleazy screamed, slashing wildly at Anton with his other hand. Stepping back from the gleaming knife blade, Anton dodged aside as the rest of the gangsters attacked.

Two of the gangsters went after Li, solely armed with wet cloths. The image of Marcus Drake and a drugged cloth rushed through Anton. This was another snatch and grab. They'd doped the cloths.

The Ramp faded and Anton slowed down. Instantly running out of space, blades came toward him from all directions. It was impossible to see and dodge everything slashing toward him.

Spontaneously ramping, Anton trapped a stabbing arm, dragging the gangster forward, and driving the knife he was holding into the lunging arm of one of the other gangsters. Using the first man's body as a pivot, he leaped over him, collecting another gangster in the face with his knee as he went over the top of the ring of men around him.

Now behind the gangster, he kicked out the man's left knee, pushing him hard back into the melee where he toppled over one of the other men dragging them both to the floor. The man with the broken knee began rolling on the ground clutching his shattered joint and groaning with agony, while another gangster dragged a bloody knife from his forearm.

To his left, he heard a guttural scream. Li was standing, poised and taut, a yard in front of the looming form of Fats. Another gangster rolled on the ground a yard behind her, his right elbow bent backward at an extreme and unnatural angle.

Anton didn't have time to watch Li defend herself from Fats. The other three gangsters had regrouped and were charging toward him. Sleazy, his right arm cradled low, lunged with the butterfly knife in his left hand. Anton blocked the lunge with his right hand and drove in hard with his left hand, his fingers extended like a knife penetrated deep into the man's diaphragm. With a great whoosh of air, he folded forward over Anton's hand, before falling away to the side. One of the other two gangsters slashed at Anton as he twisted away, catching his arm, a line of blood appearing on the outside of his bicep.

Anton grimaced, and the grinning gangster who had cut him slashed again, but before his blade could land, Anton punched him straight in the face. His nose imploded, splattering across his cheeks, he fell backward, unconscious before he hit the floor.

The last gangster, his nose already bloody after collecting Anton's knee, lifted a thick bladed chopper. He swung it overhand directly at the top of Anton's head. Ramping again, Anton stepped underneath the strike, trapping his assailant's arm and pushing forward while ducking beneath the gangster's armpit. Twisting and turning, he ended up behind the gangster with the chopper released and now in his own right hand. The man followed the arc of his arm, falling to his knees in front of Anton.

His eyes widened in helpless terror as he stared into Anton's furious face. Anton's arm snapped down, the blade following like a shining stone.

Li's foot flashed in front of him, kicking the chopper from his hand. She dragged him away from the kneeling man. He resisted for a moment, then released the terrified man and went with her.

"Come quickly," Li ordered.

Ignoring their produce on the ground, and a circle of unconscious, moaning, and sobbing gangsters, they vanished into the market crowd.

* * *

The morning sunlight streamed between the tree branches and dappled the grass beneath with patches of golden light.

Anton, Li, and Gang sat at an outdoor wicker table, where Gang had supplied a generous breakfast of Congee, boiled eggs, toast, butter, homemade strawberry jam, a selection of cut fruit, glasses of freshly squeezed orange juice, a pot of strong black tea and a jug of fresh milk.

Gang declared, "Eat first, fill your bellies, drink some tea, and then we will discuss important matters. Starting with what happened at the market an hour ago."

The three of them ate quietly for about five minutes, Gang poured three mugs of steaming tea, and followed with a dash of milk to each mug. Gang sipped his tea and said with a flourish of his right hand, "This tea is excellent. Its flavors are strong, decisive and authentic. Just like the conversation we will now have." He looked at Anton and asked, "Would you like to tell us what happened this morning?"

Taking a deep breath, Anton reflexively felt the fresh dressing over the cut on his arm. Li had sutured it ten minutes ago. He expected Gang would grill him about the brawl in the market, and was sure he deserved it. "I know Li will have spoken with you," he stated contritely. "And that's okay. We got into a brawl with the Tiger Clan, they jumped us with knives. A pair of them also carried wet hand towels which they must've doped with something. They were obviously after Li. Their boss clearly wants her and he doesn't care who he hurts as long as he can have her."

Gang nodded.

Anton paused, wrestling with turbulent emotions stirred up by the recent violence.

Gang waited patiently, sipping his tea. Li sat quietly, her tea untouched and cooling in front of her.

Anton looked at Gang, finding no judgment in his eyes, only a compassionate interest in his welfare.

Gang inquired softly, "Li's safety is important, but that wasn't the real issue today was it, Anton?"

Anton sighed and admitted, "I wanted to kill him."

Gang studied him and advised, "Anton, it is good you struggle with the acquisition of power. I would be concerned if you were not facing these issues."

"I really wanted to kill him, and I would have enjoyed it," Anton confessed. "I love the training," he grinned sheepishly at Li, "even though it hurts. I love the Ramp, and what's happening to me, the increase in power across the board. I love it all, and I want it all."

"It's good to be stronger and faster. But you must remember the average human being, even misguided ones like the Tiger Clan, are not the enemy."

Anton nodded.

"The average vampire, and I mean the average vampire is three times stronger than you are now. Some of them, like Marcus Drake, are substantially stronger than that. They're also faster, and Chloe Armitage is twice as fast as you are now. In combat, they will either push past your blade and hit you, or hit you before you can defend yourself."

Gang frowned and inquired, "Did you maintain good personal security this morning? Didn't lose your hood, hat or sunglasses?"

"Yes, Gang. Everything stayed put."

"Good work. We have to keep ourselves secret from Shadowstone and the Vampire Dominion. I must emphasize this point – it is essential we remain hidden. If we're discovered by our enemies, then we are most likely doomed."

Gang paused, sipping his tea, allowing Anton to absorb the point he'd made, then said, "It's important we don't reveal our skills in public. There are—"

"Father, they were trying to kill him," Li interrupted. "And kidnap me."

"Be that as it may, you can't be ramping in full daylight, and probably in front of a CCTV camera."

"We were quite restrained," Li argued. "In fact, anyone watching would simply see a pair of skilled Kung Fu experts defeat a gang of thugs in a Chinatown market – it's a cliché."

"Except there are six gangsters in Tufts Medical or Massachusetts General emergency rooms by now. And what's on the news? How long before a video shows up on YouTube? Shadowstone are explicitly looking for incidents just like this – and they will not see Kung Fu experts – they will see Order of Thoth operatives."

"Shadowstone?" Anton queried.

"Yes. Shadowstone," Gang said in clipped tones. "They're a very-well funded, well organized, para-military international spy organization owned and operated by the vampires, but staffed by humans. They have a mass surveillance system with artificial intelligence features called the Panopticon. They're always watching for us. It's why we must remain well hidden. ... unlike this morning."

Aha! Shadowstone are the secret keepers, snapped through Anton's mind. He was surprised by the core of tension within Gang, he'd never seen him the least bit agitated. There was a lot more going on here than he'd understood. Gang was worried about something and if Gang was worried, then Anton should be worried to. There was something bigger going on and he wanted to make sure Gang knew he would do whatever he could to help. He said, "Gang, the only reason I'm still alive is because Li and you gave me refuge. What do you need from me?"

Gang rubbed his face with both hands, then said, "Anton, this is not your fault. You've been with us for what, five weeks, perhaps a little more than that, and I know I've charged Li with beating you into shape, and she's done a great job. But you're still very early in your training, there is much you still have to learn. I have been remiss, there are things you must know before we go any further."

Anton nodded; he was all ears this morning.

"I have been trying to contact your grandfather since the day after you arrived, but I have not heard from him. Which while accounted for in your grandfather's plans, is unexpected. He may be in serious trouble."

Li rubbed her temple as if she was getting a headache.

"Is there anything we know for sure?" Anton asked.

"No. Just that he hasn't responded. It's possible he is simply in a location where he has no Internet access."

Anton looked intently at Gang, a question burning within him. *What kept my grandfather from protecting his family?* He put the question aside and asked, "Can you tell me about him? I barely remember him."

"Arthur Slayne was a prominent force leader and the obvious succession plan to George Madison, our previous head of the Order of Thoth. He—"

Anton held up his hands and asked, "I'm sorry Gang, ah, what's a force leader?"

"I will try to explain terms as I go, you will have a new vocabulary by the end of the morning. A force leader commands a team of operatives, they have total authority over their teams, and how they operate. The Head of the Order typically comes from the ranks of the force leaders, many of your ancestors have been force leaders, and quite a few have been Head of the Order."

"If a force leader has total authority over operations, what does the Head of the Order do?"

"Set policy, coordinate actions, settle internal disputes and guard the integrity and secrecy of the order. The Head cannot order a force leader to any action, but must rely on persuasion and soft methods of negotiation. The role of Head of the Order is intensely political."

"What about the third rule, operational obedience?"

"Doesn't apply to force leaders and the Head of the Order," Gang frowned. "And that's something I'm sure Ramin Kain wants to change. He'd love direct control of operations."

"Who is he?" Anton asked.

"The man who succeeded George Madison as the Head of the Order, and he's a particularly slimy political animal. You're familiar with the term 'Cui Bono'?"

"Literally 'to whose benefit?'."

Gang nodded. "Ramin Kain was the principal person to benefit from the murder of George Madison and the subsequent conviction in absentia of Arthur Slayne for the crime – by replacing Madison as Head of the Order and removing his main rival."

"What happened?"

"Officially, Arthur Slayne murdered George Madison and Mary Creeley in their sleep. Not that I believed it for a second. Arthur is no murderer; he had no motive and he was on good terms with Madison."

"How was he convicted, what was the evidence?"

"There was no evidence, there were only lies."

Anton pushed his hand back through his hair, perplexed. "How does that happen?"

"There was a coup d'état."

"What the hell? The Order is at war with the Vampire Dominion, and there is a coup d'état? Factions versus factions? You would think that people might just focus on the main game – on killing vampires."

"The Order is very high-minded. Order members either originated or advanced many of the core inventions within human history, such as agriculture, writing, mathematics and science. But there are always people who can hide the darkness within, blend in, and wear a mask in public that hides their own selfish interests. There is a cabal, centered on two men, Samuel Luther, and Ramin Kain. The Kain/Luther cabal is currently in power within the Order."

"So, Samuel Luther and Ramin Kain framed my grandfather for murder?"

"Yes. I believe so, but I can't prove it."

"So, there is no legitimate authority within the Order?"

"Only the appearance of it. Anton, please do not underestimate these men, they're in a powerful position. There are many in the Order who will follow their lead and who will defend their lives because of their own loyalty to the Order itself."

Anton frowned. "So how goes the war against the vampires with this cabal in charge?"

Li snorted. "Quietly."

"Li has it right. Since the rise of Ramin Kain, there have been no vampires of any significance killed by Order operations – especially within the northeast."

"There have been many young vampires killed, freshly turned, less than a year old," Li said.

Gang nodded. "Ramin Kain has established a reputation for finding new vampires. He claims he has a special intuitive capability, a power to 'sniff out young vampires.'"

Li touched Anton's hand and leaned toward him. "We think the new vampires are being deliberately created and then thrown to the Order for killing."

"Cui Bono," Anton said.

"Cui Bono indeed," Gang agreed. "The current regimes in both the Order and the Vampire Dominion benefit – there is a secret detente."

Li said, "Strategically, Crane gets a quiet flank while he directs his efforts at the Red Empire. Kain gets to look like a hero of the Order, and secures his own position against challengers."

"Hang on a moment, who are the Red Empire?"

Li shook her head once, and stated forcefully, "Zealots!"

"Another faction," Gang stated matter-of-factly. "The Red Empire broke away from the Order more than two millennia ago."

Li instructed Anton. "They're much larger than the Order and just as happy to kill Order members as vampires."

Gang said, "The key difference is the Red Empire has no problem killing the innocent in the pursuit of killing vampires."

Anton asked, "There is no unity amongst those who can fight the vampires?"

"None whatsoever," Gang answered.

"No wonder the vampires are so dominant," Anton said. Taking a deep breath, he let it out slowly. "So, while all this has been going on, what has my grandfather been doing?"

"Operating independently and fighting the good fight," Gang declared. "He focuses his efforts directly on Cornelius Crane. Crane has multiple labs and research centers around the world. We don't know what his aims are, but they're surely not good for humanity. Arthur seeks to find out what the vampire king is doing, and thwart his plans."

"What about now?"

"The last I heard; he is operating in Brazil."

"On the night my family was attacked by Armitage and Drake, she showed me photographs of my grandfather in Rio during the Carnival earlier this year."

Gang pursed his lips. "It's concerning that Armitage managed to have recent photographs of Arthur."

"She used them to prove my grandfather is still alive."

Gang stroked his chin, leaning back in his chair. "This throws fresh light on something that has been troubling me. As I said earlier, I have attempted to contact your grandfather and he has not replied. Clearly Armitage also knows he is in Brazil and at least one of her operatives got close enough to take photos. I now fear the vampires may have captured or killed him."

"Dead?"

"With Arthur Slayne, I wouldn't assume he was dead unless I had seen his cold corpse with my own eyes, but yes, we must consider the possibility."

Well, that would explain his absence – if he is dead. Anton mused to himself and then asked, "He was carrying a long slim black case in the Rio photos, was that a sword?"

Gang nodded. "The Black Dragon, his personal weapon. There is a story behind that sword which must wait for another day."

"What would happen if the Order were to catch up with my grandfather?"

"Probably a blood bath," Li said drily.

Gang glanced at his daughter, and then turned back to Anton and said, "The Order convicted him of a capital crime. There is no court of appeal. There is a standing kill order on him from Ramin Kain."

"Is the Order actively looking for him?"

"No force leader that I know of is trying to catch him. If they happen to stumble across him – who knows? He has a powerful reputation, he's not liked, or admired, but his skills are respected and, in some cases, feared."

"Feared?" Anton asked. The thought that people would be afraid of his grandfather seemed odd to him.

"He is extraordinarily capable in combat," Gang stated. "He was my master, and I would fear to fight him. He fought both Crane and Armitage at the same time, back in '78 in a secret vault beneath St Peter's Basilica in the Vatican – and he survived. I know no one else who could have done that."

"That's more than forty years ago, how old is my grandfather?"

"Over seventy."

"He's ripped for his age. He doesn't look seventy, more like a very fit forty to forty-five-year-old man. How does he do it?"

"A side effect of the Ramp, it slows the aging process, not like a vampire of course, but you stay fit and healthy for much longer than normal."

Li arched an eyebrow at Anton and said, "First you have to survive if you are going to get a chance to live that long."

"Speaking of survival, what about the Tiger Clan, you're expecting them tonight aren't you?" Anton asked.

"Yes. They're sure to attack and in numbers. We've wounded their honor. They will learn from this morning's brawl that we're tougher than they thought. However, that will not deter them. They're mean spirited, but not lacking in courage." Gang smiled wickedly. "I have made some inquiries, there is a fellow that owes me a favor, who is no friend of the Hu Shizu. We will have some help, of a sort, later tonight."

"Is there anything I need to do?"

Gang frowned, and ordered, "Pack your backpack. Be ready to travel on a moment's notice, and get some rest."

The tension within Gang that Anton had sensed earlier had returned.

"Tomorrow we must say goodbye to the Noodle House," Gang declared. "It probably will not survive tonight."

"Even with the helpers?"

"Even so," Gang declared. He smiled wanly and sighed. "All things must pass, even this home."

Li put her hand to her mouth, got up silently and walked away.

"This is the only home she has known," Gang said. "It is worse for her."

"Can I help?"

"Give her space. And tonight – be ready for anything."

"Yes, Gang."

Anton helped Gang clear the breakfast dishes and then returned to the garden where he laid down on a patch of sun-dappled grass, reflecting quietly on what Gang had told him. *Perhaps my grandfather is dead, or got a raw deal, but still – where was he that was so important that he couldn't protect his family?*

* * *

General Chloe Armitage sat across from James Haley in a secured room at the surveillance site opposite the Noodle House.

She listened to the recording of the conversation Gang and Li Wu and Anton Slayne had in the backyard over breakfast. She accelerated the playback on the machine to five times faster than normal. The conversation streamed through her headphones and she accelerated her mind to match the machine. In three minutes, she'd memorized everything in the recorded conversation. It was quite the treasure trove. Chloe asked James, "Have these recordings been backed up yet?"

"They're already on the Panopticon storage farm," he replied.

"Set the security level to FGEO – Personal Stamp – CA."

"Once I set security to 'For General's Eyes Only,' I won't be able to retrieve them again."

"Precisely."

James nodded. "Yes, Ma'am."

"Who else knows of this?"

There was a noticeable rise in James' heart rate directly after she asked the question, and he hesitated for a moment before responding, "Only myself, the rest were at breakfast, I didn't mention it."

Chloe smiled, "Excellent."

"Orders, Ma'am?"

That was a good question. What orders should she give him after his exposure to so much secret information? How much should she tell him? He wasn't supposed to know any of this. He was a Shadowstone operative. He was part of an organization built to protect a secret it was never meant to understand. There would always be 'situations' where one or more operatives would find out more than they should know. The praetorians typically culled them from Shadowstone – permanently. On rare occasions, on the back of great merit, the Vampire Dominion would induct them into the ranks of the vampires and disappear them to a far-flung region of the world until those who might recognize them had passed away from natural causes.

The answer was clear. Just enough to lead him to act as she required. Chloe stared at James for a long moment and ordered firmly, "Forget what you have heard today."

James nodded. "Yes, Ma'am. It's obviously nonsense – they believe in vampires."

"Indeed, obvious nonsense," Chloe agreed with a slight smile. "Be prepared to track the Wu family when they depart tomorrow – do not lose contact with them – that is all."

"Yes, Ma'am," James replied. He rose and left the room, closing the door behind him.

Gang Wu suspected that Ramin Kain was in league with the Vampire Dominion. Chloe considered Wu could well be right. However, there was only one vampire who could get away with such an arrangement – Cornelius Crane. Li Wu had made an error in thinking that such an arrangement was about allowing Crane to focus on the Red Empire. No, while that was a useful side effect, the main goal was to allow Crane to focus on the acquisition of the three Metaframe artifacts.

Her mind flashed through the most important question. Was Arthur Slayne, Brazil, and Crane's super soldier program linked? She vowed to find out the facts. Chloe paused, reviewing her immediate plans. She needed to draw the Mirovar team into the open with the Wu family and Anton as bait and take some heads. She needed to get Crane to focus resources back into the northeast and not send her back to Jerusalem. She would need a credible threat to make him do that – something she didn't yet have.

The details of Chloe's new plan had not yet jelled together. She felt a stab of annoyance at the promise she'd made back in Jerusalem. A promise she was running out of time to keep. She sighed once, stood up and walked into the operations room. James and Louise Wesson were observing monitors, the other two, Johnson and Higgins sat at their stations managing their equipment.

Chloe addressed the room, "Report."

"Yes, Ma'am," Wesson replied. "We have something unusual."

"Yes?" Chloe asked.

"Four vans have arrived," she said, "parking further down the street than they needed too. They're all registered with a local pet food company. There were twelve men in them, no women, they've all gone into the Noodle House. There are no other patrons yet, so they either have a single booking or something else is about to happen."

Chloe smiled briefly, making an instant intuitive assessment. Ms. Louise Wesson was smart and useful. She would keep an eye on her progress within Shadowstone. There were always opportunities for people with talent.

"Thank you, continue to observe and monitor the site. No matter what you see tonight, do not take any action without further orders from myself. Is that clear?"

"Yes, Ma'am," James and Louise both answered.

Johnson and Higgins also gave their assent.

Chloe left the operations room, and ascended a set of stairs to the roof. The sky was cloudless, the night cool, a full moon had cleared the horizon in the east. She stretched her arms up, arching her back, luxuriating in the experience of complete power and freedom that nightfall had brought.

The conditions were perfect for hunting. The roof of the building was flat, surrounded by a five-foot high parapet. Chloe leaped up on top of the parapet. Standing tall, her hands on her hips, she extended her senses to their maximum capabilities, and focused her attention on the building opposite. Sensing human heat signatures through the walls, she counted twelve and three. The new arrivals, Li and Gang Wu, and Anton Slayne. Anton covered the rear, the other two stood back from the kill zone before the main entrance. She listened carefully to the quiet murmur of conversations from the men in the Noodle House. *Ms. Wesson is correct. No one has ordered any food, these men are waiting, I can almost smell the anticipation from here. There will be a battle tonight.*

With a predator's patience, she settled in to wait and see what would happen.

* * *

Li held her katana sword within its scabbard at her left hip.

Her mother's ancestor, Kanenaga Yoshindo, had crafted the Green Dragon in Japan during the winter of 1675. A marble sized emerald gracing the end of its handle distinguished it from its four siblings.

The front door of the Noodle House swung open. The men of the Hu Shizu, the Tiger Clan, filed into the restaurant, immediately spreading out across the front wall. They stood, variously grinning or impassive, armed to the teeth with submachine guns, 9mm handguns, knives, short swords, hand axes, and baseball bats embossed with hard strips of gray metal. In their midst swaggered the large form of Mr. Wang. Apparently unarmed, he puffed on a thin cigar wedged between his thick lips.

"Out," Mr. Wang shouted to the men at the tables.

Gang's helpers rushed out the front door and into the street.

Li glanced at her father and thought, *that's convenient, after all, they're not here for the fight.*

Her father grinned, winking at her, then frowned and whispered, "MAC-10s, .45 or 9mm, very high rate of fire and a tendency to pull high."

There would be a lot of bullets coming their way. As the last of the helpers disappeared out the front door, it swung shut behind them. Li and Gang stood side by side at the back of the restaurant. They both let their scabbards fall to the floor, lifting their swords into attack positions above their shoulders – ready for action. The more than three hundred and forty-year-old blades gleamed in the soft light of the restaurant's lanterns, their shape and edges the very measure of perfection.

"You bring a knife to a gun fight?" Mr. Wang declared derisively.

Li promised fiercely, "When your souls enter the afterlife, you will be able to tell those you meet there that your passage was provided by the White and Green Dragons."

Mr. Wang pulled out his cigar and laughed, long and loud.

Li's eyes tightened and her lips pressed into a thin line. The Green Dragon resting in lethal stillness above her left shoulder.

The sound of glass breaking shattered the tense quiet. The gangsters had breached the back door. Anton's party was about to start. Mr. Wang abruptly stopped laughing and shouted, "Cut them down!"

Li and Gang ramped to their maximum ability.

Mr. Wang's men laughed or snarled. Their short, snub-nosed submachine guns erupted in blooms of gray smoke as streams of .45 rounds ripped through the restaurant.

Li and Gang had stood as close to each other as they could before they moved. They'd provided a single target to the Tiger Clan, and every man had aimed his gun at the same location.

Where they no longer were.

Li's mind raced, she could see the rapid puffs of smoke erupting from the barrels of the short submachine guns as each round went off. The spent brass casings were flying everywhere. The gangsters were close enough together that the gun smoke and casings were obscuring the view in front of them.

To her right, her father had already covered half the distance between the kitchen and the first of the gangsters at the far edge of the group. He was moving from table to table, his feet barely touching the surface as he flew through the room. The White Dragon held in both hands, high above his head. The gangsters reflexively started to track the moving targets in front of them, swinging their guns around.

The gangsters stared as Gang and Li moved a yard or so in front of their streams of fire. Panicked fingers pressed hard against triggers as they tried to bring their submachine guns to bear. The MAC-10 carried up to thirty rounds in a magazine. At best, it could fire a thousand rounds per minute. They would run out of ammunition in two seconds.

Li reached the wall next to a gangster, slashing the Green Dragon through his neck as she took three steps along the wall to curve in behind him and put herself in the middle of four other men.

The man's head rolled off his shoulders, his blood fountaining into the air. He slumped forward to the floor, his submachine gun continuing to fire aimlessly, clutched tightly in his dead hand.

Beyond the men surrounding her, she could see her father's sword was already red with blood as he pushed into the far side of the gangsters. At the back of the restaurant, lights flashed as gunfire erupted in the kitchen, and ricochets rang like bells off dangling pots.

The men beside her dragged their guns around as they pivoted toward her. For one of the men, it was impossible to move quickly enough as Li brought the Green Dragon down through a diagonal slash, cutting him from shoulder to hip. His suit splashed red in an instant, he started to fall away a look of shocked amazement frozen on his face.

Before he hit the ground, Li leaped vertically upward as the remaining three men opened fire. The remaining rounds in the guns opposite them cut two of the men to ribbons. The fourth man's gun ran dry, he reached for a 9mm handgun as Li landed and ran him through. He fell backward squealing as Li drew the Green Dragon clear of his gut.

The guns in the restaurant fell silent, their magazines running out of bullets. Through the gray smoke, Li veered to the right to avoid a thrown knife and assessed the situation with a glance. There had been fourteen gangsters to start with. Now reduced by five on her side, and another six on her father's side. Leaving three left, including Mr. Wang.

The knife thrower was nearest. She ran past him toward Mr. Wang, slashing the Green Dragon across his belly, disemboweling him. He had a fresh cast on his right arm, it was the gangster she'd nicknamed Sleazy. *Karma's a bitch.*

Li arrived in front of Mr. Wang. His face twisted with hate and rage, he pulled the pin on a fragmentation grenade and started to push it toward her. Li shouted a warning, "Father!"

She reversed her sword. Striking Mr. Wang hard across the face with her left fist. His knees buckled, the grenade falling at his feet. Li used her forward momentum to swing past the crime lord, landing next to her father. They both leaped behind a thick dining table, overturning it to make a shield.

Behind them, they could hear Mr. Wang groping near his knees for the grenade. He shouted, "Damn—"

The grenade detonated.

As the dust settled from the explosion, silence descended within the Noodle House.

Li checked her father, "Are you okay?"

Gang declared with a broad grin, "Never better – he definitely had that coming."

She looked to the kitchen. *Is Anton, okay?*

* * *

Mr. Wang screamed, "Out."

Anton readied himself as best he could. Gang had given him a katana sword. Anton had made great strides toward mastery of such a weapon but it seemed unwieldy and clumsy given a general lack of space within the kitchen. He put the big blade down, picking up a pair of thick bladed foot long carving knives from a nearby rack. They felt balanced and lethal in his hands. There was more conversation from the restaurant and he resisted the urge to get closer to Li and Gang. What if they needed his help? What if Li needed his help? But no, his job was here, to guard their backs.

Mr. Wang laugh loudly from the front of the restaurant.

The glass in the back door shattered, and someone shouted a harsh command from the front of the restaurant.

The back door burst apart. Six gangsters armed with submachine guns, knives, and baseball bats streamed into the kitchen, while gunfire erupted in the restaurant.

Anton ramped as the gangsters in front of him swung their MAC-10 submachine guns up and fired directly at him. He pivoted away from the guns. Rolling across the kitchen table top as bullets whipped past his head, slamming into the heavy fridge doors at the end of the kitchen. Dangling pots and pans above the table rang out as bullets plowed into them and wild ricochets flew everywhere.

Anton rolled off the table. The gangsters broke into two groups, streaming around the table. Two ran directly toward him, their guns blazing. He ducked, and rolled underneath the table. Crouching into a tight squat, he pushed up and sideways with his shoulder. The heavy metal table rose up, flipping over and smashing two of the gangsters into the floor; leaving Anton exposed to the remaining four gangsters, one of whom was the looming *Fats*.

The gangsters still standing, dragged their guns around to aim directly at him from point blank range. The nearest two held their weapons less than two feet from where he stood. He could see their fingers beginning to squeeze down hard on the triggers.

One dreadful thought raced through his mind. *I'm going to die.*

He spontaneously ramped to a level he'd never experienced before, time slowing to a crawl. Anton felt a singular sense of calm and clarity of purpose. He dropped his knives. Leaning toward the two gangsters, he flipped his hands up, catching their wrists and pushing their gun hands high as he surged between them. The bones in their wrists broke, unable to survive the sudden acceleration. Their submachine guns fired, the bullets streaming wildly into the ceiling as gray gun smoke billowed around his head. His forward momentum carried both men with him, placing the man on his right in between himself, and *Fats* and the last gangster near the back door. The man on his right shuddered as bullets intended for Anton filled his body.

Whirling in a circle, Anton dragged the man on his left into the line of fire. He collapsed, the other gangsters blowing his life away with their submachine guns. He used the dying man as a step ladder to leap high above them all before descending in front of the last two men.

The smaller one dropped his empty MAC-10, lunging with a long-bladed knife in his left hand. Anton trapped his wrist and kept moving forward. The man began to scream as his arm fractured. Anton laughed out loud and pivoted, his right foot lashing into *Fats*, catching him just below the ribcage. The big man folded around his boot, before flying through the back door and into the alleyway.

Anton half turned as he came to a halt. The last gangster's arm lay twisted at an unnatural angle. Anton struck the shrieking man at the base of his skull with an open hand, crushing his spine and sending him into oblivion.

A rush of euphoria exploded through him. *I survived, but what sort of wild Ramp was that?* He looked around, searching for threats. The other two gangsters, hit and half crushed by the table, were out cold and possibly dead. Anton turned, stepped into the back doorway and searched for *Fats*.

He lay deathly still a dozen feet away in the middle of the alley. Blood streamed from his mouth and nose, forming a pool around his head.

A blast cracked like a whip inside the Noodle House. "Li!? Gang!?" Anton shouted. He rushed into the main restaurant, the euphoria he'd felt a moment ago, blown away like a leaf on the wind.

They met in the middle of the restaurant. Li silently looked him up and down. Gang grinned at him. Anton, grabbed them by the shoulders and asked urgently, "Are you both okay?"

Li replied, "Sure, and you?"

Anton nodded, "I'm good."

Gang asked, "Is the kitchen clear?"

"I think so but there are two who could still be alive."

"Let's check," Gang directed.

They all moved back to the kitchen and Gang and Li examined the men that Anton had slammed with the table. Gang nodded and stood up. Li rose up next to the other body and declared, "This one is dead."

"Looks like you got all the ones who came through here, well done," Gang said.

"What now?" Anton asked.

"Now our helpers will start their real work."

"To clear the bodies?"

"Yes. Mr. Chan owns several businesses including a large and prosperous pet food company. He has many brothers, cousins, and nephews. Everyone who was here earlier pretending to be a patron is a close family member and entirely trustworthy. They will clear the bodies and clean up the building."

Li smirked. "You would be surprised what ends up in dog food cans."

Strings of firecrackers began exploding in the street. Anton started at the noise and Gang's smartphone began to ring. Gang answered it, and had a short conversation in rapid Chinese. Gang hung up, and said, "Mr. Chan is celebrating the removal of Mr. Wang. His crew will be here in moments. The firecrackers will mask what just happened. Casual onlookers, startled by the gunfire, will run into the street, or look around. They will only see Mr. Chan's firecrackers and it will convince them there were only fireworks." He nodded decisively. "Let's return to our home and calm down."

Anton noticed that his hands were shaking, and agreed, "Yes, let's do that."

Gang slapped Anton on the shoulder as they walked out of the Noodle House and into the Wu family home. "You did well Anton. You did the right thing. All those men wanted to kill us, and you helped save our lives."

Li said, "You watched our back. Thank you."

"Thanks," Anton replied as he walked with them. With every sense heightened and his soul thrilling with victory, he silently wondered, *Was I supposed to enjoy that as much as I did?*

* * *

Chloe had watched with interest as another set of vans arrived near the Noodle House.

Four had parked out the front, and another two had gone to the rear of the restaurant. Twenty men had left the vans. They'd been eager and energized. Their faces filled with intent. Their movements sure and purposeful.

The battle had unfolded before Chloe's supernatural senses. Gang and Li Wu, and Anton Slayne had been easy to identify from the telltale signature heat blooms of the Ramp, and their effectiveness versus the gangsters. Chloe noted to herself, *There is a qualitative difference in Anton's Ramp, he is just like his grandfather, he has the same talent. However, he has no mastery yet. They will now run from here, and draw out Francis Mirovar and his team.*

Chloe opened up her smartphone and ran an app she'd received from Dalien Morte. A cloud-based virtual phone that provided quantum encrypted untraceable secured call and text messaging services. Shadowstone was not alone in its ability to preserve secrets. She sent a text message to a number provided by Morte, it read, 'Request Contact.'

Ten seconds later a text message arrived on Chloe's display. It read, 'They have killed themselves, and are now ghosts.'

Chloe responded with another text. 'The dagger is red with their blood.'

Another text message came back. 'Contact me again in three minutes.'

Chloe waited three minutes and dialed the other phone number. A voice, depersonalized and masked by the communications software answered after the first ring and said, "Yes?"

"Tell your master there is a Shadowstone facility in Jerusalem at these coordinates," Chloe directed, and sent the GPS coordinates as a text message. "The Vampire Dominion have sent two praetorians and six enhanced Shadowstone operatives to Jerusalem. They're a direct threat to your master and they need elimination."

"I will pass this message on. Is there anything else?"

"Only this – who is Francis Mirovar?"

"My Order of Thoth force leader."

The line went dead.

Interesting, Chloe noted, *the Raven is with Francis Mirovar's team.* She then used Shadowstone technology to send a text to Marcus Drake. 'Some friendly advice, on missions, always be ready to fight, and find your own place to sleep.'

Chloe smiled broadly; her long-range plan against Crane was progressing well as Anton continued to develop his capabilities. She walked along the parapet to the side of the building. Her limousine lay parked in a back alley with her driver waiting inside. She leaped over the edge, falling the three floors to the empty alleyway below, landing easily on her feet, she made her way to the car.

Getting into the back of the vehicle, she commanded, "Back to the airport. I need to be in New York City as soon as possible."

"Yes, Ma'am," the driver replied.

Chloe relaxed in the back seat of the car as it pulled smoothly away, reflecting on what she had learned this night. *Soon the Order of Thoth and the Red Empire will distract Crane with rising threats on both sides and allow me to break my promise to him to deliver Francis Mirovar and his team. Anton, what a find he is, if he can match his grandfather, he will be the perfect weapon for my final strategy.*

Life was a never-ending thrilling adventure.

I need to keep working on Anton's motivations. He trembles on the edge of bloodlust – I need to push him over that edge and make him embrace the wild power within.

* * *

James Haley stared at his screen, replaying the video for the third time.

The result was still the same. A set of specialized cameras, telescopic microphones and motion trackers on the roof of the building provided a ghostly, but detailed video stream of the interior of the restaurant. The video showed a hail of submachine gun fire throughout the main room of the restaurant. Gang and Li Wu simply moved from the back of the room to the front of the room, and a handful of seconds later more than a dozen heavily armed thugs were on the floor.

In the back of the restaurant, Anton Slayne had taken on another six gangsters armed to the teeth with the same result; including one big brute of a man thrown through the back door into the rear alleyway as if fired from a circus cannon.

James replayed the video again in slow motion on the main screen. The gangsters moved as if standing in treacle. Gang and Li Wu moved much faster. Every step launching themselves forward, ahead of a storm of bullets that ripped apart the furniture and walls behind them.

Johnson exclaimed incredulously, "That's impossible!"

Higgins demanded with avid fascination, "Whatever they're on, I want some of that."

"Can it," James commanded harshly. "What we just saw doesn't leave this room."

"Huh?" Higgins grunted.

"Scrub the local server disks – do it now before this is swept onto the Panopticon server farm."

"Yes, Sir," Johnson replied.

"On it," Higgins responded.

"I want the disks reformatted, and run scramblers on them – this data must never be recovered."

His team worked at fever pitch to comply. The Panopticon would sweep a copy of all new data on the local server disk drives every ten minutes. To ensure the data disappeared it was necessary the reformat processes had begun across all the local disks to avoid the next sweep picking up the new data.

As the two men worked, Wesson caught his eye. Her face paled, she smiled wanly as if she'd just received a death sentence.

James looked back at his men. *Is this something we were never meant to see? Who can dodge bullets and walk away from a gun fight, and no one knows about it? And how did Gang Wu find out so much about Shadowstone? He knows who we are. What the hell is really going on here? Who is Anton Smith, or should I say Anton Slayne?*

* * *

Louise Wesson watched the replays of the fight in the Noodle House with a growing sense of horror.

She'd counted six men through the back door, and fourteen through the front door. All armed with submachine guns and an assortment of edged or blunt weapons. The front door gangsters had emptied their clips, around four hundred rounds of ammunition. The Wu family should have died, instead, they were still standing, and it was the gangsters who were lying in pools of blood.

From the first bullet to the grenade going off took less than nine seconds. She vowed to tread carefully; it is always possible to know too much. In her previous career, she'd already pulled the trigger on more than a dozen CIA operatives who had understood more than they should have. She assessed the risk. The next twenty-four hours would be critical to her survival.

James Haley ordered the destruction of the recordings of the fight in the Noodle House. It would become a data black hole, significant by its absence. There may be questions, but no one else would be able to assert what had been on those disk drives. She caught his eye, he looked stressed, but still confident and in control. He would most likely be the trigger man, the one to purge the team and clean up the mess.

She studied James, an ironic smile gracing her lips. *Will you be my killer? I guess I will find out soon enough.*

* * *

Anton sat at the dining room table with Gang and Li.

Gang opened a bottle of sake and arranged three glasses in front of them. He poured the shots and lifted his glass, Li and Anton followed his lead.

"Best done quickly," Gang urged, downing the shot and grinning at Anton.

Li followed suit. Anton drank his shot, the liquor was exquisite, a rare and aged reserve.

Gang poured a second round, and again they emptied the glasses. This time, Gang stoppered the bottle and put it aside. For a long moment, they sat there simply looking at each other.

Anton's hands had stopped shaking. The aftershocks of combat smoothed away by the physiological changes of the Ramp and the soothing effect of the sake. "What happens now?" Anton asked, his voice was quiet and reflective. "What will happen to the Noodle House?"

"Mr. Chan will look after it for me, we can trust him. Tonight, we rest and tomorrow we move to an Order safe house. Francis Mirovar will pick us up and escort us to a safe house. He is a force leader of long standing and very senior within the Order. I managed to contact him after breakfast. He has promised that he will come and I trust his word."

"They're coming here?"

"No. We'll meet them near the Boston docks. I have an address, that's all I know for now."

"Do you know where the safe house is?"

"No."

Anton tilted his head quizzically and said sardonically, "We're a bit in the dark, aren't we?"

Gang nodded, sighed and said, "It's because I have been inactive for years. Plus, neither Li nor you are officially in the Order."

"Hang on, what about those promises that I made weeks ago, just before you switched on my Ramp capability? I thought that was enough to be in the Order."

"Well, they're definitely the first steps and very much a real part of being in the Order. However, we have to wait for an Order Conclave to confirm your membership."

"A meeting of the Order; when do they happen?" Anton asked.

"In due course there will be one, and I'm sure that both Li and yourself will be confirmed as full members of the Order."

"What happens if we're not confirmed?"

Gang hesitated.

Li said, "The Order keeps its own secrets."

So, they will kill us, that's comforting to know, Anton thought sarcastically. He stared hard at Gang and inquired, "How do we make sure we're accepted and confirmed?"

Gang said, "You just need at least one force leader to accept you. Operationally the force leaders have tremendous authority. Someone becomes a force leader by common assent based on their capability to fight vampires, keep their team alive and avoid killing the innocent. Acceptance by a force leader is a sure path to confirmation."

"Speaking of Order membership, how is it you can be inactive? I thought that being in the Order was an either/or proposition."

Gang stroked his chin. "Well, it's a funny sort of situation."

Anton arched an eyebrow, and Li tilted her head and declared sardonically, "Is it now?"

Gang blinked at their reactions and laughed. It immediately became infectious and they all laughed together.

Anton felt all his tensions from the conflict evaporate away. He marveled at how Gang had a way that made him feel welcomed. *Yes, but no, it's more than that, I feel that I really belong here – with them – like family.* Anton found himself wiping away tears from his eyes, as the laughter around the table naturally subsided.

Gang mock sniffed. "Well, as usual, I get no respect."

Li got up out of her chair and hugged her father, and declared softly, "I respect you more than anyone else."

Gang's face worked with emotion as Li sat back down. He took a deep breath and instructed, "To put it simply, only a force leader can accept you into the order, and into his team, and only a force leader can throw you out. Anton, can you see where this is going?"

"Arthur Slayne was your force leader."

"He is my force leader until he is dead – conviction or no conviction. I don't have to answer to anyone else unless someone can prove Arthur is dead. The sanctity of the force team within the Order trumps all other rules."

"There are a lot of rules I don't know about."

"You know the most important ones. You have only been with us for a little over a month. You can't learn everything about a five-thousand-year-old organization in that time."

"If my grandfather is still your force leader, then you must have had contact with him. Perhaps a lot of contact with him over the years."

Gang nodded once. "Yes, that is true."

Anton sat back in his chair, shaking his head slowly and said, "I've been completely in the dark for so long." He felt a sudden wave of sadness. Did his parents not trust him with the truth? How would he ever be able to answer that question? He had to know more, and asked, "When my grandfather was convicted, what happened, did you fight?"

"I wanted to, but Arthur insisted I remain out of any conflict. I believe he anticipated this day would come. The rest of the team scattered, and like your grandfather, they're lone wolves fighting against the vampires, I have no idea how many still survive."

Anton paused, digesting what Gang had told him. "So, we will work with Francis Mirovar?"

"Yes. He has promised to shelter us until the next conclave. Have you packed everything that you need? We will leave tomorrow morning after breakfast."

"I think so," Anton replied.

Gang pushed his chair back and stood up. He caught Anton's gaze and said, "Wait here, there is something else you will need." He disappeared into his room for a minute, returning with a long case. He placed it on the table before Anton and opened it. Resting inside on a bed of black velvet was a sword identical to Li's and Gang's, except that it had a deep blue sapphire in the handle. He looked into Anton's eyes and declared, "This is the Blue Dragon. This is what you will need to kill vampires with."

Anton felt his heart jump as he realized the generosity of Gang's gift.

"This is my brother Qiang's sword, it is right that you should have it," Li declared, her eyes glistening with tears.

Gang said, "It is an heirloom of our family, inherited from my wife Tatsu Yoshindo's family line, from the island of Hokkaido in Japan."

Anton felt overwhelmed. "It's beautiful – are you sure you want to give it to me?"

Gang declared emphatically, "Yes. You have earned it tonight by fighting with courage."

Li nodded.

Anton put his hand over his heart and said, "Thank you, I don't know how to repay you."

Gang smiled. "With victory over our foes."

Anton nodded. He picked up the sword and drew it from its scabbard. The blade was majestic, flawless and beautifully balanced. He flourished it; the katana felt like a natural extension of his arm.

"Remarkable," Gang said. "You look just like your grandfather when I first met him."

Anton lowered the sword. "I do?"

"He has the Black Dragon."

Anton returned the sword to its scabbard, placed it back in the case, and asked, "How many of these swords are there?"

"Li's maternal ancestor, Kanenaga Yoshindo, made five swords during the winter of 1675. He forged them from iron drawn from a fallen meteor.

The original stone from which the metal came glowed with an uncanny light. The blades are stronger and sharper than any other swords. There are the three here, the Green, White and Blue Dragons identified by an emerald, diamond, and a blue sapphire respectively. Arthur Slayne carries the Black Dragon, which has a lustrous black pearl in the handle."

Gang paused, stroking his chin. "And then there is the fifth sword, the Red Dragon, marked with a dark ruby the color of blood."

"Who has it?"

"The vampire Armitage."

"Why on earth does she have it?"

"The Red Dragon was given to the Emperor of Japan in 1676, apparently the Imperial family gifted it to a traveler in 1897."

Anton shook his head in disgust. *How does she do that? She has everything she needs.* He frowned, took a deep breath and suggested, "You expect I will need this sword to fight her."

"It's inevitable. She has some dark purpose of her own that involves you. Why else would she leave you alive? We need to thwart her purpose, and you need a weapon that is the equal of what she carries to stand a chance against her."

"Well, unless her purpose is to see a lot of dead vampires, I don't see how my being a member of the Order of Thoth is going to work out well for her."

Gang shook his head and advised with a voice filled with cautious tones, "She is subtle, very subtle. In all things remotely associated with her, you must be fully aware of what the consequences are." The table fell silent. "One more for the road," Gang said, pouring each of them a final shot of sake.

They downed their drinks and Gang ordered, "Now everyone to bed, breakfast will be at 7:30 in the garden. It will be our last breakfast here, so don't be late."

Anton and Li both gave their assent and went to their rooms. As they walked down the hallway together, Li suddenly turned and hugged Anton fiercely. She stood on tiptoes, whispering into his ear, "Thank you, Anton, for looking after us tonight."

She kissed him quickly on the cheek, then broke away and went into her room closing the door behind her.

"Uh, sure, no problem—" Anton said half-dazed, and then realized sheepishly that he was speaking to an empty hall. He went to the bathroom, and then to bed. He found himself staring at the ceiling, his mind replaying Li's embrace, and his cheek tingling with the sensation of her kiss.

And with that in mind, Anton drifted quietly into sleep.

* * *

Chloe Armitage met privately with Cornelius Crane in his chambers on the 104th floor of the Vampire Dominion citadel.

She said confidently, "The Boston cell will run later today. Their current position is no longer tenable."

Crane arched a quizzical eyebrow and inquired, "You believe they will seek Mirovar, and draw him and his followers out into the open?"

"Yes, Cornelius."

He smiled. "It is good to see you are still on track with the promise you made in Jerusalem."

"Yes, I will have this wrapped up within the week."

"Francis Mirovar and his team are no easy marks, what is your plan?"

"We will track Gang and Li Wu to ground, and create a perimeter with Shadowstone forces. We will keep our vampire forces nearby, and then attack once Mirovar arrives."

"You will be fighting on a ground of their choosing," Crane said with a frown. "That suggests a tactical disadvantage for our forces, have you accounted for that?"

"The ground must be chosen by the Order," Chloe said. "Mirovar will not step into an obvious trap, we have to give them the ground to create confidence and foster the belief they have the initiative."

"... 'And therefore, those skilled in war bring the enemy to the field of battle and are not brought there by him.'" Crane declared.

"Sun Tzu, from the Art of War. You see my strategy here?" Chloe asked rhetorically.

Crane frowned. "Of course, but there will be losses. How many of my praetorians do you plan to sacrifice on this mission?"

Time to ask for what he will not give. Chloe shook her head and said, "I cannot guarantee that any engagement with the Order will be without casualties. To ensure success, I will need twelve praetorians, four to engage the Wu family and eight with me to engage Francis Mirovar and his team."

Crane stared at her for a long moment, and then stated decisively, "You will have six of my best. I can spare no more. We both know how you excel at combat. I expect to see blood on your blade when you return to my citadel."

Chloe responded, "Yes, Sir."

"Furthermore," Crane continued. "I'm concerned with the use of Shadowstone forces in an Order of Thoth engagement. Their primary purposes are surveillance and maintenance of operational security. Their involvement in this mission risks their unnecessary deaths and exposure of the secrets of the Vampire Dominion."

Why are these men so important to you? Chloe asked herself. Crane could and had seen millions die without blinking.

Crane frowned again and directed, "If necessary, to maintain secrecy – I will not hesitate to cleanse them all. But I warn you, do not put me in the position of having to make that choice."

"Yes, Sir."

Crane leaned toward her. "You must keep our Shadowstone operatives out of futile engagements with the Order of Thoth. Such battles are currently beyond their capabilities—"

Aha, currently beyond, but not in the future? UK Shadowstone enhanced operatives deployed to Jerusalem. Arthur Slayne conducts an operation against Crane in Brazil. Crane's network of distributed labs and research centers are working on secret projects with a single overarching goal. Chloe's mind raced as she integrated all the evidence she had before her. *He has a plan for Shadowstone super soldiers able to directly combat the Order of Thoth and the Red Empire during the day. How far away is he from completing this plan and how does he propose to control such men?*

"—I expect you to manage this engagement for victory with minimal losses."

"Yes, Sir," Chloe replied, not missing a beat while her mind spun through the implications of Crane's secret super-soldier program.

"Now there is fresh food on the 105th. I suggest that you get a bite to eat and rest up in one of our studios here. You can leave with the praetorians later this evening."

Chloe nodded. "Will do, Sir."

Crane clapped her on the shoulder and grinned wolfishly. "Good hunting General."

"Yes, Sir." Chloe stepped back, gave a small bow, turned and left his chambers. She smiled slyly as she walked down the corridor to the vault-like doors that were the only means to exit the floor. *Only six praetorians that leaves me under-resourced for this mission. A sharp defeat so close to home and a sudden attack by the Red Empire will drag Crane's attention away from the Metaframe artifacts, and give me a free hand to address matters in the northeast. As for his super-soldiers, I will bide my time and wait to see where the most fruitful path lies.*

Chloe's new plan began to come together as she left Crane's quarters.

* * *

Gang strolled through the garden at the back of his home.

He inspected his roses along the back fence for the last time. They had not received much attention over the last five weeks due to the heavy training schedule with Anton and Li. He leaned over one of his favorite plants. A Rugosa rose with a set of strongly perfumed pink flowers, he gently sniffed one of the blooms. *Beautiful, just beautiful. Who will look after you when I am gone?* Pulling back from the rose, he noticed a small object wedged against a brick on top of his back fence. It was a short cylinder that merged with the silhouette of the brick and trailed a short lead the color of aged mortar behind it. On the front of the cylinder, he could clearly see a lens.

Shadowstone! Gang's heart froze, but he kept moving. He sniffed a second and a third flower. He murmured approving comments as he spent another three minutes thinking furiously while strolling around the back yard.

He berated himself bitterly. *I have been lax! I have allowed the issues around Anton's arrival and the Hu Shizu to distract me. God knows how much Shadowstone have learned.*

Gang went into the house, catching up with Anton and Li in the kitchen. He tapped them both on the shoulder, before writing a quick note on a piece of paper. It read, 'Stay silent, we are compromised.'

Anton and Li, stared at him, shock flashing across their faces.

Gang wrote another note which read, 'Get your gear, we leave now.'

Anton and Li, immediately left for their rooms.

Gang went out to the garage and opened a safe there. Inside was a thick wad of cash and a short-barreled Glock 9mm in an ankle holster with a spare magazine. Next to the gun were a pair of incendiary grenades modified with ten-minute timers. He pocketed the cash and strapped the Glock to his ankle. He carefully synchronized the timers on the two incendiary grenades with his wrist watch. He armed and placed the first of the grenades in the trunk of the car, right next to the fuel tank. Picking up a metal jerry can of fuel, he left the garage. He carried the can into the kitchen where Anton and Li were waiting for him.

Gang put the can of fuel on top of the kitchen table. He set the timer of the second incendiary grenade to a half second behind the first grenade, armed it and strapped it to the jerry can with duct tape.

He checked his watch. *Six minutes and forty-five seconds before all this blows.* Gang mouthed, *wait*.

Anton and Li both shot worried looks at the timer on the grenade before nodding.

Gang went to his room, and fetched the backpack he'd prepared earlier that morning. Picking up the White Dragon in its traveling case, he went back to the kitchen. He reached into the backpack, pulling out an old Nokia cell phone and switched it on. As it powered up, he wrote two notes for Anton and Li. On the notes was the same message, 'Split up, be indirect and meet at this address in two hours.' He wrote the address beneath the instruction.

He scanned the timer on the grenade, it was now reading under three minutes. He picked up the Nokia and dialed 911. He got an operator and described a fire and gas explosion at his home address. He abruptly hung up, put the old cell phone next to the jerry can, and turned the gas on full on all the cooktop hobs in the kitchen.

Gang indicated with a sharp movement of his thumb that it was time to leave and they all went to the front door. He got there first, tapping his watch, he held them back. After another minute, he opened the front door. They could all hear the wailing of sirens in the distance. He held up his hand again, before nudging Li to the threshold. Anton stepped in behind her.

"Get ready," Gang whispered. "Split up and walk down the street, when you hear the first explosion, Ramp and run – you will have half a second – make the most of it to get some extra distance."

Li and Anton wore hoods, peaked caps and sunglasses. They had backpacks slung over their shoulders and carried their swords in long narrow travel cases.

Gang held up his hand, counting down the last five seconds with his fingers. His fist clenched for zero. Li exited the front door, followed by Anton. All three of them reached the street and went in different directions.

Anytime now.

The car went off first with a loud thump which blew the garage to smithereens.

Gang ramped, moving forty yards down the street. Half a second after the car, the kitchen exploded, smoke and debris from the house erupting into the air. The noise was deafening as bricks, burning wood and plaster flew into the street.

Within seconds, a fire engine rounded the street corner in front of him. He could see the grim faces of the firemen, the leaping fire and billowing smoke reflected in the truck's windshield as it passed him by. Moments later, the fire engine screeched to a stop out front of the remains of his home.

Gang slung his backpack over his left shoulder. Pulling his hat and hood tighter over his head, he held the White Dragon carry case in his right hand, and walked off down the street. He was determined not to look back.

His feet came to a halt as if they had a mind of their own. He paused, shook his head and turned around. Li and Anton had disappeared, and the fire was spreading to the Noodle House. He watched for a long moment as smoke rose high into the summer sky.

It's over now. It's really gone. Tatsu, Qiang, our home is gone.

Gang turned with a heavy heart, hurrying away to make the rendezvous with Anton and Li.

Chapter Five

Section 14.4.1 False Flag Media Posts

Summary: Normalcy bias and the poisoning the well logical fallacy.

[1] This tactic is based on exploiting the cognitive normalcy bias, and the poisoning the well logical fallacy. It relies on the target population's susceptibility for belief in the content of mainstream and authoritative belief systems, and resistance to change once a belief has been established.

[2] Secured facts that must be kept secret are published into the mass media in forms that will produce mainstream derision and rejection of their central tenets.

[3] Published secured facts should be altered in small details to enable the disassociation of belief from similar ideas and memes to ensure that whole tranches of secured discourse become mainstream taboos.

[4] There will always be a small subset of the target population who will believe the posts. The small population of believers adds to the strength of the tactic as they are able to be labeled as "fringe" and "other" in mainstream discourse. Thus, reinforcing the rejection of the central tenets of the secured facts by the target population.

[5] In this way, the target population is inoculated from ever believing that the secured fact is true, and will continue to act as if the secured fact is false.

Detail: Definitions and worked examples

The details of this tactic with worked examples is described below.

[REDACTED]

– Excerpt of Section 14, Strategic Influence and Information Disruption, Shadowstone Covert PSYOPS Manual

* * *

Boston, June 11th, 08:17

James Haley twitched, spilling his coffee as the sharp bang of a nearby explosion reached his ears.

Across the street, the Wu family garage was the center of a bright glare, reflexively James began to twist away. The Wu residence exploded in a ball of flame, with smoke and debris rising high in the air. He dived away, turning like a cat, and was face down on the floor when the windows facing the street shattered. A glittering mist of razor-sharp fragments filled the space where he'd been standing.

Higgins was neither quick nor lucky, bearing the brunt of the flying glass as he looked up from his computer console as the windows in front of him blew into the room. Rolling out of his chair, he lay screaming on the floor, blood flowing from numerous cuts across the top half of his body.

"What the hell!" James shouted, pushing himself upright and surveying the street. The fire was already leaping across to the Noodle House, and a big red fire engine was pulling to a halt in front of the Wu residence.

James pointed at the fire engine and declared in a voice dripping with derision, "You've gotta be kidding me! How long ago were they called? This is no accident!"

Higgins was still screaming when Wesson and Johnson ran back into the room. Rushing toward Higgins, Wesson shouted, "Don't pull it out!"

The warning came too late as Higgins dragged an inch-wide shard of glass from the side of his neck. The glass had missed his trachea but had caught his carotid artery. The wound began to spray blood. His eyes went wide with terror as he clutched his throat and blood sluiced around his fingers.

Johnson grabbed a hand towel from a bench, pushing it hard against the wound as Higgins lay back down on the floor.

Chaos filled the array of consoles in front of James. Half were registering static, the rest were showing fire, smoke and the arrival of a second fire engine. The one useful display was the main screen showing the Panopticon reference maps, it displayed a cluster of green contacts at the front gate of the Wu residence and along the street in both directions.

The targets had split up. *So, where and when are they going to meet again?* James watched the contacts change from green to yellow flags as they became stale. The most recent Panopticon contact on any of his targets was now older than a minute. He growled and snapped, "Damn this smoke and fire! We've just lost contact. Damn it, our targets have escaped."

"Looks like Higgins is gone," Wesson said flatly.

James looked down at the floor. Higgins lay still. Johnson grimaced as he pressed a blood saturated towel on Higgins' throat, a red pool spreading in a circle around Higgin's head and shoulders.

Johnson sighed once and stood up; his lips pressed tightly together. He turned, holding his bloodied hands away from his clothes and retreated to the bathroom.

"Wesson, get him cleaned up and ready for action," James ordered.

"Yes, Sir."

James flipped open his laptop. It was still operational; it was the machine providing the Panopticon feed on the surviving main screen. He initiated a fresh top priority search focused on the Boston region. The Panopticon would harvest feeds from every available camera, searching for Li and Gang Wu, and Anton Smith.

Slayne was so well hidden, even the Panopticon didn't know his real name. *How did they do that?* The Order of Thoth's ability to compromise the Panopticon was an unsolved mystery. One he didn't have time to solve.

A minute later, Wesson and Johnson returned from the bathroom. He now wore a fresh shirt and his hands were clean.

"What now boss?" Johnson growled.

"Okay, the three of us will have to re-establish contact with the targets ASAP," James directed. "Johnson, clear this equipment back to the van and clean all our tech from this site, including the feeds on the back fence of the Wu residence. Wesson, call in your team. Get the whole of Green-4 to Boston now."

"Yes, Sir," Johnson replied.

"Sir, what equipment mix?" Wesson asked.

"Combat surveillance operations. Bring in the nightfalcons."

"Yes, Sir, we can base the helicopters out of Logan Airport."

"Do it."

Wesson nodded, dialing her Shadowstone smartphone.

James stared at the Panopticon screen which was now a sea of red, orange and yellow, his hands reflexively clenching into fists. *They're Order of Thoth, and they're not going to get away from me.* He took a deep breath, relaxed his hands, and went to the nearby secured room. He opened his smartphone and voice dialed General Armitage.

The phone rang eight times before she picked up the call. Her voice was flat. "Yes?"

"There has been a development."

"You've lost them haven't you," Chloe said sardonically.

How did she know that? " ... Yes, Ma'am."

"You will find them again before sunset tonight," Chloe commanded with absolute certainty.

A shiver went up James' spine, it was clear that failure was not an option, and he replied, "Yes, Ma'am."

"I will be there tonight with a special forces team, now remember – do not engage the Order of Thoth. The mission is to identify them, track them, and if they go to ground, put a cordon around the site and stop them escaping again. Is that clear?"

"Crystal clear, Ma'am."

"Excellent."

The line went dead.

James Haley was not an easily frightened man, but he felt a disturbing unease as he put his phone away. *I must find these Order of Thoth terrorists or else.*

The 'or else' remained chillingly undefined.

* * *

Li Wu dodged adroitly through the traffic and crossed Bedford Street in the Boston suburb of Charlestown.

Ducking beneath a row of trees she came up against a rusty and weathered security fence. Beyond lay an apparently unused industrial site fronting onto the Mystic River. She tracked the fence for twenty yards before finding a split in the wire where it had come away from a post. Peeling the wire back another foot, she slipped through to the other side. A minute later, she'd crossed the deserted parking lot and was up against the corner of the front wall of a large warehouse.

The building was easily two hundred yards long and half that wide. Its front had two enormous steel doors spanning openings twenty yards across and half that high; both doors stood closed. Above the doors were large gantries constructed from thick steel frames with rails and access walkways, they looked worn but solid. The back third of the warehouse sat on a finger of land jutting out into the river.

Where she stood, at the front right corner of the building, Li could see a solid stone dock running forty yards past the far end of the warehouse. The whole above-ground structure comprised gray masonry stone, which up close gave the building an ambiance of solid, industrial permanence. A cold war era designed building, built to survive heavy bombardment, and possibly nuclear attack.

Li pressed her back up against the wall, cutting her silhouette to a minimum. A steel door opened a dozen feet away along the side of the warehouse. Her father poked his head out and called to her, "Li, I'm in here."

Li darted over, joining Gang in the cool dimness of the warehouse. She asked urgently, "Has Anton arrived?" She took off her sunglasses and looked around, there were numerous shipping containers on the floor and a pair of huge rolling cranes just under the ceiling, but no sign of Anton.

Gang shook his head. "No. However, it's still early, he should be here soon."

She hoped so.

"While we wait for him, we have much work to do," Gang directed with a grin. "This place is a treasure trove."

"Yes?"

"I will show you. Come this way."

Li followed her father as he walked between organized rows and lines of shipping containers stacked in pairs to make walls nearly twenty feet high.

It's like a maze in here, I wonder what Father has found.

* * *

Sergeant Detective of the Boston Police Department Homicide Unit, Luke Walker, drove his Ford SUV along Bedford Street Charlestown. He saw a young man on the sidewalk apparently waiting for a break in the traffic so he could cross the street.

Luke was about sixty yards away from him and closing quickly. He slowed his car down from thirty miles per hour to give himself another couple of seconds before he passed him by. There was something about him that piqued his curiosity. The forward tilt of the cap, the broad sunglasses, the gray long sleeve hooded top, the backpack and a long, slim case carried as if it held something precious.

Whoever he was, he was hiding something. Luke felt a sudden sense of familiarity and his 'Hunch Meter' red-lined. He was certain he should know who the young man was but he was equally sure he'd never met him before.

Recognition flooded through him and his SUV screeched to a halt directly opposite the young man. They stared at each other for a second, then the young man turned away, walking briskly along the street toward the nearest intersection.

An evidence photograph he'd resented having to hand over to the FBI and the memory of a brutal unsolved murder flashed through his mind.

Anton Smith!

Slapping a portable police light onto his dash, he switched it on. Just as someone tooted him from behind. Luke was already rolling forward to keep pace with Smith, he glanced in the mirror and saw the driver of a Toyota Corolla already backing off now that his police lights were flashing. He looked forward again, glimpsing Smith as he went around a corner and disappeared from sight.

He swore loudly, "Damn!" and floored the accelerator. His SUV lurched forward. He made a hard-left turn into the side street the fugitive had fled down. Parked cars lined the one-way street and numerous narrow alleyways branched off it. It was more than a hundred yards to the end of the street. There was no sign of Smith anywhere. He'd vanished into thin air.

Luke rolled slowly down the street, his head swiveling left and right, looking for Smith. Swearing under his breath he pulled his car over as he came to the end of the street.

"Damn it all to hell, where is that boy?" Luke growled as he shut off the police light and dialed the duty desk to call the sighting in. *What the hell, it's been more than five weeks, what is he doing still walking the streets? What on Earth are the FBI doing with this case? After all, they took every last shred of evidence from my crime scene. What are they doing with it – sitting on it?*

Luke fumed in silence as he waited for the duty desk officer to answer his call.

* * *

James Haley's laptop chimed as the Panopticon alerted him to a hit on one of his targets.

The transcript of a phone conversation of a Sergeant Detective Luke Walker of the BPD flashed onto his screen. James read the conversation in seconds, absorbing all the salient details. Walker had called in a sighting of a fugitive, named Anton Smith, wanted by the FBI in connection with a terrorism investigation.

James shook his head. Well, not actually the FBI, he would have to make some calls and squash this thing all over again. Noting the location of the sighting, James used the Panopticon mapping service to display it. The Panopticon provided real-time map data in extraordinary detail. He zoomed in on the reported location, the corner of Bedford and Mallston streets in the Boston suburb of Charlestown. The transcript stated the detective witnessed Anton entering Mallston Street before disappearing.

James whispered to himself, "If he was running away from the police, then where was he going before he was spotted?" He zoomed away from the street so that he could see for half a mile around the street corner. Slayne could have run into some of the narrow inner suburban streets with abundant hiding places. On the opposite side of Bedford Street was a broad industrial park that fronted onto the Mystic River. He ran an infra-red filter across the satellite imagery, carefully scanning the park, about half the park was active, filled with operating businesses. The rest looked empty, except for a warehouse with two very faint human contacts in it.

The building was heavily shielded. Only two people were in the building. Could it be Gang and Li Wu? Was this their rendezvous point? James set about finding out. He flipped off the filter and zoomed in on the warehouse. The Panopticon supplied situational metadata that streamed alongside the images on the screen. The US Navy originally commissioned the building into service in 1958. An armory for repairing heavy ship equipment, but decommissioned after the fall of the Soviets when Congress slashed budgets in 1991. Ownership of the building shifted to a company named Clayton Holdings, registered in Massachusetts, which was a wholly owned subsidiary of another company registered in the Cayman Islands. The local company had a managing director, a Mr. Paul Roberts, and no other staff. The utility bills and taxes were all paid on time from an account owned by Roberts. Roberts even had a rarely accessed Facebook account and looked like a genial fiftyish white male with a wife, two grown up children and a cocker spaniel.

He considered the options in front of him. The original military purpose and cold war era construction explained the shielding. However, he wondered if Mr. Roberts was a real person or just a digital phantom conjured up to cover the identity of the building's true owners.

James zoomed in on the area around the building. There were untended weeds growing in the cracked asphalt of the parking lot, but no fresh engine oil spills. He used the Panopticon to search electrical power utility logs. The site normally used only a minimal amount of electricity, yet usage today had spiked much higher than normal. Further examination quickly confirmed the building was normally deserted.

And yet there were two people in there, today of all days, and a lone detective had spotted Anton Slayne within five hundred yards of the building.

James didn't believe in coincidences.

His smartphone rang. Louise Wesson was calling him, he answered it.

"Sir," she said. "The van is fully packed; Higgins is bagged and Johnson is ready to roll."

"Good, get Johnson moving and meet me at my car. I will be there in two minutes. We have somewhere to go."

"Sir?"

"I will tell you in the car."

"Yes, Sir," Wesson replied before hanging up the call.

James looked around at the remains of the stakeout. The floor where Higgins had bled out was now the cleanest part of the room. The room reeked of too much bleach mixed with smoke from the morning fire across the street. Late morning sunlight streamed through the broken window frames, illuminating dust motes floating in the air.

James stood up, closed his laptop and slotted it into a carry case. He hung back from the front wall, glancing out through the broken window frames. The Noodle House had lost half its structure and what remained looked ready to collapse. The Wu residence was a steaming pile of wet ash. Surveying the room for the last time, he was confident his small team had eliminated any connection between the recent events in this building and Shadowstone. He sincerely hoped he would never see this dump again.

James strode from the room, descending downstairs to where he'd parked his car. Louise stood on the opposite side of his vehicle, a combat surveillance kit bag at her feet. James flicked the lock and got into the car.

Lobbing her kit bag onto the back seat, Louise sat down in the front passenger seat and turned to face him, a quizzical look on her face.

"Yes, I've found them," James declared. "Now we move."

Louise smiled. "Yes, Sir."

"What is the status on the Green-4 spectrum team?"

"They've arrived in a nightfalcon helicopter with a combat operations mission fit out, and are waiting at Logan Airport. They can be anywhere in Boston in less than fifteen minutes."

"Good. Put Red-1 and Blue-5 teams on ready alert for combat operations. What is the flight time from Fort Dix?"

"Green-4 got to Boston in seventy-five minutes."

"Wait, no, that's too long. Get those teams into the air and forward base them with Green-4 at Logan. That will give us three combat helicopters, and forty-eight troops to use at short notice."

"Sir, that would be forty-six, Green-4 is down two men, Higgins, and Johnson."

"Forty-eight counting us – I think we can expect to get our hands dirty tonight."

"Sir, there is one more thing." Wesson said, arching an eyebrow.

"Yes?"

"We also have a four-man squad from Indigo-6 in town. They have an armed rigid hulled inflatable boat we can put on the river."

"An armed RHIB, outstanding, make it so."

"Yes, Sir. Do we have new orders?"

"If we can get all three Order of Thoth in the same location, then we have to deploy a cordon and keep them there. General Armitage will be coming tonight with a special forces team to deal with them."

"I would like to see that."

"So, would I," James agreed, starting the car and driving off toward the warehouse.

Wesson opened her smartphone and started giving orders to the other teams of Shadowstone operatives. They would soon marshal at Logan Airport and along the Mystic River.

Pulling out onto the main road, the ten seconds of scrubbed video of the previous night's fight replayed in James' mind. General Armitage's special forces troops would surely be a damn sight better than the Chinese thugs that took on the Wu family and Slayne. James had no doubt the last day in Li and Gang Wu, and Anton Slayne's lives had dawned. He reflected, *Just how good are these Order of Thoth operatives? Well, we'll soon find out, my men are far better trained and armed than those triad wannabees were. I'm sure that if needed they can do the job. Vampire Dominion? They're fucking insane.*

James chaffed at the restrictions General Armitage had placed on him. This was an opportunity for real action against the enemies of society. It was why he'd signed on to Shadowstone in the first place – to make a difference in the world.

James unloaded his growing frustration on the car's accelerator, gunning the car, and speeding off down the road.

* * *

The mid-afternoon summer sun blazed in a bright blue sky.

Anton Slayne stood in the shadows of an abandoned house facing onto Bedford Street. Across the road was a disused parking lot and a large warehouse jutting out into the Mystic River. Anton carefully studied the surrounding area. He'd been watching it for hours. He hadn't seen anything that might be an indication of active surveillance. He'd identified visible traffic cameras, their orientation, and paths that would avoid them.

But what about satellites? He couldn't allow Shadowstone to find him again, but he had no way to be sure he'd hidden himself properly. He reflected on the morning, what terrible luck to run into the detective from the night Armitage murdered his mother. As soon as he'd broken visual contact by turning into the side street, he'd ramped for about two seconds, covered thirty yards, then ran down a side alleyway and hid behind a dumpster. Through a crack between the dumpster and a brick wall, he'd watched the Ford SUV trawl its way past the mouth of the alley.

Anton was certain the detective had recognized him, there was no doubt he would call in the sighting. He'd decided to stay in the area, and a few minutes searching had discovered the abandoned house he now stood in front of. He'd waited patiently; however, nothing had happened, no police cars, no helicopters, nothing at all. The secret keepers were hard at work. He didn't need to worry about the Boston Police Department, they were not the real problem. Shadowstone, their pervasive surveillance system, and the vampires they guarded were the real problem.

Anton had waited hours before risking any movement. Gang's note had said to meet at the address of the warehouse by mid-morning, he was now more than four hours late. The growing tension made him feel sick to his stomach. Four hours was a long time, Gang and Li would be worried. He hoped they would stay put and not try and look for him.

It was time to make a move. He would just have to take his chances with the satellites. A break appeared in the Sunday traffic. Anton pushed off from the wall of the house, leaped over the front fence, and walked calmly across the road. A minute and a half later he was through the boundary fence, across the parking lot and up against the corner of the warehouse.

He saw movement to his right as a steel door opened an inch and he readied himself to Ramp.

"Anton, finally you're here," Gang remarked. "Quick come inside before anyone sees you."

Anton ducked inside and Gang pulled the door shut behind him. Li regarded him with a steady gaze, her arms folded across her chest. A wave of relief washed through him. Gang and Li were safe.

* * *

James Haley watched his laptop screen.

The Panopticon satellite feed showed a third figure hurrying across the open parking lot toward the warehouse. He dialed Louise Wesson, she immediately picked up her smartphone.

"Sir?" Wesson queried.

"Was the target sighted?"

"Yes, Sir. He has just reached the warehouse."

"Good work, call in your helicopters, we will rendezvous in the parking lot. Put Green-4 on the dock, and the other two in the parking lot near the front fence. Get the RHIB to sit a hundred yards off the dock in the middle of the river."

"Yes, Sir. The helicopters will be on site in about ten minutes, and the RHIB in about fifteen."

"How long will it take you to get to the parking lot?"

"I will be there when the nightfalcons arrive."

"Excellent," James replied and hung up.

James put his laptop down and started the engine of his car. He welcomed the air conditioning, as he'd been waiting in his car for the last four hours. He'd parked about a mile back on Bedford Street underneath the shade of a large tree. He'd sent Wesson into a nearby industrial park with a suite of surveillance gear to get a clear sight of the area near the warehouse. He considered the Panopticon all well and good, but often it was best to have human eyes on the target.

A surge of relief washed through him. He'd confirmed Gang and Li Wu and Anton Slayne were in the warehouse. In less than half an hour he would have a cordon around the site that no one could escape from. He noted his unusual feeling of relief. He realized he was responding to the attitude of General Armitage. She seemed to have more than a professional interest in the operation.

The thought concerned him. He'd been reporting to General Armitage for the last eight years, and for all of those years he'd prided himself on his professionalism and skill in executing the role of Head of the United States arm of the Shadowstone organization. But this mission was different, it felt like the General had a personal agenda in play.

There was a dangerous undercurrent beneath the mission and he wondered if he fully understood what was going on. James shrugged of the momentary doubt. He put the car into gear, rolling forward into the Sunday afternoon traffic and proceeded down Bedford Street toward the warehouse.

"Time to nail this mission," he declared to himself. He spotted a shady tree just near the entrance to the parking lot and decided that would be a perfect spot to park and wait for the Shadowstone forces to arrive and deploy.

Yeah, he thought with sudden enthusiasm. *Time to pin their Order of Thoth hides to the wall.*

* * *

Stepping away from the steel door, Anton entered the cool of the warehouse.

Gang drove a thick steel bolt home to lock the door. Smiling broadly, he clapped Anton on the shoulder. Li threw her arms around his neck, crushing herself against him.

Li released him a moment later, and stepped back. Her hand flashed forward and hit him hard on the shoulder.

"Ow!" Anton exclaimed.

"What took you so long?" she demanded.

Anton grinned ruefully. "Li, you really know how to make a guy feel welcome."

Li's eyes tightened and her lips pressed into a thin line.

Anton rubbed his shoulder and said, "I had a run in with the BPD and had to make sure they weren't following me. I'm pretty sure I gave them the slip."

Li tilted her head, unimpressed with his excuse.

Anton sighed; she'd get over it. Gang and Li, were both dressed in army surplus combat fatigues, with webbing for modern weapons and a scabbard for their swords slung over their shoulders. Happy to get the conversation off his late arrival, he asked, "Looks like you're expecting company?"

"Yes," Gang answered. "We've been preparing since we arrived here. When you were late, we suspected Shadowstone must have found you. You may have evaded the Boston police today, but it is highly unlikely you have evaded Shadowstone. They almost certainly know we're here by now."

Anton pursed his lips with disappointment.

"Don't blame yourself," Gang advised, "there was only a slim chance we would get away cleanly once we were discovered at the Noodle House."

"If Shadowstone and the vampires arrive in force, isn't this place a death trap? Why don't we move out while we can?" Anton asked. "We could keep moving and escape the city."

"We already have an agreement with Francis Mirovar to meet here tonight. Moving during the day exposes us in multiple ways to detection by Shadowstone. If they catch us out in the open, and there is a pitched battle, a lot of innocent people could be hurt or killed, and you know the principles of the Order."

"Don't kill the innocent."

"Yes, exactly." Gang said firmly, "We are the aware ones. We have the ability to make an informed choice to put ourselves in harm's way. They do not."

Anton nodded and resolved to make the best of the situation. Stacked shipping containers hemmed them in. Hanging from the ceiling thirty yards above his head was a heavy framework of steel girders. The massive frame supported a crane. Steel cables, giant hooks – and a fully loaded container dangled twenty yards above the concrete floor. He followed the line of the rails the crane ran on, and they went to the very ends of the warehouse, exiting through the front and back walls.

Along the long wall and above the side door he'd just come through were a set of mezzanine levels, with offices, utility rooms, and bathrooms. Halfway along the wall was a diesel-electric power backup plant. Sets of steel stairwells rose up to the mezzanine floors, and from the top level, maintenance walkways spanned across the roof and gave access to the crane.

Realizing he might have to fight here, Anton inquired, "Okay Gang, so how does this place work?" he pointed to the mezzanines. "What's the view like from up there?"

"Excellent questions," Gang said. "Follow me. Li and I have been busy." He led Anton and Li up the stairs to the first mezzanine level. As they ascended, Gang pointed out the various equipment and utility rooms, and the backup diesel power generator on the ground floor beneath them and stated, "The US government built this warehouse during the Cold War. It has backup supplies for power and water, and the walls and roof are steel reinforced stone masonry."

From the first mezzanine level, Anton could just see over the top of the stacked containers. There was a second crane running on identical rails parallel with the first crane, but able to cover the far side of the warehouse. It too supported a large container. He also saw that at the front end of the warehouse were a pair of massive sliding steel doors aligned with the cranes.

If they'd been open, they could easily allow two semi-trailers to sit side by side for loading with shipping containers by the cranes.

"Let's go up to the next level," Gang directed. "You will be able to see precisely what we have done while you were playing with the BPD."

"Yeah, Okay," Anton agreed, following Gang and Li up to the next level. They walked along for about twenty yards before they came to a series of offices. One had lights on and an open door.

Gang led them to it, turned and waved broadly toward the warehouse floor. "Look at the floor and tell me what you see?"

Anton looked out and down across the warehouse. There were hundreds of the big steel shipping containers. The containers were stacked in pairs, one on top of the other to create a massive maze of nineteen-foot-high steel walls. The longest straight lines were about forty yards. He exclaimed, "It's a giant maze!" He pointed at the two containers suspended high in the air by cranes near the main entrance and said, "Looks like they would fit neatly into holes in the maze."

Gang acknowledged Anton's observations. "Well spotted. If dropped at the right time, we can box some people into some very tight corners."

"It won't stop vampires."

"Yes – it won't stop them or slow them down. They will simply run along the top of the maze. Which brings us to the gantry cranes and the maintenance walkways." Pointing out several key intersections in the maintenance walkways that tracked the gantry crane rails, Gang said, "There at the front, halfway along, and just before the exits at the dock are excellent locations to place a variety of tricks to distract our foes."

"What sort of tricks?" Anton asked.

"Pyrotechnics mostly – good for hazing the battlefield."

Anton's jaw dropped open.

"This whole site is a honey trap for vampires," Gang said. "This is an Order site, designed by your grandfather and developed and maintained since the mid-1990s for the purpose of collecting a large group of vampires into one location and then destroying them."

"Can we do the same with just the three of us?"

"That's not the aim today. We only have to survive long enough for the Order to arrive so we can exfiltrate with them." Turning away, Gang led Anton into the nearest office. Li sat at a desk, her fingers flashing skillfully over a keyboard. In front of her was a wide rack of eight separate monitors showing camera feeds from the outside of the warehouse and a pair of monitors displaying command line computer screens.

"Is this where you control the cranes? Isn't that going to lock you into one spot?" Anton asked.

Li turned toward Anton and smiled. She lifted her smartphone and pressed some icons on its surface. Anton heard the nearest crane rumble and he spun around – it was already moving.

Li said, "They're on an internal network with a secured WIFI router we can ping with the phones. I rewrote the SCADA code controlling the cranes. They will drop their loads based on a WIFI connect request. I select this command on my mobile, and a tenth of a second later the container on the right will drop. If I select another command, the one on the left will drop. Father's mobile is set up the same way."

Gang smiled wickedly, waving his smartphone.

"You can write SCADA code?" Anton asked.

"I've just graduated from MIT, Maths and Computer Science, I started an accelerated study program at sixteen."

"That's awesome," Anton enthused, impressed by her achievement. He reflected momentarily; *I've been wasting my time. Li and I are almost the same age, and she's already finished her first degree.* He declared, "I spent my time playing sports, collecting varsity letters and getting an Icy Hockey scholarship. What you've done is amazing."

Li smiled, blushed and laughed. "Thanks, Anton, let me show you what this system does."

Taking a seat next to her, Anton listened carefully as Li explained the details of how the warehouse operated and the locations of the various traps littering the building.

* * *

Louise Wesson pushed up from her prone position after the call from James Haley ended. She packed her scopes into her combat surveillance kit bag with practiced efficiency.

She'd mounted the industrial fuel storage tower to attain her current observation point overlooking the abandoned warehouse and had sweltered in the summer sun for the last three hours.

Louise had changed into urban camouflage patterned combat fatigues before mounting the tower. Her infiltration of the site hadn't involved killing anyone, but there was one security guard who would probably lose his job for drinking alcohol on duty and falling asleep at his post. The drugged dart she'd fired into his neck was completely biodegradable. It would soon disappear with the only remaining trace of its existence a blood alcohol reading that was similar to drinking a bottle of whiskey in an hour. When the guard recovered consciousness a day later, his memory of the twenty-four hours before the dart would be a black hole. The darts were just another trick that Shadowstone had up their sleeve to maintain operational security.

She voice activated her smartphone. The phone dialed a voice conference number for the troop leaders within the three nightfalcon helicopters waiting at Logan Airport. Once the call connected, the men identified themselves.

Louise commanded, "The mission is on. Get yourselves in the air now. Red-1 and Blue-5 bring your teams into the parking lot just before the fence line on the city side of the warehouse. Green-4 take the end of the dock on the Mystic River and hold it. Gentleman, this is a cordon operation. We take and hold a position, and enforce a line that no one crosses, is that understood."

"Yes, Ma'am," the men replied.

The Green-4 troop leader asked a question, "Ma'am, what are the rules of engagement on this operation?"

"Standard engagement model for a cordon, don't shoot unless the targets fire first."

"Yes, Ma'am."

"Any other questions?" she asked.

"No, Ma'am," they all answered.

"You have your orders," Louise declared and disconnecting the call.

With her kit bag packed, Louise carried an FN P90 submachine gun slung over her right shoulder, and a Glock 9mm holstered at her hip. Wiping away the perspiration from her forehead, she adjusted her cap over her straight brown hair, put on mirrored sunglasses and descended the long metal staircase that spiraled down and around the tower. In ninety seconds, she'd reached the ground. Hefting the kit bag over her shoulder, she lifted her speed, making for the parking lot half a mile away. She anticipated arriving at the parking lot entrance in less than five minutes.

Loping easily through the industrial estate, Louise reflected on the last twenty-four hours. Events were coming to a head. She was still alive. James Haley hadn't purged her, and he hadn't even looked like he was about to take action against her – which was a good sign. The Order of Thoth operatives were in the warehouse, which with three heavily armed nightfalcon gunships and nearly fifty fully armed Shadowstone operatives inbound looked like nothing less than a death trap for them.

A trace of doubt lurked at the back of her mind. The Order of Thoth operatives were exceptional. She was honest enough to admit she knew almost nothing about them, or their combat techniques. A quote from Sun Tzu's, The Art of War, came to mind on the topic of knowing your enemy. *'If you know others and know yourself, you will win every battle; if you do not know others but know yourself, you win one and lose one; if you do not know others and do not know yourself, you will lose every single battle.'*

She understood the capabilities of the Shadowstone operatives coming to the warehouse, but of the Order of Thoth, she knew next to nothing. *We are about to flip a coin, and the outcome will be uncertain.*

Louise hated uncertainty.

She ran on, reaching the edge of the parking lot. Haley's car sat under the shade of a large tree near the entrance to the site. He was standing next to his vehicle, still wearing his suit, smoking a cigarette and carrying a full military spec assault rifle with a red dot laser sight and an under-barrel grenade launcher.

Louise slowed to a walk to cover the final few yards. She scanned the horizon. In moments, three black specks resolved into view and rapidly expanded into the oncoming nightfalcons. Shadowstone had armed each helicopter with eight laser-guided Hellfire III and eight Stinger II missiles, an M134 Minigun at the waist, and a pair of triple-barreled GAU-19B .50 Caliber machine guns on fixed mounts beneath the cockpit. Each craft carried a full troop of sixteen fully armed Shadowstone operatives, all highly skilled ex-members of various special forces, the CIA, and the NSA. A heavily armed, superbly equipped, tough, skilled and disciplined para-military force. She frowned, and silently wondered, *How many are going to survive tonight?*

The heavy roar of the helicopters' jet turbines shattered the afternoon air as they split formation to come into land. Two came to a halt in the parking lot and the third came to rest at the end of the dock on the far side of the warehouse.

Louise shielded her face from the backwash of the rotor blades. Darkly armored Shadowstone operatives streamed from the helicopters in four-man squads. They deployed rapidly to form a perimeter around the warehouse. In less than three minutes there was a ring of armed men ready to kill anyone who might attempt to cross their line.

Louise glanced at Haley, he grinned confidently at her, his face lit with a fierce desire. She turned and studied the forbidding massiveness of the warehouse. *This place reeks of secrets – we will be lucky to survive tonight.*

She checked her P90 submachine gun, ejected the standard clip and loaded a fifty-round strip of high-velocity, armor-piercing rounds from her kit bag. She added three spare clips of the same premium ammunition, and four anti-personnel fragmentation grenades to pouches on her combat webbing. She checked the communications links with the four spectrum teams on site and the red, blue, green and indigo squad leaders all reported in.

A sardonic smile curled her lips, her eyes becoming flint like. *If tonight is going to be my last, let's make sure it's a memorable one.*

* * *

Li heard it first.

"Helicopters," she murmured, swiveling in her chair to face the direction the sound was coming from.

"… Yes," Gang agreed. "Nightfalcons."

"Shadowstone?" Anton asked.

"Yes," Gang replied calmly. "They're here."

The monitors linked to the external CCTV cameras provided a clear view of the warehouse surrounds. They watched the helicopters land and the Shadowstone troops begin to deploy to form a perimeter.

"Why haven't they taken out our cameras?" Anton queried. It was the first thing he would have done.

"A good question," Gang acknowledged. He paused for a moment, studying the displays. "Looks like a cordon. They're here to stop us leaving. They're probably forbidden from attacking us – for now."

Li turned away from the monitors and reported, "Three helicopter gunships and nearly fifty troops, all in combat armor and carrying assault rifles with grenade launchers. There are at least three snipers with .50 caliber rifles. From what I can see, the helicopters have two fixed, heavy caliber miniguns in the hull, a waist mount M134 minigun, and Hellfire and Stinger missiles."

"I've not heard of Shadowstone doing this before," Gang said with a frown. "They're armed for war."

Anton shook his head with disappointment. "They followed me here."

"Spilled milk," Li said with a shrug.

"Don't worry Anton, we're prepared for this possibility," Gang advised him. "Li, please stay here and keep watch. I'll show Anton what I showed you earlier." Gang beckoned Anton with a wave of his hand. "Follow me. Now is the time for you to pick up arms." He led Anton back down to the warehouse floor and over to an open shipping container. Nearby were thick chains and an open heavy padlock that was half a foot across.

"Anton, this was prepared by your grandfather. He gave me the key to this container when I last saw him and he told me about its contents. Now, wait here," Gang said, and entered the shipping container. He rummaged about for a long moment, and then emerged with a large military grade lock box which he sat down on the floor in front of Anton. He flipped open the lid and directed, "Look here."

Inside the box were five multi-barreled grenade launchers. Someone had daubed each weapon with a paint stripe across the barrel: two were blue, two were red, and the last one was white.

"These are modified Milkor MGLs, they carry six 40x46mm caliber grenades and have an auto-fire mode that will shoot at a rate of three grenades per second. The blue ones hold grenades with a hundred and ten pure-silver flechettes. They're an excellent weapon to use against vampires at close range. It's a lot like firing a giant shotgun round without the recoil. The red ones carry a standard high-explosive round with a shaped charge. They're best against a vehicle, but you can use one against humans or vampires in a pinch. The white is a thermobaric round – big explosion, lots of heat, and absolutely lethal within the blast radius."

"Wow! Which one should I use?" Anton asked excitedly.

"Oh my God! None of them," Gang declared. "You don't have enough training for these." He walked back into the container and came out carrying a long thick barreled gun with a large magazine in one hand, in his other hand he held a much smaller submachine gun. He gave both weapons to Anton.

Gang pointed to the large gun and said, "This is an AA-12 automatic shotgun with a thirty-two-round magazine. It's good up to about a hundred yards, and is excellent in this sort of environment."

Gang pointed at the submachine gun. It had a red-dot sight on top of the barrel, and a short magazine, and instructed, "This is a Heckler and Koch MP7 A2 personal defense weapon with a twenty-round magazine. It has a high rate of fire like the MAC-10s the Hu Shizu used in the Noodle House, but is a far more accurate and reliable weapon. It's loaded with high performance rounds optimized to deal with human body armor."

Anton studied the guns and asked, "Which is best against vampires?"

"Neither, the plan is to be out of here before the vampires arrive. In a pinch, you can use either gun against a vampire, but you need to be up close, and it is best to shoot them from behind, or else they will dodge. In fact, with all the weapons I have shown you, it is always best to shoot a vampire from behind and up close."

Gang frowned. "Except of course the grenades, you need some distance there."

Anton smiled wryly. "Makes sense."

Gang scratched his ear and said, "However, for the silver flechettes, you can use those up close as there is no explosion."

"There are a lot of exceptions."

Gang nodded, shrugging his shoulders. "What can I say – they're vampires – fighting them is a difficult business."

Anton nodded. "Clearly, but what is your best advice?"

"The trick is getting yourself in the right position to attack them. What makes that so difficult is that their senses are extraordinary. However, we can haze them with sensory clutter. Too much noise, odd smells, and lots of smoke can temporarily throw them off and give you a chance to make an effective attack. Just what the interior of this warehouse will be like tonight."

"What do you mean?" Anton asked.

Gang grinned. "I will show you shortly."

"If the environment is full of clutter, won't we be affected just the same?"

"We have less sensory power to lose, it will level the playing field."

"Okay, how do I use these guns?"

Gang proceeded to give Anton a five-minute lesson in how to hold, point, fire, reload and flick the safety switch on both weapons.

"Don't worry about learning to shoot straight, use your Ramp awareness and focus on pointing the weapon exactly where you are looking and accuracy will look after itself. We will place ammunition reloads at precise locations so you can move from one position to the next without running out of ammo. Our speed will act as a force multiplier. Anton, this is the key to survival, rely on your speed and the natural cover within the warehouse. Once combat starts, keep moving, and never stand still."

Gang looked at his wristwatch. "It's nearly six hours to sunset. That's when the Order will arrive."

"And the vampires too?"

Gang nodded. "Unfortunately, most likely."

Anton felt a mixture of fear and excitement as he chambered a round into the automatic shotgun. The weapon made a satisfying click as it became armed. It felt completely natural in his hands as if made for him. He trained the weapon on a far corner of the warehouse and sighted along the barrel. A shiver ran up his spine and he turned to Gang. "Whose gun is this?"

"It was your grandfather's, one of his favorites."

Lugging a large box from the container labeled, 'Warning: Pyrotechnics: Keep away from flame.' Gang said, "Anton, please help me with these tricks, we have some preparations to make before our guests arrive."

Fireworks, Anton noted to himself, and replied, "Sure." He stepped over to help Gang unload the box. He smiled grimly as he worked with Gang to set a range of traps around the warehouse. It was time for some payback.

* * *

The mid-afternoon summer sun beat down upon the city of Boston.

James Haley assembled the troop and squad leaders under the shade of the trees near the site entrance. He wore a discrete headset that used his Shadowstone smartphone to link with his laptop, the Panopticon, and the communication links of the assembled combat leaders. Beside him, Louise Wesson stood, wearing her own combat gear and her 'game on' face partially hidden behind her mirrored sunglasses.

The eight Red-1 and Blue-5 combat leaders all wore matt black combat armor and tactical helmets provided with an extensive suite of sensors and communications links. They carried their weapons easily and waited patiently, alert, relaxed and ready for action. The Green-4 squad leaders remained at their post on the dock; networked in by the tactical communication links.

James stood in front of the group and addressed his men, "This cordon has to be airtight. I don't want anyone or anything crossing it until we're done. Our task is to ensure that the three Order of Thoth terrorists in that warehouse," he thrust his finger at the massive building, "stay there until General Armitage arrives tonight with her special forces to deal with them."

"Sir?" One of the squad leaders asked.

"Yes?"

"I think we're attracting some unwanted attention," the squad leader remarked with a nod toward the street where small huddles of people stood watching the proceedings.

James glanced around, snorted derisively, looked at his watch, and directed, "The BPD will be providing an outer perimeter, they should be here in five minutes. Our cover is simple; this is a counter-terrorism exercise. The BPD will play ball and keep the locals from getting in the way."

James turned to his senior team leader and asked, "Wesson, what's the status on the RHIB, they're not showing up on my network comms."

"It's on station, a hundred yards off the dock."

"What's on it?"

"A single squad from Indigo-6. The RHIB itself is a thirty-six-footer. It carries a fore mounted Mk-19 grenade launcher, a rear mounted M2 .50 caliber heavy machine gun, and a quad mount FIM-92 Block II Stinger surface to air missile system amidships."

"You could start a war with that. Make sure they keep moving up and down the river and they keep a lookout for anything that could assist a river exfiltration. These Order terrorists didn't choose this site by accident. Make sure your men have their heads on a swivel, and get them connected to my comms link."

"Yes, Sir."

James faced his men and demanded, "I need two snipers and an electrical power expert. We need to take out all their external CCTV cameras and cut the power to the warehouse, who is available?"

The squad leaders responded quickly, issuing commands across secured links and five men dropped out of the cordon. Two men in pairs took up positions on either side of the warehouse. In less than twenty seconds, eight single shots rang out, reducing eight CCTV cameras into mangled lumps of twisted metal and sputtering power cables.

The fifth man ran to the Blue-5 nightfalcon, and extracted a kit from the helicopter. He went to a nearby electrical power distribution pole. Scaling it with a special climbing rig, he selected and cut some key wires. Turning, he gave James a thumbs up, before descending to the ground and returning to his position in the cordon.

James consulted the Panopticon satellite view of the warehouse, switching on a specialized filter to examine what he expected to be a dead zone of zero electrical activity. In the distance, a diesel engine came online. A soft thrumming from a hundred and fifty yards in front of him. He frowned, looking down at his screen. The warehouse was a spaghetti maze of electrical cables – all alive. He switched filters, there was a plume of hot exhaust escaping a three-inch pipe jutting out of the roof midway along the right side of the warehouse.

James grinned wryly and muttered, "Damn. Well, okay, you have a backup generator but not for long." He signaled one of the Red-1 squad leaders, gave him some quick instructions, and a minute later the Red-1 nightfalcon was lifting off from the parking lot.

James noted that half a dozen BPD cruisers and vans had shown up on Bedford Street, more than twenty police officers were setting up temporary roadblocks and police line tape to keep the public away. He sighed, *they will certainly get a show, I will need a PSYOPS crew to come in and spin this operation for general consumption.* The Red-1 nightfalcon took up a position facing the right-side wall, a hundred and twenty yards away from the warehouse. He slaved the helicopter's combat system to his laptop and fed in the Panopticon supplied location of the diesel generator. It sat on the ground level of the warehouse, butting up against the wall. The Panopticon specs for the building indicated the walls were three feet of steel-reinforced stone masonry.

The helicopter veered slightly to the left, settling about ten yards off the ground, its nose down at a slight angle. The men in the cordon backed away and gave the helicopter plenty of space.

James smiled, and gave the order to fire.

Showtime!

Beneath the cockpit of the nightfalcon, two multi-barreled heavy machine guns opened fire with the unique sound that Gatling guns make, like a thickly woven mat being torn in half overlaid with an electric whirr. The sound started and didn't stop. Gray smoke streamed from the mouths of the guns, swirling away in the wash from the helicopter's rotor blades. Spent casings dropped like confetti from beneath the spinning machine gun barrels. The bullets flashed into a mark two yards in diameter at the base of the wall, every fifth round a bright tracer, the rest comprised depleted uranium penetrators.

The stone masonry of the wall started to ablate and flake away. Disintegrating before the ferocious barrage of the twin guns. Giant sparks flew as thick reinforcing steel cables wilted under the titanic hammer of the heavy fire. Grit and dust spewed from the hole in a billowing cloud. Suddenly the bullets were through and the diesel generator exploded and a ball of flame shot out through the gaping hole in the wall.

The guns fell silent. Veering to the left, the nightfalcon made its way back to its original landing spot in the parking lot.

James heard cheers from the onlookers. They were crowding the police line and waving American flags. He momentarily considered the idea of simply letting them stay and get their minds blown away by what would go down this night, then thought better of it. He called out a quick command, "Wesson, get those BPD clowns to clear the street and the houses back to the end of the side streets. I want a clear perimeter out to a mile until we're done."

"Yes, Sir. On it," she replied, jogging off toward the police line and the BPD Officer in Charge.

James returned to his laptop, the Panopticon satellite feed with an infrared filter showed a sizable fire raging against the right wall. As he watched, the fire started to die, first slowly, and then quickly.

"A fire suppressant?" James murmured. This site was proving to be quite resilient and he mused to himself, *These guys have a lot of tricks.*

As the fire died, three faint human contacts came back into view, spread out on the far side of the warehouse. He noted silently, *Well, now you're blind and when night comes you will be sitting in the dark. Let's see what you do while we wait for General Armitage to arrive.*

* * *

Anton, Gang, and Li regrouped in the middle of the warehouse.

Acrid smoke tinged the air, but the quick response of the fire suppressant system around the diesel generator had prevented the warehouse from becoming a smoke-filled death trap.

Gang gripped both their shoulders and instructed in decisive tones, "Their strategy is clear, they want to make us powerless and keep us here until sunset; when no doubt the vampires will arrive in force." He glanced at his watch and thought for a moment. "Sunset is about twenty minutes past eight which means that we have five and a half hours before they arrive."

Anton said, "With the power out, we're not going to be able to use our crane traps."

"And once it gets dark, it's really going to be to the vampires' advantage rather than ours, it would be much better to have lights," Li remarked.

"Is there any way we can fix it?" Anton asked.

Gang frowned. "Not that I know of."

Li's face lit up and she declared with an excited smile, "Father! The fire suppressant system was operating while the generator was on fire and the main power lines were cut. What's its power source?"

"I'm not sure. Let's look."

The three of them moved through the maze, coming to the right-side wall where the diesel generator lay in ruins. They moved cautiously around to make sure they were not presenting any opportunities for a sniper to get a shot through the gaping hole in the wall where the diesel generator had stood.

They reached the wall to the left of the ruined generator. There was an array of eight silvery-gray rectangular cabinets along the wall. Each one was about eight feet high, three feet wide and about two feet deep. Heavy cables ran above them and connected at the top of each cabinet. Anton looked down the wall toward the dock, the cables ran the distance of the wall and there was another array ten yards further along.

Anton suggested, "I think this equipment runs the length of the wall."

"That's a lot of battery power," Li said.

"Anton, this is typical of your grandfather – he believed in defense in depth," Gang remarked.

"They're always watching," Anton said. "We'll need to be able to test this without letting them know that we still have power."

"Speaking of which," Li stated decisively, pressing a red button near the array. "Now they're all disconnected. They will hold their power, and not show up on some Shadowstone operative's fancy surveillance system. But testing this without giving the game away will take time, I'll have to inspect the power cables, and I can run micro-currents through the system to see that the circuits are still complete."

"Good girl," Gang declared with a grin. "You start on that. Anton and I will continue with prepping the tricks, traps and general mayhem for our much-anticipated guests."

Li left to collect the equipment she needed. Gang pulled Anton aside and suggested, "I think we should make a call; this phone of mine is not so dumb. Francis was able to send me an app, which I installed, it provides an encrypted text capability beyond the capacity of Shadowstone to decipher."

"Cool."

Gang sent a text message using the secure app, which read, 'We are at the Boston Warehouse and Shadowstone are here. Gang.'

About twenty seconds later a reply came back which read, 'We have seen it. They have you surrounded. We have a long way to come, we will be there after sunset. I will text details before we arrive. F.'

Anton read the message over Gang's shoulder, and remarked sarcastically, "So, they will arrive with the vampires – wonderful."

Gang shrugged his shoulders helplessly. "Well … there is nothing to be done to speed their arrival, or slow the passage of the sun."

Anton lifted his hands and queried, "Does the Order have a problem with daylight operations?"

"Everyone has a secret to keep,' Gang replied. "We're the same as the vampires in that respect."

"Wouldn't it be better for us to simply 'out' the truth about the vampires?" Anton suggested.

Gang smiled wryly. "Do you think you would be believed?"

Anton's shoulders slumped, then he straightened. "There must be a way to convince people of what is going on."

"The vampires own, through layered proxies, all the major media outlets. They'd squash the truth, and paint the Order as Nazi loving, death worshiping, satanic child-thieving cannibals out to drown the world in blood. They'd turn everyone against us, and we can't fight everyone."

"Then why haven't the vampires tried that?"

"They have, are you aware of the witch craze in Europe and North America from the 15th through to the 18th century."

"Yes."

"The so-called authorities of the day murdered a lot of innocent people, including some members of the Order. The vampires orchestrated the whole thing. It was a great cover; they could go into a village pretending to be witch finders, kill any Order members in the village, and then depopulate it to hide what had actually happened. The local authorities would then thank them for it."

"Vampires were behind the witch hunters?"

"One of Crane's early experiments with social control."

"Why don't they try the same tactic now?"

"Society has moved on; fewer people would believe it. I think Crane is simply weighing the risks. A public campaign against the Order risks his own exposure, so he has more to lose than to gain by such a strategy. So, both camps live in the shadows and fight our battles in secret."

Anton nodded. "It's a pretty messed up world we're living in."

"That it is," Gang agreed. He looked at his watch. "Time's getting on Anton, let's get these fireworks in place on the maintenance walkways. I also have some claymores to set up around that hole in the wall and throughout the maze, and we still have to set up our ammunition reloads so they're easy to pick up."

Anton smiled and agreed, "You're right, we can solve these problems another time – perhaps over a beer."

Gang smiled and winked.

The two men set to work.

* * *

Anton lined up the modified M18 claymore mine next to the base of a container and spooled out a net of thin electrical fibers in front of it.

The net stretched forward from the bottom of the mine, blending in with the concrete floor of the warehouse. The tripwire net created an area ten-feet wide and twelve-feet deep in front of the claymore where anyone making a single step would fire the mine on a three second 'Sneaker' delay – designed to allow more than one person to enter the area of deadliest effect. Anton circled around the net, reached down and flicked an arming switch on the mine.

He took a step back from the armed mine. It covered a square forty yards on a side surrounded by stacked shipping containers. There were two other entrances into the trap that would funnel anyone entering the square toward where Anton stood. This was the last of twenty mines he'd positioned in accordance with a map provided by Gang.

He stood between two containers, a ten-foot-wide gap in the maze wall. He prepared himself, ramped, making a vertical leap that brought his feet to the top of the first container. He pushed off again, landing in a crouch on top of the opposite pair of containers. In two vertical leaps, he'd ascended nearly twenty feet.

He rose up from his crouch and adjusted the fit of the automatic shotgun he carried diagonally across his back. The weapon rested next to the scabbard for the Blue Dragon sword. At his hip, he wore a holster for the H&K MP7 A2 submachine gun.

He looked for Gang, finding him on the second mezzanine level. The mezzanine was still accessible by stairs from the floor. The stairs had survived the partial destruction of the first mezzanine level when the diesel generator had exploded more than three hours earlier.

"Gang, I'm done," Anton called out. He only had to raise his voice a little for Gang to hear him across the warehouse.

"Good work. Meet me at the front doors."

"Sure," Anton agreed, jogging along the top of the maze toward the front of the warehouse. In moments, he arrived, jumping down to the ground below. Gang showed up a few seconds later with two of the Milkor MGLs, the ones with a splash of red paint across their thick barrel.

Anton felt his excitement rise as he recalled Gang's words. *'The red ones carry a standard high-explosive round with a shaped charge that is best against a vehicle, and can also be used as an anti-personnel weapon versus humans or vampires.'* He asked excitedly, "You need my help with one of these?"

Gang tilted his head quizzically and frowned. "Those men out there are someone's son, if they die today at our hand, it's not a cause for excitement."

"What?" Anton blinked, nonplussed by Gang's attitude. "Are you sure of that? Look at the choices they've made. As bad or worse than those triad thugs that attacked the Noodle House."

Gang shook his head and instructed, "I would be happier if you were calmer. The ideal is to find a center of peace in the midst of combat. Your excitement borders on lust for their deaths."

"A center of peace?" Anton hissed. A tight ball of fury ignited in the depths of Anton's soul. He pointed fiercely past the gates at the front of the warehouse. "What the Hell! Those bastards covered up the torture and murder of my mother and the abduction of my father to some crazy fucking insane vampire torture. They all volunteered at some point to wear those uniforms. They deserve whatever punishment I can give them."

Gang stroked his chin and then wagged his finger in Anton's face. "Shortly after I first met you, we spoke briefly about vengeance and justice. Do you remember? I see now that nothing has changed."

Anton frowned, his eyes narrowed in barely controlled rage, and he snapped, "Something about walking in the shadow of vengeance and the light of justice."

"Something like that," Gang said quietly.

"I don't see anyone else stepping up to the plate to deliver justice for my parents. It will have to be me."

Gang stepped in, clapped Anton on both shoulders and pulled him close with enough strength he couldn't resist if he wanted to. "Anton, there is no room for a personal vendetta on this journey. You must let this anger and hatred go."

"They destroyed my family. I have every right to feel this way. I promise you. I will not stop until I have destroyed Armitage, Shadowstone, and the Vampire Dominion."

Gang sighed, and his grip relaxed. "Perhaps it would be best if you were not here."

Anton shrugged off Gang's hands, stepping back, his face filled with shock. "You would send me away?"

"For your own sake – yes."

Anton's anger melted away. Gang and Li were the closest people to a family he had now, he would rather die than lose them. Working past a knot in his throat, Anton asked, "Why would you send me away?"

"Anton, you are a good man, perhaps a very good man with a great capacity for love and courage, but right now, your life is on a moral knife-edge and you could either step into the light or fall into darkness."

Gang waved at the warehouse. "Why are we here today? Why is Shadowstone assembled for war out there in broad daylight? It's unheard of. The vampires are coming tonight, and so is the Order of Thoth. There has not been a major battle in the last twenty years. What's different Anton? It's you, it's your presence here, the hidden Slayne, perhaps the last Slayne. You had a direct male line ancestor that lived in the time of Hakron the Scribe, who was part of the original post-Ahknaton Order of Thoth. Hakron entrusted your ancestor with the protection of the Papyrus of Hakron the Scribe, and it remained in the safe keeping of your family up until a few short weeks ago. Life is a strange mix of fate and choice, and I think the next few hours will be more about you and your choices than about anyone else."

A poignant sadness almost overwhelmed Anton and he asked, "You truly believe that my choices matter that much?"

Gang nodded and declared with quiet certainty, "More than you can understand."

Ashamed by his outburst in front of Gang's steadfastness, Anton said quietly, "What do you need from me?"

"Your help."

"You've got that anytime you want it," he declared solemnly.

Gang pointed to where the rails of the cranes passed through holes in the front of the warehouse and said, "The maintenance walkway up there will give you a sight on the Shadowstone positions in the parking lot. We need to thin these guys down before night falls, or else, we will have all of them and the vampires to fight at the same time. We need to take out their helicopters, they're a key asset for them, and so that's what we will use the MGLs for."

Gang gave one of the MGLs to Anton and showed him how to operate the simple weapon. He directed, "Now you take the right-hand side, and I will take the left. Watch my angles, I will show you before I fire. Fire the first three rounds only, that will take a second, then immediately pull right back to our first defensive position, they're bound to fire back at you. We have the element of surprise, but that's only good for the first shot, Li will cover our rear at the dock."

"Will do," Anton agreed, following Gang back to the mezzanine stairs. Ascending to the top level, they were able to access the maintenance walkways that spanned the roof of the warehouse. Anton took up position on the walkway next to the right-side crane rail at the front of the warehouse. He spotted Li as she took up a position on the maintenance walkway at the river end. She carried a large sniper rifle, two of the MP7 submachine guns holstered at her hips, and the Green Dragon in its scabbard over her shoulder.

Anton wanted to be at her side, but she'd her job, and he had his. He focused on the task at hand. He glanced across at Gang, who was sliding backward on his belly from the gap in the warehouse wall. He stood up, signaling Anton with a thumbs up, and pointed to his MGL, which he held at an angle up from the horizontal.

Anton mimicked his position and readied himself to Ramp. He would have to move forward, sight the target, pull the trigger, and once the first three rounds had fired, pull back off the maintenance walkway to the top of the maze below. He watched as Gang held up his right hand, counting down the seconds with his fingers, first holding up five, then four, then three, then two. Anton ramped, watching Gang move in slow motion as he held up his last finger, then Gang ramped, flashing forward. Anton moved a fraction of a second later. He came to a halt level with the gap in the wall of the warehouse. In front of him were two of the nightfalcon helicopters, the one on his side was spooling up, its rotors spinning faster and faster. In his peripheral vision, he saw a grenade shoot out from Gang's position toward the other helicopter, the noise of the shot reaching him a moment after he saw it. He raised his MGL to the same angle as Gang had demonstrated, lined it up on the helicopter and pulled the trigger. The grenade sailed away from him with a solid 'choof' sound, the revolver like barrels of the MGL began turning and a second and a third grenade quickly followed the first.

Gang's words rang in his mind. *Then immediately pull right back to our first defensive position.* Anton waited. He wanted to make sure he'd hit the target. The first of Gang's grenades struck the helicopter on the left. Its fuel tank exploded and it vanished in a huge fireball. The second and third grenades bracketed the exploding helicopter, adding to the mayhem amongst the men nearby. He saw the first of his grenades just miss the top of the helicopter, and then the second and third followed to land harmlessly along the edge of the parking lot.

What the hell? He'd missed everything. Anton's ramp stuttered, the world flicking back into normal motion.

More than a dozen Shadowstone operatives responded to the threat, swinging their weapons toward him and the other walkway. Gang had already disappeared back into the warehouse. He was safe.

He dived back into silence and his ramp took flight. The first of the muzzle flashes from the assault rifles started popping along the cordon. He lowered his weapon slightly, pulling the trigger of the MGL. It fired a fourth grenade toward the remaining nightfalcon. A couple of bullets whizzed past his head. A dozen more shattered the stone near his shoulder, sending splinters into the left side of his face. Twisting away, he leaped back along the walkway and out of the line of fire. Behind him, he heard another large explosion out in the parking lot.

"Got it!" he exulted.

There was a trickling wetness on the left side of his head. He dragged his hand across his face as he moved to the first defensive position. His hand came away covered in blood and tiny stone fragments. He blinked; both his eyes were still okay.

He laughed and exclaimed, "Hell, I got worse on the Hockey rink!"

* * *

James lit a cigarette.

A 40mm grenade looped out of the front of the warehouse and crashed into the Blue-5 helicopter. The nightfalcon exploded in a blinding glare. A wave of heat and pressure blowing over the men nearest the helicopter. Another two grenades followed, adding their destructive power to the mayhem amongst his forces.

He whirled; more grenades flew at the Red-1 helicopter which was preparing to take off for a low-level reconnaissance run around the area. They all passed over the spinning rotors, exploding harmlessly along the parking lot's fence line. His men returned fire and a swarm of 5.56mm rounds reached toward the two gaps fifteen yards up the face of the warehouse. The man who had destroyed the Blue-5 nightfalcon had already disappeared. The second man fired a fourth grenade that looped directly at the Red-1 nightfalcon. James' heart sank as it smashed into the front of the helicopter which promptly exploded in a bright ball of flame. He had to turn away, shielding his eyes from the glare. When he looked back at the warehouse, the second man had vanished.

A name rushed into his mind. *Anton Slayne – alias Smith – you're a dead man.*

"Wesson, get the Green-4 helicopter airborne, get your team back here, and move the RHIB back fifty yards."

"Already happening, Sir," Wesson replied, sprinting over to stand next to him.

"Damn MGLs," James growled with disgust.

"If they have those, they could have anything."

"Teams report," James growled into his comm links.

A rapid succession of reports flowed in. There were four dead aircrews; pilots and co-pilots. Red-1 had lost two men to flying debris from the helicopter explosion, and another two men were too wounded to fight. The Blue-5 team had operatives closer to their nightfalcon, as it had been stationary. They had lost six men from the three grenades and another two wounded and out of action. That left twenty operatives from the two spectrum teams' original strength of thirty-two men.

"Wesson, reform the teams into five squads of four, position the wounded back here and give them some first aid and water."

"Yes, Sir," Wesson responded. She rushed to comply, issuing directives through her headset.

At the other end of the dock, the Green-4 nightfalcon completed spooling up. Taking off, it veered violently away from the warehouse. It bristled with guns as the operatives on board trained their weapons on the open gates at the river end of the warehouse. Half a minute later the helicopter had parked in a deserted Bedford Street, beyond the range of the MGLs. The Green-4 operatives streamed from the nightfalcon and it took to the air once more. In moments, it had risen to a position six hundred yards above the ground and the same distance back from the front of the warehouse.

The Green-4 operatives marshaled before her. Wesson made three squads of four men and one squad of two. She assigned the three squads to join the main Shadowstone force with James and assigned the remaining half squad to herself. She turned to James and reported, "The men are ready."

"Outstanding," James acknowledged with a growl. "I want the RHIB to move into a position where it can fire on anyone coming out of the rear of the warehouse. It's got a .50 cal, and a belt fed MGL, that should be able to supply enough firepower to block any escape. Take your squad of two and block the right-side entrance, and the hole in the wall where the generator was. Make sure that no one escapes from that side."

"Yes, Sir," Wesson agreed. Turning away, she gave directions over the tactical link to the Indigo-6 squad manning the RHIB. Her two-man squad followed her, checking their weapons as they jogged after her.

James addressed his remaining men. "You know our orders. We have to hold these bastards here until the damn cavalry arrives."

The men grumbled and swore.

"I know exactly how you feel. Our standing orders are that we do not fire unless fired upon. Well, we have been well and truly fired upon." He shook his head and thrust his finger at the warehouse. "And I'm not giving these rat bastards another chance to kill us."

He stood in front of his men, his hands on his hips. He leaned forward and declared, "Now here's what we're going to do. We're going to use the remaining nightfalcon to blow the front doors off with Hellfire missiles and then take a position over the river."

He drew a circle in the air with his right index finger. "Then all of us are going in via the front door." He slapped his right fist into the palm of his left hand. "We will be the hammer and the RHIB and the nightfalcon will be the anvil."

He stood tall, his eyes flashing. "We will go in there and kill them or push them out onto the dock where the RHIB and the nightfalcon will take them apart. Now there are thirty-three of us going in, and only three of them. If they don't surrender, kill them. If they do surrender – kill them. We take no prisoners today!"

The men shouted, "Yes, Sir!"

The Shadowstone force moved out as one. Dispersing across the parking lot, they readied themselves to move forward toward the warehouse without making a target of themselves.

James tossed his laptop into his car, and picked up his assault rifle. He'd already swapped his dark gray suit jacket for a bullet proof vest. He wore combat webbing to carry extra magazines and grenades for the M203 launcher on his rifle. He cocked the assault rifle and loaded a grenade. He opened his comm link to the Green-4 nightfalcon, ordering it to destroy the front gates of the warehouse.

The helicopter barely moved, only enough to tilt its nose toward the giant steel doors on the front of the warehouse. Two seconds later a pair of Hellfire III missiles launched from their pylons to the left and right of the helicopter's cockpit. They streaked toward the steel doors, detonating with a pair of thunderous explosions and a white thermobaric glare. The heavy steel doors evaporated, the crane gantries above the gates disappearing into a cloud of flying steel fragments.

Before the smoke and dust could begin to clear, the heavy machine guns under the nose of the nightfalcon opened up. They sprayed the interior of the warehouse with a sustained barrage of .50 caliber rounds. After ten seconds and a thousand rounds, the firing stopped. The helicopter veered away to take up a new position over the Mystic River.

"Go! Go! Go!" James shouted. Sprinting with the assembled operatives toward the cavernous openings in the front of the warehouse.

In less than ten seconds they were all through the entrance.

* * *

The giant hammering of the nightfalcon's machine guns abruptly stopped, silence rushing in to fill the vacuum.

Anton lay prone on top of the maze wall about fifty yards back from the front of the warehouse. He lifted his head, just enough to sight the billowing smoke and dust obscuring the smashed entrance. Missiles had vaporized the great steel doors. Late afternoon sunlight backlit the swirling haze. The play of sunlight, smoke, metal and stone dust against the emerging torn remains of the warehouse gates and tangled crane gantries, left Anton filled with an eerily surreal awe.

The haze suddenly eddied, swirling as men clad in black body armor, carrying assault rifles, streamed over the rubble and into the warehouse. They came in pairs, their heads in combat helmets swiveling this way and that as they looked for targets. They held their rifles high, red-dot laser sights on top of the guns tracking their lines of sight. He wriggled backward, hugging the cold metal of the container. The Shadowstone operatives disappeared from view, obscured by the maze wall.

Anton glanced across at Gang, who held a similar position beneath the crane rail on the other side of the warehouse. Above and behind him, he saw that Li had left the rear of the warehouse and was lying prone on the uppermost mezzanine level near the maintenance access walkways. She had her smartphone in her hand, working it intently.

Six grappling hooks trailing solid black lines appeared over the maze wall thirty yards directly in front of Anton. Another set of grappling hooks appeared on Gang's side of the warehouse. The lines went taut as the men below began scaling them. In a couple of seconds, they would be up on the maze wall with Anton and Gang.

"Damn it!" Anton muttered. They were supposed to go through the maze, not over it. He rose to one knee, aiming the MGL at the top of the container where most of the lines were. The first of the black helmets appeared, and he pulled the trigger. The grenade flew toward them where it exploded, ripping open the top of the steel container like tearing tinfoil, and slashed through the black lines. The other operatives spotted the shot and ducked away. Anton pointed the MGL into the space where the black lines ran down, firing his last grenade which disappeared below the edge of the maze wall before exploding in a bright glare.

Someone screamed for a moment and then fell silent.

There were more choofs of launching grenades. Gang fired a volley of them across the front line of the maze, then dropped his empty MGL and ran back about twenty yards.

Anton ramped, running back across the maze toward the middle of the warehouse as Gang's grenades exploded and more screams and shouts emanated from the ranks of the operatives along the front of the warehouse. *Gang's grenades should drive those guys forward and deeper into the maze.*

The warehouse fell silent. Anton strained to hear and see anything moving in front of him. *They're not moving!* He placed the empty MGL at his feet. Pulling the automatic shotgun off his back, he trained it on the area where he expected the operatives would emerge.

Grappling hooks sailed for a second time over the container walls near Gang. More hooks and lines followed, landing forty yards in front of Anton. The black lines stretched taught, but no black helmets appeared. Instead, a dozen slim grenades flew over the maze wall, and wherever they landed they stuck as if glued to the metal containers. One landed a yard in front of where Gang stood, he ramped, blurring backward more than a dozen yards.

Anton reflexively turned his head away. All the grenades exploded in blinding glares and thunderous reports. Even though he'd looked away,

Anton found himself dazzled as gray spots flew before his eyes, and his ears rang as agonizing pain shot through his skull. Staggering backward, he stumbled over the MGL at his feet and slipped off the maze wall. As he fell, he managed to reach out wildly with his left hand, grabbing a vertical metal rail along the side of the top container. He slid down, coming to a halt with his arm outstretched above him, and his feet dangling inches above the webbed network of a trip wire for one of his own claymore mines. His eyesight was beginning to return as he looked up to see his MGL teetering on the top edge of the container above him.

Gunfire erupted in the warehouse. Staccato three round bursts from the assault rifles, interspersed by the high-speed rips of Gang's MP7s, ripped through the air.

They're on the maze wall! I have to get back up and help Gang and Li. Anton swung backward to get some momentum and then launched himself upward as a stream of rifle fire burst through the air above the container. A stray bullet hit the MGL, knocking it flying over the edge. Anton kept swinging upward, letting go as the MGL passed him on the way down to the concrete floor of the warehouse and the waiting web of tripwires for the claymore mine.

His maneuver threw him a yard over the top edge of the container. He rolled as he landed. Springing to his feet, already ramped, he ran directly toward six Shadowstone operatives five yards away on the wall.

The three operatives at the front all began firing at the same time. Anton leaped into the air, a massive ten feet up and over the flying bullets and their heads. He pulled the trigger of the automatic shotgun which answered the rifles with a fusillade of heavy shot that knocked one of the operatives off the maze wall and into the space that the MGL had fallen into. The man was still flailing in midair when the claymore mine fired – tripped by the MGL that had fallen seconds before. The man instantly disappeared in a hail of lead and gray smoke.

His following shotgun rounds struck another two operatives. Blown backward by the force of the hits, they slipped over the edge of the maze wall.

Twisting in mid-air, Anton landed on his feet facing the three remaining operatives who were sliding to a halt and spinning around to follow him. The one on the right allowed himself to fall backward and twist around, his gun was the first to bear on Anton. He dodged hard left as a three-round burst ripped past his right arm. He fired his shotgun again; a pair of rounds struck the front of the operative's tactical helmet and he dropped immediately. The remains of his shattered visor covered in blood.

The remaining two operatives stepped backward to give themselves room to bring their rifles up. Anton ran into them ramped, clubbing one in the side of the neck with the butt of his shotgun. The man silently falling backward, disappearing over the edge of the maze wall.

The last operative turned, lashing at Anton with his own rifle butt. Anton leaned backward; the rifle butt swung past over his face. Anton sprang back erect. He swung his shotgun butt up, catching the man underneath his chin. The force of the blow lifted the operative clear of the container, throwing him off the maze wall.

Anton's head swiveled around. On the other side of the warehouse, Gang was reloading his MP7s. In front of him two black-clad bodies lay limply on the maze walls.

There were no more live Shadowstone operatives on top of the maze walls. The front quarter of the warehouse exploded in multi-colored flashes, and silver sparkles. Loud whistles erupted as rockets launched and streamed down and across the warehouse from row upon row of boxes and cylinders strapped to the maintenance walkways. The warehouse became a crazed Fourth of July as light and sound battered the Shadowstone operatives in the front quarter.

Anton took advantage of the momentary chaos to back deeper into the warehouse and move to the right. Gang, having completed reloading his MP7s, did the same. He looked around for Li, she'd vanished from the mezzanine level and he could not find her anywhere.

Fear and worry for her was a cold clamp on his chest. *Damn it, where is she?* He dropped to one knee to lower his profile. Reloaded the shotgun with a fresh magazine from his combat webbing and sighted along the weapon toward the front of the warehouse which still flashed, smoked, banged and whistled with colored, sparkling mayhem. Moments later the fireworks bled dry as a final lonely rocket shot across the warehouse, exploding with a loud whistling bang in a streamer of green sparkles.

One of the operatives called out in a disgusted growl. "You've gotta be kidding me?" The warehouse went silent, and grappling hooks once again sailed over the container walls. *They're not buying it. They know we're up here now and they're going to fight us here.*

Gang signaled with his hand. The lights on the cranes came on; the right container plummeting to the floor with an earsplitting bang, a half second later, the left container followed it down. A scream of horror suddenly cut off as the second container slammed onto the concrete floor of the warehouse. Li had dropped the containers, which could only mean the operatives were now in the claymore kill zones.

The grappling lines went taut again on both sides of the warehouse. This time, Anton had to wait until the operatives leaped and rolled onto the top of the containers. Men in black body armor appeared on top of the wall on both sides of the warehouse. Gang's MP7s ripped into action. Anton started firing his shotgun. The weapon barked and stuttered. The lead operative wore a suit, a bulletproof vest, and a snarl on his face. He rolled forward and sideways with cat-like reflexes. The heavy blasts of shot striking the next operative in the chest who staggered backward and fell off the wall.

It was the suit from the night of his mother's murder. The head of the secret keepers. Rage rooted Anton to the spot, before Gang's earlier instructions ripped through him – 'keep moving.'

Anton ramped hard, moving to the right as return fire lanced past him on the left. He felt bullets whiz past his head, the suit was still firing at him with uncanny accuracy even as he blurred away. Before Anton could fire back, another two operatives fell backward in quick succession, struck by heavy caliber rounds fired from above and behind him.

It was Li, his guardian angel with a sniper rifle.

The remaining two operatives on Anton's side of the warehouse followed the suit as he led them off the top of the maze wall.

They were breaking. Anton moved again, this time backward and to his left, zig-zagging across the top of the maze. Gang's MP7s fired again as he traded streams of bullets with the operatives that had scaled the wall on his side of the warehouse. The operatives had spread out and Gang had multiple dispersed targets. He blurred, fired, blurred and fired again. Two of the operatives spun around, dropping to the floor below, another two followed them as Li claimed their lives with her heavy .50 caliber sniper rifle.

Suddenly two of the claymore mines went off, one to the right, near Anton and the other to the left near Gang. The explosions rang through the warehouse. The crash of hundreds of ball bearings smashing against the steel containers preceded the screams of the wounded and dying men caught in the blasts.

Anton ramped, backing deeper into the warehouse, Gang did the same. They both took up positions mid-way along the maze. Gang signaled Anton with his hand, pointed to his eyes and then at the rear of the warehouse. Turning, Anton jogged along the top of the maze toward the river end of the warehouse.

When he got near the river end, he took up a position where he could see the dock entrance. There was no one on the dock. In the distance, he could see a RHIB patrolling the river, above him, he could hear the distant sounds of a hovering helicopter.

He rested and kept watch, as silence descended upon the warehouse, broken only by the cries of wounded and dying men.

* * *

The injured man stopped moaning, lapsing into unconsciousness as the powerful narcotic took effect.

Each of the Shadowstone operatives carried a kit with syringes, filled with stimulants, painkillers, and other useful compounds. James threw the used syringe to the floor. Squatting, he picked up the fully armored man, throwing him over his shoulder like a two-hundred-and-fifty-pound sack of potatoes. He carried him back to the front of the warehouse where he laid him down with the other three wounded. The three remaining active operatives, Rigby and Hansen from Blue-5, and Boorman from Green-4 stood guard. They stood dispersed in a line just inside the front of the warehouse. Their rifles on full auto, scanning the maze wall for any sign of attack.

James turned away from the wounded men. He stared with flat eyes at the steel containers, now peppered with holes from the initial nightfalcon strafing, and scorched from the Hellfire missiles that had blown apart the great steel doors at the front of the warehouse. Containers that now hid the bloody remains of twenty-five of his men. All killed in a firefight that had lasted less than three minutes. He scratched his head with both hands, rubbing his scalp hard, forward and back. His mouth was a thin slash in a face that had gone tight and pale. His hands clenched into fists and then unclenched, he brushed them on his blood-splattered trousers. He lifted his hands and glared at them; the blood of his men covered them with streaks of gore.

He took a deep breath and let it out, tapped his earpiece and growled an order, "Wesson report."

"Sir, exits are secure at the river end, and on this side of the warehouse, no one has escaped," Wesson stated, her voice flat in his ear.

What a damn nightmare. James looked at his watch, it was 18:05, it would take close to a hundred minutes for more spectrum teams to get ready, and reach Boston with their nightfalcons. That still left him, at least another half an hour to re-establish the cordon before General Armitage and her special forces team arrived after sunset.

"Wesson, who is left on standby at Fort Dix?"

"The rest of Indigo-6 are available. One nightfalcon and three squads. Orange-2 and Violet-7 are on international deployment in South America, and Yellow-3 is in reserve at Fort Dix, it would take three hours to get them here via helicopter and nearly six hours by van."

"What about our forces from the other three sectors in North America?"

"Too far away to get here in any sort of meaningful timeframe, Sir."

"Get Indigo-6 here ASAP, and fire up Yellow-3 and get them to mobilize cleanup and PSYOPS crews. We'll need everyone tonight."

"Yes, Sir."

James spat on the ground in disgust. Turning to his remaining men still standing, he directed, "Move back to the parking lot entrance. Help me with the wounded, if they had wanted to kill us, they would have done it by now."

The men slung their rifles. Each man picked up one of their comrades and followed James back to the far edge of the parking lot, the big shady tree, and the original four wounded men.

James laid his man onto the thin grass under the shade of the tree. The sun was nearing the horizon and shadows were beginning to reach their dark fingers toward the front of the warehouse. He rubbed his chin, shook his head, keeping his thoughts unspoken before his men. *What a disaster. We were completely unprepared for this fight. Years of training, combat experience, and superb equipment meant nothing in that death trap. What the hell does General Armitage expect to achieve with her damn special forces when they arrive?*

James turned, inspecting his wounded, and discovered that one of them had just died. He couldn't stop himself from doing the math.

Make that twenty-six dead from the warehouse assault.

* * *

The elevator doors swished aside; overhead lights gleamed off Chloe's all-black nightfalcon as it sat in the middle of the citadel roof-top hangar.

Before the machine stood six of Crane's handpicked praetorian guards. Each wore matte black Shadowstone body armor, and combat helmets modified to protect and facilitate vampire senses. They all carried M249 light machine guns with one hundred round drum magazines, half a dozen hand grenades attached to combat webbing and an assortment of personal edged weapons composed of various long bladed swords and heavy battle axes.

She emerged from the elevator, dressed in the same style of armor and combat webbing as the guards, but instead of an M249, she carried the Red Dragon sword belted to her left hip. She strode with determined grace toward her personal nightfalcon. The guards tilting their heads in deference, parted before her. She led them on board, taking a seat facing back into the cabin behind the vampire pilot. The praetorians filed into the cabin, the last one pulling the door shut.

The helicopter's twin turbines spooled up with a low whine. In seconds, the rotors were spinning and gathering pace. Red lights strobed throughout the hangar. A klaxon sounded a steady ululation and other vampires cleared the space as the bay doors began rapidly winding back. The late afternoon sunlight slashed through the air above the nightfalcon and gleamed off the domes of the citadel's advanced air defense systems as they emerged above the roof line of the massive tower. The twin turbines roared like bound demons composed of bright steel and blue fire. The black nightfalcon leaped through the gap in the roof, speeding away to the northeast, its polished skin sparkling in the setting sun.

Chloe surveyed her troops. Each of the praetorians had been alive for more than a century, some for more than two centuries. Crane had carefully selected them from the near-dead on battlefields across the world. Their long years of service to him honing unparalleled skills in combat and warcraft. Crane had saved them all from death at the very last moment of their mortal lives and they were to a man, determined to serve their immortal master for eternity. She'd provided them with an extensive briefing of the site and the mission in a ready room off the hangar bay. She smiled quietly at them as they sat relaxed, confident, and ready to deal death once more. One particular thought ran on a path of certainty through the field of her mind. *None of you will survive tonight.*

She glanced to the side, looking through the dark transparent armor of the canopy at the hard, luminous ball of the sun descending toward the horizon. It was moments like this, from behind heavy shielding, that she could look at it without fear of crumbling to dust.

Chloe stared at the sun, shivering with a deep, heartfelt longing.

One day I will bathe in your rays again and the world will tremble before me.

* * *

Anton clicked the last shotgun round into the magazine. Ramming the full load into the automatic shotgun, he chambered the first round.

He held the gun tightly and noticed his own knuckles were white against the dull gray of the weapon. Smiling wryly to himself, he slung the gun over his shoulder, flexed his fingers and took a couple of deep breaths. He needed to ease up and get frosty.

Anton looked over to where Gang was standing on a ladder, duct taping one of the blue paint splashed MGLs to the end of one of the top-level shipping containers. The MGL lay positioned just out of sight to allow easy access by anyone running along the top of the maze who knew it was there. It was one of the vampire specials, loaded with explosive canisters of silver flechettes.

"First the Triads, then Shadowstone, and now the Vampire Dominion. It's been a busy couple of days," Anton remarked.

Gang studied Anton for a moment, grinned broadly and declared heartily, "You know what – we have been so busy that we have forgotten to eat – which is appalling." He backed down the ladder and picked up his backpack. Rummaging around inside it for a moment, he brought out a large thermos flask and three large plastic mugs in a stack, and laid them out on top of a metal ammo can. He poured the contents of the flask into the mugs which steamed lightly and filled the nearby air with a delicious aroma.

"Hmmm, I thought I could smell something good," Li said avidly, jumping lithely down from the maze wall.

"It's vegetarian, I don't recommend meat – too heavy just before a battle," Gang said.

"And no sake as well," Li queried hopefully.

"Just so, which reminds me," Gang replied. He reached into the backpack, and pulled out a polished steel hip flask. "The last of Tatsu's family reserve, we will share it together when tonight is done." Gang grinned. "Now who can I trust to look after it?"

"C'mon," Anton said, spreading his hands in a wide embrace. "That would be me."

Li blurred forward, plucking the flask from Gang's hand. "Family rules."

"Okay – can't argue with that," Anton remarked.

Li put the flask away in one of her belt pouches.

Anton picked up the mug of soup. It smelled wonderful, a thing of beauty in the midst of the blood-stained warehouse. Anton put his fingers around the mug, feeling the warmth of the soup flowing into them. He sipped the soup, discovering the delicious flavors and textures of cream, fennel, spinach and asparagus.

"This is fantastic, but I don't remember it being on the Noodle House menu."

"Well, the style of the Noodle house was a selection of authentic northern Chinese cuisine, but my personal style has always been a fusion of Chinese, Japanese, and Western flavors."

"Do you think you'll do it again?" Anton asked, wiping a stray drop of soup off his top lip.

"What, a restaurant?" Gang reflected. "Well, I would love to – I still have a passion for food and I love to cook. We'll just have to see how all this pans out. But yes, if I get a chance, I would like to do it again. But next time, not with such a low profile, more a full expression of the natural fusion of flavors from eastern and western cuisines."

Anton sniffed, drinking the aroma; and then swallowed some more of the soup which was just at the right temperature to be comfortably drunk. He said, "Gang, have you considered you just might be a genius cook?"

"Well ..." Gang stroked his chin contemplatively, took a hearty slurp of his soup and laughed. "You could be right."

Li turned to the south, her face a study in concentration and declared decisively, "Another helicopter."

"Reinforcements – and not yet dark. How many?" Gang asked.

"... just one."

"How do you do that?" Anton asked. "Your hearing is so good,"

"Just lucky I guess."

"Are we prepared?" Gang inquired glancing from his daughter to Anton and back.

"The second set of pyrotechnics are in place."

"Good work Li."

"Will they work?" Anton asked. "The last set didn't seem to impact the Shadowstone forces."

"They gave you time to reload, didn't they?" Li said.

Anton nodded, conceding the point.

Gang advised, "Vampires are natural night hunters – their senses are optimized for operating with minimal light – we can turn that strength into a weakness."

"How many will come?" Anton asked

"They know there are two or three Order here – they would aim for two to one odds. They will show up with four to six vampires. Not a big force."

"How many is a big force?"

"More than six."

"What if they know that Francis Mirovar is coming?"

Gang frowned and declared, "Then we have far bigger problems. It will be sunset soon. I don't think that the vampires will wait. This battle will be decided within an hour. Now I'm not going to give you some big speech to bolster your courage like," and Gang flourished one hand dramatically, orating in deep tones. "'Once more unto the breach, dear friends…'. As I would rather you simply survive and keep your freedom. I won't gloss over the very real danger of fighting vampires. I want the two of you to stick together, look after each other and don't play the hero."

Gang grasped both of their shoulders and stated firmly, "Just remember, tonight is all about surviving to fight another day."

Li nodded.

Anton promised, "All of us, or none of us."

Gang nodded. "Yes – we all make it out."

"Shall we check what they're doing?" Li asked.

"Yes, let's use the access walkways – just don't get shot."

Anton smiled wryly. "Great advice."

"I'll check the river," Li said, ramping away.

Anton looked at Gang, and glanced toward the west. They both ramped at the same time, blurring away to the front of the warehouse. A handful of seconds later, they were inching their way to a position that overlooked the parking lot. They watched the new nightfalcon as it dropped off its troops and immediately took to the air, with an operative remaining in the cabin, manning the waist minigun. It joined the other helicopter as both began circling the warehouse at a distance.

Anton squirmed backward, turned to Gang and asked, "How long can they keep circling like that?"

"Long enough. We need to get to our positions. They're now simply waiting for the vampires to arrive."

Anton followed Gang back into the midst of the warehouse and found his place on the right side. He stood facing the front of the warehouse. He held the automatic shotgun with both hands. The MP7 submachine gun sat holstered on his right hip and the Blue Dragon rested in its scabbard over his shoulder.

His breathed slowly and was surprised to discover how calm he felt. There was only one thing left to do; *Wait for the storm to break.*

* * *

Louise Wesson carried her military lock box away as the Indigo-6 nightfalcon roared into the air.

The box sported her name in bold letters on the lid. Her thumbprint unlocked the box. She flipped open the lid, smiling grimly as she peered inside it. In moments, she pulled off her boots and started to strip off her combat fatigues. She noticed the appreciative glances of the other operatives, and shouted a sharp command, "Eyes front." They immediately turned away, and she completed the removal of her outer clothes.

Louise pulled a matt black carbon nanotube jumpsuit from the box and put it on. It covered her sleek form from ankle to wrist, and to the top of her neck. She followed it with a matt black combat vest. The combination provided an excellent capability to stop penetrating wounds and disperse impact shock. She completed the transformation by adding additional, elbow, hip, thigh, knee, and shin guards, and a pair of gauntlets. She used the box as a stool to put her combat boots back on. Picking up her tactical helmet, she pushed her fine brown hair back from her forehead and put it on. A heads-up-display automatically activated as her visor guard came down, covering the top half of her face. A moment later the helmet reached out, connecting with the Shadowstone tactical networks and her command links to the remaining squad leaders came online.

She commanded, "Squad leaders report in."

"Green-4 Alpha in position, Ma'am."

"Blue-5 Alpha in position, Ma'am."

The three Indigo-6 squads all reported in, followed by the fourth squad manning the RHIB on the river, as did the two nightfalcon pilots circling the warehouse at a radius of a thousand yards.

Red-1 wiped out, Green-4 and Blue-5 cut to ribbons, the operation to cordon off the warehouse and contain the Order of Thoth had become a debacle. Events had vindicated Louise's earlier reservations. However, she took no pleasure in being right. She'd spent the last six months working very hard with these men, and while a cold-blooded killer when the job demanded it, she was also naturally loyal to the team. She felt the losses of her men like a knife in the guts. A knot of quiet anger burned within her. She'd only one question. Who was more responsible? Gang and Li Wu and Anton Smith for killing them, or James Haley for leading his men into an obvious trap.

Flicking her visor up, she added her P90 submachine gun, Glock 9mm and four hand grenades to the holsters and webbing on her armor.

She jammed the last grenade into position with a half-voiced snarl.

Maybe it's time to frag the boss.

She sighed, her anger loosening its grip as she restored her professional demeanor. She turned, walking over to where Haley stood watch on the warehouse.

"Sir, we have fourteen Hellfire III missiles on our nightfalcons. We could simultaneously fire the missiles into the interior of the warehouse from both ends and flatten it. The targets inside would have no chance of survival."

Haley snorted, stared down at her and said derisively, "An admirable plan Wesson, except for one small detail – that's not our mission."

It wasn't our mission two hours ago either – and that didn't stop you. "… Sir, we—"

"Enough!" Haley growled. "We hold the cordon until the General arrives. Then it's her problem." He stepped toward Louise, leaned in toward her face and snarled, "Is that clear?"

"Yes, Sir," Louise replied without blinking.

"I'm sure you've got something to do, the General will be here in thirty minutes."

"I'll check the men."

"Good," Haley snapped, turning back to stare at the warehouse.

Louise turned away and began to inspect the men in the cordon. She reflected briefly; *I'm really beginning to dislike that guy.*

* * *

Chloe scanned the report.

The Red-1 team had twelve dead and four wounded, Green-4 had twelve dead, Blue-5 had eleven dead and three wounded, and two nightfalcons lay in ruins with their crews. She arched an eyebrow in measured respect. *Two Order of Thoth and a rookie did all this. The Wu family may have been living quietly for twenty years, but they obviously haven't been idle.*

She read further, the Indigo-6 team were on site with their nightfalcon and a special forces RHIB. The Green-4 nightfalcon was also available.

Counting James Haley, and Louise Wesson, there were seventeen operatives on the ground and another four on the river. An active police cordon had been in place for most of the day and had held the public back a mile from the site. Chloe smiled. *Crane will be furious. This is precisely the sort of defeat that will deflect his attention, ensuring that he keeps me here in North America.*

Her nightfalcon swooped in to land on Bedford Street at the entrance to the site's parking lot. The street lights had come on with the onset of twilight and they gleamed off the helicopter's black skin. The cabin door opened. The six praetorians stepped down from the machine, making two lines to the left and right. Chloe was the last to emerge, walking between the praetorians as they waited for her.

James Haley and Louise Wesson stood twenty yards in front of her. Beyond them, the men of the cordon stood watch over the warehouse while the two nightfalcons circled slowly a thousand yards above the site.

Chloe pivoted, addressing her praetorians in quiet tones, "When you assault the warehouse, flush the Order to the dock where I will be waiting." She tapped a tall redhead and a lithe African-American on their chests and commanded, "Hendricks and Smithson, your target is Gang Wu – kill him." She flicked her gaze across the rest of the praetorians. "Run Li Wu and Anton Slayne out onto the dock where I will complete the engagement. Be aware the Mirovar force team is in the vicinity, we expect to draw them out with this battle. They will not be able to resist saving their own. Is that clear?"

The praetorians nodded their assent.

Chloe's eyes narrowed for a long moment as she weighed the foreseeable outcomes. *I must risk Anton's life, if he falls here, he would never have defeated Crane and I must plan anew, else I will continue with this scheme.* She turned from the praetorians, striding to where James Haley stood, she ignored Louise Wesson and took a position a yard in front of Haley.

She stared hard into his face and declared, "You disobeyed my orders!"

"We were fired upon, our standing orders—"

"Are preempted by my orders."

James stood straighter and answered, "Yes, Ma'am."

"My orders were explicit. You stated that they were, 'Crystal clear,' – did you not say that this morning."

"… Yes, Ma'am, I did say that."

"Did you understand my orders?"

James frowned briefly and then conceded, "Yes, Ma'am."

"Then please explain to me which part of, 'The mission is to identify them, track them, and if they go to ground, put a cordon around the site and stop them escaping again.', implies a frontal assault on a well-defended position?"

James' face paled in the street lights. "When they attacked it could have been a prelude to escape."

"Did they try to escape at any time today?"

"… No, Ma'am"

"Correct, they did not try to escape, and you had no justification to lead your men to be slaughtered."

"Ma'am, no one could have known they would have been so effective against us."

Chloe stepped forward. Leaning in close, she whispered tightly, "You saw the Triad attack on the Noodle House, did you not learn anything from that?"

"Ma'am? … Yes, Ma'am."

Chloe stepped back, staring at James for a long moment, everyone within earshot stood still and waited for her words. "You underestimated your opponents. You set the cordon too close to the warehouse within the range of man-portable weapons. That resulted in the loss of two nightfalcons and eight of your men. You then compounded that error by launching an ill-considered attack versus a prepared defensive position that has decimated three spectrum teams."

Chloe stared at James with her hands on her hips and declared flatly, "Given your choices and your lack of effective preparation that result was predictable."

"Yes, Ma'am."

"What you should have done after the destruction of the nightfalcons, was pull back and reset your cordon out of range of their weapons."

"Yes, Ma'am."

Chloe looked past James at the warehouse beyond and said quietly, "You are most fortunate that tonight's mission is not yet concluded, and I still need you and your men."

"Ma'am?"

"I'm a forgiving soul," Chloe said with a sardonic smile. "I will forgo punishing you for your errors of judgment today, pending your discretion and diligence to your duty tonight." She leaned in close and whispered for his ears alone, "Your redemption is still possible – make sure that you do everything necessary."

"Yes, Ma'am. I will."

Chloe smiled icily. "Of that, I'm sure."

Now he is correctly motivated, time to move forward with the main plan for tonight.

* * *

James watched as General Armitage turned and strode back to her waiting special forces troops.

They made a huddle; she gave quick sharp orders beyond his power to hear. She gave a final command and they split past her like a wave going around a lighthouse. They passed James in a quick walk, exuding confidence, purpose, and power. He turned, watching as they took up a position in a loose line a hundred yards before the front of the warehouse.

James wondered why they carried swords and battle axes, and why were they all armed with light machine guns? What were they going to do – hose the place down with lead?

He felt his skin crawl over his back. He twisted around; General Armitage stood before him again.

"I have fresh orders for you and your men."

James stood to attention and barked, "Yes, Ma'am."

"Assemble all the remaining operatives on land. When my special forces move, follow them immediately into the warehouse. Do not hesitate, the Order will fall before them or run. We will flush the game to the docks and I will kill them there."

James was shocked. *Did she just say that she would kill them?*

"Ma'am, we have the RHIB and now three nightfalcons to guard the—"

"Unnecessary – I will be there."

James felt adrift and said candidly, "They just killed twenty-six of my men, how will you kill them? It's not possi—"

A shining blade appeared an inch before his nose, gleaming in the streetlights. For the first time in his life, James felt his guts freeze in a moment of existential terror as the hairs rose up on the back of his thick neck and goosebumps rippled over his skin. *Who is she? She's faster than the eye can follow.*

General Armitage moved the Red Dragon a hands width aside. Leaning in toward James, she declared softly with supreme confidence, "I will be there." She raised an eyebrow quizzically. "Do you understand your orders this time?"

James answered, "Yes, Ma'am. Understood."

"And one final word – at the end of this, there must be no witnesses."

James frowned, pausing for a moment before nodding. "Yes Ma'am. I will see it done."

She held his gaze and nodded once. The General's nightfalcon was already spooling up. She turned away from James, strode toward it and stepped into the cabin bay. In moments, its engines reached full power, launching the helicopter into the night sky.

Beneath her soaring nightfalcon, James tapped his comms link and called his men in to form a loose rank behind the General's special forces unit. The General's men stood with a preternatural stillness. They stared at the warehouse like waiting lions with their eyes locked on a herd of nervous antelopes – just waiting for one to move before attacking with deadly effect.

James marshaled his troops. He watched as the General's nightfalcon hovered momentarily over the river end of the warehouse, its skin reflecting flood lights that had come on over the dock.

The Order operatives had restored electric power.

He saw the General's black armored form leap with superhuman power and grace from the cabin of the helicopter and disappear from view. *That's a forty-yard drop to the dock or twenty-five to the crane – who can do that?* James shook his head, whispering in sudden bewilderment, "What on Earth am I looking at here?"

Vampires? No – of course not! It couldn't be?!

A creeping sensation of dread slithered up his back as he led his men after the advancing special forces.

What the hell happens next?

Chapter Six

Sky Roman @ SkyRoman133 – 3m

'Explosions in Boston! What's happening? #Crazy #Nightmare'

John Smith @ JohnSmith1249 – 3m

'I'm on my roof. Just saw a helicopter crash and burn. #Bombs #Terrorism'

Trusted Reporter Boston @ TrustedReporterBoston – 3m

'It's a tragic accident. Training exercise gone wrong. #PublicSafety #Tragedy #Official #News.'

– Consecutive Twitter posts.

* * *

Boston, June 11th, 20:26

Anton sat back on his heels, resting on the maze wall on the right side of the warehouse.

Twenty yards to his left, Gang held a similar position. They faced the front of the warehouse a hundred yards away. Above and ten yards behind them, Li rested on the maintenance walkway with her .50 caliber sniper rifle facing forward, and the white-daubed MGL holding the thermobaric grenades beside her.

Gang fidgeted, a moment later he was reading a message on his smartphone. He glanced at Anton and Li, and reported urgently, "Francis is nearby – he says make for the dock."

Anton looked up at Li. Her eyes widened as she immediately ramped, swiveling the sniper rifle after a target. The rifle was already barking as Anton launched himself to the right. A stream of bullets and dull reddish tracers appeared where he'd been standing. They followed his movement like a stream of water from a fire hose. Before he'd moved three yards a second stream of fire reached out from the front of the warehouse, cutting through the air barely three feet in front of him – he was running straight into it. It'd cut him in half.

Collapsing, he rolled onto his front, the two streams of fire crossing above him. The burnt metal of the tracers reeked as the bullets ripped through the air above him. He pushed himself off the container. Leaping upward and to the right as the lines of fire started to swing back toward him. Pointing the barrel of the automatic shotgun toward the sources of the firestorms he pulled the trigger, his shotgun burst into action and a stream of spent shells filled the air to his left. Rising into the air, he caught sight of his assailants, three vampires in Shadowstone combat armor were rushing along the top of the maze in a reverse V formation, two in front and one behind. They broke formation as he fired at them, spreading out across the maze walls.

I can only fire on one at a time and the other two will kill me. Reaching the apex of his leap, he drew the MP7 with his left hand, aimed it at the vampire on the left and pulled the trigger while he continued to direct the shotgun at the other two vampires. The vampire watched him taking aim, and darted further left as the high-velocity rounds streamed through the space he'd just vacated.

The rearmost vampire leaped into the air, landing on the maintenance walkway. Running toward Li, the barrel of his M249 smoking as fire lanced along the length of the walkway.

Li rolled off the walkway, dropping toward the maze wall below. She fired her MGL as she fell, thermobaric grenades streaking toward the walkway and the vampire whose line of fire was swinging toward her.

"Li!" Anton screamed as he landed back on the maze wall.

The vampire attacking Li, leaped off the walkway, which promptly exploded in a blinding glare. He disappeared from sight, dropping the full distance onto the floor of the maze.

Anton started zig-zagging his way toward Li and the river, while emptying his magazines at the pursuing vampires.

A second later the fallen vampire appeared back up on the maze wall, joining with the lead vampire running forward on Anton's left, firing their M249s as they blurred along the maze wall.

"There are too many," Anton yelled, dodging violently aside as bullets and tracers whipped past him.

Gang called out, "Fall back!"

Suddenly, another set of pyrotechnics flooded the warehouse. *Li! Giving us cover,* Anton thought furiously, barely able to keep pace with events. Everything was happening too quickly to follow.

The nearest vampire, now only ten yards away on Anton's right, put his gauntleted hand up to shield his eyes. Anton pointed both of his guns at him, pulling the triggers – they both clicked on empty.

The praetorian dropped his hand and barked a short laugh. The vampire was a heavy-set blond man with a battle axe at his hip and a sword over his shoulder. He stood an equal distance with Anton to the only section of the maze wall that gave access to the river. Anton had run past it and was in danger of the vampire cornering him against the wall of the warehouse.

Snarling, the blond vampire raised his light machine gun. Anton stared down the barrel, watching the vampire squeeze the trigger, he ramped aside. The M249 fired, spitting two rounds which whizzed past Anton's head, and then ran dry. The vampire cursed, dropping the gun. Dragging his battle axe and sword from their scabbards, he blurred toward Anton.

I have no time. Reaching the junction on the maze wall at the same time as the vampire; Anton wheeled around, with the Blue Dragon in his hands. He parried the blond praetorian's attacks and stepped back along the container.

Time slowed; his sensory awareness snapping into overdrive. He felt the way he had in the kitchen at the Noodle House when surrounded by the four Tiger Clan gangsters and their Mac-10s. Suddenly calm, the Blue Dragon arced up through the air, flicking left and right just like he'd trained with Gang and Li, each time it moved it deflected a slashing strike by the vampire.

The vampire's booted left foot slammed out, catching Anton in the gut. He found himself flying through the air, back a dozen yards before crashing down onto the containers. The landing jarred the Blue Dragon from his hand. He groaned with anguish, when the bright blade flew over the top of the maze wall, dropping to the floor below.

The blond vampire blurred toward him again. Behind him came the other two vampires on his side of the warehouse firing bursts from their M249s which whipped past him.

There's a claymore mine down there, and less than three seconds before it fires.

Li screamed, "Anton! No!"

He dived over the side after the sword. He rolled as he hit the ground. There were still fireworks streaming across the roof of the warehouse, and the Blue Dragon gleamed on the floor. Across from it, the claymore stood on its squat tripod legs staring right at him. Snatching up the sword, he ran at the side wall of the nearest container butted up against the warehouse wall.

I have to get higher – now!

* * *

Gang dropped the MP7s as they ran dry.

The vampires sprinted forward, letting go of their empty M249s. They reformed into an A formation, one in front and two behind. The lead praetorian, a huge, powerfully-built man with flowing black hair, carried an oversized double-bladed battle axe. He swung it back and forth as easily as Gang could swing a bamboo Shinai training stick.

The praetorians closed. Gang flipped backward, his hands disappearing into a six-inch wide space at the end of the container. He came back up to his feet, pointed the blue-daubed MGL at the onrushing vampire, and fired from point blank range. The grenade spat from the muzzle, immediately expanding into a fist sized cloud of razor sharp, silver flechettes that carved through the chest armor of the praetorian. He froze in place as the other two vampires, a tall redhead, and an athletic African-American blurred past him. They slashed at Gang with their swords.

Drawing the White Dragon free in a flash, Gang deflected the first blows of the vampires' weapons. He blurred backward, calling out, "Li!"

Li fired her MGL, a thermobaric grenade struck the paralyzed vampire. The heavy explosion rocked the maze wall. The praetorian, now a seven-foot-tall flaming torch, toppled over, falling off the wall.

She's a good girl.

Gang's heart swelled with pride.

* * *

Chloe stood poised on top of the crane gantry, accelerating her mind and extending her senses to their limits.

A hundred yards above, her nightfalcon hovered. The other two nightfalcons circled the warehouse, their waist miniguns manned and tracking the perimeter of the site. The RHIB stood fifty yards off the side of the dock, the men on board manning their weapons and watching all directions around the boat.

The warehouse was full of pyrotechnics, the sounds of gunfire had ceased, and the clash of metal on metal had begun. The Shadowstone tactical comm links were thick with shouted commands as James Haley and Louise Wesson led the remaining operatives into the warehouse.

The praetorians and Chloe maintained a separate channel that ran on their voice prints, cutting the Shadowstone operatives out of the vampires' communications.

"Spengler is gone," Hendricks reported grimly.

Chloe smirked, *feeling your mortality, are you?* She snapped out a quick order, "Keep pushing them toward the dock."

Chloe turned, scanning the perimeter, there was no sign of Francis Mirovar and his team. *We left all the communications systems open around this site, surely you know that this battle is happening? If you wait too long, it will all be over.* Staring into the black depths of the Mystic River, she frowned and hissed, "Where are you hiding? Are you down there in the water?"

Her long-range plan against Crane hinged upon the prompt arrival of the Mirovar force team.

She couldn't afford for them to be late.

* * *

Anton ramped to maximum speed, racing along the side wall of the container.

He climbed to the warehouse wall, and then to the opposite container, literally wall running his way up to the top of the Maze. All three vampires moved onto the containers around him. A thermobaric grenade exploded within the warehouse, all of the vampires looked away, and two blurred out of sight. The blond vampire remained; his face twisted with hatred. He glared at Anton, shouting, "Come to—"

The claymore mine detonated.

Anton felt something pin his right foot for a moment, but he ran on gaining the final yard up the maze wall, stepping out onto the top of the maze. He ducked to avoid losing his head, a sword slashing through the air above him. Parrying the praetorian's second attack with the Blue Dragon, he turned aside the vampire's battle axe, which instantly embedded itself into the warehouse wall. The vampire halted, momentarily slowed as he dislodged his axe.

Blurring past him and away from the warehouse wall, Anton again moved back and sideways toward the river. On the other side of the warehouse, Gang and Li wielded the White and Green Dragons as they fought the other four vampires.

The last of the pyrotechnics faded away. There was a shout from the front of the warehouse as Shadowstone operatives clambered onto the top of the maze wall. They immediately began running toward the river end of the warehouse.

Anton wheeled around again to defend himself from the blond vampire who rushed upon him, slashing at him with a combination of sword and axe attacks. He was five yards to the right of where Gang and Li fought the other vampires. He backed away under the blond praetorian's onslaught and the two melees merged into one.

Outnumbered, Anton, Li and Gang gave ground to avoid the five vampires and the onrushing Shadowstone operatives surrounding them. In seconds, the battle spilled out of the warehouse. Anton found himself next to Li, trading blows against three vampires and edging backward along the floodlit dock. Gang had become separated and was underneath the nearer of the two crane gantries where he fought furiously with the remaining two praetorians.

* * *

Chloe watched from above as the battle spilled out onto the dock.

Anton and Li Wu were fighting Calley, Senna, and Hato while Gang Wu stood beneath the second gantry fighting with Hendricks and Smithson.

She looked once more out at the river, searching for the missing Mirovar force team. Sighing, she dropped lithely down to the dock.

She landed, drawing the Red Dragon from its scabbard. She whispered in soft acknowledgement of her life, "And so it progresses, as it must – to blood and ruin."

* * *

A figure clad in black, dropped with superhuman agility from the top of the crane gantry. They landed beyond the vampires fighting Gang near the butt of the dock.

Anton struggled to stay alive against the sudden and powerful attacks launched by the three vampires. Li blurred next to him, but so did the vampires as blades crashed again and again. He hoped the figure in black was Francis Mirovar. They needed a savior – and fast.

The Blue Dragon drew sparks as it ground along the blond vampire's sword until the two hilts clashed and Anton found himself inches away from the vampire's face. The praetorian pushed back hard, Anton half fell, half leaped back. The vampire struck again, Anton twisted violently away to the left, ducking under the vampire's battle axe as it swept vertically down. He dragged the Blue Dragon through an arc that would have gutted the praetorian except that he also turned and moved, just fast enough that the blade scored his body armor without penetrating it.

Anton spun, bringing the Blue Dragon to guard position. Attacks came from both sides, even though ramped to maximum, he was unable to avoid getting slashed across the right shoulder by the razor-sharp tip of another vampire's sword.

Anton's blood splashed. The sword wielding vampire grinned, snarling, "I will drink Order blood tonight."

The blond vampire shouted, "Senna, the Order pup is mine."

Anton blurred forward. Swinging his blade low, he dived and rolled to his feet on the other side of the blond vampire.

Screaming, the blond vampire turned away. Hopping on one foot as the Blue Dragon had sheared through his other foot.

The other vampire rushed after Anton, who met him with the gleaming meteoric iron of the Blue Dragon. Their swords clashed in a shower of sparks as Anton's blade sheared along the edge of the vampire's sword.

Anton's perception spontaneously accelerated, time slowing to a crawl, his Ramp fluctuating wildly beyond his control. The vampire in front of him leered at him with a face filled with hate. The blond vampire was steadying himself, rushing back into the battle. To his left, Li was engaged in a lethally fast war of blades with a Japanese vampire of samurai heritage who wielded a shining black handled katana. Beyond the melee, praetorians, a big red-haired one, and a lithe African-American were fighting a terrific battle with Gang beneath the nearest crane gantry. Shadowstone operatives were swarming out of the warehouse. They held their rifles high, red dot sights crisscrossing the dock in a crimson web.

His heart jumped. Chloe Armitage stood beneath the far crane gantry. Remnants of the vision at the homeless shelter flashed before him. *Armitage stood alone, her dark hair, long and flowing, a delicate golden crown on her head. She beckoned him with her outstretched hand, her eyes locked with his. Wild emotion surged, lightning crackled across the night sky, the Blue Dragon became an arc of bright, vengeful flame.* The shadows and the lights flickered – swapping places, back and forth. The momentary vision disappeared, reality reasserting its dominion.

He blurred forward, then suddenly dodged back to avoid the vampire named Senna cutting him in half with a slashing horizontal strike.

Armitage stepped forward, shouting at the operatives, "Hold your fire!"

The Shadowstone operatives pulled to a halt, their guns remaining fixed on the three targets of Li, Gang, and Anton. The five praetorians continued to press their attacks.

Why doesn't she order us shot? Anton asked himself, nonplussed. The three praetorians continued to push hard against Li and Anton's defenses. The Blue Dragon, once again bright steel, snapped left and right in his hands.

Armitage! What's inside my head? He stopped thinking, devoting himself to keeping Li and himself alive for as long as he could.

* * *

Chloe caught James Haley's gaze and shook her head.

The barrel of his gun dipped. A scowl briefly crossing his face before he hid his disappointment.

She turned back to stare at Gang as he fought the two praetorians. Both vampires had cuts, Hendricks more than one – Gang was unharmed.

They cannot touch him – how interesting. Intrigued, Chloe waited, watching as Gang Wu fought the two praetorians, she'd sent against him. Behind him, the other three vampires pressed hard against Anton and Li Wu. Her senses expanded to their maximum; she accelerated her mind to its full extent. The world slowed down and she watched Gang's techniques in detail, absorbing every nuance, learning every move.

Experiencing the moment with every fiber of her being, she consumed everything she witnessed. Without effort, she would be able to repeat Gang's techniques perfectly. This was the second of the powers she kept hidden from her master, Cornelius Crane; the power of muscle mimicry.

Fascinating, he is a beautiful exponent of the katana. I have not seen such mastery since I fought Arthur Slayne in the secret vault beneath St Peter's Basilica.

The diamond on Gang's sword drew her attention as she focused on the blade's familiar, perfect form. Her breathing quickened. *He has the White Dragon.* An electric thrill shivered along her spine. Smiling broadly, her body and soul sang with the opportunity. *This is a challenge, a test of mastery – who will survive tonight? He is one of Slayne's students, the innovations, clarity and purity of technique is a signature of the master's influence.*

A genius worked his magic with the blade before her. A rare excitement rose within her, anticipation edged with fear – she would attempt to take Gang Wu's life tonight – but there was a shadow of doubt as to who would be the victor.

"How rare," she whispered.

* * *

Li had begun her training on her third birthday.

Drawing on everything she'd mastered over the last fifteen years, she beat back the samurai vampire's sword with a set of flashing strikes, forcing him to give ground. With the vampire on the back foot, she reversed direction, charging toward Anton and the two vampires that had him surrounded. The blond vampire was preparing to plunge a chrome bladed battle axe into Anton's head. With every ounce of power she possessed, she launched a flying kick at the base of the praetorian's skull. Connecting with a sickening crack, the vampire flew limply through the air, landing with a mighty splash in the Mystic River.

Li landed on her feet, deflecting a slashing, overhead strike by the Japanese vampire who had followed after her. Rushing past him, she slashed hard, but he managed to roll over the Green Dragon and avoid Li cutting him in half.

Li found herself back-to-back with Anton, as all four combatants simultaneously paused as if taking the time to consider options after the removal of the blond vampire from the fight.

Anton and Li circled in place, the two vampires stalking them just beyond striking distance.

"You're bleeding," Li said. "I thought I taught you better than that?"

Anton grimaced. "Thanks. I'm sure I needed reminding."

"And your foot as well—"

"Huh?" Anton grunted, glancing down in surprise.

"Don't look down," Li hissed.

The vampire named Senna was in front of Anton. He arched a waxed eyebrow, and promised confidently, "Don't worry young fellow. In moments, I will free you from your wife."

"We're not married," Anton and Li shot back in unison.

They struck out at their opponents, and the fight rejoined as they fought back and forth across the dock.

* * *

Squad Leader Harvey West commanded the rigid hulled inflatable boat and his small team of Indigo-6 operatives.

It'd been a long day, cruising up and down the river opposite the warehouse, making sure no one crossed the perimeter in either direction. They'd all watched the battle unfold. Jacked in with the Shadowstone tactical comms links they'd heard everything their fellow operatives had said. His fingers itched to aim his assault rifle and take a shot at the terrorists now fighting on the dock. He could see them clearly in the warehouse's flood lights. It seemed crazy to him the fight was still ongoing. Why were they fighting with swords? There were three nightfalcons armed with heavy weapons – just lay down a barrage on the dock and kill them all.

He'd been excited earlier in the day to discover they'd cornered a team of Order of Thoth terrorists, and then shocked when the first engagement had destroyed two helicopters, killing their crews, and another eight good men. Then there'd been the ill-fated assault on the warehouse where another twenty-six had died. What a disaster, nothing like that had ever happened before in the history of Shadowstone.

"What the hell!" Harris shouted from the bow of the boat where he manned the Mk 19 automatic Multi Grenade Launcher.

West watched as a blond Shadowstone special forces soldier flew end over end to land in the river with a splash.

"How did she do that?" Martinez demanded at the stern, his hands on the .50 caliber machine gun, swinging it to aim at the melee on the dock.

"Who knows? Some sorta crazy Kung Fu," Jenkins said from amidships next to the quad mount FIM-92 Stinger missile system.

West growled, "Stow that crap, and keep your eyes peeled – our job is to keep watch – not provide a damn sports commentary."

West checked that his safety was off, surveying the shoreline about five hundred yards opposite the warehouse. The police had evacuated the park beyond the shoreline. The Boston Police Department enforced a cordon to make sure no one would approach from that direction. He'd a strong suspicion that if the rest of the Order of Thoth were as capable as the handful of terrorists fighting on the dock, then the BPD would be pretty much useless in this fight.

The RHIB rocked for a second.

Harris yelled, "What—"

West looked forward to the bow of the RHIB. Harris was falling limply into the river.

There was a loud splash and he twisted back to the stern. Martinez had vanished.

Jenkins stood up, pointing his rifle at the river, firing and screaming, "They're in the water!"

West swung around lifting his gun. Something flashed through the air, striking Jenkins in the back of the head. It was a knife; Jenkins fell forward, toppling over the edge of the RHIB and into the river.

"Oh my God!" West whispered, pulling the trigger on his assault rifle, firing blindly around the boat into the water. He emptied his magazine and the gun clicked dry.

There was a sudden pressure on West's back, and a bloody blade erupted from his chest as pain flared through his body. There was a powerful push from behind and he fell forward off the blade, pitching head first into the river.

Underwater he could hear a dull roar as the throttles on the RHIB's engines surged to full power. The boat disappeared as a darkness far greater than the murk of the river overwhelmed him.

* * *

Gang's sword crashed against the praetorian's blades.

The praetorians fought with skill and power, they pressed hard against Gang and he had to give ground, shifting backward toward the melee along the dock. A dozen yards away, Chloe Armitage waited with glistening eyes, her attention focused on him. The Red Dragon lay naked, its point carried in perfect stillness an inch off the concrete surface of the dock.

First these two, and then Armitage. Gang reassessed the battle, as the two vampires circled around him, probing his defenses without success. *I can't allow her to get to Li and Anton — they're not ready to face her — I must protect them.*

Plunging his mind deeply into silence he became one with space, flow, and time. Power surged through his body, the White Dragon arcing through the air, shearing through the red-headed praetorian's sword in a shower of brilliant sparks. The vampire's eyes widened in terror as Gang's blade continued past his shattered defenses, driving deep into his chest. Gang drew the White Dragon back, cutting the vampire's heart in two.

The second praetorian's blade whispered through an overhead arc toward Gang's head like the hammer of a dark god.

Blurring with blinding speed, Gang continued the motion of drawing the White Dragon from the dying vampire. Sweeping it through a horizontal arc and striking the second praetorian beneath the armpit. The White Dragon continued easily through ruptured armor, flesh and bone before exiting in a spray of bright red blood.

The vampire, his mouth gaping with shock, slid off the lower part of his body, crumpling into a writhing heap.

The sound of sincere applause erupted ten yards away and Gang looked up, straight into the vivid blue eyes of Armitage. She declared sincerely, "Such mastery of the blade. I've not seen it's like since I fought Arthur Slayne."

Walking toward her, the White Dragon moving in slow arcs in front of him, Gang declared in tones of absolute conviction, "You have nothing to say to me – vile filth."

Armitage smiled again, but her eyes hardened into azure ice. She flourished the Red Dragon and blurred forward.

Shadows blurred; Gang and Armitage faced each other barely eight feet apart. They each held their swords with both hands poised over their shoulders. A mirror image study of purity and purpose. For a long moment, stillness reigned. Two great masters facing each other in perfect silence.

Armitage leaned forward slightly, whispering in heart-felt tones, "Gang Wu, I see you."

Gang's eyes flashed without a trace of mirth. "And yet, you understand nothing."

Both moved at the same time. Their blades flew through elegant arcs, crashing against each other with utter fury and power. The uncanny meteoric iron comprising the White and Red Dragon's blades flexed and shivered, and withstood forces that would have shattered any other weapon. A moment later, having neatly traded places, Gang and Armitage faced each other again. Both were untouched, their defenses equal to the task before them.

Gang's mind plunged once more into deep silence. The future and the past dissolved as he became one with the moment. The Ramp flowered into crystal being, golden light coruscating along every nerve and muscle fiber. He surrendered to the effects of long years of dedicated training, engaging Armitage in mortal combat without regard for safety, hope or deliverance.

Gang wielded the White Dragon with dazzling mastery, the blade glimmering in the floodlights over the dock as he struck blow after blow against Armitage's formidable defenses. Time and again they blurred and shifted position, engaging in a deadly dance of razor sharp metal. In the depths of his sinews and nerve fibers, Gang began the unique sequence of moves he'd developed over the last twenty years for this one specific task. This would be the test of his life's work. A test of his ability to innovate beyond the martial gifts of Armitage and claw away her life with a blood-soaked blade.

A test whose result would be determined before the passing of another minute with either her death or his own.

* * *

James Haley let the barrel of his gun drop down, and took a puzzled step backward.

Next to him, Louise Wesson lowered her P90, a quizzical look on her face as she also took a step back. The rest of the Shadowstone operatives maintained their positions, their guns held high, a net of red dot sights focused on the available targets. Li and Gang Wu, and Anton Slayne.

James took a deep breath and slowly exhaled. The battles on the dock continued to evolve. In a sudden movement, Gang Wu killed two of the Shadowstone special forces operatives, and Chloe Armitage rushed forward with her blade. In moments, they'd engaged, their blurred movements impossible to track.

"This is insane!" Wesson exclaimed. "Look how fast they move, all of them – this is why we were slaughtered in the warehouse."

"It's like the Noodle House, but this time, we have special forces that match them."

"It's another world," Wesson whispered.

"It is, isn't it?" James agreed.

Something caught his eye out on the river. The RHIB was under full power, charging toward the end of the dock. It was about sixty yards away and approaching fast – something was very, very wrong. He reflexively pushed Wesson aside, diving to the left. He shouted, "Incoming!"

The Mk 19 MGL on the bow of the RHIB started firing grenades toward his men. James and Wesson fell to the ground, the grenades fell amongst his men, exploding with devastating effect. In less than two seconds a dozen grenades destroyed his team.

James lifted his head, looking out at the battle, his hand on his assault rifle. The RHIB stopped at the far end of the dock, five Order terrorists leaped from the boat and blurred along the dock firing MP7 submachine guns. One of the special forces soldiers fighting Li Wu froze. She blurred past him, her sword flashing through a high arc. The man's head flew off his shoulders and rolled along the dock. Bizarrely, the man's headless body remained stiffly upright. *What the fuck? What the hell was going on?*

Stinger missiles fired from the quad mount in the middle of the RHIB, streaking up into the night sky toward the circling nightfalcons.

Damn the orders. James got to one knee, swinging his rifle up to his shoulder. Sighting down the barrel along the dock, he looked for a clear target. *This mission has gone to hell. I've got to do something to fix it.*

Chapter Seven

"Flavor is a universal language understood by everyone." – Chef Gang Wu, the first and last lines of the Noodle House Menu

"If you love others, life will of necessity be tragic, beautiful, but tragic." – Gang Wu, father, husband, and widower

"Effective innovation is the child of mastery of both technique and self." – Gang Wu, Ramp master, wielder of the White Dragon

* * *

Boston, June 11th, 20:29

The grenades boomed, and cracked.

The Shadowstone troops fell away in disarray, annihilated by the surprise attack from the RHIB. Defensive flares streamed through the night sky as the circling helicopters attempted to evade the missiles streaking toward them. First one, and then another helicopter exploded in balls of flame, falling from the sky in showers of burning debris. One helicopter survived as both missiles simply stopped working within a thirty-yard radius of the black nightfalcon, before tumbling harmlessly away.

Anton scrambled to defend himself, parrying, blocking and backing slowly along the dock as he dodged the rain of blows from the praetorian facing him.

The vampire reversed, moving backward, as two men in combat fatigues and carrying long katanas rushed past Anton to engage him. The vampire's eyes flattened with grim determination, he picked up his pace as he furiously defended against the two Order warriors. In a moment, Anton found himself able to take a breath and assess the broader battle.

In the brief respite; he took in the RHIB at the end of the dock, a single warrior moved from the bow where the grenade launcher was to the stern where a heavy machine gun stood ready for war. Near the RHIB, three Order members and a dripping blond practorian with a battle axe in one hand and a sword in the other traded blows.

I thought he was dead – he's back.

Above the crane gantries, the surviving Shadowstone helicopter hovered, its waist gun unmanned. Beneath it on the dock, Gang and Armitage were blurring around each other in a display of awesome mastery.

Li walked away from the strangely upright, headless body of the Japanese samurai vampire. The Green Dragon was red with his blood. Flicking her sword, she cleaned it, while heading toward where her father fought Armitage.

Before the gates of the warehouse lay the smashed remains of a score of Shadowstone operatives. However, one was upright on one knee at the edge of his fallen men. It was the suit who had led the Shadowstone team on the night Armitage murdered his mother. Vengeful fury flooded Anton's soul.

The man pointed his assault rifle down the dock, his head tilted to sight his targets. The under-barrel grenade launcher fired and the assault rifle smoked as the operative followed the grenade with a withering burst of fire.

Anton yelled, "Grenade!"

The grenade exploded at the end of the dock, bullets streaming toward the RHIB, the Order warriors, and the blond vampire.

I can take him out, then join Li and Gang against Armitage – we can kill them both tonight.

* * *

The General's helicopter swooped down, looming above them, as Gang Wu and Chloe Armitage continued their one-on-one combat.

Gang rested deeper into the silence as his sequence of attacks and defenses neared their ultimate expression. The world shrank, the smoke and the screams of the wounded and dying drifted away, and time slowed to a crawl. The White Dragon met the Red Dragon in another clash of blades and the White Dragon's blade slid down to the Red Dragon's Guard.

Gang stepped back and they broke away from each other. Armitage raised her sword up, revealing the intended gap, and Gang drove through it with the White Dragon.

This is it.

The White Dragon pierced Armitage's black armor just below her left breast. The blade drove deep into her, its point erupting in half a dozen blood-soaked inches from her back.

The first strike would not kill her, but with the edge of the White Dragon facing next to Armitage's heart, the reversing cut as he pulled the blade free would fatally slice her heart in two.

Gang began withdrawing his blade. Pulling back on the White Dragon, it began to bite further in toward Armitage's heart.

In a sudden movement that blurred before his eyes. Armitage's left hand fell from her sword's handle, grabbing his left wrist before he could continue to pull on his sword.

The bones in his wrist instantly gave way before Armitage's titanic strength. He ignored the agony of her crushing grip, focusing all of his power on completing a fatal cut.

His movement halted, frozen in place.

Swinging his free hand wide, he knew he'd lose his left hand.

The Red Dragon flashed before his eyes, instantly severing his hand.

The sequence was over – it had failed.

Ignoring the shock that raced up his arm, Gang crouched, sweeping with his foot. Armitage leaped over the attack, drawing the White Dragon from her chest as she flew over him.

Lightning quick, Gang rose, turning and leaping backward a dozen feet.

Armitage was faster; flying through the air, she landed in front of him, lunging forward with the White and Red Dragon swords.

Gang grimaced as the blades sheared through his chest, pushing out through his back in a spray of blood. He tried to gasp but wheezed as blood rushed into his lungs.

Armitage and Gang stared at each other in a moment of deadly intimacy and then she drew the blades out. He fell backward and lay still on the cold concrete of the dock, his blood rapidly pooling around him.

Armitage staggered, a trickle of blood breaking past her lips. Dropping the White Dragon, she clutched at her chest. Above her the nightfalcon hovered lower, its rotors perilously close to the top of the gantry. With inhuman speed and power, she leaped upward into the open cabin of the helicopter. The nightfalcon's engines roared, it veered up and away from the battle.

* * *

Li screamed with horror.

Anton spun back around. His rage evaporating, he dashed forward toward her. In front of him, Gang slid off two sword blades as Armitage staggered back, dropped the White Dragon and then leaped upward into the cabin of her hovering nightfalcon. A hard knot engulfed his chest, choking his throat.

He ran forward silently, bullets zipping past his head. The surviving Shadowstone operative was retreating back into the warehouse, firing short bursts of covering fire as he left the dock.

Above the gantries, the black helicopter's turbines roared under full power as it leaped upward, veering away over the Mystic River. He got a glimpse of Armitage standing alone within the cabin bay, blood covering the left side of her chest armor. She was staring at her gauntleted right hand pressed tightly under her left breast.

Gang had got her?

A line of tracers erupted from the .50 caliber machine gun on the RHIB. They sparked off the armor of the helicopter and with them appeared a row of holes, stitching along the hull of the nightfalcon from nose to tail. The armor piercing bullets struck Armitage just as she looked up and she vanished in a cloud of pink mist.

The helicopter's engines stuttered, black smoke pouring from their sides. It dropped like a stone into the Mystic River, landing with a huge splash, and sinking beneath the surface in seconds.

Anton's throat loosened, he exulted, "She's dead! She's dead!"

He ran over to where Li cradled her father's head, dropping to his knees opposite her.

Blood soaked Gang's chest. Anton's heart sank, his throat constricted again. The nightmare of losing his parents rolled back over the horizon and swallowed his world.

Steepling his hands over his nose and mouth, he whispered, "Oh no!"

* * *

Li cradled her father's head. She gently stroked his face with blood-stained hands as tears streamed from her eyes.

Gang blinked, gurgling as blood trickled from the edge of his mouth. He whispered weakly, "Lift me up."

"Father, lie still, stay with us," Li pleaded.

Gang snorted, coughing blood, and smiled wanly. "Always the disobedient one."

"Father! Don't leave us," Li cried, bending her head over her father and crying with terror.

Gang began to push himself up, grimacing with pain. Li and Anton both reached beneath him, bringing his shoulders up so that he was almost sitting. Anton moved his knee behind him, supporting him with his thigh as Gang reclined back. His face was pale with blood loss. Dragging in a breath, he turned to face Li and smiled at her, his eyes glistening in the flood lights.

The sounds of combat on the dock faded away as Li trembled with shock. Old memories flooded her mind. Of a thirteen-year-old girl holding her father's hand with too tight a grip. Of the coffins of her mother and older brother standing on rails before her. Of attendants removing the supports and the coffins descending into graves cut from the snow-covered ground. She remembered tears freezing on her cheeks before they could fall. The cold of that day was a pale echo of the frigid depths of sorrow that now brushed her heart with icy fingers.

Gang struggled to breathe. Each breath was harder than the one before, and each gap longer before he drew the next breath. He stared at his daughter's face, never moving his gaze.

Li scooped up the White Dragon, ramped and flicked it so all the blood on it flew away. A moment later she was walking beside Anton, reaching out, she put her hand on her father's head.

Anton followed Francis as the team formed into a group around Li, and himself. The Order members held their MP7s ready, scanning the horizon for any activity.

"How can you be sure more praetorians will come?"

Francis glanced at Anton. "Brutal experience." He suddenly stooped, picking up a smartphone off the dock, he frowned, fingering a slash across his left chest pocket.

"That was close," Francis said.

"Yeah, you nearly lost your phone," cracked a burly, heavyset man with thick red hair, who looked like he would fit in perfectly as a linebacker in any leading NFL side.

Francis raised a quizzical eyebrow, his lip curling wryly. He put the phone into a thigh pouch on his combat fatigues and continued forward.

They reached the RHIB, and everyone climbed on board. Anton gently laid Gang down on the floor of the RHIB just in front of the operator console and sat next to Li.

She picked up her father's hand and cradled it with her own.

Francis directed, "Peter, take us to the pickup point, it's time to go home."

The burly man replied, "Sure, Boss." Pushing the throttle forward, he steered the RHIB into the river.

And where is home – really? Anton studied the team, while slowly rubbing Li's back.

I have no home.

* * *

James Haley emerged from the shadows of the warehouse.

The RHIB had vanished along with the Order of Thoth. The wreckage of the two nightfalcons continued to burn where it lay in two piles on the edges of the site. Since there had been no order to lift the BPD cordon, the Boston Fire Department would not attend. The third nightfalcon had fallen into the Mystic River and presumably was on the bottom of the river.

And General Armitage with it?

James checked the bodies of his men first. They were all dead, killed by the grenades from the RHIB. He was thorough by nature, he double checked, finding one of his team still alive – Louise Wesson.

She was still breathing, but with few visible marks on her body. He assumed the explosions had concussed her. He rolled her over, placing her into the recovery position. He picked up her smartphone, as his own had lay smashed by a piece of shrapnel from the grenade attack. It accepted his thumbprint as all North American Shadowstone phones did.

James dialed the lead operatives from the Yellow-3 spectrum team at Fort Dix and the Shadowstone PSYOPS crews. He confirmed a massive cleanup operation on the Boston warehouse site. It would be a piece of work to clean up the physical mess and spin what happened tonight for the media. No one in Shadowstone would be getting any sleep in the next twenty-four hours.

Once the gears of the Shadowstone machine were in motion, he returned to check on the special forces operatives that had arrived with General Armitage. The closest were the two killed by Gang Wu. They were obviously dead, especially the African American, who lay cut in half through the chest. The other, a large red-headed man lay on his back, his jaw agape in apparent shock.

In the warehouse floodlights, something odd with the red-head's mouth drew James' attention. He crouched next to the body, checked the upper teeth, and exclaimed with shock, "What the hell?!" *He's got canines like a dog or a wolf.*

James stood up, his breathing accelerated, a very unfamiliar shiver of dread racing up his spine. He deliberately took a couple of slow, deep breaths, turned and checked the special forces operative chopped in half. *He's got fangs too.*

James checked the other three bodies on the dock. There was the weird one that still stood upright. He circled warily around it. Some blood had leaked from the headless neck. It struck him that there should have been a lot more – then he laughed out loud with a touch of hysteria, quickly stopped and shook his head. *What's stranger? The lack of blood or not falling down?* He pressed on the corpse's chest, pushing the body over. Blood sluiced from the open neck wound like a tipped bucket, spreading out in a pool. *Was the heart stopped? The body was stiff from the get go – paralyzed.*

James checked the severed head and the other two bodies. They all had a pair of prominent one-inch canines that were clearly not human. His mind whirled, he felt dizzy; his world spinning out of control. *Superhuman speed and strength. Why did we have to wait until night for them to arrive? Have I ever seen General Armitage in daylight?*

James rubbed his chin, and muttered to himself, "Looks like I'm not in Kansas anymore."

No witnesses – now that makes a lot of sense. He looked around. *There are still our wounded in the parking lot, there is another one of these – vampires – still in the warehouse. There is the nightfalcon in the river and its pilot who is probably also a vampire, and where is General Armitage?*

"At the bottom of the river? Still alive or dead?" he whispered. James frowned, his disciplines kicking into gear, his voice raised to normal volume and he declared, "I'll have to do something about this. I can't leave these bodies here for anyone else to find."

James walked back to the dead Shadowstone operatives and collected a satchel of hand grenades. *These should do it.* He stared at the closest of the dead vampires. He pulled a pin on a grenade, lobbing it so that it rolled to a stop next to the vampire's head. The grenade exploded, obliterating the head, leaving no evidence of anything inhuman.

Yes, that will do.

James pulled the pin on a second grenade.

* * *

Memories flashed through Chloe Armitage's mind.

The violent impact of the heavy machine gun rounds as they tore through her torso, throwing her backward in a mist of her own blood. The edge of the cabin door smashing into the side of her face as she fell out of the helicopter. Her combat helmet coming free as she hit the surface of the river. The dreadful sight of her own nightfalcon coming straight at her, and finally the concussive force of the armored front of the helicopter as it smashed her into oblivion.

Now she was awake, half buried in the mud and drowning in the dark. Panic rose within her, driven by the hemorrhaging from the two .50 caliber bullets that had drilled holes beneath her lowest left rib, and through the bottom part of her right lung. The sword cut that ran through her upper chest burned, adding to the blood loss. Her heart raced. She closed her eyes, willed herself to relax to quell the panic and shock. She slowed her heart to a level that would stem the flow of blood leaking from her body. The world collapsed around her as her perceptions shrank to a single focused point. Her left leg lay trapped beneath the nose of the helicopter – she must move it or die.

She drew upon the ancient training of the Order of Thoth and ramped. She activated the third of the three secret powers that she possessed. The power to achieve a supreme Ramp, a level of capability above that achieved by the Order of Thoth and the Red Empire in the last five thousand years. Time slowed precipitously, her heart pausing between beats. New energy exploded from the base of her spine, flooding through her body. Sinews like steel cords responded, bone stronger than iron bore forces that would crush any other vampire. Stiff, unyielding fingers punched through the metal armor of the nightfalcon and with a single convulsive movement she ripped the nose of the helicopter apart.

With her leg free, she swam upward through a murky darkness that could defeat even the vision of a vampire. She slowed as she reached the surface. Letting only her face break out into the night air, she expelled the bloody water in her lungs and took a single ragged breath. Allowing herself to sink back down, she turned, swimming away from the remains of the battle toward the far shore of the Mystic River.

The pain grew, threatening to overwhelm her, but she crushed it with her will. She covered five hundred yards underwater in just under five minutes. Her head emerged out of the river. She took a shallow breath, then another, and another. With each breath, she expanded her lungs a little further. She gritted her teeth, hissing in agony on each exhale. She glared and spat blood. Her wet hair clung to her scalp. Her eyes were black and bloodshot, and a dark bruise shadowed her right cheek.

Wading slowly through the mud to shore, she staggered out of the river and onto an open expanse of well-maintained lawn and trees. The park was clear of people except for two Boston Police Department cruisers sitting with their lights strobing at opposite ends of the grassy reserve.

She gravitated toward the nearer of the two vehicles. She could already smell the delicious aroma of the men inside; they were both young, fit and fresh. Her throat burned with thirst. A desperate desire filled her body, threatening to overwhelm her mind.

Behind her, she heard the distant crump of an exploding grenade. She glanced backward. James Haley rolled another grenade next to the head of one of the fallen praetorians. It promptly exploded, erasing the visible evidence of vampirism from the corpse.

She'd been right not to kill him.

Chloe turned back toward the police cruiser. It was only twenty yards away and both of the officers had emerged from the car. They seemed unsure of what to do.

Was she friend or foe? They couldn't know. With her damaged body armor, she looked like a wounded special operations soldier, who was clearly in need of help.

The vampiric thirst was upon her. She needed blood or she would die of her wounds within minutes. Her hand brushed past her sword scabbard and found nothing there. A pang of loss ripped through her. *Damn ... the Red Dragon – it's back in the river.*

She staggered, dropping to one knee, putting out her hand in supplication. She implored the young officers, "Help me. Please help me. I've been shot."

The officers both moved forward, in a moment they were beside her, each taking an arm to support her.

"Who are you?" the first one asked.

"What happened? Where are you shot?" the other said.

"'What are you?' would be a better question," Chloe remarked coldly. Snapping both of their necks before they could react. A second later she plunged her fangs into the throat of the nearest of the men as he lay slumped on the ground and proceeded to drain his blood. He died of blood loss before his fractured neck and severed spinal cord could kill him.

She stood up, her body feverishly processing the fresh, hot blood. Immediately she felt better, stronger, refreshed. Pushing a finger through one of the bullet holes in the front of her body armor, it came to a halt against her flesh knitting beneath the ceramic plates.

She looked longingly at the expanse of black water. The Red Dragon sang a siren song in her mind. She considered swimming back out and retrieving it from the bottom of the river.

Did she have time to get it?

She looked across the park, the other police cruiser still waited. With the cruiser's flashing lights stealing their night vision, and given the distance, the police officers probably didn't know their colleagues were already dead.

She would have to make sure.

Her smartphone vibrated, she laughed with surprise. Pulling it from its pouch on her combat webbing, she opened it up. There was a message from Marcus Drake that read, 'The Red Empire have attacked and destroyed the Jerusalem Shadowstone facility, only Haras Mosule and I have escaped. M.'

"Excellent," she whispered, closing the phone and putting it away. She took a deep breath and let it out, her lungs felt whole again.

Chloe looked down at the fallen officers, searched them and found the car keys and their Glock 9mm handguns. Carrying the men to the cruiser, she stuffed them into the trunk. She had to bend and break their bodies in several spots to make them both fit into the available space. She went to the cabin, ripped out the camera system and crushed it with her bare hands. She smashed the GPS, and all other systems that could track the vehicle. She then got into the car and drove it to where the other police cruiser waited on the other side of the park.

She could see the two men in the car looking at her without seeing her. With both police cruisers running their strobe lights, it was impossible for a human to see into the cabin past the reflection on the windscreen.

Chloe stepped out of her car with a Glock pistol in each hand, emptying both clips as fast as she could pull the trigger into the cabin of the police car. For good measure, she pulled a pair of grenades from her combat webbing, lobbing them through the shattered windscreen and into the cabin of the BPD cruiser.

She was already back in the stolen car, pulling away with a roaring engine and screeching tires when the grenades ripped the second police cruiser apart.

There would be no witnesses.

Chloe plotted a course to the Boston Shadowstone facility housing the R.I.S.C front company. It had a small permanent staff who could be relied upon to dispose of the police cruiser and a pair of bodies. It also had a helicopter pad on the roof of the building that would allow for easy transport to the Vampire Dominion citadel in New York City. She pulled her smartphone out again, set it to hands-free, and voice dialed James Haley. There was no answer. She then voice dialed Louise Wesson's phone, and James answered it.

"Yes?"

"You recognize my voice?"

"Yes, Ma'am. I'm glad to see you're still alive."

Chloe laughed sardonically, "I'm sure you are."

"Ma'am?"

"Status report."

"Gang Wu is dead. All the other Order of Thoth members have escaped with his body. I have already initiated a cleanup detail using the Yellow-3 spectrum team and I have activated a PSYOPS crew. They will be on site in about two hours. In another five minutes, there will be no witnesses. Do you have any new orders?"

"It is imperative you clean up properly. Get divers into the river. There is a nightfalcon on the bottom. Use the GPS logs from the Panopticon to recover the craft and the pilot. You will also find a sword nearby. I must emphasize, do not stop looking until you have the sword, once you have it secured, call me immediately on my personal line."

"Yes, Ma'am," James answered.

There was only one reason why he would be dropping grenades onto dead praetorians – he knew the truth – dead vampires do tell tales.

"James, you have done well to survive tonight. Keep doing your job, ensuring you wipe all evidence clean and recover my sword, and I'm sure your career in Shadowstone will continue to prosper."

"Yes, Ma'am. Thank you, Ma'am."

Chloe heard a trace of uncertainty in James' voice, it was clear he was still coming to terms with his discovery of vampires.

She hung up the call and relaxed, setting a tiny fraction of her mind to operate the police cruiser while she reflected upon her plans. With the battle done, it shocked her how closely she'd come to dying. Death had brushed her in the past, more than once, but this was the closest she'd ever come to her own end.

Gang Wu was a genius with the blade, he almost had her. Then the helicopter, if she'd stayed unconscious a little longer, she would have drowned or bled to death.

It was a shame to kill someone who handled a blade as beautifully as Gang Wu did. She'd felt something like regret at the end when she drew the blades out. Such a waste, but what were her options? The plan must progress.

She sniffed and then laughed out loud. The past was gone. She'd watched Anton and Li during the battle, they had fought hard to protect each other. Love? Or something close to it.

Chloe smiled, factoring the possibility of using Li Wu as another lever with which to move Anton toward her own desired goal.

Anton is now with the Mirovar team, he will most likely find a place within it. His skills and power will increase. I must keep the pressure on, I do not have time to waste. I feel certain Crane will have done with me once he has all the Metaframe artifacts or discovers my plan. I must be certain of the relationship between Crane and the Order, is Ramin Kain a traitor as Gang Wu believed, and if so, how can I turn that to my purpose? I must make best use of the Red Empire agent within Francis Mirovar's team; the Raven must be put to work.

With the Red Empire attack in Jerusalem, and this defeat by the Order so close to home, Crane will be distracted and off-balance, he will not see the subtle agency of my plan.

Chloe shivered in anticipation; her pulse quickened. *There is a reason for my gifts, a purpose beyond my life. Crane will be defeated and a new order will come to this world, an order based on the truth that I will reveal.*

Her eyes glistened as she drove the police cruiser into the basement parking garage of the R.I.S.C building.

Time to go to the citadel, I must manage Crane's fury and turn it to my advantage.

* * *

James pulled his Glock 9mm from its holster at his hip, and crouched next to the unconscious Louise Wesson.

No witnesses. The General's orders had been explicit, and he wouldn't fail her again. He put the Glock against Wesson's temple, his hand trembling slightly. He pulled the gun away and took a breath. He then placed the gun back to an inch from her ear and now it was steady as a rock. He began to pull the trigger.

Her eyelids fluttered and she moaned. "What … happened?"

He lifted the Glock away, placing his left hand gently over her head and asked softly, "What do you remember?"

"Owww," Wesson moaned. Her hand came up and rubbed her forehead. "The teams … Red, Blue and Green … they've just arrived. Where am I?"

"On the dock. There's been a battle. It went badly for us. We're the only survivors."

James stood up, holstering his gun.

Wesson convulsed, vomiting the contents of her stomach, the mess splashing across James' boots.

He sighed; took off his flak jacket and made a hard pillow for Wesson's head. He directed, "Rest here, I'll be back soon."

Wesson murmured an answer he couldn't make out.

James strode away. He pulled a silencer from a pouch at his belt, fitting it to the barrel of his Glock. He walked around the warehouse and back out to the parking lot.

The wounded men, patched up as much as they could be, waited patiently for medical extraction.

James strode up to his men as they rested under the big tree near the site entrance. They looked at him with curious eyes. He hid the silenced Glock behind his back.

Another seven good men who will have to make the ultimate sacrifice.

James pulled his gun up, firing until the twenty-round magazine lay empty.

He shook his head, turning back toward the warehouse and Louise Wesson. Fragments of the recorded conversation from the previous morning flitted like ghosts through his mind, the words of Gang Wu prominent amongst them.

Who the hell am I really working for? The Vampire Dominion?

* * *

It was a clear summer night as the RHIB powered along the Mystic River.

With his emotions grinding their pitiless way through his soul, Anton looked up at the stars, questions hurtling through his mind. His wild ramp on the dock, visions in the midst of combat, a crowned Chloe Armitage. There were no answers, only the raw emotions of loss and a driving need to act. *Gang was like family. No – he was family. He treated me like a son and now he's gone.*

Rage struck him, a red wave that rocked him to his core. He glanced at Li, she sat next to him, her hands resting limply in her lap. She'd arranged Gang's remaining hand over his chest, his other arm lay along his side, hiding the fact that it ended just above the wrist. His eyes lay closed, someone had put a jacket over his chest. He looked peaceful like he was asleep – except for the deathly pallor of his skin.

Anton wrapped his arm around Li. She shivered and he pulled her closer. She turned her head, crying quietly into his chest.

She's torn to pieces.

Anton clenched his teeth, a dark fury boiling within him.

Li put her arms around him, turned her head on the side in his lap and squeezed him tightly. He stroked her hair, brushing it away from her forehead. He felt the dark fire within wither and retreat. His eyes filled with tears, he bent his head forward, weeping quietly.

A slender woman with dark, wavy hair approached and suggested gently, "Your shoulder needs suturing and I think we should check your right foot, there is definitely something wrong there."

Anton looked up, wiping his face with his hand and said, "Thanks, I'm Anton."

She nodded. "I know. I'm Juliette Mirovar."

Anton looked at her more closely. "Are you, his wife?"

"Yes," she replied with a warm smile. "We make quite a team."

Anton undid his combat webbing and pulled off his top without disturbing Li, who continued to rest her head in his lap. He grimaced as he pulled his shoulder clear of his clothes, dropping them to the side.

There was a nasty gash on his right shoulder. Juliette opened a black case and pulled out a pre-filled syringe.

Anton frowned and asked, "What's that?"

"Painkiller. We can do this without it if you would like."

"No, that's okay, go ahead."

Juliette put a LED headlamp on her head and with its light shining on Anton's shoulder she used the syringe to inject Anton several times around the wound site. She counted ten seconds and then rapidly set to work stitching the edges of the cut back together with black thread. Two minutes later she completed the task by tying off the thread and applying an antiseptic herbal salve.

She smiled at Anton, moving to sit opposite him.

"That was quick and painless, you're a bit of a miracle worker."

"I've done battlefront tours with Médecins Sans Frontières, do you know about them?"

"Yes, Doctors without borders."

"So now you know a little something about me. Let's have a look at your foot."

Anton lifted his right foot up, placing it on the seat opposite. He'd not checked it before, but now that he did, it looked a mess. Something had gone through the top of his combat boot.

"I didn't really feel anything. I think it may have been a steel ball from a claymore mine."

"Well, we'll soon find out."

Juliette undid the straps of his boot, gently peeling it away from his foot. She cut away the sock with a pair of scissors, revealing a raw puncture wound that'd penetrated the instep of his foot and exited just behind the ball of his foot. She picked up the syringe, applying more of the painkiller around the wound entry and exit sites.

"You could have some foreign material in the wound, we will have to make sure it's clean."

Li sat up, staring at Juliette as she pushed a sterilized probe through the hole in Anton's foot.

"Does it hurt Anton?" Li asked.

"I can just feel it – like pressure."

"Our medications are very effective, and now that you can Ramp, your physiology is changing. Your capacity to heal is accelerated, nowhere near as fast as a vampire, but much faster than a regular human. Now you have completed your mastery of the Ramp, your body has completed the physical transformation. You will heal in a day what would normally take ten."

Li shook her head. "Anton is still mastering the Ramp, he only started six weeks ago."

Juliette shook her head, momentarily perplexed. "I'm sorry – what did you say?"

"Six weeks, my father used the pressure point technique for switching on the Ramp capacity of Anton's body."

Juliette paused for a moment, frowning at Anton, and then her face relaxed into a broad smile. "Well, you're a very lucky young man, it is rare for anyone to survive the process, which is why we rarely use it. But still, you were holding your own against Crane's praetorians when we arrived, you must have mastered the Ramp."

Li shook her head again and said, "No he hasn't, his speed fluctuates, but sometimes he is very fast."

"You've never mentioned this before," Anton said.

"Instability is typical of a student, but you must have been consistently operating at a mature top speed to be able to survive against vampires, especially skilled and experienced fighters like praetorians," Juliette declared. She picked up her needle and thread, and started sewing the wounds in Anton's foot. She pursed her lips in thought and then said, "It is highly unusual to be so fast with only six weeks for the body to transform, you should be only about halfway there. Perhaps you have a talent."

Peter leaned over from where he was steering the RHIB and remarked, "Don't tell him he's got talent. He's just survived a fight with half a dozen vampires and the Witch Queen herself, he'll get a big head."

Francis sat down next to his wife and said, "Stay with us, fight with us, and if you do well, I will sponsor you at the next Order Conclave."

Anton glanced at Li, she stared back at him with a look on her face that said, 'don't say no.' He looked within his own heart, feeling a resonance as he looked into the faces of Francis and Juliette Mirovar.

These people are honest and good.

"Thank you," Anton replied with a nod. "I will join your team."

Francis put out his hand, and Anton shook it. Francis had a firm, powerful handshake.

Anton let go, the RHIB slowed, pulling into a pier. A nondescript van waited there. Two men stood next to it. They wore black overalls and balaclavas to cover their faces.

"Order helpers," Juliette said softly to Anton and Li.

"We're here," Peter stated, leaping onto the pier and lashing the RHIB to a bollard with a stout rope.

Everyone got out of the RHIB, with Anton carrying Gang's body in his arms, they moved over to the van. The two Order helpers gave Francis the keys to the van, and got into the RHIB, driving it away from the pier and back out onto the river.

Francis and Juliette got into the front of the van. Anton got in the back with the rest of the team, laying Gang's body gently to the floor of the van. In moments, the van was on its way.

"Where are we going?" Anton asked.

"To a safe house," Peter replied.

Anton suddenly felt a wave of fatigue overtake him. He realized just how tired he was as he fitted a seat belt, put his head back and closed his eyes. As he dozed, a thought kept recurring to him.

How can anywhere be safe when the vampires are in charge of the world.

The van sped off on its way and Anton drifted into fitful sleep.

* * *

The Raven sat in the back of the van, studying Anton Slayne and Li Wu.

They'd recognized Anton immediately for who he was. Their Red Empire instructors had briefed them extensively on the key figures of the Order of Thoth and the Vampire Dominion. Anton's striking resemblance to his grandfather had given his identity away. The Raven reflected upon these new members of the team. *Who is Anton Slayne? The grandson of an outcast with no place in the Order, and Li Wu, someone who has hidden away from the fight for years, and yet they both survived the praetorians and it would seem – Chloe Armitage herself. What difference can they make to my mission?*

The Raven sat with the other team members in the back of the dimly lit van. The van cruised along route I-95 past Salem, toward New Hampshire, Portsmouth and the state of Maine. They held a smartphone; the screen was dark as if the phone was off. The Raven had taught themself how to operate the phone with the screen dark through memory and touch alone. The phone was the same as the rest of the quantum encrypted smartphones that the Order team members all carried, except for one thing – it hosted a set of Red Empire applications written by a deeply hidden cell of the Red Empire operating out of the city of San Francisco.

The Vampire Dominion and their Shadowstone lackeys have no awareness of the presence of the Red Empire on this continent. Now to test the trojan inserted into Francis

Mirovar's phone during the chaos on the dock. The Raven had been waiting months for a chance to access Francis Mirovar's smartphone, seizing the opportunity the moment it had arisen.

The Raven's fingers ran lightly over the dark surface of the smartphone, activating a specialized Red Empire application. The software ran for three seconds, in that time, it compromised Francis Mirovar's smartphone. In another two seconds, it decrypted the contents, filtered the accounts and delivered the quantum signature of Ramin Kain's smartphone to the Raven's smartphone. The Raven attached the contact details of the Head of the Order of Thoth to an encrypted message and sent it to the smartphone of Shabbah al Ahmar's secret ally. Questions burned within their mind. *Who is Shabbah al Ahmar's other operative? Who is his ally?* The Raven didn't know. The Red Ghost had forbidden it.

With another critical step in the mission accomplished, the Raven put the smartphone away in a waist pouch and rested with their eyes closed.

The Raven had found the years of hiding within the Order difficult. Inserted as a child and only partially trained, it had been a risk for the Red Empire that the Order would not accept the Raven, or given their young age, they would in time transfer their loyalty to the Order.

Shabbah al Ahmar himself had decided the Raven had all the right prerequisites to fulfill the mission and become a highly placed agent of the Red Empire within the Order. He'd taken steps: constructing a detailed background identity, assembling a fake family, creating a plausible and believable story to wrap around the Raven's arrival on the Mirovar's doorstep. The Raven had baited a hook – a hook swallowed by the Order.

From the day of their arrival, the Raven had excelled at blending into force leader Francis Mirovar's team. They'd grown to adulthood within the team, absorbing all the Order had to teach them, blending the Order's training with the intensive early instruction provided by Shabbah al Ahmar and the best instructors of the Red Empire.

Shabbah al Ahmar expected the Raven to rise to become the Head of the Order, and from that position, to subvert the operation of the Order to his will.

The Red Empire know me as Al Ghurab, the Raven, and one day, perhaps one day soon, I will bring the Order to its knees before the rulership of Shabbah al Ahmar and together, the true children of the way of the Ramp will conquer the Vampire Dominion.

It was a noble cause, which fueled a passionate fire within the Raven's heart. *Our cause is both right and just, we will prevail over our enemies.*

The End

The story will continue with the next instalment of The Metaframe War.

A Traitor's War

After the desperate battle on the Boston docks, Anton Slayne finds refuge amongst the vampire hunters of the Order of Thoth. Anton discovers the Order of Thoth harbors a traitor who could get his new friends killed. While a secret alliance between the Red Empire and the vampire General Chloe Armitage, threatens to do the same.

With threats, both within and without – will Anton be able to stay alive long enough to save his friends, or will his circling enemies destroy everyone he loves.

www.ingramcontent.com/pod-product-compliance
Lightning Source LLC
Chambersburg PA
CBHW050529260626
47157CB00004B/1525